RAINBOWS WAIT FOR RAIN

By Allan C. Kimball

[signature: Allan C. Kimball]

Cover Art By Mark Kneeskern

Sun Country Publications
Wimberley, Texas

Rainbows Wait For Rain by Allan C. Kimball

ISBN 0-9649407-9-5

Cover art by Mark Kneeskern

Note: This is a work of fiction. Although some characters are historical figures they are used fictionally in this novel. A Calamity Creek does exist in Brewster County, Texas, a Woman Hollering Creek exists near San Antonio, and a Second Coffee Creek exists in the Texas Hill Country but they are not the ones described within. Also, the reader should note that the village of Lajitas was not as developed in 1879-81 as it is described here. All of the events described in Chapters 4 and 5 are taken from actual historical encounters with various Comanches in Texas, and John Ringo's background is historically correct. Nothing remains of the ranch cabin at Mule Ears Peak, but some of the corral exists.

Lozen was, indeed, a woman warrior and the sister of Apache chief Victorio and the leader of her own band. She was in West Texas in 1880 searching for her brother. Wyatt Earp often frequented the Texas town of Brackettville during this period. The community of Burgess Springs later became the city of Alpine.

Alsate was the last chief of the Chisos Apache, and some visitors to Big Bend National Park have reported seeing his ghost roaming the mountains.

All the locations are exactly as described.

Calamity Creek, Woman Hollering Creek and Second Coffee Creek were originally published as individual novels.

Second Edition
Sun Country Publications, Inc.
P.O. Box 1482
Wimberley, TX 78676
512-842-5162

DEDICATIONS

To the real Bryce, Dutch Dave, and Joaquin—men of great integrity, enthusiasm and optimism. I am proud they are my friends.

•

To my Cowboy Action Shooting pards; a greater bunch of folks never existed.

•

To my wife, Madonna, whose belief in me has made me a better person.

BOOK ONE
CALAMITY CREEK

SPRING 1879

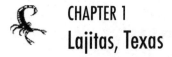

CHAPTER 1
Lajitas, Texas

Dutch Dave was the first person to see it early that Sunday morning. The sun was just rising and the infernal racket from the roosters across the Río Grande had already begun. Dutch hated those roosters. They always started their sunrise serenade just when he was getting ready to get some sleep. He swore that one day he'd convince his friend, Ethan Allan Twobears—the old Army scout—to sneak across the river and snatch up every one of those roosters and bring them over to the American side so Dutch could cook up a few free lunches for the evening crowd at his Mejor Que Nada Saloon.

His last customer was, as always, Twobears. He drank his last beer at about 4 a.m. according to Dutch's railroad watch; then went to his rock house to pass out. Dutch had then gone about his normal early morning routine: tidying up, wiping out dirty glasses, organizing the inventory, and counting his money. After totaling up the day's receipts in an old ledger book, he opened the secret trap door in the floor behind the bar and put the cash away in the small safe he had stolen from his last legitimate job as a ticket agent for the Santa Fe.

The safe didn't have a lot of money in it when Dutch disappeared that night in La Junta, Colorado, nine years ago, but it had been sufficient to stake him to enough whiskey and one whore so he could open his first saloon. That had been in Del Rio. But the competition was too great in Del Rio. The city was too large and the Mexicans across the river could always undercut prices on the American side even if their whiskey tasted of kerosene and chile peppers. And the Mexican whores worked for far less. So after just a month, Dutch packed up his inventory and equipment and his one whore into his wagon and headed west.

He established his number two saloon outside of Fort Clark, hoping to corner the business on the troopers stationed there, but he couldn't seem to attract many of them. Too many of the Seminole porch monkeys lounged around outside his rented clapboard house that served as his saloon, making use of the free shade. For the first few weeks, he chased them away perhaps a dozen times each day, but they kept coming back. He finally gave up. In a couple of months of making no profit, he packed up and headed west again.

Dutch's number three saloon was on the outskirts of Langtry and the Judge tolerated his presence as long as Dutch proved to be no real competition. Besides, the Judge's wife wouldn't let ol' Roy Bean hire on any whores for his Jersey Lilly Saloon, so Dutch's place was allowed to do business as long as the Judge got a free one every now and then. But Dutch eventually had to skedaddle out of Langtry, too. The Judge heard from a number of townsfolk that Dutch was dallying with Mrs. Bean, a lie spread by Roy's better half herself in order to make the good Judge jealous and pay more attention to her. As angry as the Judge could get, Dutch was thankful he escaped with his life. He'd heard the Judge bellow, "Get a rope!" to a chorus of cheers. Dutch ran to his mare and galloped off as quickly as the four-year-old could move. He heard shots and laughter, but he never turned around. Gracey, Dutch's whore, followed the next day in their buckboard with his cash, his saddle, and her daughters Corazon and Alma. That act of loyalty stunned the saloonkeeper so much he almost considered giving up cynicism as a way of life. He hoped she wasn't falling in love with him—that could cost him as much cash as she saved.

So here he was in Lajitas, a dusty place with not much reason for existence. He heard more than a few of its citizens describe the place as Godforsaken. Named for the flat rocks that served as the bed across the shallow ford on the Río Grande, this was the place where raiding Comanches used to cross on their autumn raids into Mexico. That historical fact alone made this an unlikely place for people to settle. Those old Spaniards never even built a presidio here, and they were likely to build one of those fortress missions just about anyplace; even Apaches and those Comanches were just passing through. The land surrounding the river here was too rocky and in many places too steep to grow crops like land up river a few miles. And the same reasons meant it was no good for grazing. Most of the land north of the river here rose steeply into rugged foothills, steep canyons, and mesas—good for nothing but ocotillo, lechuguilla, mesquite, creaosote, candelilla, various types of cactus, cat-claw, cenizo, and the occasional cholla. With the Comanches all safely on a reservation up in the Nations, little settlements had recently grown up on each side of the trickling river, with most residents inter-related, everyone usually failing to make some sort of a living in this desert but scrambling nonetheless. Dutch loved it. He had a monopoly on the beer, whiskey, rooms to rent, and whores, and it seemed like everyone who lived here except for Old Man McGuirk who ran the town just loved to partake of each one of the commodities Dutch had for rent.

Even though the town had one small Catholic chapel, it didn't take to religion much. The Mexicans and the McGuirks went to church on Sunday mornings—assuming the itinerant padre had made it down that week—and when couples did bother to get married, they got married there but otherwise the church was an empty place.

So Dutch was quite surprised to see the new chapel appear on Comanche Mesa, just east of town. It was no church and it wasn't exactly a chapel either. It was kind of a miniature chapel, Dutch thought when he saw it. Or maybe the steeple of a church that had sunk into the dirt and rocks of the hill. It stood only about as tall as two men but had a full-sized door. The door was open and the rising sun illuminated the stained glass window of the crucified Christ in the chapel's back wall in a true blaze of glory.

Dutch decided to see what was going on with this strange chapel and began walking toward the mesa. About halfway up the hill, he heard noises behind him and turned to see a small crowd gathering to follow him up onto the small mesa.

The preacher emerged from behind the chapel. He was a tall German with sun baked skin and hair so blonde it was almost white. He looked like fire and brimstone itself.

"What the hell's going on here?" Dutch asked. He didn't want any revival meetings going on in Lajitas. He'd seen what they could do to an honest business of whiskey and whores, at least while they were in a town and for a couple of weeks afterwards.

"Sinner!' the preacher sang out as the crowd of about ten people gathered around the chapel. A couple of children peeked inside. Dutch noticed there was only enough room on the inside for about three people.

"I think you need to get your damn ass out of town and right now," Dutch told the preacher, pointing a finger in the taller man's face. But the preacher had a faraway look in his eye, looking through Dutch and the crowd or perhaps past them, focusing on the shacks in town.

"Sinner!" the preacher sang out again. "Have you repented your sins? God is watching you. God has seen the evil that you have done. He will forgive, but you must ask for His forgiveness. Sinner! Have you repented? Pray with me now! Repent now!"

"What's all this?" Joaquin Jaxon, the newly assigned Texas Ranger, asked Dutch.

"Some son of a bitch wanting to deprive an honest man of an honest living," Dutch said, turning to leave.

"And you're the honest man?" the ranger asked with a smile.

"As honest as you'll ever find down here, lad," Dutch replied. "And I'll bet far more honest than this snake oil salesman. Y'know, ol' David said he wanted to be a housekeeper in the house of the Lord. That was just so he'd be near the door when the preaching started. Now excuse me. I'm slap out of sleep and I'm goin' to catch up on it."

Dutch strode down the mesa and back into town and Joaquin thought he could hear the saloonkeeper mumbling to himself the entire way.

The preacher continued to pray loudly, holding his Bible in his hand, reading a passage from it in a normal voice every minute or so. It was effective, Joaquin had to admit.

"'Mind not the deceit of a woman. For the lips of a harlot are like a honeycomb dropping, and her throat is smoother than oil. But her end is bitter as wormwood, and sharp as a two-edged sword. Her feet go down into death, and her steps go in as far as Hell,' says Proverbs. And 'His own iniquities catch the wicked, and he is fast bound with the ropes of his own sins. He shall die, because he hath not received instruction, and in the multitude of his folly he shall be deceived.'"

Although the preacher stood in the open doorway of his chapel, he didn't block anyone curious enough to peek inside. Joaquin looked in, noticing the back window that was obviously a high quality of stained glass. In front of the window was an altar hand-hewn from oak, left unpainted, and the ranger bet the preacher had done the hewing. To the right of the altar was a lectern, similarly hewn from oak, upon which the Bible probably rested when it wasn't in the preacher's hands. To the left was an old copper plate, streaked with verdigris, used to collect offerings. A shiny seated-Liberty dime was alone in the plate.

Perhaps a hundred feet away, a narrow wagon was parked. Nearby, a short but wide hobbled draught horse grazed on what little grass he could find. Joaquin walked over. The canvas top of the wagon was pulled back to the seat, covering a wooden box. He reached in, opening the box, and saw it was divided into three parts. One held tools, another socks and undergarments, the third cheesecloth-wrapped salted meats.

Several strong ropes were carefully coiled in the wagon bed. Joaquin figured the preacher manhandled the small steeple into the back of the wagon, tied it securely, and wandered about on his ministry. It wouldn't have been an easy job for one person, but the preacher had the youth and size for it.

"Sinner! Repent and be saved!"

The preacher said his now oft-repeated line with such force, his eyes wide with such urgency, that Joaquin thought the tirade was directed at someone specific in the gathering, but the eyes focused on no one and the words blew by them all.

"Luke says: 'Unless you repent, you will all perish.' Matthew says: 'You must change your hearts and minds.' And James says: 'But each one is tempted when, by his own evil desire, he is dragged away and enticed. Then, after desire has conceived, it gives birth to sin; and sin, when it is full-grown, gives birth to death.'"

The crowd sated its curiosity and, confused by a Scripture with no instruction, ambled away, most of them shaking their heads at the spectacle they'd just seen.

The preacher stood silent for a while.

"Joaquin Henry Jaxon," the ranger introduced himself, holding out his hand. The preacher grabbed it and shook it with sincerity. The power of the man's grip and the roughness of his hands clearly showed he'd not been a preacher all his life.

"Brother Karl," the preacher said, his voice cracking a little. He closed the Bible and placed it on the lectern inside the chapel, turned and pocketed the ten-cent coin on his plate. The money had failed to prime the pump of giving from the little crowd. His clothes were wrinkled but recently scrubbed, as was the preacher himself. Joaquin guessed Brother Karl had arrived well after dark, placed his chapel on the mesa, then went down to the river to clean himself, his black suit, tie, and white shirt. He noticed the preacher's boots were dusted off.

"Joaquin seems to be an odd name for someone who doesn't look Spanish," the preacher said.

"Not a drop of Mex blood," the ranger replied. "My father was a hand on the XIT up in the Panhandle and on one drive he started choking on a tobacco plug and this old cocinero saved his life. Man's name was Joaquin Guerrero and when I was born just two weeks later, my pop insisted I be called that. The Henry's from my mother's father, so that satisfied her."

"Well, I am Brother Karl Adolph Weichkopf of Luckenbach," the preacher said. "And I do not have any good stories about my name."

"Long way from your parish," Joaquin said, pulling his hat down a little more over his eyes as the sun rose above the chapel.

"My ministry is an evangelical one," the preacher said. "I have no congregation. I travel and minister to those who need to hear the Word of God. I search for the sinner."

"Shouldn't be hard to find sinners these days on this frontier."

"We are all sinners," Karl said quietly. He removed his jacket in the growing heat, folded it neatly, and placed it over the Bible lectern. "Only when we come to that realization, is salvation possible."

"Forgive me if I don't philosophize with you, brother, but my stomach is carrying on a more important conversation. Can I buy you breakfast?

"Having sustenance we shall be content," Karl replied with a broad smile.

•

Dutch's anger simmered by the time he got to his apartment behind the saloon, but percolated up a little when he saw Lizard Teats in his bed.

Ingrid Jarrell appeared in the saloon one day last year, bedraggled and filthy after what was obviously a very long journey, and immediately joined Graciela Salgado as one of Dutch's whores. She told him she walked from the train depot in Burgess Springs, intending to stop only at the river. He didn't believe that tale for a moment. Burgess Springs was a hundred miles to the north, a hundred miles of mountains and canyons and, most importantly, desert. Everything out there either pricked, sticked or stung and it was highly unlikely this waif of a white woman strolled across it carrying a large carpet bag. But it was obvious she'd walked a considerable distance.

Once cleaned up and in a new dress, Ingrid should have been Dutch's main meal ticket. She was young, blonde, thin, and had chiseled beautiful features. A poet would have described her eyes as "cornflower blue," but almost everyone thought of them as "ice blue." She didn't speak much and her attitude was aloof and uncaring. Unlike Gracey, who took to her carnal duties with a true passion each and every time, Ingrid went through the motions, her eyes closed not in ardor but languor. As an attractive, young white woman, she should have been the most popular whore between Del Rio and El Paso. Instead, Ingrid did about half the business that Gracey did and most of the local cowboys took to calling her Lizard Teats for her coldness.

She took to Dutch right away, as women often did. He may have been paunchy and bald, but he had openness to him, and an innate kindness that women instantly recognized and appreciated.

And he recognized that Ingrid carried around a deep sadness inside of her. A woman like this—with manners and bearing and looks—didn't turn to prostitution on a whim. A bad affair of the heart, a dead husband, perhaps she was abandoned by a husband or her family, a dead child or children. Who knew? She wasn't likely to ever say. She would just suffer and earn her money in perhaps the only way she knew. She didn't look like someone who ever had to learn a skill or trade, uncommon enough for a woman anyhow even on the frontier. Gracey, now she was just a natural. She enjoyed the act and decided when she was very young that she might as well get paid for doing what she would be doing anyway. She had no regrets, no remorse, no reticence at all.

Ingrid and Gracey were almost exact opposites and Dutch often wished he could shuffle some of their traits around so Gracey might talk just a little less, and less loudly, and Lizard Teats would smile and say a few words of endearment to her clients who were, after all, mainly looking for just a kind word and a shoulder to lay their heads on for a few moments.

When she was saddest, she came to his bed almost like a small child frightened by a storm or a nightmare, needing to be held and soothed.

Right now, Dutch just wanted to go to sleep, but understood he would have to give up some of that precious sleeping time to Lizard Teats. He undressed and quietly got into bed, hoping that perhaps she was asleep and he wouldn't wake her. As he pulled the sheet up to his neck, she moved over and wrapped her arms and legs around him, pulling him close.

"Now what's the matter?" he said, aggravated but quietly.

She didn't reply. Her left hand rubbed softly against the thick hair on his chest.

"I'm not going to get to sleep anytime soon at all, am I?" he sighed.

She cocked her neck up and kissed his neck. He felt her quivering, like a small animal, with fear.

"Tell me what's botherin' you?" he asked.

"Protect me," she said.

"From what?"

"Everything."

Women are the salt of the earth, he thought. That's why they drive men to drink.

CHAPTER 2

Comanche Reservation, Fort Sill, Indian Territory

Temumuquit sat naked on the east bank of sacred Medicine Bluff Creek, watching dragonflies flit over the reflections at the tips of the small waves the balmy wind kicked up. He ran a yucca-stalk comb through his long black hair over and over again.

He listened to the grasshoppers and the burbling of the water, letting the sun warm his wet face. At times like this, he didn't feel like a prisoner. But all the Kwahadi Band of the Nehmehneh were prisoners here at the Americans' fort, and not just the Antelopes but all the other bands of the Human Beings as well. Even Medicine Bluff itself was a prisoner. He could not understand how part of the very earth could be a prisoner, but he knew it was. The white soldiers didn't like Human Beings coming here. He liked this spot because the west bluff blocked any view of the Americans' buildings. Bathing in the creek, listening to Ta'ahpu in all of the sounds around him made him forget for a few moments that he could not roam free like Comanches from the beginning of time did.

He stopped combing his hair, lifted his face to the sun, and said a prayer: "Sure Enough Father created man. He created his body from the earth, his bones from the stones, his blood from the dew, his eyes from the depth of clear water, his beauty from His own image, the light of his eyes from the sun, his thoughts from the waterfalls, his breath from the wind, his strength from the storms. Aho."

His hand moved quickly but quietly to the quiver and bow near his right knee. He held the bow in his left hand, strung it quickly; then plucked an arrow with a forked tip from the painted, rawhide quiver. He pulled the arrow back on the bowstring and turned quickly to his left and loosed the arrow. He did it again and again, using all three of the specially prepared arrows he brought. He stood up in one quick motion, walking about 20 feet where all the arrows lay in the tall grass. In the fork of each arrow was a plump grasshopper. He smiled, gave thanks, "Aho," and popped each grasshopper into his mouth before he put the arrow back in the quiver. A good, light meal but nothing like buffalo, he thought.

This skill with bow and arrow had earned Temumuquit his name: Hummingbird. He could draw an arrow and shoot down a hummingbird or grasshopper or small mouse with great ease. Taking a grasshopper or mouse in this fashion was remarkable enough to others in the band, but they knew of only a couple of others who had been able to knock down hummingbirds darting in the air.

Returning to his former spot, he stood for a moment letting the sun wash over his body of eighteen summers one last time before he left. He ran his hands over his broad chest, down his rippling abdominal muscles, onto his thighs. He sat down, putting his comb in the rawhide bag next to his quiver. He slowly braided his hair on each side, working in a strand of blue beads made for him by his only woman, Jucuni. He smiled when he thought of giving her that name, a quiver for his manhood. He fastened the end of each braid with small pieces of beaver fur and long buckskin thongs that Quiver had painted small red dots on. He buckled on an old American army belt given to him by his father, Kiyou, then looped his buckskin breechclout over it and between his legs. He pulled on moccasins, picked up his bag, bow and quiver; then walked home.

"Your father is looking for you," said Kwitapu, rushing up to greet Hummingbird as he entered the village. "I think he's worried you might be on an outbreak."

Kwitapu's name meant Shit, short for Crazy Enough to Eat Shit. He was shorter than Hummingbird, and much thinner. He was dressed only in a breechclout and moccasins, his hair flowing loose below his shoulders. If his hair weren't so greasy, it would have been light brown. That and his light blue eyes gave him away as the captive he was, taken from a Texas farm house on the Canadian River when only a baby. His Comanche mother nursed him, and he took his place among five brothers and two sisters. No one in the band, no one at the agency, and none of the soldiers thought of him as white.

"Let him look," Hummingbird said. "I'm grown. I have a wife and son. I do not answer to him."

"That is what I tell him when he asks me where you are, but he doesn't like to hear me say that. He worries," Shit said.

"Since when are you my father's confidant?"

"I am just there when he comes out of his lodge this morning and asks about you. He goes to your lodge and Quiver is outside rolling up the sides a little to air your lodge out and she tells him she does not see you since last night."

Hummingbird stopped and looked around. The village was quieter than usual, only a couple of children playing and a dog barking. Only a few old men and old women would be around because today was agency day and most of the band traveled to the store for their monthly ration of beef and other supplies. He imagined his father was at the head of the line.

"Why are you here?" he asked. Shit shrugged with his lips, shaking his hand back and forth quickly a couple times. Hummingbird knew why Shit remained in the village; he was a notorious gossip and loved to stir things up. It was his way of relieving the boredom of reservation life.

"I should leave," Hummingbird said after a while. "I would if enough men would follow me. We've lost what we were. Is it better to sit around this village day after day and wait for the Americans to give us whatever they think we should have or should we be like Human Beings have always been and take what we need? Take what we want to prove we are warriors? My father had his day. Quanah Parker had his day. Now my father is an old woman and Quanah Parker is becoming an American."

"You say this and you say this," Shit said. "You know I'll follow you anywhere you want to go. I'll do whatever you wish me to. You know this is true. But you talk about leaving and yet you never say what we do if we leave."

Hummingbird started walking toward his lodge again. "We would behave like Human Beings," he spat. "We would do what we have always done. We would follow the War Trail into Mexico and take what we want. If we happen by any Americans they will feel our wrath and we will count coup—"

"You say these crazy things," Shit said, shaking his head. "You know from the elders who tell us these American's don't understand coup. They all want to kill us. Show your face off this reservation one time and see what happens. Count coup… You pause to count coup on some American and he'll have your scalp hanging from his belt in no time. What do we know about raiding into Mexico? You and I can't remember ever being off this reservation. We are too young when we come here. I do not know how to track and neither do you. We hunt only a little. I do not even know where Mexico is, or how far, and neither do you despite all your talk."

"You are content to become a woman, a slave?" Hummingbird said, turning abruptly as he faced his lodge. He crossed his legs and sat down quickly at the lodge door. Shit sat next to him, placing his hand on Hummingbird's thigh.

"We may not like it, but do we have a choice?" Shit said quietly.

"All things are possible," Hummingbird said. "If we are Human Beings we do still have choices."

"And consequences."

"Yes," Hummingbird said. "Every day I come closer to be willing to pay those consequences. If the white soldiers follow us, let them try. If the Americans want to kill us, let them try."

"I sense you're serious this time."

"Why should I eat grasshoppers and carrots and maggot-filled beef when I can have buffalo?"

"The buffalo are gone," a deep voice said above them. They looked up to see Esarosa—White Wolf—one of the band's elders. "A Human Being accepts what is and does not long for something different." He limped around to face the two young men. He wore buckskin leggings painted blue and decorated with silver beads. The leggings were heavily fringed and dragged along the ground behind him. He wore heavily painted moccasins, a purple muslin shirt, and carried a long staff decorated with wolf fur and feathers and beads—once it had been a lance but now it served only as a crutch. He wore a stovepipe hat with a star on it. The young men knew from stories that the star came from a sheriff that White Wolf had killed many summers ago in Texas, and it was his proudest possession.

"That's what some say," Hummingbird said, his eyes now lowered.

"That is what is true," the old man replied. "You forget? I was with the group that had permission just one summer ago to leave here and hunt buffalo again. The colonel gave us that permission and we were grateful because the beef had not come on time and none of the Americans could tell us when it would come. It was a bad drought that summer, too, after a bad winter. So we took our weapons and some the soldiers loaned us and we left, roaming over our old hunting grounds." The old man sat down in front of the two friends.

"We roamed many suns. Remember? Because we were gone so long the soldiers were worried we had broken out and were sent to find us? But we found no herds. What we found will forever be seared into my memory and it was the saddest thing I have ever witnessed and I tell you now I wish I had not gone. Buffalo bones scattered the plains as far as we could see. Much of the meat had been left on their bones, left to rot on the ground. The flies. The flies were the worst. We could not get too close to the buffalo because they were so covered in flies that the flies would get into our noses and mouths and ears and eyes. It was a terrible thing, I tell you.

"The buffalo are gone. The way of the Human Beings is gone. The way of the Americans has come. I am too old to change, but you are not. If you are smart, you will do as Quanah does and learn to be an American."

"I do not want to be an American," Hummingbird said.

"If you are smart, though, you will do so," White Wolf said, using his staff to help himself rise. "Human Beings are more intelligent than the Americans and we can be better Americans than they can themselves if we want to. Quanah will never leave here; memories of the war times are still strong between both our peoples, but you might. You are young enough. You can go to an American school and live in an American village and become the best of the Americans. Perhaps you or your son can even become the chief of the Americans. That is the only way the Human Beings will triumph." He turned without waiting for a reply and shambled away.

"Crazy old man, thinking we can become an American chief," Shit said. "We don't even have a chance to become an Antelope chief because the old ways are gone."

"That's the first smart thing you have said all day," Hummingbird said. After a few moments, he added, "Do you think all the buffalo are really gone? Forever?"

"White Wolf is a wise man and is a brave Human Being in his

time."

"We can be brave, too," Hummingbird said. "The buffalo may be gone from here but they cannot be gone from every place. Perhaps they are way to the west in Apache country. Many of the Apaches are still free; they must still hunt the buffalo. Or maybe they are far to the south, maybe even in Mexico. No one here has been to Mexico in many summers. I have heard the soldiers talk. None of them wants to go deep into Texas because it's too hot and too empty a place. We no longer go there. The Apaches roam mostly far to the west of there. The Kiowa are here with us. The buffalo could be thriving in such a place empty of both us and the whites. I say we find out."

"We'll go?"

"When the band comes back from the agency, gather up our friends and I'll talk to them. I'll convince them this is what we must do," Hummingbird said, nodding his head.

The night was made for an outbreak—no moon, a cold north wind, the sky covered in thick clouds that drizzled enough rain to keep the Americans close to their stoves. Hummingbird, Shit, and six of the friends they had been able to convince to go along, moved quietly south from their village, behind the officers' quarters at the head of the fort's parade ground, then behind the enlisted barracks to the stables. They were disappointed the Army had no pintos among their stock, but were thankful for ones they did find in good shape.

•

Sergeant Major Jefferson Hays banged on the door to Lieutenant Colonel John W. Davidson's quarters, startling the commanding officer awake and frightening his wife. He swung out of bed, grabbed a pistol from its holster on a nearby chair and walked to the front door in his underwear.

"You've got no compunction at all waking me up in the middle of the night," the colonel said. "You better have a good reason."

"Begging your pardon, sir, but it's nearly morning," the sergeant said. "Sorry, sir, but one of our scouts rousted me a moment ago and said eight horses were missing from the stable and his wife, who is the cousin of the wife of one of our worst troublemakers, said eight of the young bucks have broke out."

"When did this happen?" Davidson said, placing his pistol down on a table by the door and lighting the lamp. He went back inside to get his uniform.

The sergeant remained in the doorway and spoke loud enough for the colonel to hear him in the next room while he dressed. "Near's he can figure they've been gone since sometime before midnight, sir. Five, six-hour head start."

"Head start?" the colonel said, returning to the living room fully clothed. "You think we're chasing after these savages now?"

"Well, sir, I assumed you would send out a detail to bring them in."

"Do you know who they were?"

"Only the one they call Hummingbird, him and that crazy one they call Feces or some such and some of their buddies. Eight in all is what they say, sir."

"No women and children?"

"No, sir."

"Well, I'm not inclined to rush off and chase them right now," the colonel said. "I'll send messages out to several of the other commands telling them to be on the lookout, but unless they commit some sort of depredation I'm more inclined to wait. They'll be back soon. Especially if they left their wives and children here. They're out kicking up their heels."

"But, sir, what if they do raid a ranch?" The sergeant was confused by his commanding officer's nonchalance at this. Old Bad Hand Mackenzie would've hunted them to the end of the earth. Even Mexico never stopped Mackenzie.

"You say these were all young men?"

"Sir, between 14 and 18 years of age. No experienced braves."

"Were you ever that age, sergeant major?"

"I vaguely recall it, yes, sir."

"Well, I think they're behaving typically. They'll go out and blow off steam and try to find some buffalo like their fathers did last year and when they don't find any, they'll be back. These kids don't know how to be wild Indians. Now if Quanah Parker or Horse Back or even old White Wolf went out with their friends, well, then I'd be right worried, sergeant. I understand what happened up at Fort Reno last year when those 300 Cheyenne ran off to the Yellowstone. Colonel Lewis was a good friend of mine and we lost him when he tried to bring those hostiles back in. But this just isn't the same situation. What I will do is send out a couple patrols to look around and if they run across these boys, they'll round them up. Otherwise, I expect they'll be back in a few days, like I said. Now you go wake all the line officers and tell them I'm having a meeting in my office in, say, half an hour. You stir my cook and have him make coffee and maybe doughnuts for us. I'd be partial to some hot doughnuts about now."

"Yes, sir!" the sergeant said, saluting and happy to be taking some sort of action.

CHAPTER 3
Austin, Texas

The six men sat around a table in the Phoenix Saloon, four of them playing whist. Five of the men drank beer. The sixth—the tall, thin one with the auburn hair peeking out from his broad-brimmed hat—was drinking a gin fizz. He was also the only one dressed casually, although he did have a short, thick tie knotted at his collar and his vest, though well-worn, was made of the finest green and black brocade. He had a prodigious mustache, one that would have overwhelmed his narrow face except for his piercingly blue eyes.

This was John Ringo.

Everyone in the saloon knew him. They knew him as a cold-blooded killer who had escaped justice in the deaths of a deputy sheriff and several others in the recent Mason County Wars. The local fish wrapper, the *Daily Democratic Statesman,* took to calling the conflict between old-time German pioneers and American-born settlers off in an obscure corner of the Hill Country far west of Austin the Hoo Doo War, a reference to the bad luck that befell more than a dozen citizens and lawmen. The conflict began over cattle rustling, which had become Ringo's specialty. It was aggravated by the fact that the Germans had all been Northern sympathizers during the War Between the States while the others had been loyal Texans, fighting for and supporting the Old Lone Star. The fracas escalated into a blood feud. It became a small civil war wherein, according to the *Statesman,* "people are shooting each other with renewed energy." Even the Texas Rangers failed to quell the clash that went on for about two years until the leaders on each side had been killed. Only one person ever went to jail in connection with all the violence. Ringo was arrested several times on various charges related to the war, and he spent time in three county jails, but was never tried for any offense. Once he was arrested for threatening the life of the Burnet County sheriff when the sheriff reported his name incorrectly—as "Ringgold"—to a Lampasas newspaper. He was proud to be a Ringo and knew his heritage, proud to be following in the grand footsteps of Jan Ringo, one of his ancestors who had been a notorious pirate.

Ringo's companions at the table knew he had a pistol tucked into the waistband of his trousers—he'd shown it often enough in the past couple of days. Just the sight of it and the man's reputation won him any argument. The gun was a Colt's Model 1873 in .44 caliber with a 4 3/4-inch barrel enabling it to be worn discreetly yet drawn quickly. It was fresh from the factory's Custom Shop, nickel-plated and heavily engraved, with ivory grips. He carried the revolver even though carrying firearms was against a city ordinance in Austin. It being the state capital, the city fathers didn't think it was dignified for people to go around heeled, and given the heated nature of political arguments in the growing village, usually prompted by the legislators gathering in the capitol that very moment, the prohibition was probably a smart move.

This group had been drinking and playing cards off and on for two days now. Three of the men were long-time partners in various illegal enterprises, mostly cattle rustling, which is how they'd met Ringo. John Anderson, the man they all called Bad Back, was the leader of the three. Jim Parsons and Bad Back grew up together near Del Rio on a ranch where their fathers had been hands. Hal Bryce was the newcomer in the group, joining up last year. Given the way he spoke, they figured him for a Yankee. The other two men—twins Miguel and Ronaldo Burleson—they had all met two days before when they first sat down in the saloon. Dressed in suits, they nonetheless looked like men who didn't much care how they made a few dollars.

Ringo pulled a jack of spades from his hand smoothly and placed it over the other cards on the table. Bad Back was on Ringo's left and smiled when he saw the jack. He slammed an ace of spades on the jack.

"Trick's mine," Bad Back said, smiling.

"That it is," Ringo said softly, gulping down his tumbler of gin as if it were a shot of whiskey. "But in the future, I'd be a little more careful about holding on to an ace of spades. "It is, after all, a harbinger of death."

"What in Hell's a hard dinger?" Bad Back asked.

"What you get when you go see Miss Mae," Parsons said.

"Naw," Bryce said, tilting his bowler back on his head and suddenly looking rather proud of himself. "It's one of those new base ball words. It's when a batsman hits the ball out of the field."

"I was pert near right," Parsons said, throwing down new cards.

Ringo shook his head and pursed his lips. "Har-binge-er," he said, motioning to the bartender for another drink. "Means something that tells you what might come to be."

"Well, maybe so," Bryce said nodding his head, adding a card to the pile. "But a hard dinger is a ball that's hit off the diamond."

"You think anyone here gives a shit about base ball?" Bad Back said, straightening in his chair as he played his card.

"It's the coming thing. They've even gotten up a professional league back east," Bryce said. "If I'm right, there's even a team in St. Louis."

"Shut up," Ringo explained. He took the trick with a nine of diamonds. "That's the fifth one for me and Parsons. Y'all up for another round?"

"I'm pert near bored myownself," Parson said.

"Yeah," Bad Back agreed. "I think I've been sittin' way too long now." He stood up and stretched his arms over his head.

"I don't think Ron and me got to play too many hands," Miguel said, pulling the cards toward him, shuffling them around in the process, but he had to stop for a moment when he got dizzy from moving too quickly, feeling his beers.

"Missed your chance," Bad Back said. "I'm getting some sunshine."

Ringo swallowed another gin and left with Bad Back, Parsons and Bryce. Miguel gulped down the last of his beer and slammed his chair back. He and his brother stumbled after the others out of the saloon.

The late afternoon sun assaulted their eyes, the smell of horse manure assaulted their noses, and the heat almost took their breaths away. They all stepped back into the shade provided by the wooden awning jutting out from one side of the saloon. Ronaldo sat down with his back against a wall and promptly fell asleep. Ringo leaned against the "Ice Cold Lager Beer" sign, one foot propped up behind him.

"I don't know 'bout you, Johnny, but I'm pert near broke," Parsons said. "When we goin' to make some more cash?"

"What do you want to do? Rob a bank?" Ringo laughed as if his suggestion was an obscene one.

"Something," Bad Back put in. "I'm down to about $25 and when I get that low, I feel like I'm plumb broke."

"I forget what $25 even looks like, it's been so long," Bryce said, rattling coins in his trouser pocket. "I could only throw junk now after I bought that first round of beers."

"Use your imagination a little," Ringo said. "Trick is to either do something no one's ever done previously or do it in an innovative way."

"I'm not even going to ask," Bryce said.

"Me too," Parsons added.

Ringo stepped out on the sidewalk, crooking his finger for them to join him. All but Ronaldo, now snoring, did. "Look up there," Ringo said, using his chin to point several blocks away to the squat, stone capitol building with its skinny dome looking like a too-small derby worn by the state's biggest fat man.

"We're gonna rob the Lege?" Bad Back said.

"No," Ringo sighed. "I'm just trying to illustrate a point. Just imagine all the money that's gathered up there right now. Only the richest of Texans get to be elected to the Legislature or serve as governor or heads of all the various agencies and departments. The state's money is locked up in vaults that we couldn't ever get to, but those politicians have got more money than Croesus. We just have to figure out a way to get some of it from them."

"How do we pull off that play?" Bryce asked, stepping back into the shade. All but Ringo followed.

"I told you," he said. "Be innovative. Use your imagination."

"Wisht he spoke more English," Parsons said to Bryce. "I can pert near understand what he says, but not all the time."

Ringo just shook his head slowly. He looked diagonally across Congress Avenue at a two-story building. The bottom floor proclaimed itself the "Milwaukee Beer Agency" while the top floor housed *Statesman* offices. A young boy walked up and down the block, trying to sell newspapers to passersby.

"Paper!" Ringo yelled to the boy. The boy raced across the busy street, just in front of a horse-pulled streetcar that was moving slowly, and narrowly missed being run over by a faster moving carriage.

The boy handed Ringo a paper, gasped a couple of times to catch his breath, then said, "One penny, mister," while holding out his hand.

Ringo withdrew several coins from his vest pocket, looked through them with his index finger, chose the three-cent piece and gave it to the boy whose eyes lit up when Ringo said, "Keep it. And be careful crossing that street." The boy ran back as recklessly as he had crossed.

Ringo walked over to the group, glancing at the stories in the newspaper as he walked.

"Here is a fount of information, gentlemen," he said. "Passenger train service has been suspended between Austin and Hempstead... Willie Allen, colored, was charged with disturbing the peace but the article doesn't say how he disturbed it... Constable B. P. Woodridge of Hill County suicided... the Zulu chiefs submitted to British military authority over in Africa—"

"Well, that's a big relief," Parsons said.

"As I was saying... 2,500 longshoremen remain on strike for higher wages in New York City... They had the May Queen coronation over at the Graded School... Charles Freeman of Pocasset, Massachusetts, in a freak of religious frenzy killed his five-year-old daughter because he said the Lord told him to—"

"Oh, my God," said Miguel crossed himself. "That poor little innocent girl. This is a horrible thing."

"Maybe this is more your bailiwick: Mrs. Smith has just received her spring stock of millinery," Ringo continued.

"Maybe my imagination ain't up to snuff, but how does any of that help put money in our pockets?" Bryce asked.

"They may not, but this might," Ringo replied. He pointed to a story on the front page, nodding his head. He read the headline and first part of the article.

Governor's Wife Will Tour Texas

Austin (Special)—Frances Wickliffe Edwards Roberts, wife of our popular Gov. Oran Roberts and the First Lady of our fair state, will embark on a good-will tour of the State of Texas.

Along the tour, the lovely Mrs. Roberts will see every corner of the Lone Star State, enumerating among her stops sojourns to Jefferson in East Texas, Amarillo in the Panhandle, El Paso in West Texas, and Del Rio in South Texas. The First Lady is expected to call on the state's lustrous cities and its scenic vistas, including guided tours in such remote areas as Palo Duro Canyon where our brave Col. Ranald Mackenzie defeated the Comanche Nation, and the mostly unknown wilderness of Big Bend where hostile Red Devils only recently roamed wild.

The governor, whose assurances come from the experience of a hero of the Confederacy, downplayed any concerns that the First Lady will not be as safe as any other Texan traveling in our state and that, in fact, one of the purposes of her tour is to demonstrate that Texas is now as civilized as any of its Eastern cousins. The governor reports that while his wife will travel with a considerable entourage, the number of armed guards, drawn from among the ranks of the bravest of our Texas Rangers, will be kept at a minimum.

Mrs. Roberts will travel in a personal railway car providing her with all the comforts of our Capital City and, when railroad access is not possible, in a custom carriage that will be transported with her.

"And the story goes on to describe how the railway car and carriage will be outfitted, and what her itinerary will be," Ringo concluded.

"So the governor's lady is going on a trip," Bad Back said. "I still don't see —"

"If you would just open your eyes," Ringo said. "Follow me, if you can, here. The governor's a wealthy man. He's a big war hero, was on the Texas Supreme Court, got himself elected a United States Senator and would probably still be serving there except the Yankees threw him out of Washington so he came back here and ran his own law school. Imagine how rich a man must be in order to teach other attorneys how to get rich?"

"I don't —" Bad Back tried to interrupt.

"If you can't follow it, then shut up until I explain it," Ringo said. "You ever heard of kidnapping?"

"Ever'body's heard of kid's napping, for Christ sake," Parsons said, spitting tobacco juice into the street. "The governor and his wife have got kids and they'll pay us to get them to take a nap? I pert near thought you was the genius of this outfit?"

"Kidnapping is when you grab somebody and hide them away until one of their family ransoms them out," Bryce said, taking off his hat to wipe out his sweat from its band with an old rag he took from the back pocket where he always kept it dangling, using the same rag to wipe sweat from his face and neck.

"You get a gold star for today," Ringo said. "The governor, I'm told, has a beautiful wife and she's many years his junior. She is probably the apple of his eye. Well, if we steal that apple, I'll bet Mr. Roberts will pay us a pretty penny to get Mrs. Roberts back home."

"How we do that?" Miguel asked.

"This trip," Ringo explained. "In Austin, the Governor's Mansion is full of guards and every place the First Couple goes they have guards around or nearby. And they're always in crowds of people. Couldn't grab her here. But while she is on the road, especially in some out-of-the-way place traveling in that carriage of hers, I'll bet we can surprise her guards and make off with that fair matron."

"How we keep from being found?" Miguel asked.

"Choose a locations that's too inaccessible, like out in the Big Bend. I've passed through there, and it's not only inhospitable, it's covered in mountains. True mountains, not hills like around these parts. Full of hidden canyons and caves. I even know the whereabouts of a secluded cabin now abandoned. If we kidnapped the First Lady down there, perhaps along some lonely trail or, better even, stealing her away from a room in one of those small towns, we would never be found." Ringo said, the plan forming as he spoke the words. "We get to a town ahead of her entourage, spy out our escape route and hiding place, then wait for the delicate rich woman to go to bed. We sneak into her room and carry her off. Not only will we probably not have to fire a shot, but the others won't even know she's gone until the next morning and by then we'll be long gone. We get into those mountains and even the best scout or tracker won't be able to find us."

"I think I pert near understand it all except how to get the money?" Parson said.

"After a week or so, we start traveling back to Austin," Ringo replied. "We keep Mrs. Roberts incognito and quiet. We find some old line shack someplace in the hills west of here and send one of us down to give a message to the governor asking for the money. How much... she should be worth $50,000." At this figure, the men gasped. None of them had ever contemplated a number that high. "No," Ringo continued. "Let's make it $100,000. In gold coins. We tell him to go to some location and make certain he's not being followed. At that place we have another message that tells him to go to a third place. That's the shack. He comes in, drops the bag of money and we hand over his First Lady. We skedaddle on horseback, leaving the governor and his wife to walk back to a road. By the time they can notify the law, we'll be half-way to New Mexico."

They were all silent for a while.

"Think it'll work?" Bryce asked Bad Back.

"Might," he replied. "I've never known Johnny to be wrong yet. Sounds like he's got it worked out." He turned to Ringo, "Count me in." The others all agreed; they were going to be richer than any of them had ever dreamed. It was a plan.

●

Governor Oran Roberts stormed into the office of Buchanan Frass, editor of Austin's *Daily Democratic Statesman*. By his side were two Texas Rangers, the largest ones he could find on short notice. They stood in the doorway, suit coats pulled back behind the grips of their Peacemakers, but it was the white-bearded, red-faced old man who commanded the editor's attention.

"What in the name of all that's holy do you mean by publishing this?" the governor howled, tossing that day's newspaper into the editor's face, knocking the man's cigar to the floor.

"I... I... I don't understand, Your Honor," Frass stammered, retrieving the cigar and standing up. He was dwarfed by the governor and right now the governor's wrath, flowing white beard and mustache, and thick white hair that haloed around his head made him look downright Godlike to the editor.

"That story about my wife," the governor spat. "What gave you the right to print that, you ignoramus?"

"But... but, governor, your office called us about the story. We thought... well, we thought you wanted publicity about your wife's trip."

"The trip, yes," the governor said. "But you printed her entire itinerary. How could any human being be so stupid? Oh, I answered my own question. You're a newspaperman not a human being."

"Was something wrong in the story?" the editor asked, now regaining his composure after the insult. How dare a politician, of all people, insult a journalist?

"No, her itinerary's all completely accurate. You weren't supposed to print that part of the story. Now any knave in this state who might wish to do her harm will know precisely where she will be and when. You idiot!"

"I'm sorry, Your Honor, our reporter must have misunderstood the directions from your office and I will certainly take him to task over that. But, the story is now in print. What can we do?"

"You can shrivel up and die, you piece of shit, because there's nothing else you can do. What I should do is cancel the entire trip, but I can't do that now you've publicized it all across the state. So what I will have to do is increase the number of Rangers accompanying my wife and completely change up her itinerary, maybe cancel some of the more remote stops," the governor said. "But don't you dare print another word about it." He turned quickly on his heel, nodded to the Rangers, and stormed out of the room. The Rangers lingered to break all of the editor's fingers on his right hand. "And this never happened!" the governor hollered from down the hallway.

CHAPTER 4
Terlingua, Texas

The first ray of morning light shined through the only window in Ethan Allan Twobear's adobe and stone shack and drifted slowly over his eyes. It was enough to wake him from a deep sleep.

This was how he'd planned his jacal when he built it—the window faced east, looking out over the Chisos Mountains, while his bed was built into the west wall of the shack. Every morning when he was at his small home, he woke up the same way and at the same time: sunrise.

He rolled over to sit on the stone platform—covered by a thick bearskin and several blankets—that was his bed. He rolled his head around from one shoulder to his chest to the other shoulder then towards his back a couple of times, working the kinks out of his 50-year-old body. He rose, slipped on his boots, and went outside to relieve himself.

He stood at the edge of a tall cliff comprised of loose dirt and small rocks, looking towards the Chisos, taking in the whole range from the big rock they called Casa Grande looming over the giant "V" formation in the mountains, south along the Sierra Quemada to the distinctive Mule Ears Peak then the bare stone of Castolon. The mountains were a deep purple this early in the morning. The blazing orange and yellow sunrise washed out any definition he might have been able to see in the formations. He'd chosen this particular tall hill just west of Terlingua both for its view—he never tired of it—and its isolation from the settlements in both Lajitas and Terlingua. He was a little aggravated that mining engineers were beginning to wander around both locations, looking for silver and cinnabar. He had even talked to one engineer who'd heard stories of gold over in the Chisos and was committed to spending six months investigating the possibility. He hoped they never found anything. Mines would destroy his solitude.

He went back inside, pulled on his wool trousers then his old buckskin shirt. It was his only shirt and although it was impractical much of the year in the desert heat it now felt like a second skin to him, made a deep brown and very soft by years of wear. The trousers were one pair of two he owned, cotton for hot weather and wool for cold and this morning it was cold. The wool trousers were what was left of his old uniform, with a broad sergeant's stripe running the length of each leg.

Ethan quit the army three years ago, amazed he was still alive. He joined in 1861 to help preserve the Union, fighting at Leesburg, Brandy Station, the Shenandoah, Gettysburg, and many other battles with the 1st Vermont Cavalry. He even got to watch Lee hand over his sword to Joshua Chamberlain at Appomattox. After the Civil War he was reassigned to the Scout Service and Fort Clark when a clerk in Washington noticed that his enlistment papers said he was Indian. He'd tried to correct a different clerk, the one back in 1861, that he was half white and half Mic Mac, but he clerk didn't know what a Mic Mac was and when Ethan explained it was an Indian tribe prominent in the Maritime Provinces of Canada and in northern Maine, New Hampshire and his native Vermont, the clerk just shook his head and wrote down "Indian" in the space provided for race. So when the Indian Wars heated up again after he Civil War and commanders in the West desperately searched for scouts who could track down hostiles, Ethan got shipped out even though he knew absolutely nothing about the frontier of Texas and New Mexico.

He tried to explain that to his first commanding officer, Lt. John Bullis, when he reported for duty at Fort Clark.

"I'm from northern Vermont, sir. Before I joined the Army I was a timberjack," Ethan told the lieutenant. "I don't know Texas and I don't know Apache, sir."

"I'm from Macedon—Upstate New York, so we're almost cousins, not too far across the lake," Bullis told him. "I learned. You'll learn."

And he did. But he had nothing in common with the Seminole Negroes who made up most up his scout unit nor the lone Mescalero, and the white soldiers wouldn't have a thing to do with him even though he was a first sergeant. To the whites, excepting Bullis, breeds were worse than a full-blood and if it hadn't been for their hatred of the black Indians, Ethan might have felt their full animosity.

He never fit in, no matter where he was. He was much taller than the average, well over six feet, and his black hair had now turned almost white. His features were hard but handsome, looking like a typical white man except that his skin was dark brown as were his eyes. He grew up in the north woods, raised by his maternal grandfather, and he took his name when he was very young. He never thought of himself as Welsh, even though that's what he looked like. At his grandfather's insistence, he accepted an Indian scholarship to Dartmouth and studied civil engineering but discovered after he graduated that almost no one would hire him or keep him on a job once they found out about his racial background. Taking work with a lumber company was all he could find before he enlisted in the Army.

After the fiasco at the arroyo near Langtry, he left the service and sought retreat in this desert. He'd just seen too many people die over the years for no purpose he could fathom.

Ethan took the big Bowie knife from its beaded sheath on his belt and slammed it into the top of a can of peaches with the palm of his hand. He opened the tin. Using the tip of the knife to spear each piece, he ate the peaches then drank down the syrup. He chased that with a beer he'd kept cool on the outside windowsill. This was his usual breakfast. It was also his usual supper unless he killed and jerked some meat.

Checking to make sure his pistol was loaded with five rounds, he clicked open the loading gate of his Model '75 Remington, spun the cylinder and made certain an empty chamber would be under the hammer, closed the gate then returned the pistol to his holster. He grabbed a handful of cartridges and his Spencer carbine in case he saw any game along his walk. He rarely did, but he knew to be prepared.

Then he set off on his daily twelve-mile walk to Lajitas. No matter how many times he traveled along this route, the landscape of plateaus and hills and desert rolled through the lower realms of his consciousness like distant thunder—barely noticeable but oddly soothing.

•

Lajitas

By the time Dutch Dave got out of bed, Lizard Teats was already up and dressed. She was slightly taller than most women, thin but shapely. Her blonde hair and alabaster skin only accentuated her aristocratic features. She always kept herself up, no matter how busy she might be during the day—the opposite of Dave's other whore, Gracey, who tended to get more and more disheveled as the night wore on. She wore navy slippers and a powder blue chemise, the bodice fitting loosely around her breasts, and the petticoats were so clean they rustled when she walked.

She sat in the east window of Dutch's apartment behind the saloon, looking up at Comanche Mesa.

Dutch splashed water on his face, felt the stubble on his chin and figured he was good for another couple of days before he would shave, then ran his wet hands through what little hair he had left on the sides of his head.

"One good thing about being bald, your hair's always neat," Dutch said. Ingrid didn't give that little, sharp chuckle like she usually did at his jokes. He walked over to her. "You've been moping around even more than usual the last couple of days. You going to tell me what's ailin' you or not?"

She didn't answer; didn't look at him.

"You don't fill me in, I might have to make Gracey my favorite," he said. Her head snapped around and he saw a deep sadness in her eyes.

"Please, no," she said, reaching out a hand to his. "You can't ever leave me."

"Well, then, 'fess up. We can't have this."

"Dave, you just wouldn't understand. Honestly. You couldn't. This will pass."

"Christ, I hope so," he said, pulling on his trousers. "I'm slap out of patience." As Dutch laced up his shoes, he realized that he would probably be a lot more patient with Ingrid than he would ever tell her. This was the most beautiful woman he had ever seen, let alone been with. She had class. She had bearing. What she was doing here, and prostituting herself, he could not imagine. She belonged in a stately mansion in a large city, with servants and handmaidens and half a dozen wealthy suitors who called on her daily leaving their engraved buff-colored cards in a little silver tray to be carried into her private parlor by a colored maid.

"Listen," he said after a while. "If you can't confide in me, who can you? Lord knows I'm the last person to be judgmental and I'm the eternal optimist, I can always see the bright side of somebody else's problems."

"I know you're trying to help," she said, standing up and kissing him on the nose. "Maybe some day I can explain, but I can't now." She shook her head as her eyes teared up. "I can't."

"Fine," he said. "Let's get somethin' over t' Tio José's. I've got a package for that ranger that came in on the wagon yesterday and he's usually over there when I'm not open. Maybe Twobears'll be there, too. I've got a box of air tights for him."

Tio José's was a four-table, no-window adobe café adjacent to Dutch's Mejor Que Nada saloon. It was the last of several nondescript buildings above the short bank overlooking the Río Grande. A quarter-mile up river was the famous San Carlos Ford, one of the two major crossings of the old Comanche War Trail that served as the major raiding highway for the Comanches from the Llano Estacado into Mexico. The river here was narrow, barely a dozen feet across, and was usually very shallow. The flat rocks made crossing easy.

Every morning before dawn, José carried several white sheets down to the river to soak them. He tied two sheets to each wall of his shack, three more to the ceiling. This kept dust to a minimum and the evaporating water cooled the inside just enough so the heat wasn't unbearable.

José served simple meals for breakfast and lunch; then closed when Dutch opened his cantina in late afternoon.

Brother Karl and Joaquin made it a point to eat here once a week when the ranger was in town. Both in their late 20s, both from the Hill Country, they had enough in common to begin liking each other. Joaquin found the preacher serious but amusing. Karl found the ranger a good listener.

"I know you're going to get tired of me asking, but I'm going to until I get a good explanation. What's the story behind that tiny chapel?" Joaquin asked Karl.

"Believe me when I tell you that you would not understand," Karl replied. "It is probably more interesting to hear how you got here."

The ranger laughed and shook his head. "I go where they tell me to go," he said, taking a plate of pork and onion-filled tortillas from José. "It's that simple."

"And becoming a Texas Ranger?" Karl asked, rolling up one of his own tortillas and taking a bite.

"It's just as simple," Joaquin said. "My father ran a goat farm some miles south of Mason. I tried that for a while but I was bored, then I hired out as a hand on a ranch in the Bandera Mountains. But what I really wanted was some adventure in my life before I got too old and before all the red Indians were rounded up and bandits all behind bars. So I joined the rangers. Now my sergeant up in Fort Davis, his story is interesting. Sergeant Rush Kimball. He joined up because his lady friend told him she wouldn't marry him unless he spent three years as a Texas Ranger. So he did it. His time's up in '81 and he plans on quitting the day after he makes three years and marrying the lady."

"Must be a wonderful lady," Karl said wistfully.

"Never met her, but I've seen the photograph he carries with him everywhere and she is one of the most beautiful women I've ever seen. Sarge's deep in love with her."

"How beautiful thou art, my love, how beautiful art thou. Thy lips are as a scarlet lace; and thy speech sweet. They cheeks are as a piece of pomegranate, besides that which lieth within. Thy two breasts are like two young roes that are twins, which feed among the lilies. Thou art all fair."

"Yeah," Joaquin said slowly. "I never asked him about any of those things. So now you've got my ranger story, at least tell me how you became an itinerant preacher."

"Fair enough," the preacher said. "It was simple for me, too. I heard the voice of God. I was lost in the wilderness. I had my Bible with me and one time while reading it, I dropped it and the hand of God moved the pages to a passage that was meant for me. I picked it up and read Isaiah, 'Then I heard the voice of the Lord saying, "Whom shall I send? And who will go for us?' And I said, "Here I am. Send me!"' That was clear enough for me. I immediately took up the work of the Lord. God sent me."

Dutch and Lizard Teats stepped into Tio José's, hesitating for a moment to let their eyes adjust to the interior darkness from the noonday sun. Karl saw Ingrid and bolted upright from his chair.

"Ingrid!" he said.

Her hand went to her mouth covering a silent scream. Her eyes were panicked; she turned and ran away, bumping into Ethan who had walked in behind her and Dutch.

Dutch and Joaquin stared at the preacher who sat back in his chair as if he were a bag of potatoes someone had tossed.

"You know her?" Joaquin said.

"I have known her," Karl said.

For a moment, Dutch couldn't decide whether to chase after Ingrid or ignore her. He was tired enough of her attitude lately that he preferred ignoring her. As clinging as she could be, maybe she needed some time by herself to sort out whatever was bothering her. Besides, he wanted to hear what this preacher had to say about knowing her.

Ethan grabbed a chair from another table, turned it around and sat down at Joaquin's table, his arms resting on the back of the chair.

"What was that all about?" Ethan said.

"We were hopin' the preacher would tell us," Dutch said. No one spoke again for nearly a full minute.

"Yeah," the ranger said. "You can't just let this pass."

Preacher Karl stood up. "I am sorry," he said. "I just cannot explain it well enough for you to understand. Perhaps soon." He left.

"You think he's the reason Lizard Teats took to whoring?" Joaquin asked Dutch.

"The heat addled my think box long ago, so I slap don't know. That woman's been acting the strangest I've ever witnessed any woman act. But the worst of it did start when that damn chapel appeared on Comanche Mesa," Dutch said. He turned to Ethan, "Any ideas?"

"Affairs of the heart are beyond me," the scout said. "I just came down to get a horse."

"It's 'bout time you got yourself a horse. It's been, what, a year since that sorrel you had forever gave out? And, hey, I've got you a new case of air tights, all peaches just like you wanted and they'll be a lot easier to carry horseback than walking like you been doing," Dutch said.

"Ten months, actually," Ethan said. "I didn't miss him at all, not like I thought I would. Walking's been good for me. Clears the head, exercises the body and the mind."

"I had one horse I would have been happy to sell you if I still had him, but I got riddance of him 'cause he was just too stupid," Dutch said. "Dumbest animal I've ever owned. One night I'd had way too much to drink and passed out. That old nag picked me up in his teeth mind you and slung me on his back and carried me ten miles to home. When he got me there, he pulled off my boots and nosed me into my bunk. Then he went into the kitchen and fixed up a pot of coffee, and brung me a cup all fixed up with cream and sugar. Then the next day I had a hangover like you couldn't imagine, and he went out all by himself and laid rail for me on the line so's the Santa Fe boss would let me sleep in. When I woke up and found out what that fool fleabag had done, I cussed him for two days and just gave him to a greenhorn passing by. It was good riddance, too."

Joaquin smiled, "Sounds like that was a real smart horse to me, not dumb. Why'd you ever part with him?"

"Smart? You ain't dry behind the ears you think he was smart," Dutch said. "Who ever heard of a decent human being using cream and sugar in his coffee? No wonder I had such a terrible headache."

"Since Dutch no longer has his string, maybe I can help you," Joaquin said to Ethan. "I've got three mares, I don't seen why I can't part with one."

"Why three?" Ethan asked.

"Old habit from being a wrangler," Joaquin replied. "I like more than one mount. The filly was born a year ago to my favorite mare. I haven't ridden her much. I guess if you're afoot, I can part with her for a decent price."

Ethan reached into a large leather pouch hanging from his gun belt, pulling out two gold coins. "This enough?"

"What are they?" the ranger asked, looking at the large coins.

"Spanish," Ethan said. "I found them over the years."

"They good?" Joaquin asked Dutch. Dutch took one and looked

it over carefully, chuckling a little at the portrait of a hook-nosed fat man on one side. The reverse showed a crown and a crest. Then he bit into the edge, which gave way a little.

"They're pretty funny lookin', but I'd say the gold was real pure," Dutch said. "Two probably worth a lot more than that filly."

"Two's what I'm offering since I'm putting you out a little," the scout said.

"Done," Joaquin said. "You got tack?"

"Saddle and everything back at my jacal."

"I guess today's Christmas for ya," Dutch said to Joaquin, handing him a book-sized package wrapped in heavy brown paper. "This came for you on the wagon this morning."

Joaquin noticed the return address was "Sgt. R. Kimball, Company E, Texas Rangers, Fort Davis." The package was this year's "bible," the master listing of wanted criminals in Texas. He opened the package. On top of the wanted bible were several wanted notices.

"Anythin' interestin'?" Dutch asked.

"This is, kind of," Joaquin said. "Was an Indian raid on a farm house near Tascosa. Witnesses said it was Comanches. They stole a beef and a pie cooling off on a windowsill. Says the father was off hunting and the mother and two daughters were picking beans and they hid until the Indians were gone."

"I thought all the Comanch were rounded up in the Nations since Mackenzie killed off all their ponies," Dutch said.

"They sure it was Comanche and not Apache?" Ethan asked.

"What it says," the ranger said. "Besides, isn't that out of Apache raiding territory?"

"Mostly," the scout said. "But you can't ever tell with Apache. But if it was Apache, they'd never have left those folks alive. I'd much rather have to deal with Comanche than Apache. You can count on Comanche. They travel down trails they've traveled on for generations. They go where their grandfathers went. You face them, and they're fierce fighters, but you can count on them to do certain things, behave in a certain way. They'll kill you quick enough if you get in the way of what they want, but that's just a means to an end for them. Apache, killing gets to be a thing in itself. They'll kill for sport. Apache are unpredictable. Maybe one time they'll take a baby captive to raise as one of their own, maybe another time they'll just bash its head in. A Comanche will take young children to raise, take a woman as a wife or slave. But they don't kill for amusement. I'd rather face Comanche any day. How many did they say?"

"Somebody sees an old Krank riding down the trail and all of a sudden he's being chased by fifty blood-thirsty braves led by Geronimo himself, so who knows what's true," Joaquin said. "The report says a dozen."

"Any other raids?" Ethan asked. If it were an isolated incident, the Comanche would return to the reservation. If it were a full outbreak, they'd continue on the War Trail.

"No more I can see," Joaquin said, searching the package for other notices. He leafed through the wanted bible and stopped cold at an entry. "Well, that's interesting."

"What's that?" Ethan asked.

"Says here," the ranger said, showing his tablemates the handwritten entry, "that a Karl Weichkopf is wanted in Fredericksburg for 'theft of church.'"

CHAPTER 5
Renegade Comanche Camp, near Big Spring, Texas

For the first time in his life Hummingbird felt like a Human Being. He was riding free; he had raided an American's farm three days before; he was now following the War Trail. His band of eight warriors gorged themselves on the steer they took from the farm, not wanting to waste any of the meat but having no way to preserve any of it while they traveled.

If they were followed, they didn't know it. They hid one day in a narrow canyon that split off a larger one, laughed, told stories they'd heard their elders tell, and ate beef. The second day after the raid, they were back on the trail.

They were able to kill rabbits and one stray dog, so they ate well enough, but they craved something more substantial and craved the excitement they felt during their first raid.

No one told me it would be like that, Hummingbird thought as they walked their horses in the early afternoon sun. He and one other warrior, Small Snake, brought rawhide shields they strapped over their shoulder to shade their heads from the heat. The others tried to walk in the shadow of their horses, but since the sun was high the shadows were slim. No one told me I would be frightened, he thought. He had a taste of metal in his mouth as he and six others raced in to the ranch while Shit stood guard on a small hill. His stomach roiled and he was afraid he would soil himself as he approached the corral adjacent to the ranch house. The blood pounded in his head, but he saw so clearly, better than ever before. He noticed cracks in the farmhouse door, he saw spittle at the corner of the steer's mouth, and he heard the American shush her children in the bean field away from the house. He heard the steer chewing its cud, smelled the cud, smelled fear and sweat and rose water on the females lying in that field. He saw the woman's husband on a hill a long way off, waving his arms and running towards them. He saw no threat anywhere, yet he was afraid. They pulled apart one side of the corral and Hummingbird roped the steer; then they raced away. He felt exhilaration, a better feeling even than when he was with Quiver. He passed the steer's rope to Shit, turned, and galloped back to the farmhouse.

He had smelled the food before—a familiar scent he couldn't place. He rode around the sod house until he saw the pie on the windowsill. He grabbed it, holding it in his lap with one hand while he guided his horse with a rope in the other. The heat of the pie added to his excitement. By the time Hummingbird caught up with Shit and the others, he was laughing so heartily his face hurt. He held up the pie as if it were a trophy. The others gathered around, reached in and grabbed handfuls. He was left with one portion and ate it as they rode, its warmth filling his spirit. He never tasted apples so good.

He wanted more pie, more beef, more excitement. He knew what to expect now and would understand the fear next time.

The next time came soon. The day after they avoided a small American village, Small Snake, who was the best tracker in the group, reported a ranch not far from their trail. They rode to look it over.

A man and a boy looked after horses in a corral behind the ranch house. A cow heavy with milk was tied with a long rope to a post near the corral. They didn't see any cattle, but horsemeat would suit Hummingbird's band just fine.

They rode in steadily, slowly. The man and boy saw them. The man waved the boy off and the young one ran to the house, emerging with a long barreled shotgun, his mother and an older sister. The boy gave the shotgun to his father, who walked to the corner of the ranch house as the boy ran to his mother's side. Hummingbird broke away from the band, walking his horse up to the rancher. He pulled his feet from the rope tied around his horse's waist and slid off the mount, holding only his reata in his hands.

Hummingbird knew only a few American words—me, you, family, want, need, give, take, food, horse, cattle, trade, name, now, bye-and-bye, yes, no, come, go, and Christian. He doubted this man knew the language of the Human Beings.

"Food-me-want," Hummingbird said carefully, making sign for the words as well.

The rancher cradled the shotgun in his arms, not pointing it at Hummingbird. He looked around at the rest of the band that was standing on their horses at a distance. The rancher shook his head and said, "No;" then went on at some length with words Hummingbird didn't understand.

"Food-me-need," Hummingbird repeated, indicating the horses behind the rancher. At this, the rancher raised his shotgun, pointing it at Hummingbird who raised his hands in front of him.

"Food-me-take," Hummingbird said, turning on his heel and leaping onto his horse. He dropped his reata down on the off side so the rancher didn't see what he was doing, maneuvering the loop so it rested in the palm of his right hand. The American said something else unintelligible, motioning with the shotgun. Hummingbird kicked his horse forward; then turned it after a single stride, throwing the reata loop toward the American who fired his shotgun. One of the pellets burned across Hummingbird's cheek and he could hear others buzzing by his head like a swarm of bees, but nothing else touched him. The loop dropped cleanly over the rancher and Hummingbird pulled it tight, grabbing the American under one armpit and across his chest to his neck. He kicked his pony again, turned and raced off as the others in the band yelped their approval. He hollered directions to them. They raced in and took the three horses. The American woman and her children slammed the door of the ranch house and Hummingbird could hear the children crying and the woman screaming as he dragged the man through the mesquite and cactus, bumping over rocks.

That elation washed over him again. He kicked this horse into a gallop, racing around the house. Suddenly, the rope went slack. He looked back to see that the American had tried to get the loop off but only succeeded in moving it to his neck where it had tightened again and eventually decapitated him. The body was still in the dust behind Hummingbird's horse; the head rolled across the prairie. Hummingbird whopped as loudly as he could, coiled in his lariat, and trotted over to his enemy's head, sliding over to touch it with his hand, saying "Aihe," loudly counting coup. Then he raced off to join his friends.

That night they camped after slaughtering one of the raided horses. The band lauded Hummingbird on his courage as they ate.

"I never can stand up to that American the way you do," Shit said. "He is armed but not you. You just wave the bullets away. I cannot do that."

"That's why they won't be telling stories about you in the Old Men's Smoke Lodge," Hummingbird said, running his finger over the cut on his left cheek that would heal to a prominent scar. The scar would give him the opportunity to tell this tale the rest of his life.

•

Captain June Peak of Texas Ranger Company B was an experienced Indian fighter, the only one of the six others who was. They came for a long campaign and not just a bravura chase to make themselves look good. They brought along two pack mules loaded with food, water, blankets, and several boxes of ammunition. The only thing missing, Peak thought, was a good tracker, but he should have enough know-how to fill that role himself.

The Comanches weren't hard to find. They camped near the head of the North Concho River, having a celebration. The area was a jumble of boulders and the sky was turning dusk, giving the rangers the perfect cover to sneak up on the hostiles. Peak hobbled the mules and horses and lead his men forward after a brief instruction. He knew these men would not falter. The seven men moved in a semi-circle toward the Comanche camp, rifles at the ready. Peak planned to take these Indians back to Big Spring tied across the backs of their horses, dead but a better fate than the way they had treated Robert Leffingwell and his wife Ursula who might never recover from the shock of having to search for her husband's head so it could be properly buried with his body.

Almost as one, the seven rangers levered cartridges into their Winchesters but when they raised their rifles to fire they discovered their targets had vanished. Peak knew Comanches were crafty, but how was that possible? In about one flat second, the hostile band took refuge behind large rocks and began firing back at the rangers. Two of Peak's men fell before they knew what hit them. The remainder returned fire. Flames and smoke from rifle barrels filled the confined space and the sound was like constant thunder overhead. Two of the men took bullets from the Comanche camp but continued to fight. Each ranger expended fifty rounds through the Winchesters in a very short time, running out of cartridges. Peak sent one of his men back to retrieve more ammunition from the mules. The Comanches fired almost as often as the rangers, so Peak knew they should be running low on ammo, too. When they were out, he thought, they would have no resupply and the rangers would take them all. As they waited, they drew pistols and each fired another ten rounds until the pistols were empty as well. The ranger Peak sent reappeared, clearly frightened and empty-handed.

"Whur's th' cahtridges?" Peak said.

"Dunno," the ranger said, trying to catch his breath. "The mules is gone and so's our mounts."

"Mother a Christ," Peak said. He paused for a bit and looked around. "We've gotta rurn fer it, boys, and we've gotta rurn fest an' herd. Don't be lookin' aback, y'might not wanna see what's a-gainin' on ya. Just get."

The rangers stumbled through the boulders as quickly as they could and ran through the tall grasses by the river. The Comanches didn't follow them very far, but they laughed and fired more rounds their way, wounding Peak in the shoulder and another ranger in the neck. Peak's command now numbered two dead, four wounded, with lost supplies, horses, and mules.

"We got whupped real good," Peak said, panting as he ran with the others, hoping they weren't his last words.

•

Hummingbird couldn't believe how much Ta'ahpue smiled on them yesterday. He faced down an American, stole some ponies, stole more food and blankets and ammunition and more horses and two mules from Texas Rangers, killed some rangers and chased the rest off. Who among the Human Beings had shamed Texas Rangers? Yes, it had been a good day. His power was growing. He felt so good, he oddly didn't care whether he lived to finish this adventure or not. A brave man dies young anyway, he thought.

His band was almost caught, but they heard the rangers creeping up on them and once they heard the rifles being cocked, they moved behind boulders and fought back while Shit—putting his sneaky skills to work—immediately stole around the rangers to catch them in a crossfire but had discovered the mules and horses and brought them back instead.

Yes, it was a good day.

Today began well, too. The sky was clear and a little cool, and a scent of rain hung in the air. The grasses were so dry, he knew they could use a good rain. His band rode steadily, leading the two ponies that remained from the raided ranch and the seven horses and two mules from the rangers. Each of the warriors had placed ranger blankets across their horse's back, under the ropes that served as their saddles. Hummingbird wished now he had brought Quiver with him, let the others who had women bring theirs, because he saw his little group as the beginning of his own band.

They stopped suddenly, each of them smelling smoke. Shit motioned them to join him on a nearby hill. From that vantage point they saw the beginnings of a prairie fire.

Hummingbird saw a small wagon loaded with goods with two adult Americans standing beside it with three children. A blanket was spread out by the wagon with food on it, indicating the family had stopped for a noon meal and somehow had probably started the fire. Lucky for them, the north wind was blowing the fire away from them. But he noticed they looked panicked. The woman clung to the man and the children clung to her. The woman pointed to the fire. The man kept shaking his head.

Hummingbird rode along the hill, looking at the expanding fire's leading edge. Bobbing up and down, barely above the deep grass, he saw a dark-haired head. One of the American children was running from the fire and the fire was gaining on it. He kicked his horse into action and raced down the hill. He chased one edge of the fire; then cut directly through it until he emerged just behind the child. He could see now it was a girl. He could hear her screams. He galloped next to the girl, reached over, grabbed her and swung her up in front of him. He turned to see which way the fire was moving and saw a break to the west. He rode for it, cutting through the fire again briefly. The child, to her credit, he thought, was quiet as he did this, holding tightly to the neck of his horse. Out of the fire, he slowed, trotting around its edge back to the Americans.

The family stood stunned when Hummingbird slipped off his horse, reached up and took the child down. She immediately ran to her mother who hugged her wildly. The man said something to Hummingbird, but he recognized none of the words. The girl turned away from her mother and walked boldly up to Hummingbird. She said a few more words, and he recognized "name" when she pointed to herself and said, "Frances." She pointed to him and he heard "name" again in her words.

"Temumuquit," he said, pounding his fist against his chest, standing tall. She reached up to his hand and pulled him down towards her. She kissed Hummingbird then ran back to her mother. Hummingbird nodded at the girl's family, jumped back on his horse and rode back to his band, singing yet another song. His power just kept growing, he thought.

CHAPTER 6
Along the San Antonio-San Diego Road, near Uvalde, Texas

They sat in the shade of several pecan trees a few miles west of Uvalde. The steep hills they rode through over the past few days gave way to these rolling hills and broad brushlands. Ringo drank steadily from his silver flask. They were waiting on the stage that ran between Fort Clark and Del Rio down the old Jackass Mail Route. They needed some cash to fund Ringo's kidnapping operation and they hoped to carry some away from this hold-up.

"So where exactly we going?" Bad Back asked.

"I've gone over this itinerary a few times looking for a remote location and I keep coming back to the Big Bend," Ringo said. "The exact spot is both far-flung, tiny, and right on the Río Grande. If anything goes wrong, we can be across the border to Mexico in an instant. The right place is Lajitas."

"Ever been there?" Bad Back asked.

"No," Ringo said. "I've ridden through the area before but I don't recall anything about Lajitas. Maybe it wasn't even there then. The only community I can recall is Presidio, but I think that may be too large for our plans and even it's miniscule."

Parsons rolled his eyes.

"OK," Bryce said. "We get to Lajitas, but then what? None of us even knows what the governor's wife looks like."

"Do you have any idea what the people down there look like?" Ringo snapped. "They're mostly brown. Even the white people are mostly brown. Who would live in such a place? Only people on the run or those who can't make it on their own in the regular world. These are Mexicans and the dregs of white society, gentlemen. Finding the governor's lady will be the easiest thing we ever do; all we have to do is look for the most beautiful, whitest woman around."

As he finished off his flask, Ringo realized his last statement made him angry. Why did governors and other wealthy people have all the most beautiful women? They had fancy houses and good educations and enough money to do whatever it was they wanted to do. They looked down their noses at people who had to work for a living, like his family had always done. He reached into his vest and withdrew a small leather portfolio to look at the photographs he always carried with him of his sisters—Fanny Fern, Mattie Bell, and Mary Enna. They were attractive certainly, as his mother was, but not beautiful women like governors' ladies were with their finishing school educations, sheltered from the harshness of weather and making a living and from the cold realities of life.

His father, Martin, was certainly every bit of Governor Roberts' equal, he thought. But because he didn't have the money or the formal education, he never had a chance to be the governor of any state. But Martin read the classics and instilled culture in all of his children and Ringo still valued it. Many people, especially the newspapermen who did stories about him, thought he had attended a college, probably a well thought of one like Harvard or Yale but Ringo was self-educated with his family's books.

Ringo wished his father was still alive, but wishing didn't make a thing so. He recalled the day exactly, an image that would never leave him. When he was fourteen, his family packed up from Missouri and headed to California, but before they had gone too far in the wagon train they were part of, they faced an Indian attack. His father stepped off their wagon with his shotgun in his hand, stumbled and blew the top of his head off. Mother Mary was pregnant at the time and gave birth to a stillborn, disfigured son. Ringo always blamed that on his mother watching the terrible accident to his father. Ringo swore then nothing similar would ever happen to him and spent the next year getting as familiar as possible with firearms. He got comfortable with them, got extremely accurate with them, got so that he could repair them and make their actions smoother and quicker. He began to appreciate fine weapons and when he became able to afford to, purchased custom-made firearms.

Now he was sitting by the side of the road with what could only be termed a gang of outlaws, waiting for a stage to come by to rob. He knew his father wouldn't be proud of this, but he didn't care. Ringo had come to understand a great truth that eluded his father about wealth. Those who had money had the power to keep others from getting any. Unless you were born into their circles, the wealthy kept you out and poor, working for them. They had theirs. The railroad magnates and industrialists robbed and pillaged, killed and raped as often—no, more—than any outlaw ever did. Certainly their gains were better, and just as ill gotten. But the elite had the power. What they did was not only approved of but also applauded because they did it in the name of big business and that was the business of America. What chance did anyone like his father have?

No, people of Ringo's class could acquire wealth only one way. They had to take it. If that meant rustling cattle from those Dutchmen in Mason County, then so be it. Anyone who tried to stop him better be fearful. He killed at least two of them he knew of, probably more since in a couple of ambushes he couldn't be certain whose bullet struck which man. One of those two was old Charley Bader and that was a mistake, Ringo knew, but mistakes happen. How many mistakes had Governor Roberts buried over the years? he wondered. All it takes to get what you want, Ringo knew, was to have the balls to take it.

Ringo stood up to put his empty flask away in his saddlebag. He turned to the others and recited:

I want a free life, and I want fresh air;
And I sigh for the canter after the cattle,
The crack of the whips like shots in battle,
The medley of hoofs and horns and heads
That wars and wrangles and scatters and spreads:
The green beneath and the blue above,
And dash and danger, and life and love—

Bryce whispered to Bad Back, "Are you sure he's not way off base? Sometimes I think he's out looking for the horse he's riding."

Parsons nodded agreement. "Times he seems pert near jackass-able."

"That tarantula juice he swigs makes him a little light-headed sometimes, but there's no one I'd rather have side me in a fight and he's the smartest man I know. He's stood us in good stead over the past couple years, y'all know as well as I," Bad Back said.

Ringo pulled his bandanna up over his nose and pointed down

the road at the stage that was just rounding a corner in the road about a half-mile off. Bad Back kicked Miguel and Ronaldo who had fallen asleep. They all took their time checking weapons and pulling masks over their faces, then hid behind rocks near the crest of the hill. The stage would be moving its slowest here.

When it arrived, Bad Back stood in the road and hollered, "Hold!" while brandishing his rifle. At that moment, the others came from behind their rocks, pointing Winchesters at the driver and messenger on the boot.

"Discretion is the better part of valor," Ringo said to the messenger who, he could see, was trying to determine what his odds were if he were to let loose with his 10-gauge. "Break open the weapon and drop it on the ground, then dismount."

The driver wrapped the reins around the brake handle as the messenger dumped the shells from his shotgun and tossed it to the side.

Bryce opened the stage door. "Get out!" he ordered. Five passengers stepped down as the driver and messenger did. "Hands high!"

Bad Back scrambled onto the stage and tossed down the box from the boot. He used the butt of the messenger's shotgun to smash open the lock on the box.

"Some greenbacks, a couple big gold coins, and a lot of adobe dollars," Bad Back said. "We can get those changed around in Del Rio."

"How much?" Ringo asked.

"Hard to tell," Bad Back said. "Hundreds, mostly cinco pesos." He counted the paper money and said, "Folding stuff is five thousand, Fifties and Twenties. Four $50 gold pieces. Didn't even know they made these."

"Why so much cash?" Ringo asked the messenger.

"I wouldn't touch it I were you," the messenger said.

"You're not," Ringo said, hitting him on the side of the head with his pistol barrel. The messenger fell to the ground and got up moaning, holding his ear. "This pistol has a hair-trigger and you're lucky it didn't blow your head clean off. Do you want me to repeat the question?"

The messenger shook his head no. "The pesos are a bank transfer, we have them mebbe once a quarter. The folding money belongs to the governor."

Ringo's eyes lit up. "The governor?"

"Yeah," the messenger said, still massaging his head. "He's building a vacation hacienda at San Felipe Springs near Del Rio. The cash is for the contractor to get started."

Ringo doubled over in laughter and almost lost his balance. "Well, I imagine he can spare it."

Bryce was at the rear of the stage, untied the luggage, tossed the bags to the ground. He cut open each bag and went through the contents. He threw clothing left and right.

"Must you do this to my clothing?" one of the women passengers said.

Ringo was tempted to buffalo the woman as he had the messenger, but thought better of it since the rules of etiquette in the West required treating women with much more respect, although he doubted many of them actually deserved it. "Bring your nose down to our level, m'am," he said to her. "We're all equal under our clothes. That fine silk and lace doesn't mean a thing. Get your clothes off."

"Lord!" the woman said, her hands over her mouth.

"You serious?" Bad Back said.

"Deadly," Ringo said. "All you, get in on this naked fandango."

"I think this kinda violates the rules," Bad Back said.

"Did I ask what you thought?" Ringo said. "There are no rules, and you'd better not break any of them." He motioned to the stage passengers with his pistol, "Let's get equal." Slowly they complied.

"This way they can't hide anything from us," Ringo told Bad Back. Miguel and Ronaldo watched with great interest. Parsons walked to the far side of the stage, out of view.

"What's in the luggage?" Ringo asked Bryce.

"Clothes. One small pistol in with men's clothes. Got some jewelry in a box, looks pretty nice. Got a box here in with the luggage I haven't opened yet; pretty heavy."

"Take the jewelry and pile all the clothes over here," Ringo said. "The rest of you, put your clothing in this pile."

"Look at all this," Bryce said after opening the box.

"More cash?" Bad Back asked.

"Nope. It's a lot of newspapers," he replied. "Like the jackpot."

"A jackpot of newspapers?" Ringo asked.

"Yup," Bryce said. "They're all the *Sporting News*."

"A newspaper about gamblers and pimps?" Ringo asked.

"No, no gambling," Bryce said, taking a copy to Ringo. "It's a whole newspaper about base ball. Look at this."

Ringo grabbed the paper and tossed it, the sheets blowing away with the wind. "Take a couple if it'll keep you quiet, but I'm tired of hearing about this base ball."

"I think with my cut I'm going to go east and buy me a team," he said.

"Do whatever you want, but right now pay attention to what you're doing."

The stage passengers and crew stood naked by the side of the red and green coach. The men held their hands over their crotches. The two women held one arm across their bosoms, a hand at their crotches. The men and women had turned away from each other. Miguel and Ronaldo laughed in Spanish, pointing out attractive or unattractive body parts to each other.

"Bryce, get the jewelry off them," Ringo ordered. Bryce did so, removing rings and necklaces. He went through the clothing and removed pocket watches, brooches, and pin watches. "Parsons, get me a bottle of whiskey out of my saddle bag."

"We going to have a party?" Bad Back said.

"No, but not a bad idea," Ringo said. "I've got a partner in Arizona where I'm headed once we're finished in Texas who did that. Curly Bill cut in to a dance in Charleston one evening, maybe two dozen townfolk having a celebration of some sort. He made them all strip down, including the band, and made them continue with the dance. I wish I could have seen it."

Parson handed him the bottle. Ringo poured it over the clothes pile, snatched the cigar from Parsons' mouth, and dropped it onto the pile, which whooshed into flames.

"Lord!" the woman who spoke earlier said. "What are we to do now?" The other woman was crying in fits, losing her breath.

"I imagine, if you're polite, you'll get back in the coach and travel on back to Uvalde and see if you can't get someone to buy you some new clothes," Ringo. "If you're not polite, I'll take the team with us to sell and you can walk back."

"Lord!" the woman said.

"Right now, I'm your Lord," Ringo said. "Give me thanks that all I'm taking is your clothing, money and jewels. I think a couple of my boys might like to take substantially more."

The passengers returned to their coach, the driver and messenger climbed to the boot. The driver slowly turned the stage around and headed back to Uvalde, thinking that perhaps his wife had been right the past few months. It was time to go to California.

CHAPTER 7
Lajitas

Joaquin soaked up as much sauce as he could with the last piece of his tortilla, ate it, and washed it down with the weak lemonade that was the only beverage José served. Dutch had gone, following Ingrid back to his saloon.

"I guess I'll go talk to the preacher man," Joaquin said to Ethan.

"Mind if I go along? I'm kind of curious about him, plus you can cut out that filly for me on the way back."

"Sure. Never know, I might need your help if I have to arrest Brother Karl."

The two left and walked toward Comanche Mesa and Karl's small chapel.

"Mind if I ask you something?" Ethan said. Joaquin shrugged. He had an idea what was coming. Everyone eventually asked. "With that ash hair and blue eyes you're about as white as they come, except for maybe the preacher, so how did you get that Spanish name?"

"Me and my brother got all our looks from my father. We're both tall and lean and fair like he is. His father came over from Denmark. My mother is half-Irish and half-Mexican, and she's pretty fair except for her brown eyes. My three sisters got the looks from that side of the family; they're kinda squat and dark-haired. My grandfather's name on that side was Joaquin and he'd died maybe a couple months before I was born so my mother passed along his name. Simple as that really."

Ethan nodded. "You really think the preacher is a thief?"

"I've heard odder things happening," Joaquin said as they approached the base of the mesa. "But I just don't see him as a criminal. Got to be a good explanation and I plan on getting it. If I need to take him up to Fort Davis, I will. But I'd rather not."

"So you don't think you might need my help subduing our Brother Karl," Ethan smiled.

The ranger stopped and shook his head. "But that's not why you came, is it? I don't think you care anything at all about Karl or what he's done or not."

"You're right," the scout said. "That Comanche report has gotten me a little spooked. A little spooked and I didn't want to panic everyone else by talking about it in José's. How many rangers are up at the Fort Davis detachment these days?"

"It varies too much to give you an accurate count. Maybe a dozen at the most, but they come and go. You think the hostiles will come here? Out in the middle of this desolation? Even the Mescalero won't live out here."

"It wasn't that long ago that the Comanche War Trail crossed over the San Carlos Ford. I figured you knew that."

"I guess I recall," Joaquin said. "But it's been so long since they raided into Mexico and the break-out group is pretty small. Why would they come here of all places?"

"Comanches are creatures of habit. My guess is one of three things happened. One, a couple experienced warriors talked some young ones who haven't been off the reservation into going along for a little glory from the bygone days. If so, they'll have to travel the War Trail, because that's what all their stories are about. That's what the young ones would expect and the older ones want respect... and that's the one thing a Comanche desires more than anything... They'll follow the trail. The other possibility is that they're all young and inexperienced looking to live out the stories they've heard since they were children. If so, they'll hit the Trail as soon as possible and follow it into Mexico like their grandfathers' grandfathers did. Three, perhaps it's just a small group out to kick up their heels a little and they're probably already back on the reservation."

"You don't think the last is a good proposition?"

"Nope," Ethan said. "I can't imagine a Comanche out for a little fun. They'll generally accept whatever the situation is, so if they left the reserve they did it for a good reason. The best reason is to become real Comanche again and not be blanket Indians anymore. I think at the very least you need to alert your sergeant up there, maybe even ride up yourself and bring a little help back with you."

"They're not going to do that," Joaquin said. "I've always been surprised they let me roam around down here along the río. This is just too far away from the big ranches and the railroad and the highways and the settlements. We're not worth it."

"You may be right," Ethan said. "You may be right, but at the least we should be ready for anything."

Joaquin nodded his agreement. They scrambled up the short mesa to the chapel but didn't see the preacher at first. Joaquin thought maybe Brother Karl had run off as quickly as he could, but realized he'd have no reason to. He didn't know about the wanted notice. Besides, the chapel, wagon and draught horse were still here and Joaquin doubted he'd leave them behind. Where would he go on foot?

Ethan pointed to the inside of the chapel. Karl was on his knees in front of his Bible open on the lectern, mumbling prayers. The two of them stood silent, watching for a while. Then Joaquin said, "Say good-bye to God for a bit and talk to me."

Karl stood, touched the Bible, and walked out.

"Confess, therefore, your sins to one another, and pray for one another, that you may be saved. For the unceasing prayer of a just man is of great avail," the preacher said, walking to the east side of the chapel, leaning against the wall in what little shade was there. Ethan took up the remainder of the space in the slim shadow, squatting down. Joaquin pulled his hat down as low as it would go across his eyes, facing Karl.

"You stole this church," Joaquin said.

"No, I did not," Karl replied, shaking his head firmly, slowly.

"City marshal in Fredericksburg says different."

Karl shook his head again. "I took this chapel but I did not steal it. It was given to me by the Lord and I turned it into a chapel."

"Look, you better give me a good explanation for all of this or I'm shipping you back to Fredericksburg and let them sort it all out. Leave God out of it."

"That is not a church, not even a chapel really," Karl said. "What it is, is the steeple from Christ the Redeemer Lutheran Church in Fredericksburg. One night last October there came a fearsome storm with thunder and lightning and rains so heavy it seemed like the wrath of God. Lightning struck the church. It was the most terrible lightning strike I had ever seen. It knocked the steeple off the building and it fell into a deep puddle. The rest of the church burned to the ground, even in that driving rain. The rain was so strong and the thunder was almost non-stop, so the fire brigade never even tried to put it out. I doubt if they could have done much good even if they had been on the scene immediately because the heat and fire was so intense that church turned into ash very quickly.

"That steeple sat on the side of the smoldering ruins for days and days. I believed no one wanted it," Karl paused a little, his eyes looking up for a bit then back at the ranger. "That storm frightened me to the core of my being, Joaquin. That is when I wandered in the wilderness north of the village and that is where God spoke to me. When I returned, the steeple was still unclaimed. That night I claimed it. I did not know how the congregation could use it, and if they could, certainly they would have salvaged it by then. I took it home and repaired it and made the door in place of one of the stained glass windows that had broken in the fall. I put it on my wagon and left on my ministry. As God is my witness, that is the truth. If I thought that old steeple belonged to anyone, I would have paid for it.

"I've wandered since October to find this place and now that I've found it, I will not leave."

"Lizard Teats," Ethan said.

"You have no need to slur her," Karl snapped.

"I didn't know I was," the scout replied.

"You and Ingrid were close?" Joaquin said.

Karl nodded, looking down. "We were," he said. "But she was a married woman. She became frightened and fled. I did not know where she had gone or what became of her. I have been searching for her since I started following the path of the Lord."

"Didn't expect this, did you?" Ethan said.

"I do not expect you to believe me, but none of this matters to me. We are all the children of God. Christ suffered and died for our sins. If she repents she can be saved, as I was, and I will not be complete without her nor without her repentance."

"I see how God, you and her figure into all this, but what about the inconvenient husband," Ethan said, still not looking up at the two men standing nearby but watching the movement of a deep green velvet ant carrying a bit of food across the sand and stones.

"He got a bill of divorcement within the month and has since remarried," Karl said. "I do not believe he cares if he ever sees her again. We will not tempt his anger, though, because we will never go back to the Hill Country. I do not believe either of us wants any of the memories there."

"The way she reacted to you, I don't think she's of the same mind as you about getting back together or even repenting," Joaquin said.

"True enough now," the preacher said. "People change. I am living proof of that. Once I was lost and now I am found and just as she is lost now, she will be found."

"Amen, brother," Ethan said, standing, his knees crackling as they straightened. "You going to arrest him?"

"I don't think I will," Joaquin said. "Seems like a big misunderstanding. You still willing to buy that steeple?"

"I am."

"I'll write to the Fredericksburg marshal and tell him you made the offer and we'll see what happens. But in the meantime, you mind your manners. I don't want any trouble here between you and Liz— Ingrid— or with Dutch."

Karl nodded his agreement and turned back into the chapel, saying to himself, "Christ redeemed us from the curse of the Law."

•

Gracey busied herself making biscuits, beans and bacon as she always did about this time of day. Being a Thursday, she also grilled some pork. This would do until Monday when the main menu item would become beef. Dutch would let her make only traditional Western fare. The lone concession he made to the Mexicans who were the majority of his clientele were the two jugs of pickled jalapeños at each end of the long bar. His main business was drinks anyway, not food. In an hour, Tio José's would close and Dutch would open, a long-standing agreement between the two.

Dutch paid Gracey a little extra for her cooking and also let her work as a curandera for the locals and let her keep all the money. After all, she had two other mouths to feed.

The Mejor Que Nada was the largest building in Lajitas, after the

McGuirks' home, even larger than the Catholic Church on the hill near the road that ran to Presidio. Dutch had twelve tables with six chairs around each of them—never had the saloon been filled to capacity, however. The bar was actually a series of heavy planks that ran the length of one wall, set on old whiskey barrels from which aromatic smells still filled the nostrils of anyone leaning at the bar. Behind the bar were shelves filled with bottles of various spirits, some of them actually containing what their labels proclaimed. Dutch left a large space in the center of the bar wall for a mirror he planned on buying one of these days.

Dutch sat with Ingrid at the table furthest from the front door.

"I'm slap out of patience. What's goin' on with you and that preacher, and why are you so scared lately?" Dutch demanded.

She held her head high, looking at his eyes, her eyes tearing up. He'd never seen her this emotional. "We knew each other in Fredericksburg. That's our home. We grew up on neighboring farms near Luckenbach so we've known each other since as long as I can remember. My father betrothed me to a banker in Fredericksburg when I was only ten years old and I had to honor that when I turned sixteen. But Karl and I kept seeing each other and never stopped being lovers. Then… then… One night we were caught…"

Ingrid being a bed swerver didn't surprise Dutch. "Your husband found the two of you together?" he asked. Dutch rolled a hard-boiled egg between the palms of hands then methodically peeled it, something he'd done so many times in this same place that it was like breathing.

"I don't think Augustus knew until after, no. We were caught by the hand of God."

Dutch had never heard Ingrid mention God before, and didn't expect to hear her suddenly speaking like the preacher. In fact, he realized, she was speaking more at one time than he'd ever heard her speak before. She kept staring at him, tears rolling down her cheeks.

"Was this Brother Karl a preacher then, too? He defile a member of his own flock?"

"No. I don't think either of us was ever very religious," she said after a while. "We went to church with our parents every Sunday but we never listened, we just played around with each other. Maybe that was our downfall. We should have understood we were in the house of God."

"You planning on gettin' back together with him? Gonna leave with him?"

"Oh, no, Dutch, no," she gasped, touching his hand. "I need you to protect me. I don't want to be anywhere near him. If I am, God will surely punish me. He will punish me."

"Karl ever harmed you?"

"No… the only harm that's ever come to me I've done to my-self."

"Well, don't you worry none," Dutch said, holding her hand. "Nobody'll ever hurt you while I'm around. Not some crazy preach-er, not cow-boys, not drunken greasers, not heathen Indians, not God Himself."

Ethan walked in, letting the low afternoon light stream in behind him, illuminating all the dust floating in the saloon. He walked over to Dutch and Ingrid who were sitting at his usual table. Dutch motioned for Ingrid to go and she left to help Gracey prepare food.

"Interesting day," Ethan said.

"If there is a God, He's got a strange sense of humor," Dutch said. Ethan nodded in Ingrid's direction. "If you talked to ol' Brother Karl, you probably already know, my friend. She was married, had relations with him, they got caught, and she ran off in shame and he's a-chasin' her."

"Says he won't leave Lajitas without her," Ethan said.

"Then we better get used to havin' him around 'cause he's gonna be here all his life," Dutch said. "Hey, I had Gracey mix you up some Arkansas wedding cake."

"Some what?"

"You know, think you called it johnny cake last time you asked about it. She's made it up all sweet and moist just like you care for it."

"You're a man's best friend," Ethan said, slapping him on the shoulder.

"Women, too," Dutch said.

CHAPTER 8
Lajitas

Brother Karl lay on his back in his wagon. The canvas was pulled back to the seat so the bed was open to the stars. As part of an almost nightly ritual, he named the constellations and what stars he could, as his father taught him many years ago. The moon wasn't up yet, so the Milky Way glowed in a wide band across the sky, looking so close that he believed he could reach up and swirl it with his hand. A shooting star flew past, on the edge of his vision.

He lost his breath a little, thinking about those days last year…

Ingrid and Karl often met at the Lutheran Church after dark. No one was ever around and the building was situated at the end of a street with the nearest neighbor separated by a playground for children and a picnic area under a thick stand of oaks. They would sneak in, strip down, and enjoy each other in the quiet darkness just inside the front door of the church. Every time they met, Karl urged her to run away with him. She and her husband had no children yet, and Karl knew he could provide for them wherever they would go. She always hushed him and said she would never do so as long as her father lived. Once her father passed, however, she would leave Augustus and be with Karl forever. It was enough to calm him and give him hope. Forgive him, but he also wished God would call her father home soon. In the meantime, they would continue their adulterous passions without guilt because their lust was too much to overcome.

This night rains had begun early, but they were light. In their passion, Karl and Ingrid didn't notice that the rains got heavier and heavier, that lightning was gathering in the West. They finally did hear the thunder and the rains that drummed against the church roof, but nothing prepared them for the strike that came while they were wrapped up in each other.

An observer would later say that two, wide bolts of lightning struck the roof of the church. Inside, Ingrid and Karl only saw a blinding light that filled their world. When they looked up, the only thing in the church that they could make out in that light was the large crucifix above the altar. The light made the crucifix seems as though it hovered directly over them. The thunder sounded in a deafening roar, rattling the walls of the church, threatening to shatter the lovers' bones. The steeple toppled in an explosion to the ground. The ceiling was on fire, burning quickly and brightly. More lightning and thunder followed. Ingrid screamed and screamed and screamed. Karl was dumb struck, confused, looking around in a panic. They stood up, naked to the rain, illuminated by lightning flashes and the fire spreading towards them, clutching their clothing to their breasts, expecting the finger of God to come from the sky and point them out to the city. They finally regained enough of their wits to dress. The rain eased a little, but the thunder and lightning did not. The booms made Ingrid's heart skip beats. They stood in awe as the fire consumed an entire wall of the church, shattering stained glass windows. They moved to the opposite wall.

Ingrid screamed herself hoarse. Her eyes popped. She shivered uncontrollably. Karl was still confused about what was happening.

"We have to get out of here," he said to her, grabbing her arm. She pushed him away, frightened of him. "No, don't touch me. Oh." She looked down at herself in disgust. The rain had now soaked them both; the fire was consuming the back wall and the entrance wall; burned rafters fell from the roof.

Ingrid bolted through the front door as flames licked at her. Karl tried to follow, but the door was engulfed in a matter of seconds. The only two exits were in the front and the rear of the church and both walls were covered in flames. Thunder rattled what was quickly becoming a ruin. Karl removed his coat and wrapped it around his left fist, turned and broke one of the windows behind him. He punched out as much of the shattered glass as he could, placed the coat over the windowsill and pulled himself through.

Ingrid was gone. Karl moved across the street and joined a small crowd gathering on the porch of a nearby home. He searched the street for Ingrid, but he was certain she'd fled. He watched the church burn and burn. Most of the crowd finally left, but he stayed until dawn when the building was nothing but steaming embers and charcoal beams. He knew what he and Ingrid had been doing—had been doing since they were quite young—was wrong and now he knew with a certainty he had never experienced that God saw them and was angered by their remorseless sinning. He sat on the top step of the porch and sobbed.

With morning light, townspeople gathered to see what was left of the church. The steeple was intact, a couple of boards cracked where it had hit the ground, but it was otherwise unharmed. The church was demolished and Karl caused it to happen.

He and others walked through the smoldering wreckage. He saw them express surprise and sorrow, even heard one say to another that this had been God's will. If they only knew, he thought. His guilt overwhelmed him and he began sobbing anew. Someone tried to comfort him. He didn't know who it was or what they said. He kicked at the burned wood, the splintered life-size crucifix with its plaster Christ smashed on the ash-covered floor. In one corner he saw the church's Bible, soaked with water but unburned. He picked it up and carried it with him. He staggered away from the church wondering what to do. Should he confess? Should he find Ingrid and flee as far as possible? Should he just start cleaning away the debris and rebuild it with his own two hands—a thing he knew how to do. It was the only thing he had in common with Jesus, he thought; he was a carpenter, too. He never believed much in Jesus as a real person before. Never believed much in God, certainly not as a father figure who watched over His flock but more as a disinterested Creator. He never saw the hand of God in anything. Until now. The hand of God was unmistakable. But what to do? How could he repair what he had done to himself, to Ingrid, to her husband, to the church, to God? God spoke loudly last night, maybe He would speak again.

Karl went to a store and bought a water jug and some crackers, then walked away from Fredericksburg. He asked around and discovered Ingrid had packed a bag and taken a stage into San Antonio. He knew she had nothing in San Antonio, but where else would she go? Should he even try to find her? If so, where would he begin?

He started walking. He didn't know where he was going until he arrived, just before sundown. Here, some 20 miles north of the city was Comanche Rock—a giant rock, the largest rock anyone had ever seen or even heard of. It thrust over 400 feet above the surrounding oak-thick hills—a lone, naked stone the Indians called a spirit or enchanted rock. Perhaps if he climbed to its summit so he could be closer to God, perhaps God would listen to him.

The rock was so massive Karl could walk up it and didn't have to climb even though the sides of the rock were steep enough to take his breath away. He stopped several times, noticing how smooth the rock was. The colors seemed to change, from granite to deep reds to light gray to a motley of browns, punctuated here and there with green and yellow lichens. Near the top, getting exhausted, he stumbled once or twice over fissures in the rock where grasses and flowers grew in the collected dirt and moisture.

At the summit he sat to catch his breath, surveying the hills below him. The rock must cover an entire section of land, he guessed. He gulped down some water and ate two crackers, realizing for the first time that he still carried the church Bible. He set the Bible down carefully by his knee. It was dry now, but many of its pages were thick and crinkled after recovering from the rains.

He didn't remember lying down but he must have because he awoke flat on the top of the rock. A noise woke him and he struggled to bring himself fully awake to figure out what it was. Although no hostile Indians were reported anywhere near the area and Comanches had a steadfast treaty with the white settlers of Fredericksburg that had never been broken by either side, he still worried. He knew that long before he was born his father and several other Texas Rangers had been attacked at the base of this rock and his father's story of that harrowing day, told over and over again over pints of beer at dinner the whole time he was growing up, had put fear of Indians at this place into him.

What he heard was a deep groaning or moaning. It sounded as if Goliath were suffering from his fatal wound. The sound floated over the rock, fainter then louder then gone. It returned a few times, giving Karl chills. He thought at first it was the wind—but the wind howled or cried, it didn't moan softly as if in pain. The moaning moved around a little, but never seemed to get closer or farther away. On his back, staring up at the Milky Way in the starry sky, he decided the moaning was the voice of God, expressing His disappointment. This frightened him more than the thought of Indians.

He stayed awake all night, listening to the moaning that he heard less as the night went on, finally going away altogether. He watched the stars move in their imperceptible way. God was upset with him, but was also showing him that he was part of all creation. All night when he thought of the church, he thought only of Ingrid's nude body those many times they had been together there then saw the light of God then the charred remains of the house of God. Now when he thought of the church, he recalled lessons heard there over the years he never thought he listened to.

He was a sinner, yes, but Christ had been born, suffered and died for sinners like him. If only he repented, he could be forgiven and saved. God was giving him another chance.

Before dawn, the eastern horizon turned blood red, then lighter, then orange, then yellow before giving way to the sun. Karl cried deeply with remorse, sat up and drank some water. The wind blew softly in from the West, just a little more than a breeze and it warmed him along with the sun. He picked up the Bible, holding it open in his hands, intending to read the whole book if necessary to understand what God wanted him to do. But the answer came quickly. A gust of wind blew the pages over, a hawk screeched overhead, a rock squirrel scampered nearby, and he looked down at the passage in Isaiah: "Then I heard the voice of the Lord saying, "Whom shall I send? And who will go for us?' And I said, "Here I am. Send me!"

Karl realized he must find Ingrid so she could be saved as he had been. He would carry his ministry wherever he had to go. He would thank God by praising Him. And he would find Ingrid.

…and now Karl had found Ingrid, but she was frightened of him and probably frightened of God. He couldn't blame her for either, couldn't blame her for giving up her dignity when she gave up her hope, but he had to convince her she did have hope. "And hope does not disappoint, because the charity of God is poured forth in our hearts by the Holy Spirit who has been given to us," he said. "For why did Christ, at the set time die for the wicked when as yet we were weak? For scarcely in behalf of a just man does one die, yet perhaps one might bring himself to die for a good man. But God commends his charity towards us, because when as yet we were sinners, Christ died for us."

•

At some time past midnight Ingrid sat on a stool at the saloon's bar. The scout and the ranger sat around Ethan's usual table in the back. Joaquin sipped slowly at whiskey, knowing how much and how slowly to drink so he wouldn't become too drunk. Ethan just guzzled his beers and ate his peaches, like he always did. Three Mexicans sat around another table getting very drunk; one could hardly hold his head up. It was Thursday—no ranch hands tonight. Ingrid knew she wasn't going to make any money, but she didn't really care. She would still sleep in Dutch's bed, be warm, and eat his food in the morning.

Ethan rose from the table, said goodbyes to Joaquin and Dutch then left. He left somewhere around this time every night… or morning, really. Now that he had a horse, perhaps he'd make it all the way home regularly instead of waking up by the side of the road like he often did, according to Dutch.

Joaquin remained, sipping out of an almost empty whiskey glass. Dutch passed Ingrid another full glass and she brought it over to the ranger.

He thanked her and patted the chair next to him. She sat down.

"Looking for company?" she asked.

"Not the way you intend," he replied. "I don't think would be right, considering Brother Karl."

"He's nothing to me," she said.

"But you are to him," he said.

"Are you going to arrest him? I heard you weren't."

"Not now," he said. "I don't see any clear reason."

"You should. You should arrest him and put him in jail far away. He's done terrible things and he shouldn't be here."

"You just don't want him here."

She shook her head no emphatically.

"It's a free country," he said.

"But Dutch said he stole that chapel he's carting around. Aren't you the law? Shouldn't you put him in jail?"

Joaquin took another sip and scrunched up his face in thought. Finally, he said, "Most rangers believe in justice. Sometimes following the law doesn't get you justice. I don't think we help anyone by putting Brother Karl behind bars."

"Helps me," she said, looking directly at him for the first time. "And I'd be grateful."

"Naw," he said. "We'll just see that the good preacher behaves himself while he's here and eventually he'll move on. That's what he's been doing, moving from one place to another."

"He won't leave now he's found me."

"We'll see about that, too."

"Will you at least keep him away from me," she said. By this time the three Mexicans had left and Dutch walked over and sat down next to Ingrid.

"He won't harm you," Joaquin said.

"Neither of us will let him," Dutch said. "But I don't think you have any real thing to fear from him."

She touched the ranger's arm, leaned over and kissed him. This concerned Dutch a little. He'd never seen her do that with a customer before, never seen that level of emotion in her before. This ranger was a much younger man than Dutch, handsomer, stronger, and probably knew how to handle himself. Maybe Ingrid was beginning to think of him as a better protector.

"Thank you," she said. "You know, I don't even know your name. Everyone just calls you 'the ranger.'"

"Joaquin Jaxon," he tipped his hat to her.

"You don't look Mexican," she said.

"Naw, " he said. "My mother hails from Contra Costa County, California, and she's a hopeless romantic and fell in love with all those Robin Hood tales about Joaquin Murrieta when she was younger so she named me after him."

"A ranger named for an outlaw," she said. It was the first Dutch had ever seen her smile.

CHAPTER 9
Lajitas

Dutch was happy today was cold as a dead snake. Not that he liked cold—he didn't—but he knew from several years of experience living here that this would be the last cold, even cool, weather for many months to come. The pattern seldom varied after the New Year: cool, warm, rain, hot, cold, then roasting until November when the first norther blew in.

People lived in the desert for many reasons, he'd discovered. Some were born here and knew no other life, desired no other life. Jobs brought others here, like the ranger or the soldiers who drifted through. Some, like the McGuirks, were speculators on the land, what could be raised on the land, and what was under the land. Some, like Ingrid, came here running from something. It seemed to Dutch that he was always leaving places so sudden that he forgot to take his right name with him. That's why he stuck with simply "Dutch Dave," so he didn't have to remember which name he was using in which place. But he stayed here because of the weather. The Chihuahuan Desert made the years longer than in a city. Life moved gradually here and the days themselves moved more slowly when the weather was always the same, as it was most of the year. He knew Ethan was here because he was running, too, running away from himself and most of the world. Out here, even when sitting in Dutch's saloon as he did almost every evening, Ethan didn't have to socialize with anyone he didn't want to. No one would ever bother him. Dutch had known him for several years, since they met in Langtry. That was a bad time for him, and Dutch tried to be his friend, but Ethan was only interested in drinking his troubles away, which, Dutch knew, only irrigated them.

So when the six hardcases walked into the Mejor Que Nada, the first thing Dutch thought about was why they were here. One of them, the best dressed of the lot, had a mean look that would make an icicle feverish. Only one of them—the man wearing the bowler and town coat—didn't wear chaps. But none of them looked like regular hands.

He'd bet they were cow-boys with sticky ropes, looking for other folks' livestock to admire.

"What's your pleasure?" Dutch asked.

Ringo ordered a gin fizz, Parsons ordered whiskey, the others beer.

"We're slap outta gin," Dutch told the tall man. "In fact, we haven't even seen any fizz in these parts for years."

"Scots whiskey?" Ringo asked politely.

"Oh, now that I do have. I've got a pony cask of scotch that I've had for a couple years so it's aged right good. But it's expensive as Lillie Langtry's underwear," Dutch said.

"Give me a glass for a taste," Ringo said. "If I like it, I'll take the remainder."

Dutch couldn't remember what the scotch originally cost, not that it cost him anything when he took it back in Langtry, so he was unsure what to charge Ringo. The newcomer seemed well enough off, so Dutch guessed at a fee.

"Maybe half-a-cask," he said. "Cost you $50."

"Forty," Ringo said.

"Fifty. This is rare tanglefoot in this desert. Came from all the way across the ocean."

"Forty," Ringo repeated.

"You seem a cultured gentleman, how about $45?"

Ringo slid his pistol from his holster so quietly that Dutch didn't know the gunman had done so until the engraved barrel was pointed directly between his eyes an inch or two away. Dutch heard the cylinder rotate and the click of the pistol's hammer; all he saw was the lead peeking out from the chambers.

"Forty," Dutch said. Ringo de-cocked the pistol and holstered it with a little spin.

"I knew you were a reasonable gentleman," Ringo said. Dutch retrieved the small cask from under the bar and poured Ringo a shot-glass full of the scotch. Ringo sipped it while everyone watched.

"It'll do," he said, taking the cask. He flipped an old $50 gold piece to Dutch who barely caught it. "And keep the change."

Dutch smiled and got the other men their drinks. They continued to lean against the bar, their backs to him. Dealing with these boys were going to be as dangerous as squatting bare-assed over a nest of rattlers, he thought. He motioned to Gracey.

"Find the ranger and ask him to wander over here," he whispered to her. She looked at the new men and nodded; then left.

Joaquin walked in with Ethan at his side and Gracey behind them. As soon as the ranger saw the men at the bar, he knew why Dutch fetched him. They walked to the back table, asking Gracey to bring them two beers.

"Any good places to stay around here?" Ringo asked Dutch.

Dutch shook his head. "Good? No. The only places to rent are a couple of rooms behind this saloon. That's it. Can't be fussy if you want to stay indoors."

"Any important visitors been through lately?" Bad Back.

"Important? Here?" Dutch laughed. "Why I believe the Queen of England and the Archduke of all the Russias passed through last Thursday. If mem'ry serves I believe the King of the Jungle and the Queen of the May were in their entourage, too."

"Sarcasm doesn't become a beertender," Ringo said.

"Stupid questions get stupid answers is all I know," Dutch said. "Important people? The most important person who ever came through here was probably that old Comanche Chief Iron Shirt before the war. Important people... Are you lost? Don't you know where you are?"

"I'm fully aware of where we are," Ringo said. "Are you expecting anyone of circumstance?"

"If so, it's a surprise to me," Dutch said.

"Then why's that ranger hanging around?" Ringo said, nodding toward Joaquin.

"Why don't you ask him," Dutch said. "I've got better things to do than palaver with you."

"Hey, ranger," Bad Back hollered. "You lost out here?"

Joaquin nodded to Ethan. He got up and walked to the bar. The scout stayed in his chair but eased his pistol out of its holster into his lap. "I think you boys might be the ones lost," he said. "Where you headed?"

"How do you know we aren't headed pert near near here?" Parsons said.

"Nearest ranch to here on this side of the river is more than fifty miles off, and he's got all the hands he needs," the ranger said.

"We're headed to Arizona Territory," Ringo said. "We've got jobs at a ranch near Tombstone."

"What ranch?" Joaquin asked.

"Can't tell you the name because I don't know it. Family named Clanton runs it on the border," Ringo said.

"Don't know the name," Joaquin said. "Which reminds me, what's yours?"

"John Ringo," he replied, giving Joaquin his hand, knowing the name would impress the ranger. He could tell by the surprised look that it did. "I'm not wanted anymore for anything in Texas."

"I know," Joaquin said. "What about the rest of you?" Ringo gave their names, pointing to each with the hand that held his shot-glass.

"Any of them wanted?" Ringo asked.

"Not that I recall, but I'll check my bible."

"And what do they call you?" Ringo asked, pouring another drink.

"Joaquin Jaxon," the ranger said.

"Look here, boys, we've got an actual beaner ranger," Parsons said. "I guess that's why they've got him pert near hid away out here by the river."

"No beaner blood flows through these veins," Joaquin snapped. "My mother was a very religious woman. She gave me the name because I was born on July 26, the feast day of San Joaquin—Saint Joachim—the father of the Virgin Mary. You making fun of my mother?"

Their voices were getting louder, so Ethan holstered his pistol, not snapping it in, and walked over to the bar just in time to hear Joaquin ask Ringo if he had insulted his mother.

"Ah," Ringo said, smiling. "The hand that rocks the cradle is the hand that rules the world."

"Mater tua criceta fuit et pater tuo redoluit baccarum sambucus," Ethan said almost under his breath, his hand casually resting on his pistol.

"You're not as mangy as you look, insulting me in Latin," Ringo said, touching the grip of his own pistol.

"Insult? Quien sabe? Depends on your point of view," Ethan

said, cocking his head to one side.

"What does it mean?"

"I guess you're not as educated as you pretend," Ethan said. "You'll just have to learn Latin to find out."

"I will."

Dutch slammed down a glass of beer on the bar, spilling a little of it, and pushed it over to Ethan. "Look," he said to the group in front of him. "Why don't y'all just whip out your dicks and slap 'em on the bar and we'll take a measure to see who's biggest? If not, then drink up or get out. This saloon is a big investment for me and I won't stand still to see it busted or shot up over nothin'."

"I think I'll keep my pecker right where it belongs," Ethan said. "I think these cow-boys will do the same."

"For now," Ringo said. "But I'll be ready to skin it anytime you are. I'm certain we'll meet again in the wild open spaces and then we can determine which dog gets to stay on the porch."

Ethan lifted his beer glass in salute and walked over to his usual table. Ringo poured another scotch while his friends ordered new drinks.

"So what's a Texas Ranger doing way out in these parts?" Ringo asked.

"I'm ranging," Joaquin said. "Out of the Company E detachment in Fort Davis. They gave me all of the Big Bend and I had to live someplace so I chose here. It's pleasant enough and certainly has more people than any other place out here."

Ringo didn't believe him. Rangers protected communities of white people and this wasn't much of a community and had only a couple of white people he could see. They didn't range alone. When rangers came this far, they were chasing somebody—bandits or hostiles—and traveled in large groups. No, this ranger was here either as an advance man to spy out the town for when the governor's lady was driven through, or he was a bodyguard for the lady who was already here but whose presence wasn't yet known. They would need to keep their eyes open and wait.

"Well, you won't have problems from us," Ringo told him. "As I said, we're just passing through and we'll likely be gone in a day or two. We've been riding a good deal."

"I guess you have," Joaquin said. "This ain't on the road to Arizona, or anyplace for that matter. You've got to mean to come here."

"We just wanted to see the country," Ringo said. "Traveling is the best education, you know."

"I'm sure your boys here are all fine scholars," Joaquin said. He turned and joined Ethan.

"What do you make of them?" Ethan asked.

"I don't know," the ranger said, drinking his beer and continuing to look at the six men at the bar. "You ever had that many white men come here in a group that size before?"

"Only when the soldiers ride through," the scout said. "Even when crazy William Brocius had his ranch out near the Chisos, all his hands were Mex 'cept for one mulatto Seminole."

"They're here for a reason, but I'm stumped why. No cattle to rustle. No banks to rob. The train's a hundred miles north. No regular stage, only the supply wagon from Fort Davis twice a month and they're not going to be after carrots and kegs of beer and bolts of cloth."

"Maybe they are just travelin' like ol' Mark Twain."

"You believe that?"

"Not for a second."

•

Ingrid wore her best clothes because the temperature was freezing outside and her fancy woolen dress and shawl were all she had that would keep her warm. When she left the apartment she intended to go into the saloon, but changed her mind. She didn't feel like working tonight and she knew Dutch wouldn't mind. She was startled by a figure that walked around the corner of the saloon.

"Didn't mean to alarm you," Joaquin said, tipping his hat. "Just came out for a breath of fresh air." In reality, Joaquin and Dutch were both worried about her. She hadn't been around tonight and with these new scoundrels in town, she shouldn't be left alone. Dutch needed to look after the bar, so Joaquin volunteered to find Ingrid.

"It's OK," she said. "I was just going for a stroll."

"In this cold, after midnight, and you're going for a stroll?" he asked.

"I've never minded the cold as long as I could dress for it," she said, extending her arm to him. "Will you walk with me?" He took her arm and they walked down to the river.

"Whenever I get a little melancholy I like to come down and listen to the water. It's soothing."

"You really shouldn't be walking out here alone."

"Why? I do it all the time."

"Bunch of villains rode into town today. They've been over to Dutch's most of the night and just cleared out a little while ago. I don't know what they're up to, but it can't be any good."

"Arrest them."

He laughed. "I don't think so. None of them is wanted for anything, and I'm not going to try to run them out of town all by my lonesome either. One against six is bad enough odds but one of them is Johnny Ringo."

Ingrid nodded understanding. Joaquin noticed how her features stood out in the bright moonlight. He wished both Dutch and Karl didn't claim her.

"Why don't you leave this place," Joaquin said. "You don't have to go back to Fredericksburg and all of that. You could go back east, or head west to California maybe. Start all over."

"With what? How? Do you know options a single woman has out in the West? Wife, whore or schoolteacher. I don't have the education to be a teacher and I failed at being a wife. And back east would be even worse. The gossips would wag their tongues non-stop wondering why a woman my age wasn't married. With no money, I'd have to earn a living somehow, but how? Washing laundry? I suppose I could marry some wealthy gentleman, but I'd rather earn my money honestly than let some oaf hump on me in return for an allowance and respectability."

"Get a black dress and go to California and change your name. You could be the Widow Smith or whatever."

"I know what I am," she said, inhaling deeply and patting his hand. "God knows what I am and I'm just not fit to be around polite society anymore."

"We're not polite out here?"

"Not mostly, no. But everyone I've met out here is at least forthright. You know where you stand. They don't look down on me, they accept me for what I am and I accept them. It's much simpler that way than having to put on one face after another in the polite society of a city. I can't deal with the hypocrisy."

"What about going with Brother Karl. I believe he loves you as much as any man can love a woman."

She shook her head quickly. "Maybe he does, but he's in the wrong profession to marry a whore."

"You don't have to be—"

"Stop," she said. "I am what I am and I can't go with Karl. My love for him brought me the wrath of God and brought me to this place. Karl is not what I need. I'm getting colder now, take me home."

"I didn't mean to upset you," he said as they turned to walk back up the bluff.

"You didn't," she said. "I do it to myself several times a day. You just happened to be with me this time."

He left her at the apartment. She knew that in many ways Joaquin was right. Her current situation couldn't stand. She felt an urgent need to speak to another woman, someone who could understand her feelings, but didn't know who it could be. Certainly not the Mexican slut she worked with. But who? Maybe she was just trapped and had to accept it. No, that's what she had for more than a year now. Something had to change.

•

Ringo and Bryce leaned against the wall of Tío José's café, drinking and smoking. The others had gone to their campsite across the road, too drunk to stay awake. They stayed back in the dark when they heard voices to the west of them. Slowly, Ingrid and Joaquin came into view then walked around the corner of the saloon out of sight.

"You see that?" Ringo asked.

"Yah," Bryce said. "That's the most beautiful woman I ever saw."

"Yes, she is. A gorgeous woman in an exquisite dress, accompanied by a Texas Ranger. Now just who do you suppose she is?"

"The governor's wife?"

"Who else?" Ringo said. "This is where she's supposed to be about now according to what we read in the newspaper and she certainly doesn't fit in with this other riff-raff and she's being escorted by a ranger."

"What now?"

"Tomorrow, as soon as we see her again. No sense in wasting time."

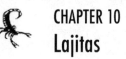

Ingrid rose as soon as she heard the roosters crowing across the río, dressed in her warm clothing as silently as possible and left Dutch snoring in bed. She walked to the Catholic Church, a solitary adobe structure painted white. The church was directly in line with the McGuirks' large adobe and stone home, also standing by itself on the east edge of the town. She knew Mrs. McGuirk came down every morning to pray in the church her husband built for her. She didn't know if the woman would speak to her, ignore her, or be insulted that Ingrid would even dare approach her, but she had to try.

Josefa Navarro McGuirk, a woman twice Ingrid's age, knelt before the altar with her head bowed fingering a rosary. Ingrid slid quietly into the last pew. Finally, the woman crossed herself, stood, and walked toward the church door. She was surprised to see another person inside, something that rarely happened. And this was a white woman, dressed well, and carrying herself as a woman of substance, all of which surprised her even more. As she drew near, Ingrid stood to greet her.

"How do you do? My name is Josefa McGuirk," the frail-looking woman said. Her eyes were bright, her smile wide and engaging, her gleaming white teeth a sharp contrast to her dark brown skin.

"Hello," Ingrid said. "I've seen you but we've never met. I'm Ingrid Jarrell. I work at Dutch's place."

"Oh, my," Mrs. McGuirk said, lifting her eyebrows about as far as they would go before disappearing into her bonnet.

"Please, I need to speak to another woman about something distressing me, and if you would only listen I would appreciate it very much."

"Certainly, my child," Mrs. McGuirk said, placing her arm in Ingrid's. They left the church and stopped in front. Mrs. McGuirk rarely got to talk to another woman and was happy to speak to Ingrid even if she was a fallen woman. Besides, it might make for an exciting story when she and her husband visited her relatives in San Antonio.

"Would you like to breakfast with me?" she asked Ingrid. "I have some strawberries that came in on the last wagon that are quite exquisite. My cook Inez whips cream up into something quite delicious. And we have several kinds of tea."

"Thank you very much," Ingrid said. They turned to go to the McGuirk's house but were confronted by a wall of four men.

"O, Dios," Mrs. McGuirk said, now afraid her exciting story was going to go very badly.

John Ringo tipped his hat to the women. "I'm afraid I'll have to ask for the pleasure of your company, m'am," he said to Ingrid.

"I'm not working," she said.

"M'am we're not here to listen to you give a speech," Ringo said, taking her hand, squeezing it tightly. "You're coming with us." He twisted her hand a little, to give her just enough pain to make her compliable. He turned to Mrs. McGuirk. "We'll be leaving with the First Lady, here, and you can tell the governor we'll be getting in touch with him on how he can get her back."

Mrs. McGuirk was confused by what the man said, stunned by what was happening, and watched speechless as the men pushed Ingrid onto a horse that was brought by two other men and the seven of them rode off.

"Socorro! Socorro! Help! Por favor, rápido!" Mrs. McGuirk screamed as she ran toward the heart of the village. Almost no one was around. She banged on doors, screaming for help, until finally Joaquin stepped out of his apartment, pulling his trousers up, a pistol in his hand.

"What's all the noise about?" he asked.

"La chica!" she said.

"What girl?"

"That girl who works with Davíd. Ingrid, I think. They stole her."

"Who did?" he asked, but he knew.

"No sé. I don't know. Several men, mostly ruffians. We were leaving church and they just grabbed her, put her on a horse and rode off."

"How long?" he asked, looking around, but not seeing any sign of riders, nor any dust. But with all the hills and mesas surrounding the town it would be easy for anyone to ride behind one and completely disappear.

"Just a couple of minutes. Oh, you must save her."

"We'll get her back," he said. "Which way did they go?"

"Why, I don't recall. It all happened so quickly. They were all around us and, I must tell you, I feared for our lives. The good looking man grabbed Ingrid and they were gone."

Dutch and several other townspeople had gathered around now.

"Mrs. M.," he nodded to her, tugging his suspenders up over his bare torso. "Did I hear you say someone took Ingrid? Against her will?"

"Si, absolutely. I don't think they knew what they were doing at all."

"Why's that?" Joaquin said.

"Well, el guapo, he said to tell the governor he would let him know how to get her back. Why would such a gentleman as Governor Roberts care about a woman such as she?" Mrs. McGuirk said.

"The governor?" the ranger asked.

She nodded. "That's what he said, to tell the governor."

"While we're here jawin', they're getting' away," Dutch said.

"We don't know where they went," Joaquin said. "Get your horse and I'll get mine and we'll ride around but I don't think we're going to catch sight of them by the time we get mounted. We need a tracker."

"Ethan is nearly fifteen miles away!" Dutch said, anxious to do something immediately.

"Like I said, get your horse. Maybe we'll get lucky. If we don't see them right away, we won't have any choice but to get Ethan to help."

Dutch didn't answer. He ran back to his apartment to get his shotgun and hat, ran to the corral and saddled his horse. Joaquin saddled his, sliding a Winchester into the scabbard tied to the saddle. Dutch noticed the ranger had a second pistol stuffed into his gunbelt.

"From here we can see quite a ways to the east and when I came out when Mrs. McGuirk was screaming I didn't see any dust in that direction," Joaquin said. "Leaves us three choices. Maybe they crossed the river, but I don't think so because Mrs. McGuirk would have at least heard the noise the horses would make splashing across the water. That leaves west and north. West follows the road to Presidio, north is just this jumble of hills. I'll go north, you take the road." Dutch didn't even acknowledge what the ranger had said, he just road off to the west. "And don't try to take them all by your lonesome! Follow them and we'll find you!" Dutch waved and kept riding.

●

Ringo was quite happy with himself. He had estimated the governor's lady would be an early riser and she was. He estimated she would probably be staying with the only wealthy family in town and she was; they caught her with one of them. They'd gotten lucky when the ranger wasn't with her, probably didn't see any danger in her going to church. And the rest of the town was asleep except for a goatherd family.

He'd planned the getaway well. Just to the north of the road was a hodgepodge of various sized hills in front of the towering Lajitas Mesa that overlooked all the area. They rode quickly behind the hills then turned east, riding in a barely wet ditch that would cover their tracks and eliminate any telltale dust. Once they got a little further east, they could cross over to Comanche Creek which had bluffs high enough to hide them and follow it to the broad plain that stretched out in front of the Mesa de Anguila then follow the edge of the mesa into the Sierra Quemada. The tall, dark cliff of the mesa would mask any dust. Once into the burned hills that flowed from the Chisos down to the Río Grande, no one would ever find them. The desert was too confusing, the hills and mesas too irregular to give anyone a clear idea of where they might go, even if they managed to follow them this far. And he knew the perfect hideout that Curly Bill had showed him the last time he rode through these parts.

"Why are you doing this?" Ingrid shouted, her heavy dress bunched up uncomfortably beneath her.

"You'll get the story when we're safe, Mrs. Roberts," Bryce told her. "Meantime, save your energy."

"I'm not Mrs. Roberts," she shouted.

"Then I guess we've whiffed," Bryce laughed. "You're just a poor little saloon girl."

"Yes!" she said. Yes!"

•

Hummingbird's band made a cold camp on the highest mesa above the crossing the night before, surprised that a town full of Americans had grown up around it. They woke to a woman shouting. Hummingbird and Shit darted to the mesa's edge, crouched low, and watched several Americans ride off leading a horse that a woman was tied to.

Hummingbird thought the woman was truly a worthy prize. His raid so far had been a thing of beauty and seeing the woman changed his plans. They would not continue into Mexico for slaves and cattle and horses. They would take this woman and she would be his second wife. Her skin was whiter than any he had ever seen, her hair like spun gold.

He told his band of his new plan. All agreed but Shit who said, "I think this is a mistake. Why risk fighting more Americans?"

"Do you forget the Texas Rangers we sent running with their tails between their legs? These men will be taken just as easily."

"Then what? What can you do with this American woman? You can't take her home with us, the American soldiers will take her from you and hang you for it."

"We are not going back to the reservation," Hummingbird said. "We are now free Human Beings and we are amassing our wealth. Look how many horses we have, this food and weapons and ammunition. We will become a new band of Human Beings, our own band. We will find a place where the Americans haven't come yet and live there with our women and raise our families without anyone telling us what to do, when to come, when to go."

"I don't think we can find a place without Americans," Shit said. "They are like lice. Once they begin an infestation, they cannot be stopped."

"We will find it, and it will be full of buffalo because the Americans aren't there. I will go and bring Quiver and my son to be with us. We can raid more and find wives for the rest of us. It will be glorious."

Shit shrugged his lips and eyebrows as the others shouted,

"Aihe!" claiming Hummingbird's dream.

"How do we do take this woman?" Shit asked.

"We follow, then strike them when they least expect it," Hummingbird said.

They fanned out. Small Snake would track the running Americans from about two miles behind so he could not be seen. Shit would ride parallel to Small Snake, about a mile to his north to keep him in sight. The rest would ride parallel to Shit another mile out, keeping him in sight. When the Americans stopped, Shit and Small Snake would ride to the band and they would determine their course of action from that point.

•

When Ethan rode into Lajitas, Dutch and Joaquin rode up to greet him. They were covered in dirt, their horses covered in sweat. Brother Karl was placing a borrowed saddle on a borrowed horse by the corral.

"Que paso?" he asked.

"Them hardcases snatched Ingrid and made off with her," Dutch said.

"Why?"

"They didn't hang around to explain it," the ranger said. "We tried to find them, but we can't find their trail. I found where they rode into the hills north of town but then they turned into the ditch and I lost them. We don't know if they went east or west from there."

"This is crazy," the scout said. "Insane."

"Mebbe so, but wonderin' about it ain't getting' her back," Dutch said.

"Eh-yeah. Show me where they went into the ditch," Ethan said. As they rode across the road, Karl joined them, looking uncomfortable in his borrowed saddle.

"Where you going?" Ethan asked.

"With you," Karl said.

"I don't think that's a good idea," Ethan said. "Not a good idea. You'll only slow us down. Same with Dutch. The ranger and I will find them and bring Lizard Teats back."

"You're slap weak north of your ears you think you can leave me behind," Dutch said.

"Me either," Karl said.

"I can't force you not to follow, but you had better understand—and this includes you, Joaquin—that from this point on I'm in command. I'm in command and you do exactly what I say, when I say, no questions and I don't care whether you understand what I'm telling you to do. This isn't a democracy from this point on. You don't have a say in anything."

They all agreed.

At the ditch, Ethan swung off his horse, signaling for the others to stay mounted and not move. If he only knew why they took the whore, he might know which way they were likely to go. West didn't lead much of anywhere, except Presidio, only slightly larger than Lajitas, then hundreds of miles across desert into El Paso. If they grabbed her just to use her up and throw her away, that's the direction they would go. East led eventually to larger towns like Del Rio and San Antonio, even Austin. Would they be kidnapping her? Didn't make sense. But then, Mrs. McGuirk said Ringo told her to tell the governor they had Lizard Teats. Why the governor? Who knew? But they did mention the governor and the governor's mansion was east. He walked east alongside the ditch, leading his horse. The overturned stones that Joaquin didn't see were obvious to Ethan, along with several indentations in the mud just below the dark surface of the stagnant water.

He motioned for them to follow. He walked along the ditch for a ways longer then mounted his horse, picking up the pace, keeping his eyes on the water and the dirt alongside it. Long ago his grandfather taught him how to use his sweeping vision, to see all that he could and take it all in at once, and he saw where the group exited the ditch long before he got to the spot. The tracks took them across the road to the south and into the rocky creek where about half a foot of water flowed.

"You stay in the creek and follow it at my stride," Ethan told them, then spurred his horse to the bluff above the east side of the creek. They rode along for some time until the scout motioned them out.

"They're headed almost due east now," he said. "Due east, ahead of us by maybe two hours judging from this horseshit. They're not really trying to hide their trail anymore. Couldn't if they wanted to, really, given the way they're going. Normally, tracks are temporary things but they last a lot longer in the desert unless it rains. A rock out here can go undisturbed for a hundred years; then a horse comes along and flips it over. It stands out. They're kicking over rocks and trampling grass and cactus like crazy, moving fast now. Seven horses, so it's the six men from last night and Lizard Teats for sure."

"Let's get them," Karl said.

"Can't," the scout replied. "It's getting too late in the day. My guess is they'll be in the Sierra Quemada by nightfall and we don't want to go wandering around there after dark without knowing where they might go. Can't catch them before that. Don't worry. At the end of these tracks men are moving and they're leaving behind all sorts of information about where they are. They're leaving behind information and I won't lose the tracks and the tracks will lead us to them. We'll be on them tomorrow."

"Any clue where they might be headed? We could cut them off," Joaquin said.

"Hard to say," Ethan said. "Hard to say. If they're headed back to a city, they'll turn north before they reach the Chisos. If they're looking for a hideout, they'll go east or south. I'm guessing, just guessing, that they'll want a place to rest a while, maybe even a place to hide the whore away where she won't be found. If I were doing that I'd go to Brocius's old place by the Mule Ears."

"Why there?"

"His stone cabin is still standing," Ethan said. "Maybe a little drafty without much of a roof, but decent shelter last time I was there. Even has a stone corral to keep your mounts from roaming off. It's difficult to get to. Difficult and the view commands everything in front of it and it backs up against a cliff above it to one side and a cliff below it to the other. And it has one of the few springs in the Quemada, cold, pure water. We'll know for sure tomorrow."

They continued following the tracks, planning on camping out just before sunset. When the shadows got long and the sky ahead of them started to turn reddish from the reflected setting sun, Ethan dismounted and walked over to the tracks.

"This is odd," he said, mostly to himself.

"What'd you find?" Joaquin asked.

Ethan pointed to a group of hoof prints. "We've been follow-ing seven horses until now. Now we're following eight. Eight tracks. Came in from the north and the new one is keeping to one side of the main tracks. He's not making many tracks himself, but enough to tell."

"You mean someone else is following Ringo?" the ranger asked.

"Eh-yeah, that's my guess," the scout said. "But don't ask me who."

CHAPTER 11
Mule Ears Peak, in the Sierra Quemada, Texas

The ride to Mule Ears Spring wasn't difficult on horseback; just up and down and up and down over the many foothills into the burned mountains. The heat was dry and suffocating, making the men gasp every now and then to get enough air into their lungs. The ground itself was all loose pebbles, reflecting the heat back up to the riders. Shade was impossible. The tallest things growing along the trail were three-to-four-foot high mesquite bushes. The rest was all grasses, prickly pear, lechuguilla, and the random candelilla, cholla, or ocotillo. The horses moved slowly, picking their way through this landscape, avoiding the lechuguilla points that could stab deep into their legs and cripple them. The purple pods on the prickly pear pads were all that was left of the yellow flowers that bloomed a couple weeks earlier. Most of the ocotillo were bare now, but a couple still had orange blossoms at their tips, like candles in the desert.

Each man carried a canteen full of water plus they had two large water bags strapped behind the saddle of the horse Ingrid was riding. As they rode, they soaked bandanas in canteen water then tied the silk cloths around their necks providing some relief from the heat. But the dryness of the desert kept evaporating the moisture from the bandanas so quickly they had to constantly rewet them. That meant stopping twice along the route to refill their canteens from the water bags. Ringo promised a spring at the end of the trail, and they all knew if it were dry they would be in fatal straits.

The route couldn't have been any easier to follow, though, because the two looming stony points dominated the landscape. They were aptly named. It was impossible to look at them and not think you were seeing the ears of some giant mule just over the top of a high hill.

Ringo knew enough about geology to know they formed when lava spurted up through the ground then hardened in the air. They got their shape, he guessed, from high winds chipping away at loose rocks until they looked like this. He was impressed by it all.

"You're making a mistake," Ingrid said to Ringo who was leading her horse.

"You keep saying that, m'am, but I'm not about to take your word for it," he said. "Now shut up about it or I'll shove your lace petticoats down your throat."

When they arrived at the old shack, Ringo was not happy. The last time he'd been here, the small stone cabin was intact but now the roof made of octotillo stalks, grass and mud was broken in and scattered, and the door was missing along with many of the stones that comprised the walls. The tallest of the remaining walls was the front one, but it wasn't even belt-high. He looked around quickly but didn't see any of the stones, so he guessed others building their own shacks salvaged them. How far, he wondered, would someone have to carry those heavy stones? How desperate would they have to be? The stone corral, though, was completely intact.

The spring was obvious, flowing near the ground from a rock cliff and surrounded by deep green ferns. The men let the horses drink for a bit, then knelt down and scooped the cool water up into their mouths and splashed it on their heads and necks.

They unsaddled their horses and shooed them into the corral, then sat around on what was left of the cabin's walls.

"Well, it's pert near a hideout," Parsons said. Ringo said nothing.

"What now?" Bad Back asked him finally.

"Same as before," Ringo said. "No change. We just don't have a roof over our heads. I believe we've all slept in the out-of-doors before. And I can't imagine anyone trailing us out here."

"You don't think they'll put together the biggest damn ranger posse anybody's ever seen and take us deep?" Bryce asked.

Ringo shrugged. "They have to find us first. It'll be dark before long. Let's get some sleep and figure the rest out tomorrow."

He tied Ingrid's hands behind her back, tied her feet together then carefully set her down on the ground inside the walls. He tied another rope loosely around her neck and fastened the other end to his wrist. He sat with his back against the far wall, pulled his hat over his eyes, and told Ingrid, "Sleep tight, Mrs. Roberts. Or as well as you can on these rocks."

"I told you, I'm not—"

"Hush," Ringo said.

When morning arrived, none of them were still asleep. None of them got much sleep during the night.

"I'm in desperate need of some coffee," Bryce said. "I'll get us a fire going."

"Not yet," Bad Back said. "We don't know if anybody followed us or not."

"We're safe," Ringo said, untying the rope from Ingrid's neck, feet and hands.

"We need a look-out, regardless of how safe you think this place is," Bad Back said. "Somebody needs to climb up on one of them peaks. They'd see somebody coming miles before they ever even got close."

"Can't," Ringo said.

"I'm good enough to scramble around them rocks and get to the top and I'll bet everybody but maybe you is, too," Bad Back said.

"Can't," Ringo repeated. "You go right over that hill and you'll see. You keep thinking those peaks are just over the next hill, but there's always another one in the way. Once you do get close, the ground kind of drops away before you can get to the base of them. So you have to climb your way down by a significant number of feet, then turn around and start climbing almost straight up by a lot more. It'd take you a couple days to climb one of them from here. Just send somebody down the path we just came up. If they see anybody, which I doubt seriously will happen, they can get back here and warn us. We can ambush anybody on that trail from the hill just in front of us if we have to and they wouldn't have any cover."

"If you say so…," Bad Back sighed. He sent Miguel and Ronaldo out—silent Ron always went with his younger brother—giving Miguel instructions to walk out to the third hill in front of the cabin, hide as well as they could behind the top of the hill, and keep a sharp eye on the trail.

•

The Americans weren't even trying to hide their trail, making Small Snake's job as easy as it could be. It appeared to him they were either heading to the strange horse-ear-shaped peaks to the east or were skirting the base of the tall mountains. Either way, they were going to be easy to follow.

Suddenly, the Comanche squeezed his legs tightly on his horse to stop it, dropped to the horse's neck and listened as intently as he could. The sound was unmistakable: Americans were walking toward him. He knew that at any moment they would crest the hill in front of him. He wasn't certain how many there were—Americans always made such a terrible noise when they walked, it could be two or twenty. But he knew it was at least two. Hummingbird told him not to be seen, but Small Snake didn't think he was going to able to avoid it. He was small, even for someone with only fourteen summers, and he might be able to go undetected for a short period of time, but he couldn't hide his pony out on this desert. The tallest things growing out here were ocotillo and you could barely hide a war lance behind an ocotillo stalk. Clumps of candelilla or the mesquite shrubs were thicker, but not very tall.

He quickly slid the rope halter from his horse and fashioned a loose hobble from it to keep his horse nearby in the event he had to escape quickly. He yanked the rope off from around the horse's girth that he used to keep his balance and control the pony; then slapped the horse's rump to get it moving a little away from him. Perhaps the Americans wouldn't see the hobble, and think his was a wild horse. He ran quickly to the largest mesquite bush he could see and made a decision to use his bow if he had to defend himself, making as little noise as possible. In his low crouch, the rifle strapped to his back with plaited rawhide stuck up higher than he did. He strung his bow and waited, hoping he wouldn't have to use either of his arrows.

The two Americans strode over the hill almost in a swagger. Just over the crest, one of them nudged the other and pointed to Small Snake's horse. The other said something Small Snake couldn't understand and they both walked toward his horse. Just as he thought they would have to see the hobble, they did. Both men raised their rifles and looked around. Small Snake notched the arrow onto his bowstring and drew it back. When the second man pointed to Small Snake, the

Comanche rose slightly and loosed his arrow which found it's mark in the American's throat just as the man fired. The rifle shot hit him in the upper thigh. Small Snake expected the first man to fire also, but he didn't. Instead, he dropped his rifle and bent over the fallen man, his face in agony. Without hesitation, the first man pulled the arrow from the second's throat. It was a crazy thing to do, Small Snake knew, but sometimes Americans did crazy things. Being pulled backwards through all that soft tissue, the arrow caused even more damage and blood gushed out of the American's neck. The first man tried to stop the flow of the blood by covering the now gaping hole with his hands. Small Snake took advantage of the situation and raced to his horse. He quickly tied on the belly rope and refashioned his halter, jumped his horse's back and flinched just a little from the pain in his leg. He was about to ride off when he noticed the surviving American turn towards him. The man's face was red with anger and blood, but he didn't say anything. He grabbed his rifle and fired it from his hip as quickly as he could work the Winchester's lever, but all the shots went wild. Small Snake, knowing the element of surprise was long gone now, swung his rifle into his hands and fired one shot that caught the American in the chest. The man crumpled to the desert beside the other.

Small Snake kicked his horse and galloped toward Shit.

•

"They are shooting," Karl cried. "What are they shooting at? Oh, God, please let Ingrid be safe."

Ethan motioned for them to stay where they were. He dismounted, walked a few yards to his right then ran quickly and silently parallel to the trail. He kept running down the hill and up another and stopped. Something disturbed his vision on his left, far away. It was a light haze, smoke or dust. It moved and grew smaller—dust from a rider going away from him. Another puff of dust joined that one and continued to the north. At least a mile, he thought, maybe more. He turned to look down the trail and saw two bodies motionless near the top of the hill past the one in front of him. He squinted his eyes and waited. He saw the bodies a little clearer, recognizing the clothing of one of them, one of Ringo's gang from the saloon two nights ago. The half-breed Mexican. He assumed the other dead man was his brother. He continued to wait. Nothing moved. The cabin was only one more hill beyond where the bodies lay. He turned and ran back.

"Whoever's been tracking Ringo killed a couple of his men along the trail," Ethan said. "He killed them and then he rode off."

"Just one?" Joaquin asked.

"Eh-yeah, just one was tracking them and he was alone for the fight, but he joined up with another rider some distance from here and they both rode away. Maybe to get some friends, maybe just high-tailing it. I still can't tell who."

"Comanch?" Dutch asked.

"Possible," Ethan said. "The tracking horse was shod, so it wasn't an Indian pony. But remember that report the ranger got said the band that broke out from Fort Sill stole Army horses on their way out. So it could be them. Could be."

"What're they doing out here? You said yourself they came this far south they'd cross into Mexico," Dutch said.

"I don't know," Ethan said shaking his head. "None of it makes sense to me. But they're gone for now."

"So what do we do? With all the shooting, Ingrid could be harmed or already has been harmed. We have to go." Karl said.

"We'll go, but slow and easy. Slow and easy," Ethan said. "They're likely to come out and investigate those shots themselves."

"I don't like this at all," Dutch said.

Ethan nodded. "Joaquin, you and Karl ride along over there and Dutch and I will go on this side of the trail. "Keep your weapons ready."

"But, be careful," Karl said. "We do not want to go off and shoot without knowing if Ingrid is safe."

"She could be dead for all we know," Ethan said.

"Don't say that, buddy," Dutch said.

•

"I didn't have a choice," Small Snake said to Hummingbird; then explained what happened.

"Did you see the woman with the gold hair?" Hummingbird

asked. Both Small Snake and Shit said no.

"But a second group of Americans is following the group that has her," Shit said. "They must want to take her back. What do we do?"

"Get closer," Hummingbird said. "Then wait. Whatever happens, both groups want the woman so they won't injure her. They'll fight it out and when that fight is over, we'll have a lot fewer Americans. We can make our move safely then."

If all these men were after this gold-haired woman, she must certainly be a grand prize, Hummingbird thought, solidifying his desire to have her for himself.

•

"You son of a bitch!" Bad Back said to Ringo. "This is some safe hideout you've led us to. Somebody's following us and they're close. We can only hope Miguel and Ron have them pinned down."

"Likely to be that big posse of rangers," Bryce said. "I knew this was a bone-headed idea from the beginning."

"No you didn't," Ringo said. "It was a good plan and it still is. The rangers couldn't have gathered up this quickly. That has to be those townpeople from Lajitas."

"We need to know," Bad Back said. "We can't wait for them to come waltzing in here."

"Then you take a look," Ringo said.

"I will, by God," Bad Back said, feeling for the first time in weeks that he was the leader of this outfit again. "Parsons, you come with me. Ringo and Bryce, you get some fortifications set up in case we do have to defend this place."

"Be better if you saddled up," Ringo said as they left.

"And waste a lot of time," Bad Back said as he and Parsons walked off.

Whatever Bad Back expected to find, he expected it further down the trail not just over the first hill from the cabin. As he and Parsons topped the hill they saw two riders to their right and two to the left. They hesitated. Parsons wanted to run back to the cabin, but Bad Back caught his arm saying, "No time. Cut loose and when they duck for cover, then we'll get back."

But they already wasted too much time. The saloonkeeper emptied both barrels of his 10-gauge shotgun into Bad Back. The blast eviscerated Bad Back, who dropped backwards into a sitting position. He looked down at the mass of blood and intestines in his lap and tried desperately to remember a prayer before he died. He failed and slumped forward.

The ranger emptied his pistol at Parsons and the scout fired his Spencer at the now fleeing kidnapper. The Spencer round caught Parsons in the back of his shoulder, one of the pistol rounds caught him in the side and another caught him under his left shoulder blade. He kept running toward the cabin, sprawling on its floor when he got to it.

Parsons gasped for breath as Bryce turned him over. "Where's Bad Back?" Bryce asked.

"Blown to kingdom come," Parsons wheezed.

"You OK?"

"Pert near," Parsons said and was dead in Bryce's arms.

"A few minutes ago we were six good gun hands and now we're down to two with our backs literally to the wall. Any suggestions, ace?" Bryce said.

"Negotiate," Ringo said.

"Just let me go," Ingrid begged. "I'm what they want. Just let me go."

"Not on your life," Ringo said.

"Maybe she's what she says she is," Bryce said.

"You just said you thought we were being trailed by all the Texas Rangers in the state. You think anybody cares about a common whore from down at the end of the civilized world?" Ringo said, standing up with his pistol in his hand, watching the trail. "She's the governor's wife I'm telling you. She has to be."

Ingrid went to Ringo, pulled his head down to hers and kissed him as deeply and as passionately as she knew how. While she was kissing him, her hand went down into the crotch of his trousers, fondling him. Then she abruptly pushed him back and spat.

"Would the governor's lady do that?" Ingrid said.

Ringo went from shock to confusion to anger in the space of a second. He brought his revolver up to Ingrid's chest and cocked it.

"Don't continue choking," Bryce said. "She's our only ticket out of here."

Ringo uncocked the pistol and shoved it roughly in its holster. He went to Parsons' saddlebag, pulled out a whiskey bottle and took a long draught from it.

"Negotiate," Ringo said, nodding his head. He drank again from Bryce's bottle, letting the remainder of the liquor burn down his throat until his insides grew warmer. "Negotiate."

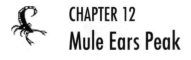

CHAPTER 12

Mule Ears Peak

"Hello, the shack!" Ethan hollered from the top of the hill. He stood on the ground, behind his horse, his rifle trained on the cabin ruins.

"What do you assassins want?" Ringo yelled back. "You've killed four of my best friends."

"Only two. Only two; somebody else rubbed out the brothers," Ethan said. "I imagine they all needed killing."

Ringo was confused again. The Lajitians had killed only two of the four. Who else was out there? Then his anger returned.

"What do you want?" he yelled.

"You know," Ethan said. "Send the woman out unharmed."

"What do we gain from that?"

"You get to live."

"And just what guarantees do we have of that?"

"Got our word."

"And what's that worth?"

"We've got a preacher and a Texas Ranger here with us, you can take their word. And I don't lie much."

"Just let me go," Ingrid said quietly to Ringo.

"I have a mind to carve you into little pieces and toss them out one by one then go out of this miserable world in a blaze of glory," Ringo replied.

"You'll have to tag me out first," Bryce said, pointing his rifle toward Ringo.

"I can do that," Ringo said. "And I promise I can do it before you can squeeze that trigger. But I probably won't. You have anything to drink?'

"You drunk up everything we had," Bryce said. "I'm a little surprised you're still vertical."

"Maybe the world would be better off if I just put a ball into my own head right now," Ringo said.

"Maybe so," Bryce replied.

"Not today," he said. Then loudly, "I'll tell you what we'll do. We'll hold onto this whore of yours and you get to purchase her from us."

"Just send her out," Joaquin said. "If you don't, you're not getting out of there alive. Simple as that."

"You're not begrudging us a little profit are you?" Ringo said.

"How much?" Karl hollered out.

"Damn it, I told you to follow orders, now keep your mouth shut," Ethan told the preacher. "Shut."

Karl pulled a large bag of coins from his pocket and handed it to the scout. "If this will buy Ingrid's safety, it will be worth it. It is all the money I have left in the world. I have about $300 here."

"You think they'll take that and leave? That Ringo has a serious case of big behavior," Dutch said. "That's not enough money to quiet his nerves."

"It would be an insult, especially if they thought they'd gotten the governor's lady," Ethan said.

"Maybe it would be a way for them to save face," Karl said. "I shall help thee in the time of affliction, and in the time of tribulation against the enemy."

"All we have is $300," Ethan shouted out.

"We've done all this for three hundred junk dollars?" Bryce said to Ringo.

"I believe we can either take the offer or a couple of holes in the ground, assuming their preacher is Christian enough to bury us," Ringo said. He turned to the hill and hollered, "How do we know you'll honor the bargain?"

"Told you before," Ethan said. "Take it or leave it."

Ringo wished desperately for a drink, but wishing wouldn't produce one and that prospect depressed him a little more than his current predicament. He'd fought his way out of enough gun battles before; he had confidence he could do it again. But if he did, to what end? Then he would have nothing. He'd have to leave the woman behind, perhaps even his saddlebags with what was left of the stagecoach money. Maybe even his horse. He might fight his way out only to have to walk who knew how many miles across the desert to a town with a decent saloon. The pistol in his hand was his friend and it felt comfortable there. He knew when his time came it would be a violent one. Why wait and let someone else determine the time and place? He could control that right here and now. He could do it himself. Or he could take some of them with him, perhaps even all of them. That would make for good newspaper copy. It would make the front page of both *Harper's Weekly* and the *Police Gazette* and he would become a legend. Or he could take the money and run away, living to fight another day, perhaps in a bigger and more famous fight than this.

That was the great tragedy of life, he knew: Who knew? This might be the high point of his entire life or perhaps bigger and better things were waiting. If he ended it now, he would never know, but if continued on and nothing happened he would always regret it. Forget being forced from the Garden, this was the true punishment for the Original Sin. Never knowing, but knowing you didn't know. It was the way God or Nature or whoever was in charge had of leading you on. It was a way for God to have the last laugh. Well, you don't quit whist after the third deal.

"Let us saddle up and ride on by," Ringo yelled. "As we pass, you hand me the money, I hand over the reins to the whore's horse. We don't get the money, we ride off with her."

"Agreed," Ethan said.

Ringo and Bryce saddled all seven horses. Each carried three canteens full of water hanging from their saddle horns, a large full water bag strapped behind each saddle. Ringo led the horse Ingrid rode; Bryce held lines to the four riderless horses. They rode slowly up the hill.

Karl handed up his bag of coins; Ringo gave him the reins to Ingrid's horse. As the two bandits rode off, Ingrid jumped down and rushed to Dutch's arms. Joaquin and Ethan watched the men ride off, their weapons ready.

"Don't do that no more," Dutch told Ingrid as she cried into his shoulder.

"Are you OK?" Karl asked her. She didn't reply.

"You think they'll be waiting for us down the trail?" Joaquin asked Ethan.

"Doubt it," the scout said. "Doubt it. They know ol' Lizard

Teats ain't worth much and have to figure they got all our cash. But I wouldn't let my guard down until we get back to our own beds."

●

Hummingbird watched the two men ride away. They didn't have the gold-haired woman with them but they led four horses. He wanted the horses but didn't want the other group of Americans to get too far from his band.

"How is your wound?" Hummingbird asked Small Snake.

"The bleeding has stopped and it doesn't hurt too bad now," he replied. "I don't know what it'll be like tomorrow."

"Do you feel comfortable riding?"

"I can. Where?"

"Follow the woman with the gold hair. We're going to get those other Americans' horses then we'll find you, so leave us a good track."

Small Snake nodded quickly, walked to his horse, vaulted up and rode off.

"I have a dream last night," Shit said quietly to Hummingbird. The leader believed dreams were a way for God to speak directly to men if only men could figure out what God was saying. He nodded for Shit to continue.

"We collect a huge herd of horses, more than we can count. To celebrate, we have a feast. We eat well and sing and dance and then we all fall asleep and while we sleep our horses run through our camp and trample us all to death. So many horses run over us that our bodies are stomped deep into the earth until we become the same as the dirt."

"Have you thought about what this means?" Hummingbird asked.

"I lack the imagination you have," Shit said. "The only thing I can think of is that if we continue on the path we are following we will all die."

Hummingbird was thoughtful but impatient. He wanted to catch the Americans before they got too far away, but the dream disturbed him a little. Shit wasn't known for having dreams.

"Perhaps it means just that by the time we die and become one with the earth again we will have captured untold numbers of horses and be wealthy beyond the dreams of our parents," Hummingbird said. "It's clear that's our destiny. Look at the horses we have now in such little time and we shall capture more before the sunsets. We're wasting time. Let's go."

The band mounted and rode after the men with the horses.

•

It was a simple pursuit that Ringo and Bryce could tell the Comanches were enjoying all too well. They whooped and hollered, sometimes firing a gun in their general direction, but it mostly just a big show.

"You're in one hell of a slump," Bryce said to Ringo as they spurred their horses on. "Now we've got red Indians chasing us."

"Blame me for that, too?" Ringo said.

"Damn straight."

"Let the horses go."

"That's too much money to let go."

"Make a choice, those horses or your scalp."

"What makes you think they'll stop chasing us if we let the horses go?"

"It's what they're after. What else?" At this point, Ringo was out of breath from trying to talk and ride his horse at a gallop at the same time. He didn't feel much like arguing anymore. He drew his pistol as he reined up his horse. The horses slowed, Ringo aimed quickly and fired. The bullet cut through the reins Bryce was holding, releasing the other horses. He spurred on with Bryce. Looking over his shoulder, he could see all of the Comanches chase after the loose horses.

Ringo and Bryce rode quickly over a couple more hills, then across a broad plain in front of the mountains. When they reached the top of one of the few hills ahead of them, they reined in, dismounted and walked the horses.

"How far you figure?" Bryce asked.

"If memory serves, about 60 miles, maybe 70," Ringo said.

"Then what?"

"Train depot. I'm heading on west into Arizona Territory. Tombstone. It's supposed to be the richest silver strike ever and a thriving cattle area. From what my pal Curly Bill told me, it sounds like a significant amount of money can be made there. Like to come along?"

"With you?" Bryce laughed. "Not on your life. I'm finished with you and finished with the West. It's too unpredictable and violent for me. I'm going home."

"To where?"

"Illinois," Bryce said. "I just might try to get on with that Chicago base ball team. I think I might do right well as a batsman."

Ringo shook his head. "Base ball… OK, we've got a long, hot ride ahead of us. Tell me everything there is to know about this base ball."

CHAPTER 13
Calamity Creek at the Mesa de Anguila, Texas

"Your leg looks bad," Hummingbird said to Small Snake. After capturing the horses the fleeing two Americans let go, the band followed Small Snake's track to a point ahead of the other group of Americans. The young warrior sat against a rock, his left leg stretched out in front of him. His upper thigh was different shades of purple with streaks of red and black. They all knew the poison would take Small Snake soon.

"At least it doesn't hurt," Small Snake said.

"If we leave the horses with you, can you guard them?" Hummingbird asked.

"That will depend on how long I have. How long I have to guard them and how long I have left to live. Do you know?"

Hummingbird shook his head. "The task is important. Once we capture the gold-haired woman and the rest of the horses, we can leave for a better place. It shouldn't take us long."

"Promise you'll tell my grandfather how I died."

"The bravest of warriors," Hummingbird said. "And a brave man dies young."

Hummingbird and Shit strung the horses together on ropes, then staked them to the ground below one of the rolling hills to the west of their ambush point. After all their raids they collected more than two dozen horses and they would be difficult to look after until they found a good camp. The rest of the men climbed into the adjacent hills.

Hummingbird didn't think the Americans expected an attack and he determined this location was perfect for an ambush. The Americans were heading back to their village, crossing the broad, empty plain that stretched out from the huge mesa. The band would wait here, where the plain ended and the jumble of foothills leading up onto the mesa began. A small creek with steep sides stood between the hills and the plain. It had a little water in it and the Americans would be likely to stop here, rest and water their horses. Facing the creek were three hills, each higher than the other. The band made camp in the saddle between the last two hills. From the top of the second hill they would have command of the creek and the plain. The Americans would have no place to go. Turning around on the plain would leave them completely exposed. They couldn't pass the hill without being fired down on. They couldn't head toward the mesa because there was no way out, and no way up unless they climbed on foot and climbing the steep cliffs would also expose them to fire. They could hide in the creek, but not for long. Hummingbird's band had several days worth of food on the pack mules, and even more ammunition.

Since leaving the reservation, the band was successful in everything. They behaved bravely and followed his orders perfectly. They became true Human Beings. They became free men, and they were being rewarded by Ta'ahpu. Hummingbird could barely contain his joy.

●

Ethan returned to the group after riding behind them for a couple of miles.

"See any sign?" Joaquin asked.

"Not directly," the scout replied. "But there's a lot of activity out there. A lot." He pointed to the north. "Whoever they are, they're being very careful to stay hidden in the gullies and ditches crossing the plain and I don't think they're white men. Apache or Comanche; most likely that renegade band from the Nations. But they've got a lot of horses with them—a small herd. That makes trying to figure out how many they are almost impossible. But let's say your report was right and there are eight of them."

"Why would they follow Ringo then come back and swing wide of us?" Joaquin asked, guessing the answer.

"They could be just trying to avoid us to get across the ford into Mexico or they could want to take our horses. That's probably what they were after from Ringo. Looks like they're collecting quite a herd, in fact. If they went after his horses, they'll certainly come after ours is my guess," Ethan said. "They'll come after ours."

"What do we do?" Dutch asked.

"Well…" Ethan said, pausing quite a while. "We have a problem.

We're at their mercy right now on this open plain. We're only a few miles from town but along the way are at least three, four good places for an ambush since we'll have to ride through those hills up ahead."

"Where would you ambush us?" Joaquin asked.

"The creek. We'll have to water the horses in the creek there. Opposite the creek are several hills they can hide on."

"So what do we do?" Dutch said again.

"Well... like I said, we have a problem. We can't turn around and we can't go north because that would mean riding more on the plain and if they fired on us or chased us, we wouldn't stand much of a chance. We can't go south because the mesa's in the way. We certainly can't get by them going west without a fight. We either make a stand or ride like hell and hope we can get by them. Either alternative can be fatal. Real fatal."

"If we continue, then we endanger Ingrid more than if we make our stand," Karl said.

"I think if we continue we put all of us in danger," Joaquin said.

Ethan reined in his horse and dismounted. He scanned the land in front of them quickly, and then scanned it again with his eyes squinted. He squatted down and sifted some of the desert dirt back and forth in his hands. "They're going to expect us to go into the creek," he said. "And that's our best alternative."

"Do what they expect?" Dutch said.

Ethan stood. "Eh-yeah," he said. "It's our only cover. If we're lucky, they'll put on a show of keeping us penned in. Then we let them have our horses."

"What?" Dutch and Joaquin said at the same time.

"Look, we're about four miles from downstreet Lajitas. We can walk that in a couple of hours. We have enough water. If it was Apache we're up against I wouldn't suggest it. They'd take the horses and wait around for our scalps. The Comanche are more likely to take what they want and leave, especially so close to the crossing. They'll take the horses and leave."

"Can we count on that?" Karl asked.

Ethan shrugged his shoulders. "Nothing's certain in this desert except dyin' and fryin'. I think it's our best chance."

"How do we do it?" Dutch asked.

"Keep riding like we don't know they're out there. We get to the creek; ride down into it. The walls are maybe ten feet high at this end and they'll be good protection. Once in the creek, we unsaddle the horses and let them drink their fill. Then we wait. If the Comanche show, we make them look good by firing at them for a little bit, then we chase the horses out of the creek. They should get the horses and leave, insulting us all the way."

"I pray you are right," Karl said. "At my first defense no one came to my support, but all forsook me. But the Lord stood by me and strengthened me. And I was delivered from the lion's mouth. The Lord will deliver me from every work of evil, and will preserve me for His heavenly kingdom."

"You and all the other preachers I ever did hear spend so much time talkin' 'bout the Kingdom of Heaven and how you can't wait to be with the Lord, but none of you are ever in a terrible hurry to get there," Dutch said.

"All we need is a little luck," Ethan said.

"Luck always seems to favor those who don't need it," Dutch said. "We need it." Then, very softly to Ethan: "You sure you want us to go into a creek bed? You going to be OK?"

"No," he replied quietly so the others didn't hear. "But want has nothing to do with it."

They reached the creek quickly and rode their horses down the steep embankment. The creek was wet only in patches. The horses drank while the men unsaddled them and set their gear down against the west embankment. They drank from their own canteens, watching the hills above them. Ethan saw the Comanches first, his head back drinking. He nodded towards the hill and they all immediately sought the cover of the west bank just as the Comanches opened fire.

"The heathens are nothing if not reliable," Joaquin said.

"Toss a few shots at them, but don't waste your ammo. Don't waste it. What we have is all we've got. And don't aim to hit any of them. If we have any chance it's going to be with the horses but if we kill one of them then vengeance kicks in and we're in real trouble," Ethan said.

"Like we ain't now," Dutch said.

Dutch, Joaquin and Ethan returned fire for a few seconds then stopped. Karl tried to shield Ingrid but she pushed him away, turned and buried her face in the bank wishing she could disappear.

The Comanches reloaded their rifles twice and laid down a withering fire, but the bullets struck either just at the lip of the embankment or against the east wall.

"They're using a lot of ammunition," Joaquin said. "I wouldn't figure them to be using it all up. They must have quite a cache." Ethan nodded his agreement, then dashed over to the horses shooing them up and out of the creek bed.

"Take the horses and leave us in peace," Ethan yelled. "Tome los caballos y nos sale en paz."

The horses had a difficult time getting out of the creek, but they managed. Ethan ran to the collapsed dirt they left behind and watched. It took only a couple of minutes for a Comanche to run low across the plain and drop loops over the horses' necks and lead them away. He was tall and his long black hair flowed behind him like a horse's mane. The way the Comanche smiled and moved with confidence, Ethan guessed he was either the best warrior of the bunch or its leader.

"How long you figure before they leave?" Joaquin asked the scout when he returned. Ethan only shook his head.

•

Hummingbird took the horses to the string Small Snake was looking after.

"Four more," he said to the boy who smiled but didn't rise to help Hummingbird add the horses to the herd. "How do you feel?"

"Well," Small Snake said. "I'm tired, but that's all."

Hummingbird touched Small Snake's head then ran up the backside of the hill to the rest of the band. As soon as he arrived, Shit said to him, "We've got their horses; I think we should leave."

"I will have that gold-haired woman for my second wife," Hummingbird said.

"We may have to pay for that," Shit said. "The creek provides good fortification for them and I don't think they'll give the woman up easily. They just fight one other battle for her."

"We'll be as triumphant as always," Hummingbird said. "We

haven't lost a warrior yet and will not."

"Small Snake?"

"We haven't lost him yet. If we do, he will die as a brave Human Being. He killed two Americans all by himself and helped us win all their ponies."

"I still don't like this."

"Questioning isn't like you. Why do you doubt? Is it your white blood finally coming forward in battle?"

"I'm as much a Human Being as you are," Shit snapped. "That's why I'm not sure we should continue this fight. Some of us are going to be killed."

"They are cornered. They have no horses. They'll give the woman up."

"These Americans are not cowards."

"No, but is a woman's life worth their own? You know it's not."

"Is a woman's life worth one of ours?" Shit said and turned away.

Hummingbird decided to resolve the situation quickly. He walked to the top of the hill and shouted down to the Americans, "Woman-give." His answer was a quick pistol shot that grazed his arm and he jumped back behind the hill. He rose up just enough to shout again, "Woman-give. You-go." He'd already ducked down by the time a rifle bullet sailed over him where his head had been.

The band looked at him for direction. "We wait until dark, then we kill the Americans and take the woman and go into Mexico." They turned and unwrapped some jerky they took from the Texas Rangers and ate and drank, then dozed off while Hummingbird watched the creek.

•

"Jesus, we're dead men now," Dutch said.

"Not as long as we have a breath," Ethan said.

"We're not getting out of here," Joaquin said. "The only possible way is towards the mesa and we can't climb that."

"We could, but it'd be trying," the scout said. "No we'll wait to see what they do. See what they do. Maybe they're just seeing what they can get away with."

"Why would they want Ingrid?" Dutch asked.

"Pretty woman," Ethan said. "The leader probably thinks he can get him a trophy."

Every now and then, the Comanche leader hollered down to them with the same message followed by several rifle shots.

The sun began to set. "Dutch, you and Karl look after Lizard Teats, Joaquin you come with me down the creek," Ethan said.

"I thought you said we couldn't get out that way?" Dutch said.

"I could, maybe, and if I could I'm worried they could get in," Ethan said. "We'll spend the night down there. You and Karl try to take turns getting some sleep, but one of you stay awake and watch that hill and across the plain. Watch."

"We're not goin' to see any Comanche sneaking 'round in the dark," Dutch said, shaking his head.

"You could get lucky," Ethan said. "But I can almost guarantee they won't be coming straight at us. Comanche aren't stupid."

"It's that word 'almost' that bothers me," Dutch said.

The scout and the ranger moved down the creek bed that wound snakelike across the desert. They stopped at a narrow point, the embankment only half as high as it was where the others stayed. Ethan sat on the east side, motioning Joaquin to the west.

"Try to rest," Ethan said. "We may need all the rest we can get. Just sit back and rest your head sideways against the bank. Make sure your ear touches the dirt. If you doze off, don't worry. If there's a sound you'll hear it. At least, I'll hear it." Joaquin nodded and did as he was told, holding his pistol in his lap.

Ethan settled back and sighed deeply. The others were worried about the Indians, but he was more concerned about the weather. The skies got cloudy just as sun went down and he felt a slightly cool breeze, not a good sign at this time of year. If it rained, the water would flow off the mesa and out of the desert into this creek and that would be a calamity. He didn't know if he could survive that happening again. Maybe it would rain further off.

•

Hummingbird sent two of his warriors out across the hills with instructions to move quietly into the creek bed from near the mesa. The rest would lie across the top of their hill, shielded from view by the several candelilla plants clumping together. They would wait and at first dawn catch the Americans in a crossfire.

•

Ethan's leg snapped forward as if in a spasm, suddenly and hard, striking Joaquin on his foot. The ranger was wide-awake in an instant, adrenalin pumping in his throat and beside his eyes. He strained to see into the darkness of the creek, making out the shapes of rocks, candelilla and the sides of the bank. The smells of a desert rainstorm filled their nostrils, the sweet creosote almost intoxicating. Ethan hoped the storm was far off, hoped it was to the north where runoff wouldn't come their way. He inhaled as deeply as he could, turning his head slowly from side to side. It was stronger from the north, and he relaxed a little. He nudged Joaquin again then cocked his pistol. A flash of lightning lit the area up faintly, but they heard no thunder. A second flash came and Joaquin fired at two figures illuminated just up the creek. No return fire came. Ethan motioned Joaquin to remain where he was, then he crouched down and moved carefully up the creek bed.

He found two Comanches. The ranger's quick shooting resulted in two chest wounds. One was through the heart and the Indian was probably dead before he hit the ground; the other was hit in the lungs and blood bubbled up from his sucking chest wound. Ethan bent over and cut the Comanche's throat, then returned to Joaquin.

"That was some shooting," Ethan said.

"I got them?"

"Eh-yeah. Both."

"You think any more will come down here?"

Ethan shrugged. "I doubt it, but we'll remain here until morning."

"Twobears!?" Dutch yelled from down the creek bed.

"OK," the scout replied. "You go back to sleep."

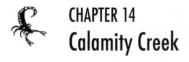# CHAPTER 14
Calamity Creek

Joaquin and Ethan joined the others at daybreak. The Comanches tried no other sneak attacks during the night, but that didn't let anyone but Ethan sleep well. After a while the Comanche leader repeated his demand for the woman, following it with more heavy gunfire, then a lull.

"These guys got an armory with them?" Joaquin said once the shooting stopped.

"Well, assuming that ranger report was right we were facing eight Comanches and after last night we're down to six. To six. We're getting the odds down. We just need to keep lowering them."

"How? We can't see them most of the time?" Joaquin said.

"What they're doing is lying on the top of that hill using the candelilla as cover to watch us but we can't see them. Every so often they let loose but the fire's so heavy we can't get in a shot of our own." Ethan pointed to the hill. "Watch the candelilla on the far left for a bit." Joaquin didn't seen anything except for the bunched-in pencil-thin stalks of the plant, but after a while noticed the small portion of a head peek out from around it then drop back. "You saw him?" Ethan asked.

"I did."

"You're the good shot here, bust a cap on him."

"My pistols won't reach the top of that hill; use your rifle," Joaquin said.

"I'm not very accurate with the Spencer that far," Ethan said. "My eyes aren't quite what they used to be. Not what they used to be. You've got a rifle, use that instead of your pistol."

"I'm better with my pistols. I can shoot but it's mostly instinctive. I killed a lot of prickly pear out on the range. But I'm not too sure about the rifle. I hit and miss with that. Takes too much concentration."

Ethan reached over and took the ranger's '73 out of its scabbard, chambered a round and handed it to Joaquin. "Then don't concentrate.

Just stand up and fire a couple rounds."

"Where?"

"Aim just inside the right side of that candelilla, low."

"Give it a try," Joaquin said. He held the rifle at his waist and stepped back so he could see a little better over the embankment. He quickly snapped the Winchester to his shoulder and fired two swift shots, then jumped back with the others.

"Anything?" he asked.

"I saw arms go flying up," Ethan said. "Maybe you killed him, maybe wounded, but if so the wound is serious. I'd say you took him out of commission. So now we're down to five. Odds are getting better all the time. The odds are better."

•

When Pony Far Away fell over backwards, a slice of his ear gone and a hole to the left side of the bridge of his nose, the band shot back at the Americans.

"I tell you," Shit said to Hummingbird when they stopped. "This quest of yours is going to get us all killed. Is that woman worth it?"

"I don't know," Hummingbird said. "But now we have three dead to avenge."

"We should leave."

"We stay. If you want to leave, go."

"You know I won't."

"Then don't complain."

"I won't."

"Good, "Hummingbird said. "Now, we need a good lookout. Go up that steep hill and keep watch from up there. You should be able to see the area and warn us if any of the Americans try to get out of the creek from the far end."

Shit knew Hummingbird didn't actually believe anyone could come at them from that position, he just wanted to get Shit away from him before their disagreement developed into an argument that could develop into a fight. "What is your plan now?" he asked.

"We wait," Hummingbird replied.

●

"May the Lord deliver us," Karl said.

The shadows were very long, indicating the sun would be down again soon. They withstood several more short onslaughts of fire from the hill, returning only a few shots. They all knew this standoff couldn't last much longer. Their ammunition was running low, Dutch's shotgun was useless at this range, and Karl had no weapon and barely knew how to use one anyway. They had plenty of water—the creek wouldn't go completely dry for another couple of weeks—but they had no food. Soon the Comanches would lose patience and do something, or they would. A pitched fight would only result in most, if not all, of them losing their lives.

"Deliver me from my enemies, O Lord; from my adversaries defend me. Rescue me from evildoers; from blood-thirsty men save me. For behold, they lie in wait for my life; mighty men come together against me. Not for any offense of mine, O Lord; for no guilt of mine they hurry to take up arms."

Ingrid recoiled at Karl's words as if he struck her. Sitting against the embankment, she leaned forward and wrapped her arms around her head, her head on her knees, and sobbed.

Karl was in league with God. God who clearly showed how angry He was at her for her lust for Karl and her a married woman. If you angered God, what hope was there for you? And now that Karl found her in Lajitas, she was reminded every hour of everyday of just how disgusting she was. She was honestly glad he discovered something to believe in and apparently believed he was redeemed. But she knew what life was like and knew redemption was a fantasy, a method people used to feel good about themselves and feel superior to others. All were sinners. Some sinned more than others. And some sins could not be redeemed. She might have been able to trick herself into believing in redemption, except for the very real proof she had from God's own hand that she could not. She never heard or read of anyone feeling that wrath as she did. While lying there in the house of God, copulating like a jackrabbit, her lover inside of her, naked to the world and to God, God spoke. God spoke clearly. How could you avoid the anger of God? No, Ingrid knew what she was and had no choice but to play out the hand she dealt for herself. She had no one to blame but herself.

"Let me go," she said, looking up at Dutch.

"Whad'ya mean? You studyin' to be a half-wit?"

"Give me to the Indians. Living with them can't be any worse than the life I've lived so far. If I stay, they could kill you all and I'm not worth it. So just let me go to them. Then they'll let you go, and I'll just go on the way I have been."

"Won't work now," Ethan said. "Not now."

"Why not?"

"We've killed two, maybe three of their band. They won't leave now until we're all dead, then they'll take you if you're not dead, too," Ethan said.

"Hell of a thing," Dutch said.

"Just one big calamity," Ethan said.

As the cicadas sang in the twilight, the Comanches fired again.

"Our father who art in heaven, hallowed be they name. Thy kingdom come, thy will be done on earth, as it is in heaven. Give us this day our daily bread. And forgive us our debts, as we also forgive our debtors. And lead us not into temptation, but deliver us from evil," Karl prayed alone, in the dark, his large frame on his knees.

"I'm about ready to pray askin' God to make me deaf so I don't have to listen to that man pray all the time," Dutch said.

"Religion is for people afraid of hell," Ethan said. "Spirituality is for people who've been there." He took several long drinks from his canteen; then began taking his clothes off. He knew if you didn't have a choice, you might as well be brave.

He cut a long, wide strip of buckskin from his shirt, buckled his belt on backwards so the buckle was in the middle of his back, then looped the buckskin strip inside the belt and between his legs. He cut two other small strips and tied his large Bowie knife to the back of his right calf. Even in the dim light they could see his chest was covered in black tattoos of intricate, almost flowery designs.

"The devil's bakin' biscuits in your head," Dutch said.

"I don't know what you're planning, but you're crazy to go out there," Joaquin said.

"Time to play Injun," Ethan replied.

"I'm not worth it," Ingrid said.

"I know," Ethan said. "But the others are." He walked off in a low crouch to the head of the creek.

He knew this wouldn't be easy, but maybe he could lower the odds enough to be in their favor. He guessed only five Comanche remained and believed he could take out three, maybe even four of them before they were alerted and got him. That would leave only one, maybe two, and Joaquin and Dutch might be able to deal with them. He knew it was their only hope. Besides, this would give him the chance to do a little penance before he met his Maker.

•

Shit sat on his hill aside from the others and brooded. Perhaps he was feeling the white blood in him, but he had a hard time truly believing that. He never knows his white parents. He never knows American society. Only the ways of the Human Beings. His mother gets him when he is still an infant and only recently does he wonder how. Do some Human Beings kill his white parents? If so, how could he now live in their midst as one of them? But it is the only way he knows.

Now Human Beings no longer roam free, they are like prisoners on just a small portion of the land they once command. The Americans have taken over. They are everywhere you go. It is almost as if day after day the earth vomits out another American city where only the ground is before. The American soldiers grow in numbers, the farmers grow in numbers, the ranchers grow in numbers; they are like grains of sand there are so many of them and only a handful of Human Beings left on the whole earth. To survive, the Human Beings would have to become Americans. They would have to be happy in one place. They would have to rip apart the earth and sow seeds and harvest the grain and corn. Women's work would become men's. It seemed inevitable. He hears stories from some of the soldiers back on the reservation who tell him about cities larger than he can imagine with thousands upon thousands of people crowded into them and these cities cross the countryside in the east and they are quickly spreading west like a prairie fire.

Now the band of eight friends becomes five and Small Snake will not survive another day if he isn't already dead, so they will be half their original number and it is all because Hummingbird is infatuated with this American woman. He follows Hummingbird hoping his friend is right; that they can reclaim the Human Beings' past glory. But it is only a dream. The reality is that the way to survive is to become an American. That's what White Wolf tells them should be done, he remembers.

It is something he feels he can do. If he cuts his hair and washes himself and his hair, he will at least look like an American. He can speak some of their words, and even more Spanish. He can learn and survive on this frontier as an American. That's what he will do. Tonight when the band is fast asleep, he will creep over to the horses and take a few of them and ride away. The horses will pay for his transformation into an American. All he needs, he thinks, is to come up with an American name. He thinks for a little bit, rolling around different names he knows from soldiers and the sutler's store. Billy, he decides, Billy will be a good name. He'll cross the Texas border to the west into the place they called New Mexico and become an American.

"Billy," he said aloud. Yes, he definitely liked the sound of it.

At that moment a hand clasped over his nose and mouth and Shit felt a stinging sensation across his throat. He gasped for air but only swallowed blood. He could not yell out a warning. His hands went to his throat, hoping to stop the flow of blood, but the shock set in too quickly and he fell unconscious. Then he bled to death on the desert hill.

CHAPTER 15

The Foothills of the Mesa de Anguila

One down, Ethan thought. Comanche feared having their throats cut because they believed the soul left the body through the mouth and if the throat was slit the soul would be unable to free itself. The scout was sorry for this, but it was the only way he could succeed. He must kill in silence.

He hoped this was the only outlier, that the others were relying on him to keep watch, that the others would be asleep now. He guessed it was past midnight. It took him since sunset to get this far—no more than a quarter-mile—moving slowly and carefully down the creek, then up the bank and up to the highest hill. If the Comanche had an outlier, he would be up here, Ethan knew. And he was. The walk up the face of the hill was slow and difficult. The hill was mostly loose rock, lechuguilla, and candelilla. Each time he took a step it was the same—first the heel touched the ground then slowly rolled forward until he was on his toes, and repeating this over and over he never dislodging a pebble. The trick was never to walk; just keep shifting your weight from one point to the other. He moved wrong a couple of times and his legs ran into the point of a lechuguilla, stabbing painfully into him. In a way he was glad for the pain; it kept him alert.

He looked up at the sky for what he knew might be his last time. No moon, but the stars were bright enough to cause faint shadows. Some saw things in the stars, animals and people, but not Ethan. The stars were just haphazard, the way the rest of the universe was, and that's how Coyote scattered them. He liked Coyote. Coyote acknowledged that God was much bigger and more important than he was, but bragged that God wasn't around much.

He descended the hill on the opposite face the same way. His low crouch was beginning to cramp his legs and hurt his lower back. Even his neck hurt. He moved from one candelilla to the next. They weren't even knee-high, but in the darkness he could merge with their shapes. The hard part was getting from one to the other across open ground.

To be invisible he had to merge with nature, keeping low and finding the natural shapes, the dim shadows, the bends of the grounds. At least none of the Comanche would be looking this way since he was now behind them. Without another outlier, he was safe for a little while.

He prepared as well as he could, wearing no clothing that could be caught by cactus or one of the other prickly plants out here. The pricks and stings he could endure, and with no clothing nothing would stick. The small loincloth would protect his only vulnerable parts; its buckskin worn smooth from years of wear would slide over the rocks without sound. His high buckskin moccasins would protect his feet and shins and would also be silent in the darkness. His tattoos would protect him from harm.

But now the dreadful part began. He wouldn't be able to walk into the Comanche camp. He would have to crawl, moving even slower than he moved before, transform himself into a snake. He lowered himself to the ground. He knew how to do it. He had to remain alert yet send his mind away, remove himself from the pain that was coming...

How had Margaret fallen in love with him? Maybe it was because they were the only native Vermonters within hundreds of miles. Maybe because she liked rugged men who feared little. Quien sabe? He was stationed at Fort Clark and she was the local schoolteacher. Just after Margaret moved in, Lieutenant Bullis told Ethan to go over and welcome her.

"If you didn't know, a lot of Vermont women get recruited for these positions. I don't know why, but I've met several. Ride by and say hi," Bullis told him. He did, and they talked almost non-stop the remainder of the evening and into the night. They didn't even realize they talked without stopping for supper. He told her of his past and gave her tips on how someone from the Kingdom could survive in this desert while she brought images of home back to him. Even the sound of her voice reminded him of October apples and December snows and March maple syrup.

He felt like he tricked Margaret into thinking he was better than he was.

"Mi loa aloha," he said to her a week after meeting her. He explained he picked up some pieces of language when he accompanied a military attaché to the Kingdom of Hawaii, setting up Army and Navy liaisons with officials there. Her schooling taught her about the Sandwich Islands, but she never imagined she would meet anyone who saw them. To her it seemed as far away as the moon. He told her stories of his escapades, of all the strange and beautiful places he had seen, promising to take her to see them, too. He tricked her into becoming his wife.

They married after only a month and had a son soon after. They named him David after Ethan's only friend.

A year after David was born, Margaret decided she needed to return home because her mother was ill. Ethan wanted to go, but couldn't. Apache raids were getting more frequent and Colonel Grierson up at Fort Davis wanted every man in the field. He got one more letter from her; then a letter from his sister-in-law who wrote Ethan that Margaret and David were dead. The same influenza epidemic that was sweeping the northeast and attacked Margaret's mother had attacked them, too.

Ethan buried himself in work, volunteering for every patrol he could. And he began drinking; it was the only way he could sleep.

This patrol was guarding a small group of settlers from the railhead at Del Rio into the Langtry area and Ethan was the guide. Only one of the homesteaders had a wagon; one couple traveled in a buckboard, the rest on horseback with pack mules. On their first night out Ethan recommended a campsite in an arroyo. It was narrow and had steep walls about four feet high. The sandy bed of the arroyo was soft so the tenderfeet would sleep well, the mesquite shrubs would provide firewood, the banks would provide protection from winds and the prying eyes of bandits or Apache.

He told Second Lieutenant Carrey he would sit up on a nearby hill and keep watch during the night, but his real reason was that he wanted to be alone. When the rains came, he was glad. The large stinging raindrops and some hail took his mind away from thoughts of Margaret and David. When he heard the low rumble he didn't know what it was at first. When he realized what it had to be, he jumped up, ran down and screamed to the camp but his warnings were drowned out by the incessant thunder just as the lives of the 15 homesteaders and five soldiers were drowned out by the flash flood that swept into the arroyo before anyone was aware of what was coming.

He retrieved the bodies and loaded them into the big wagon after tossing its waterlogged contents into the arroyo. A few of the horses survived. He hitched up two and roped the others together and drove the wagon back to Del Rio.

When he made his report at Fort Clark, he offered his resignation to Bullis who brushed the idea aside.

"How can you control an act of God?" Bullis said. "Pull yourself together and try to get some sleep."

The only way to sleep was drink even more.

…The memory was blasted out by a sharp pain in Ethan' shoulder blade. He knew immediately what it was when the pain spread out, burning at first then sapping his energy. A scorpion stung him. He took a couple of deep breaths. It was just one more thing to endure on this crawl. He felt the scorpion walk across his shoulder and down his arm, across his hand. He could have crushed it, but he didn't. The scorpion was just being a scorpion, and it will be alive tomorrow but several human beings will not. Eh-yeah, God wasn't around much. It was almost as bad to kill a man as be killed. It was never easy, never forgotten. The faces, even when you never saw them, always haunted your dreams. If you dreamed.

He continued his slow crawl forward, guessing now he was about 50 yards from the camp. The closer he got, the slower he would have to move. He hoped he would be there before daybreak. At one point he dragged his leg over a horse-crippler, the cactus' sharp, long needles tearing into him. He turned over and checked his leg, pulling several needles out. At least he was low enough to avoid lechuguilla and prickly pear. A live, sharp rock ripped into his chest. Some rocks were alive and some were not, he knew. This one was alive and belligerent. The rocks he pulled himself over hurt more than he thought they would at this point. Too many rocks behaving badly. He'd hoped he would get used to that pain over time but it turned out just the opposite. He needed to clear his mind…

He and his grandfather often sat at this point of rock near the top of the mountain. Maples and sycamores provided good shade; pines provided a perfume he never tired of. They sat and looked out across the sweeping valley below them. The could see a few roofs of houses but the prominent feature was the steeple of a Congregation church lurching up from the trees that covered the village. He liked winter best, watching the snow swirl and fall softly in faint light, hearing the bells on the reins of the teams that pulled townspeople's sleighs.

Sometimes his grandfather would ask him questions that led into lessons. Sometime his grandfather told Mic Mac stories.

"A long time ago lived a man and woman and their three children, two boys and a girl," his grandfather said. "Their family is very poor and the younger son tells his brother they should go traveling because they might find something better than what they had, maybe they would find wives in this better place. But the older brother didn't want to go, but told his younger brother to make a large deerskin bag and that when he found a girl he wanted, he should put all sorts of pretty things into the bag. Tell her, he instructed, that to see all of the pretty things she must get inside the bag and when she does you tie up the bag and run away with her. The younger says he'll do it. He makes a bag and sets out on his travels.

"The first place he comes to is a camp where the people still make tools from stone. The younger brother asks to see the chief but the people tell him they have no chief and have no need for one. We don't like strangers coming here. If you're looking for people like yourself, you must travel further.

"So the young man went on, coming to another village. The men in that village sat around making stone arrows, and one of the elders tells the younger brother that they have no need for all the new inventions like metal for arrows. They preferred the old ways like the people in the first village. The elder tells him to continue on.

"After a while the younger brother comes to a deep, broad river which he crosses and then comes to a lake. He finds a village and as he walks in all the people come running to greet him because they welcomed strangers. The young man asks for the chief's lodge and they take him to it. The chief asks him where he has come from and why he is there. The younger brother says he has traveled a very long distance to pay them a friendly visit and perhaps find a wife.

"The younger brother sees the prettiest girl in the village who is the chief's daughter. He goes out and finds pretty things to put in his bag. He finds beautiful stones and pieces of mica and flowers and berries and other strange and curious things and puts them all in his bag. When he sees the chief's daughter he tells her that she is as beautiful as the beautiful things he has in his bag. He tells her to go inside and look, to see the things for herself. He gives her a quick peek at all the wondrous things inside. She is curious. He opens the bag completely and she climbs into it. He quickly ties the bag up and ignoring her pleas, he runs away with her in his bag.

"When the young man lets her out of his bag, she is far from her village and she begins to cry. He tells her to stop because if she comes with him further on his travels he will show her strange and beautiful things, just as he promised, and that the things he would show her were larger and more beautiful than the small things in his bag. She agrees to travel with him and becomes his wife."

…Killing the first three Comanche was easier than Ethan anticipated. They were sound asleep as only young men can on such rocky ground. He moved carefully to each one, and slit their throats—nearly severing their necks—letting their blood soak into the earth. But as he approached the fourth man, the one he'd seen earlier, he must have made a noise because the Comanche leader stirred from his sleep and sat up, a knife in his hand.

Ethan leaped onto the Comanche. They struggled only a little then, at the same time they plunged their knives into the other. The Comanche leader stabbed directly. Ethan stabbed, twisted his blade and pulled it up a little, then lost consciousness just as the first ray of morning light fell over the camp.

When no shouting or gunfire came from the hill, Dutch and Joaquin decided to climb out of the creek to see what happened during the night. Walking around the hills on the flat desert, they saw the Comanche herd of horses, sniffing and pulling at their ropes a little with morning hunger. One warrior sat against a rock, obviously dead for some time.

"Gangrene got him," Dutch said.

Still silence from the hill. Dutch called out to Ethan but heard no reply. The two of them climbed the hill, stumbling frequently. Once into the saddle between the two hills, they saw three Comanche bodies all with blankets pulled around them, the ground dark with their blood. Joaquin noticed another body at the edge of the tallest hill. Then they saw Ethan entwined with another Comanche, neither of them moving, more darkness over the ground around them.

They rushed over and moved the bodies apart.

"This Comanche is dead, too, but he bled to death from a stab wound," Joaquin said. "Looks like they fought it out."

"Ethan is breathing," Dutch said. They saw the stab wound low on Ethan abdomen.

Joaquin laughed a little. "That Indian didn't know how to knife fight," he said. "He just stabbed and pulled out his knife, probably trying to stab again. If he'd stabbed a number of times, maybe he'd hit some vitals. But just this one, the wound closes up quick and you don't lose a lot of blood. If the blade doesn't get any vitals, you can make it. Look at the Comanche's stomach, that wound is a big hole, ragged and he had no hope past that point. Bled out."

"Hell of a thing," Dutch said. "Man's part Injun, part Welshman, and all hard son-of-a-bitch. He's going to make it, but he's going to need attention and we can't give him much here." He looked around the camp and spotted a water bag. He brought it over and poured some water in his hand and rubbed it on Ethan's face. The scout's eyes flickered open and his mouth tried to move but no sound came out. "Take it easy and drink some." Ethan did.

"I used to be relentless and redoubtable," Ethan whispered. "I thought that was all gone, but I must have some of that relentless left."

"Shut up and let us take care of your sorry arse," Dutch said. Ethan managed a small smile and closed his eyes.

"I'm too old for this shit," Ethan sighed.

"He can't walk back," Joaquin said. "I'll go and bring back a wagon."

"No," Ethan said. "You can't leave. The rest of them need protection."

"We'll all go together," Joaquin said.

"We can't move as fast as you can," Dutch said. "Ingrid would slow us way down and me, too. My rheumatiz slaps me way down.

You can protect yourownself out there and back; we'll stay here with Ethan. Just leave me your long gun."

"Dutch's right," Ethan said before he passed out again.

"No," Karl said. The preacher followed Dutch and Joaquin while Ingrid stood at the base of the hill looking up at them all. Karl displayed Ethan's pistol that he'd stuck in his waistband. "I will go. We need Joaquin to stay and protect him and you and Ingrid. I have always had a talent for running. I can get to town quicker. And, Dutch, I promise you that I will use this gun as a peacemaker if I have to. And I do know how."

"Get 'r done," Dutch said.

CHAPTER 16
Lajitas

Karl was indeed a talented runner. He covered the five miles to town in fifteen minutes, gasping for breath, He returned with H.W. McGuirk himself driving his buckboard. They loaded Ethan in the back, his stomach wrapped in a makeshift bandage torn from Ingrid's petticoats to keep the wound from opening, his head propped up with a blanket. Ingrid rode in the back with him, doing her best to hold him steady as the buckboard traveled over the desert. The others saddled horses and led the Comanche herd behind the wagon into Lajitas.

Gracey quickly nursed Ethan back to health. McGuirk gave the scout a new shirt and pair of trousers. It didn't take two weeks until Ethan was out of the bed Dutch gave him in one of the few rooms for rent at the Mejor Que Nada. He walked around Lajitas normally, but with little strength at first. That grew quickly with Tio José's pork and tortillas; he refused the meat biscuits of the canned beef Dutch had.

Joaquin traveled to Fort Davis with the horses, sold them and made a report to Sergeant Kimball. He stayed a while, enjoying the coolness of the town, putting off returning to the heat of the desert as long as he could. When he returned, he shared the money with Karl, Dutch and Ethan. The scout joined him and the preacher in their daily lunch ritual as Ethan mended. He and Dutch tried to convince Ethan to come down off his hill in Terlingua and settle in Lajitas, but the scout would have none of that telling them he couldn't wait to sleep in his own bed.

Ingrid kept her distance from Karl as well as she could. Mostly she stayed in Dutch's apartment during the day, going to the saloon only at sundown. Dutch told her to stop whoring and just be his woman. He'd send off to a man he knew in El Paso and get another whore sooner or later. Maybe two more now that he had some extra cash. He knew even a black African would generate more income than Ingrid ever had. Ingrid could be the waitress he always wished he had.

Karl refused to leave. The couple of people who had initially attended his services were gone now; the newness had worn off. And most of the town was Catholic anyway. He knew they would never come to pray with him.

On the day before Ethan Allan Twobears left to return home, he walked up the mesa to Brother Karl's little chapel.

"I'm sorry I couldn't convince Ingrid or Dutch or even Joaquin to come up with me," Ethan said. "They wouldn't come."

"That is fine," Karl said. "I knew when I started this quest it would not be easy. I have learned to be patient."

"Eh-yeah," Ethan said. "But you and I are the whole congregation."

The preacher smiled and opened his Bible, saying, "It's a beginning."

Book Two
WOMAN HOLLERING CREEK

Fall 1880

CHAPTER 1
Lost Mine Peak in the Chisos Mountains, Texas

He rewarded himself with a can of peaches.

He sat on a cliff edge on a long point of land jutting out from the Chisos Mountains that reminded him of a point his grandfather often took him to in the Green Mountains of his native Vermont. Except this point was barren of trees, and the view that awaited him didn't overlook the vastness of Lake Memphremagog. It was all desert.

The walk up was long but not arduous; most of the time he was in the shade of trees that grew thick in the high Chisos. The trees gave way just below the top of this ridge. The trail itself played out a little further up. It was a game trail and the bears, lions, deer, raccoons, and other critters that created it followed the path of least resistance so the resulting trail was often a series of switchbacks up what would otherwise be a very steep mountainside. The higher the trail got, though, the fainter it became until about a hundred feet from the top it disappeared.

He ate his peaches, drinking down the juice when he was finished. Below him stretched the rest of the world. From this perch he could look down on mile-high peaks. One time he looked down on two eagles gliding in an updraft. It wasn't often a person got to look down on eagles.

The sky was clear and deep blue this October morning. The view included some of the Chisos range to his right, the burned mountains of the Sierra Quemada and the rest of the Chihuahuan Desert below him. In the distance to the south was Mexico. If he squinted, he could make out the Río Grande, a narrow ribbon of darkness snaking across the desert. The air was so clear he could see mountains across the river that he knew were more than a hundred miles away.

Time to go to work, he thought, standing up and tying a thick rope around one of the boulders near the edge of the cliff. Holding the rope, he dropped carefully over the edge using his feet to guide him down thirty feet to a small ledge barely large enough for him to stand on. His back to the cliff, he slowly moved to his left until a large mesquite bush blocked his progress. He slowly squeezed between the bush and the cliff, trying to avoid as many thorns as he could, and ducked into the fissure cave behind the mesquite.

The light inside was faint, but he didn't need much. He'd been here many times before. He walked bent over to the back of the cave, grabbed a slab-sided rock and pulled it out. The hole was barely large enough for him to fit through, but he did. Inside was almost totally dark, but he knew what was here and where it was. He moved two steps forward until his foot hit one of the chests. He knelt down and reached out to make certain he had the chest on the right and not the one on the left that contained jewels and gold ornaments. He opened the right chest and filled a bag with gold coins.

This was the "lost mine" people spoke of. He knew it wasn't really a mine, but a stash of Spanish treasure. He couldn't do much with the jewels and ornaments and trinkets, but the coins spent as well or better than American money. He had one checked once in El Paso and was told it was nearly pure gold.

Ethan Allan Twobears, the old scout, took only enough to live on each time he visited. His needs were few and he wasn't greedy. Except this time. This would be his last time here, so he filled his bag with coins, figuring to take enough to live on for the rest of his life. Communities in the Big Bend were growing, engineers were looking for valuable minerals and were certain to find some and that meant mines, and the miners to run them. Too many people meant too many risks each time he returned to this cave, the cave an old Mescalero told him about several years ago, making him promise he would never reveal its location to any undeserving man...

He saved the old man's life. While scouting for a cavalry squad from Fort Clark out on a routine patrol, he discovered the old man lying on the side of the road with a broken leg. It was difficult to tell his age, but he had white hair — something Ethan never saw on an Apache before.

When the squad rode up a few minutes later, Corporal Alfonse Meckel wanted to kill the old man. Being so far from the reservation, the squad leader reasoned, made him a hostile. Ethan asked the corporal just how much of a threat he thought this old man with a broken leg was and the corporal replied that it didn't matter. When the corporal dismounted, walked over and drew his pistol, Ethan grabbed the revolver and punched the corporal hard enough in the face to knock him straight back to the ground and break his nose.

"I may be wearing this buckskin instead of my uniform blouse today, but don't you forget my sergeant's chevrons," Ethan said. "Now sit up and lean forward and hold your bandanna up to your nose with one hand and squeeze the top of your nose hard with the other."

He went to the side of the road to cut down a sapling to use as a splint for the old man's leg. He set the leg, strapping a piece of sapling on both sides. The old man didn't even flinch.

"Where's your horse?" he asked the Mescalero. The old man just stared at him.

"Caballo?" Ethan asked. The old man pointed down the road.

"Gerharter," he called to one of the troopers. "Get down the road and bring back the old man's horse."

"Ja," the trooper said and rode off around the hill in front of them.

Ethan and the old man then had a conversation in broken Spanish. The Mescalero told him he was deathly ill and traveling to his home near Sierra Blanca to die in peace with his family. He said he doubted he would make it because he thought he was too ill for the miles to go before he could sleep the long sleep. But, he said, that didn't bother him. If he died while on the right path his spirit would return home to be with the spirits of his ancestors. He just needed to stay on the right path.

Ethan asked him if he could ride and the old man said he would manage. Ethan boosted him up on the pinto Trooper Gerharter had retrieved.

"Buenos suerte," Ethan said to the old man. The man reached down and touched Ethan's shoulder and whispered his name, asking him never to reveal it. He nodded a promise. Then the old man whispered a place to him, telling him he would find riches there.

Ethan didn't believe or disbelieve the Mescalero's story of Spanish treasure, he just filed it away in his memory as one more story. He'd heard the tales of various treasures and mines the conquistadors left behind; everyone who ever traveled in the Big Bend region heard those stories. Some took them seriously and spent years searching for one or the other. Ethan just didn't care. He'd never seen anyone with wealth who was happy. Besides, if you had money all you did was spend the rest of your days worrying about someone else trying to take it from you.

Ethan decided the spot was a good one for a camp with shelter from some trees and the hill. Corporal Meckel's nose finally stopped bleeding, but he continued to throw daggered looks at Ethan the rest of the evening.

The next morning they continued down the road. Ethan spied the old man's pinto off the road, grazing on the thick grasses. He looked around and found the old man, dead by the roadside.

"Keep on the road and I'll catch up with you," Ethan ordered the corporal. "Take the pinto with you."

He carefully lifted the Mescalero's body across his saddle then walked his horse back to the hill about a quarter-mile behind them. He walked the horse to the top of the hill and pulled the old man down and carried him to a large rock. The ground was soft enough for him to dig a hole, so he placed the body in it then covered it with rocks. He made certain the body faced to the west, to Sierra Blanca so far away.

…Now he struggled with another rock. It was always the most difficult part of the trip to the cache, lifting that heavy slab of stone back into place on the cave wall. He left the cave, scooted the ledge, climbed back to the cliff edge. He coiled the rope, slung it over his shoulder, picked up his canteen for the walk down the mountain then back to his jacal some forty miles away in Terlingua.

He only found the treasure cave when looking for something to do one day while visiting one of his favorite places in the Chisos. It wasn't until he sat down, snacking from one of his cans of peaches, that he remembered the old Mescalero's tale. He saw a boulder that looked like it could be the right one, near a split of rock. He followed directions to the cave, the cave with all that wealth.

If Ethan still had a family, he might have taken all those coins and taken them away from the brushlands and desert. He would have taken them to a good city, with good air and good people. He would have built them a good house. Margaret would want for nothing. David would attend the best of schools. Perhaps they would even have more children; they'd be able to afford it. They'd be able to afford anything.

But the influenza stole his wife and son from him so he didn't care much about money anymore. After he quit the army, he found a comfortable spot for a comfortable jacal on top of a hill, only returning to the cave when he ran out of money — no more than once a year. He could carry enough in his trouser pockets to last him at least that long thanks to his simple needs and wants.

Every now and then he wondered who, if anyone, he would pass this information to. Maybe it was best to be forgotten. He also wondered if anyone would get suspicious of the coins and follow him to the cache or attempt to rob him of what he had. So far, no one had. And this was his last time here.

CHAPTER 2
Brackettville, Texas

"Step right up, ladies and gentlemen, boys and girls, puppy dogs and pussy cats, and you horses should be paying attention, too, yes, folks that's because my Ever-Cure Elixir is a bona-fide miracle of the modern age. This cure-all elixir was concocted by Alexander Graham Bell, America's greatest scientist, and by Mary Baker Eddy, America's greatest spiritual leader. Let me remind you that Mr. Bell is the great mind who invented the telephone and other boons to our modern society and, just this year, had bestowed upon him the honor of the Volta Award from the country of France for his contributions to the advancement of science. And let me remind you that Miss Eddy — so far advanced on a spiritual level that she has founded her own religion — and it was she, you may recall, who penned the great book *Science and Health* which laid the groundwork for the merger of science and medicine that led to this amazing discovery. Yes, ladies and gentlemen, only our esteemed and honorable President of these United States Rutherford B. Hayes could have brought these two geniuses together. President Hayes took this bold and unprecedented step in order to take advantage of the flood of new techniques, new materials, and new remedies that are just now coming to the fore."

Doctor Extraneous Hudspeth crouched down on the bally platform and motioned with his hand for the gathering crowd to come closer. Doc was a good blower and knew he didn't need to be bombastic all the time; it was better to vary the approach. Get the towners to make a commitment of their attention. Get them wanting to know more. He continued in a normal voice.

"Ladies and Gentlemen, this was not an easy task. At first they concocted a potion that would cure the pox. Then one that cured cholera. One that cured lock-jaw. One that cured consumption. One that cured cancers. One that cured chronic onanism. One that cured boils and sores and scratches and scrapes and cuts. One that cured idiocy. One that cured distemper and dyspepsia."

Doc stood abruptly, regaining his bally voice, "But then, ladies and gentlemen, these two brilliant individuals discovered this elixir." He pulled a medicine bottle smoothly from a coat pocket and held it high over his head. His serious face broke into a broad, toothsome, smile.

The smile caught Cynthia Laroch off guard. She was watching the presentation from the porch of the hardware store, hugging a post on the boardwalk. She had been moving back and forth from one side of the post to the other, but now she stopped and stared at Doc. She never saw a man smile that way before. It was happy and engaging. She didn't know it was possible for a man to smile this way. She couldn't remember ever seeing her father smile, and the only smiles she'd seen on any of her three brothers were either mean or lewd.

Of course, she hadn't seen many men at all in her seventeen years. She left the family farm in Castroville only to go to church with the family on Sundays and then not even every Sunday. The old Alsatians in church were hard farmers and pioneers who couldn't recall how to smile and had no reason to. As the families walked to their wagons after the service, some of the younger boys would run around and play and some of them would smile, but their fathers caught them quickly by the necks of their shirts or waists of their trousers and with a swift hand to an ear or back of the head quickly put a stop to playing and smiling.

No young men called on her. Her father wouldn't allow it. The boys, he said, didn't want her — she was too plain for other men to want — they wanted the Laroch farm, the most extensive in the area. It stretched for several sections. On it, the family grew corn and wheat and raised cows and hogs and chickens. Her older brothers took wives and brought them to the farm to work the fields, slop the hogs, milk the cows, gather the eggs, and get children. Her mother toiled all day in their kitchen, making the meals for the family that now numbered sixteen with all the men, wives and children. She was worn out and never said much, rarely even looked up from the stove or cook pot or table, and when she did she also never smiled. Cynthia was the one meant to look after her father when he got too old to work the farm, and she couldn't do that if she had her own family to look after.

Doc turned slowly right and left to flash his amazing smile at each segment of the crowd.

"This is an elixir that not only cures all the things I just mentioned to you, as you know, but it is a virtual cure-all for every ailment known to man, woman, child or animal," he continued. "This is the greatest achievement of mankind and it was brought forth by two of our finest Americans and the world will long owe our free and bold country a huge debt of gratitude. And now, with special arrangement with the Harvard University, the most prestigious college in this fair land, where this elixir finally came to fruition, I am able to offer this elixir to the general public, ladies and gentlemen, to each and every one of you for the very low prices of $2 per bottle."

"Why that's almost a week's wages for me," a man hollered out.

"Yes, sir, it might be because I can see you are a hard working man. In fact, I can see you work harder than the wages you earn, but let me ask you this, sir, if your wife was frigid towards the marital bed would you not work a week without pay to gain her warmth and affection? You, madam, if your mother suffered from dementia, would you not be happy to toil for a week so that your dearly beloved mother would once again be the person you knew and loved? You, marshal, if you suffered from hemorrhoids and saddle sores from long, hard days in the saddle bringing nefarious criminals to justice, would you not work for a week without pay in order to rid yourself of these burdensome tribulations? Yes, ladies and gentlemen, a bottle of this elixir is high-priced but worth-every-penny because of all the time and development and experimentation that went into it, not to mention the time of the two geniuses who toiled long and troublesome hours to arrive at the proper recipe, not to mention the facilities of the foremost font of learning in this great land. Yes, I tell you every bottle is worth every penny, every dollar."

Cynthia continued her rocking back and forth around the post, enthralled now by the painted canvases that hung on the bannerline at the back of the platform. They were garishly colored, almost lurid, with elaborate lettering on them to identify each as Maximo the World's Strongest Man, The Amazing Sword Swallower, Jo-Jo the Dog-Faced Girl, The Spectacular Fire Eater, Tiny Alice the World's Fattest Woman, The Wild Man of Borneo, and, simply, The Magus.

She wondered why the sword swallower, fire-eater, and wild man didn't have names but the others did. She wondered what a magus was — the canvas depicted a man fully engulfed in a dark cape holding a glowing stick in one hand and a glowing ball in the other. What could that possibly mean? The world was a more amazing place than she had imagined. She never anticipated people could eat fire or swords, or that women could look like dogs. And just where was Borneo? Back east or out further west? It sounded almost like the name of one of the German settlements her father traded with in the Hill Country, but it wasn't the same, she knew. Maybe Mexico, she decided.

If Mexican men looked like the Wild Man shown in the painting, she would have to change her plans. Mexico wasn't the kind of place she thought it was. It certainly offered her no haven, nothing different than what she left.

"Will it bring the dead back to life?" a heckler laughed.

"I'll be brutally honest with you, sir, no it will not," Doc responded quickly. "But, confidentially, I must also add that I am currently working in concert with Mr. Bell and Miss Eddy in order to come up with a concoction that will do just that very thing. Who knows what glories await mankind?"

A woman in a ruffled, powder blue ballgown emerged from an adjacent wagon, walked over to the platform and quietly stepped up. Cynthia noticed the wagon had wider wheels than any she had seen before. The side of the wagon was painted bright red with "Dr. Extraneous Hudspeth's Odditorium and Cavalcade of Wonders and Ever-Cure Elixir" painted in flowing, gold letters on the side.

Cynthia stopped rocking and gasped a little when she noticed the woman had a shiny brown nose and dark hair sprouting all over her face and from the sleeves of her gown. This must be that Jo-Jo woman, she thought, mesmerized. The woman slowly pulled several boxes from the rear of the platform to the front edge, to Doc's left.

Doc didn't acknowledge Jo-Jo's presence, continuing his bally: "Now this elixir will cure small troubles in just a day or two but larger problems, like the pox or cancers, may take longer. Up to a month. But no malady, no matter how severe, will ever outlast the efficacy of this elixir. Yes, ladies and gentlemen, I give you my words as an elder doctor of medicine, I give you my personal guarantee that if you do not feel at least a little better after the first day of drinking this Ever-Cure

Elixir then I will happily refund your money. If you have a small problem, one bottle should suffice. Follow the directions on the bottle and drink one-half cup twice a day. If you have more severe problems, drink the same amount per day, but it may take as long as a month to cure the problem, so you will need to stock up on several bottles since I must move on and offer this amazing elixir to as many people as possible across our great and wonderful country. Now, step right up, ladies and gentlemen, and the lovely Jo-Jo the Dog-Faced Girl will fill whatever your needs happen to be. And remember that you may meet Jo-Jo personally along with all these other stalwarts and oddities depicted behind me for a mere extra dime after you have purchased your life-saving elixir."

The crowd pushed forward to buy bottles. Doc took money and distributed elixir on one side of the stage while Jo-Jo handled the other side.

Cynthia couldn't take her eyes off Jo-Jo. The woman was dressed so elegantly yet did possess all the features of a dog. Jo-Jo knelt with one knee on the platform, leaning over to make her sales. Cynthia noticed the woman's low-cut bodice displayed full breasts in danger of falling out of the dress as Jo-Jo leaned forward when she handed a bottle to a buyer. The woman also made certain to hike up her skirt every now and then so her bare ankles were visible above her velvet slippers. If a man jostled around a little, he could also catch a glimpse of Jo-Jo's smooth, white calves. If he were directly in front of her, he could see considerably more. Cynthia wondered why these areas of Jo-Jo's body were not also covered in hair like a dog's would be. None of the men appeared worried about that, as they crowded around, money in hand, so they might bask, however briefly, in this glory.

•

When elixir sales were completed, Cynthia watched many of the crowd pay another dime and disappear into the large tent behind the platform. She waited until the crowd was gone then timidly handed over her ten cents and took a place well behind the crowd.

The inside of the tent smelled of coal oil and sawdust and the sweat of the crowd. A long platform stretched the length of one wall.

Doc emerged from a slit in the canvas and took to the platform.

Cynthia listened intently as Doc explained that, in addition to being an esteemed doctor of medical science, he was the only white man in the world to have earned an appointment as a magus by the very sultan of the Ottoman Empire himself. He explained that magi had roamed the world for centuries, performing miracles for cabbages and kings, and, in fact, three prominent magi had visited the Christ Child at the very beginning of recorded history, giving the magi imprimatur to the entire Christian religion and the very heart of Western civilization.

She watched him take small items from the audience and, without touching them, enticed them to float around his body. He pointed a short, black stick at a young woman standing next to her boyfriend. He waved the stick a little and, suddenly, a bouquet of flowers appeared where the stick was and he presented it graciously to the lady. Finally, he produced a crystal ball out of thin air — where could such a large sized ball come from? — and caused that to float above the platform in a magical dance, then, suddenly, drop to the stage with a resounding thud. The wonders she had witnessed today were all a puzzlement to Cynthia.

Doc bowed to the applause. When the clapping subsided, he introduced the performers one-by-one as they took the platform from the same curtain slit. Jo-Jo and Tiny Alice came first, taking chairs at opposite ends of the platform. Neither of them said a thing. Jo-Jo looked pitiful; Tiny Alice looked jolly. Men — mostly the soldiers from Fort Clark — teased each of them and made vulgar remarks about their looks, but neither of them reacted. Tiny Alice grinned, nodded and waved. Jo-Jo looked sad, as if she understood all the rude words better than the men who made them. Cynthia couldn't take her eyes off Jo-Jo even as Maximo took the stage and lifted several large dumbbells, bent an iron bar, and juggled an anvil back and forth from one hand to the other.

Doc went backstage for a moment and emerged rolling a cage that held the Wild Man from Borneo. The Wild Man raged and frightened women and children while husbands and fathers chuckled nervously and Doc extolled the crowd on the Wild Man's history, how he was captured. But Cynthia heard none of the words. At one point, her eyes met the Wild Man's and his snarl evaporated for a moment. She thought she detected a little bit of a smile at the edge of his mouth as he roared and tugged at the bars. Every now and then, when she glanced over at him she caught him looking at her. At least, she thought she did.

Cynthia also caught Jo-Jo looking over at her, so much that she thought something was awry in her dress and quickly checked her clothing. She was all in place.

For a moment she feared Jo-Jo and the Wild Man recognized her. But they couldn't. They didn't know her, didn't know of her. She was just a plain young woman in a gray bloomer dress with a green bonnet that didn't match.

The Spectacular Fire Eater stopped her quandary — he was a young man but had a wooden peg where his left leg should have been and as he walked onto the stage, the leg was lit up with sparklers sticking out of it from all sides. As he lit up a half-dozen small torches, holding three in each hand one between each finger, the sparklers fizzled out. He waved the small torches about and jabbered on in a sing-song manner about how he acquired this talent when visiting a volcanic island in the Pacific Ocean. Again she didn't hear many of the words, but did wonder where the Pacific Ocean was and what, indeed, an ocean was. It sounded like it would be a body of water, but how would it be different from a lake or a pond or a river or a creek?

One-by-one the man brought the small torches up to his mouth where he spit fire onto them. The fire flared up, astonishing the crowd with each. Then the man put each one in his mouth, picking up speed with each, and each emerged with the fire still blazing. How did he do this and not burn his mouth, Cynthia wondered. She burned her mouth on too-hot meats and soups. How could a man eat fire and spit fire? This man did. Finally, the man put each torch into his mouth and apparently swallowed the fire because when he pulled it out, the flame was gone.

Doc made a big production out of introducing the Amazing Sword Swallower and Cynthia didn't hear a word. While this tall, handsome man carefully pushed knife and sword blades down his throat to the gasps of the crowd, she continued to stare at Jo-Jo. Jo-Jo continued to stare at her and, when she glanced over, saw that the Wild

Man was staring as well. She might have been embarrassed by all this attention, but wouldn't have understood the word.

•

When the show ended and the crowd dispersed, Cynthia sat down on the bench in front of the hardware store. The sun had set while they were in the tent but the few street lamps cast enough light to walk around safely. The noise and bright lights from the Bucket of Blood saloon a block away commanded the attention of most of the townspeople who hadn't gone home.

After a while, Cynthia rose and walked as quietly as she knew how around the show wagons. She saw Doc go into one. Maximo, the Fire Eater and the Wild Man went into another. Only two of them had windows. One belonged to the Sword Swallower. The other was Jo-Jo's and Tiny Alice's.

Cynthia lifted up on her toes and peeked into Jo-Jo's wagon. Alice was already in her bed, snoring. Jo-Jo sat at a small table in front of a mirror, daubing some lotion on her face. After just a little while, Jo-Jo took a soft cloth and wiped away the lotion which also carried away her dog-like hair and the brownness of her nose.

Jo-Jo was a fraud, Cynthia realized. And instantly she saw her salvation.

CHAPTER 3
San Antonio, Texas

San Antonio was a busy city so no one noticed when the tall, handsome, sandy-haired man with the brilliant mustache and cold eyes stepped off the Southern Pacific train at the depot. He carried a large, well-traveled, green and rose carpet bag. His black suit was tailored to fit his athletic frame.

He strode immediately over to a boot-black, sat in the chair and lit a cigar. While the old Negro cleaned and polished his calfskin boots, he settled back to watch the comings and goings of passengers, railway workers, stevedores, newspaper boys, and a chili queen pushing a gaudy yellow cart up and down the platform. He observed people, partly out of habit and partly because he enjoyed the imaginative process of guessing each person's story.

Everyone had a history but most of the people they met had no interest in that, only in gaining something, usually money. People mostly saw each other as commodities or meal tickets, especially in cities or boomtowns. He was interested in their stories, though. Once he knew — or guessed correctly — a person's story then he could predict how that person would act and react. That was valuable information in the two chosen professions of his life. Studying people made him money and kept him alive.

"All done, massuh," the elderly boot-black finally said.

He stepped down and gave the man a new, seated-Liberty dime, more than twice what the boot-black charged.

"Thank yuh, massuh, thank yuh, verah much," the boot-black said.

He picked up his bag, nodded his head at the boot-black and walked away deliberately, glad to be rid of the ten-cent piece. That engraving on the front just looked too French to him, and he didn't care for the French or many things French, except for their sexual attitudes.

He walked through the station, stopping for a moment at the ornate front doors to drop his spent cigar into an iron receptacle.

"Direct me to the express office?" he asked a porter going by.

"The next building to your left, sir," the porter replied.

He nodded, touched the flat brim of his hat in thanks and walked to the adjacent building, his long stride and tall-heeled boots making a distinct sound on the boardwalk.

The interior of the Wells, Fargo & Co. office was crowded with people jostling for position in two lines that led to harried clerks wearing the green eyeshade badge of clerks everywhere. One window was marked "Express," the other marked "Flocke's San Antonio-El Paso Stage Co." Affixed to the iron grating adjacent to the stage line window was a large poster that read, "You will be traveling through Indian and Bandit Country and the safety of your person cannot be vouchsafed by anyone but God." Light filtered down into the large room from windows more than twelve feet above their heads. Each window was propped open, letting the heat from the crowd flow out. He looked around, seeing another clerk behind a desk behind the bar that separated the customers from the two clerk positions. The clerk was busy copying numbers and information from a stack of handwritten papers into a light green ledger.

"Excuse me," he said to the clerk who took a moment to look up.

"I'm sorry, sir, but you will have to stand on line as the others are and await your proper turn," the clerk said politely but tersely.

"Bartholomew Dodge," he told the clerk. The clerk looked at him directly for the first time and correctly decided this was no regular customer for no customers knew who Bart Dodge was.

"I'll tell him he has a visitor, sir. May I tell him who's calling?" After a moment's silence that told the clerk the man wasn't about to divulge his name to him, the clerk rose and said, "Be just a minute."

He nodded, placing his bag on the bar to take the weight off his hand that was getting a little cramped. The clerk returned, sat back down at his desk and continued his copying. "Mr. Dodge will be right out," the clerk said without looking up.

A man dressed in a dark blue suit with a silver brocade vest stepped out of an office and walked toward him. The man extended his hand and they shook across the bar.

"Bartholomew Dodge?"

"Bart. You must be Wyatt Earp."

"That's a fact," Wyatt replied. "Your brother said you were in need of help on a sensitive Wells Fargo matter."

"That I do," Bart said. "That I do. But we shan't talk here. Please, come into my office; it's more pleasant and more quiet."

The pair walked into an office where two more clerks sat shuffling papers around between filing cabinets and their desks.

"Barney, pour us two of the good whiskeys," Bart said to one of the clerks.

"Branch is fine for me," Wyatt said.

"Oh, that's right. I forgot. Brother Fred said you didn't drink spirits. Don't cuss, either, I recall he said."

"I see no reason to do either," Wyatt said.

"Pour me a whiskey and bring my associate an iced water," Bart ordered as the two men went into an inner office.

Wyatt placed his bag in front of Bart's desk, pulled out a chair with rollers on it from the side of the desk and sat down, resting his feet on top of the bag. Bart sat behind the desk.

"You arrived quickly, Mr. Earp. I only telegraphed Fred four days ago."

"He said it was the first time you had ever asked him for assistance so he felt it must be vitally important. I was unengaged at the time, and I often spend time in Brackettville during the winter months so when he mentioned this involved that village, it piqued my curiosity. When Bob Paul recommended I should assist, well, that sealed the deal for me."

"Did he give you any of the details?" Bart asked as the clerk arrived with two tall mugs, one half filled with an amber liquid, the other filled to the brim with water, the ice chips in the mug clinking together. The clerk left.

"Ice is a luxury most places in the West," Wyatt said gratefully after sipping a little from the mug. "No, we all thought it best that you tell me directly what the problem was. That way I get only one version of the story and I don't let any important information slip."

Bart nodded. "That's what I would've done. Well, here is my dilemma. The United States Army here has contracted with Wells Fargo to distribute payrolls to several of the more remote forts in west and south Texas. At least until we have proper railroad service to those areas. If we ever do. The last two payrolls that left this office were taken by highwaymen, even though no one but me and the Army knew which stage the payrolls were on."

"Inside job," Wyatt said, taking a large drink from his mug. He set the mug down on the walnut desk, slowly wiping the condensation from the glass down the side as he rotated the mug absentmindedly.

"I'm afraid so," Bart said. "I know I'm not the source and I trust General Ord explicitly. Only two other soldiers here are aware of when the shipment goes out, Major Horne, the dispersing officer, and his assistant, Lieutenant Shepard. Ed Ord has expressed his absolute trust in the two of them."

"Well, that trust doesn't mean a thing until it's proven out," Wyatt said softly.

"I know."

"Even Ord."

"Well… I've downed too many bourbons with Ed not to know his mind. He's a stiff-necked son of a bitch and too much of a Presbyterian, and I liked Chris Auger much better when he was in charge of the Department, but I do trust him. The other two officers I know just to talk to."

"Which forts does the payroll go out to?"

"Clark, Duncan, Stockton and Davis."

Wyatt blew a long whistle. "That's a long run. Where have the previous two been held up?"

"Between here and Brackettville. Fort Clark's the first stop, so that way the highwaymen get everything."

"Seems likely that the insider is either here or at Fort Clark, then. Who is privy to this at Clark?"

"Just Colonel Bill Shafter and Quartermaster Sergeant Paschal Erny."

Wyatt sat quietly for a while, finishing his mug of iced water. "When's the next payroll going out?"

"We haven't set a date as yet."

"Today's Friday. Make it Monday. Where's the money kept in the meantime?"

Bart pointed to the large, gray Hall's Safe to the left of the office door. "The payroll was supposed to leave here a couple days ago, but

I've been too frightened to send another one out. We're talking many thousands of dollars, Mr. Earp, and that kind of money could tempt anyone."

"Even you."

"Are you insinuating—"

"Relax, Bart. Fred and Bob both vouch for you and I take Fred's word as the Gospel and Bob's nearly so. But we can't rule anyone out. Show me the money."

Bart had a questioning look, but rose from his chair and opened the safe anyway. Inside the safe were four treasure boxes made of dark green wood with straps of metal wrapped around them, each one tagged for a different fort. Bart removed four keys from his jacket pocket and opened each of the one-by-two-foot boxes, displaying the coins and paper money.

"How many people have keys?"

"Only me and Ord have all four keys. The senior officer at each fort has one key corresponding to his box."

"So here's what's going to happen," Wyatt said. "Give me your keys. Then tell me the combination to this safe and close everything back up again. I'll be eating and sleeping in this office until Monday morning when I'll drive the stage out. I'll have my own messenger guard with me. No one from Wells Fargo goes along. You tell no one you don't usually tell when the stage is leaving. We tell the regular driver and messenger only at the moment the stage is ready to leave, and they'll ride along inside. And you tell no one about me driving."

"I'm really not comfortable with that, Mr. Earp. I have a responsibility—"

"So far what you've tried hasn't worked. If you want my help, this is the way it happens. If you don't want my help, I'll ask for a night's lodging in the Menger, compensation for a good supper, and a ticket home. Fred vouched for you; didn't he vouch for me?"

"In the highest manner," Bart said, handing over his keys.

•

"Gentleman to see you, Mr. Earp," one of the clerks said on Saturday afternoon. "Says he's your brother."

"Show him in," Wyatt said. In a moment, a thinner, younger version of Wyatt walked through the door and shut it behind him. He tossed two pair of empty saddlebags on the floor and the two men embraced.

"Morg, how've you been?"

"Pretty good, Wyatt, pretty good." He looked around Bart Dodge's office, scowling a little.

"In that cabinet under the window," Wyatt said, sitting down behind Bart's desk. Morgan opened the cabinet, removed a bottle of whiskey and poured himself a tall glass. He sat on the edge of the desk.

"You living here?" he said, taking a long gulp of the whiskey.

"Yesterday, tonight, and Sunday. I drive the stage out early Monday."

"Everything going to plan?"

"So far. I telegraphed Bullis at Fort Clark yesterday after I talked to Bart and he's sending me someone. Supposed to be here late tomorrow. Nobody knows a thing. Nobody suspects anything."

"Sounds pretty slick to me."

"Simple, actually, when you think about it. And we can be back home in a couple days at the most. We'll do well for just a few days work."

"I gotta hand it to you, Wyatt, you always were the brains of our outfit."

Wyatt smiled and walked to the safe, spinning the dial. "Let's get to work."

•

An hour after the sun went down, Wyatt was finishing a dinner of chicken, peas, and biscuits at the desk with Bart. Wyatt dealt a hand of poker using just his left hand, dropping the cards beside their plates.

"I'm glad that you relented and agreed I could ride along in the stage," Bart said.

"It's a compromise I'm not too happy with," Wyatt replied. "You don't normally travel on the stage and I would prefer everything go as usual."

"But as I said, I often do travel along. I haven't been on any of the stages that were held-up, but I've often been a traveler on the route to make quarterly inspections of the substations. This will not be out of the ordinary."

"Just make sure you keep your mouth shut about what we're carrying and no matter what happens out there, you don't try to be a hero."

"Well, if the highwaymen do, indeed, show themselves, I'll not sit idly by and watch them abscond with the Army's money. I will be armed and I am more than able to help you and your friend deal with whatever we encounter."

Wyatt collected his chips, shuffled the cards and dealt another hand. "You'll go unarmed and I'll search you before we leave to make certain of that. Same goes for the regular crew. I'll keep their weapons in the boot with me. And neither you nor they will interfere at all, regardless of what does or does not happen."

"Now, really, Wyatt—" He was interrupted by a loud banging on the front door.

"Folks can't read the sign says we're closed," Bart said, angry to be disturbed at a Sunday supper, and playing cards with Wyatt Earp to boot. As he walked out, Wyatt wiped his greasy hands on a napkin and retrieved his shotgun from the floor by his feet. He cocked it, keeping the barrels below the top of the desk, and faced the door.

"Get the hell out of here," Wyatt heard Bart say at the door.

"Ah'm here t'see Mistah Earp, suh," another voice said.

Wyatt uncocked the shotgun, put it back on the floor, then walked to the front door.

"Lieutenant Bullis send you?" Wyatt asked the barrel-chested man at the door. The visitor wore obviously old but clean clothes and held his hat in his hands clasped over his gun belt buckle. The man's chocolate face would have disappeared in the night except for the office light reflecting on it.

"Yas, suh. Ah'm Sar'nt Benjamin Factor, suh. The light'nt said not to wear mah uniform, but Ah took me the liberty to carry mah sidearm."

"Smart thinking, Ben, come on in," Wyatt said, shaking the soldier's hand and closing the door behind him. He pointed to the inner office.

"What's the meaning of having this... man... here?" Bart said.

"My shotgun messenger," Wyatt replied. Wyatt pulled up another chair for Sergeant Factor and motioned for him to be seated. Wyatt and Bart sat, Wyatt pushing the basket of food over to the sergeant.

"Eaten tonight?" Wyatt said.

"Nah, suh."

"Dig in and get what's left," Wyatt said. He poured the soldier a drink from Bart's half-empty whiskey bottle.

"Now that's top drawer bourbon," Bart protested. Wyatt ignored him.

The soldier took a sip and saluted Bart with the glass. "Tis that, suh."

"You know John Bullis at Fort Clark?" Wyatt asked Bart.

"Never met the man, but just about everyone around here knows his whirlwind reputation."

"He's a good friend of mine. Sergeant Factor here is one of his best men and he's agreed to help us out."

"A nigger Indian's going to help us out how?"

"I told you. He's my shotgun messenger. What's the going rate for that these days?"

"We pay $30 a month and that's top wages for top men," Bart said, visibly uncomfortable to have a Seminole Negro savage seated next to him, and eating to boot.

"Since this is such a special run I expect you'll be offering the good sergeant here a month's wages then for this particular trip."

"Now, Wyatt, I made a financial deal with you. A lucrative one. I don't see any reason to pay out any more money, especially not to this... man."

"We're a package," Wyatt said smiling. "But we don't came at package rates. I need the sergeant and so do you."

"Whatever you say," Bart mumbled.

Benjamin sucked a chicken bone clean then bit into half a biscuit. "Be in advance, suh, iffen yah doan mind."

Bart opened a drawer, opened a metal box in the drawer, and withdrew a ten-dollar bill and twenty silver dollars. "Whatver you say."

CHAPTER 4

Wild Cow Mesa, New Mexico Territory

Lozen was lost. She knew where she was — she always knew where she was and where she would lead her band — but she was lost without her brother. If what Wolf Rising told her was true, then Beduiat, the man the Pale Eyes called Victorio, died just a few suns ago at the hands of Mexicans. This was not reasonable.

Wolf Rising and three other Mescalero rode into the camp that morning. They had been with The Conqueror and his band made up mostly of Chihenne warriors.

"Little Sister, everywhere we went, Pale Eye soldiers were before us," Wolf Rising said. "In my life, the Pale Eyes were always behind us. They pursued and we mocked them and ran away and lost them. But now, they were ahead of us. At every water hole, the Pale Eyes were already there. We ran to the south and the Pale Eyes were there; we ran east and the Pale Eyes were there. We crossed the long river, and the Pale Eyes were there, too. Pale Eyes soldiers and Rangers and Mexican soldiers met us. We ran for the stronghold but they surrounded us. We rejoiced for a little while when the Pale Eyes soldiers and Rangers rode away, but then more Mexicans came. The fight was a long one and The Conqueror and many of his band fell. We escaped. Maybe some others, too. But The Conqueror did not."

Lozen separated from The Conqueror nearly four moons ago to help a cousin in childbirth. Her band followed her, as always. They had agreed to meet up again this moon, at Rattlesnake Springs several days to the south of this camp. She refused to believe The Conqueror would not be there as agreed.

"I will join your band," Wolf Rising said, removing his turban of owl feathers and sitting by the fire. His friends nodded and sat next to him.

"You are welcome," Lozen said.

She turned and walked up a nearby hill, the tin cones on her sleeveless top tinkling in the twilight. Although her top was made of buckskin, it was cut low at the armpits and the front reached only to just below her breasts so that the breezes riffled through the loose garment, cooling her skin. In battle she would shed her skirt to wear just the warrior's breechclout. She had rubbed the sacred hoddentin in the buckskin herself and treated it over a low fire to give the clothing a soft, brown color and make it water repellant. She had no wife to do these things for her as other warriors did.

Lozen had been a warrior as long as she could remember. She rode, roped, tracked, hunted, shot, stole horses, and ran as well or better than most boys her age when she was growing up. And she only got better. All she had to do, she would tell people, was mimic her brother.

When she came of age, a band of warriors formed around her. They came, she knew, only partially because of her skills. They also came in part because she was The Conqueror's sister, and they came in part because of her Power, and they came in part because she remind-ed them of White Painted Woman, the great mother who begat all the Indeh.

She had taken only one man to her bed, despite urgings from The Conqueror. That had been Gray Ghost many summers ago, but he stayed for just one moon and then disappeared as quickly as he had appeared. He called himself a Seneca Hebrew and said he was trav-eling from near the great Pale Eye cities to the far northeast. He even said he came from a city named for the buffalo. He said his name, but she had trouble pronouncing it so she called him Gray Ghost, because he seemed to arrive on his wagon like a ghost in the night and his hair was very gray. She did not speak this Seneca Hebrew tongue and he did not speak Chihenne, but they managed to have conversations using bits of English and Spanish. When they were intimate, they needed no language. He told her that the Pale Eyes were more numerous than colonies of ants, and lived just as crowded in on each other. That's why they traveled west, he explained: they were too crowded in the east and as they made more and more people they needed more and more room for them. He explained the Pale Eyes had always done that. He said they had originally crossed a great sea in great boats from the original homes that lay several moons from the eastern cities they now occupied. This did not seem reasonable. But because he said it, she accepted it. And she accepted her most precious belonging from Gray Ghost, a gold dragonfly pendant she never removed from around her neck.

At the top of the hill, Lozen stood still to catch the last bits of light from the setting sun. She heard a bird squawk nearby. When she looked, she saw the bird dart from one mesquite branch to another, then to the top of an ocotillo, then back to the mesquite. She saw the long bit of food in its beak and knew what the bird was doing, making certain it was safe to enter its nest to feed its young. Odd, she thought, the young birds should have hatched and flown a few moons ago. She wondered if this was a sign she should pay attention to. She moved quietly to the shrub and spied the nest, an almost perfect circle of dried grasses and twigs on the fork of two branches. Birds make their nests in circles because they have the same religion as we do, she thought. So these late birdlings must have a meaning. But what?

Did it simply mean she was too late, or did it hold out some kind of hope? She would have to think on it and pray on it. But not now. She had her band to think of.

She stood to face where the sun had set and raised her arms beside her, palms up.

"Upon this earth on which we live, Yusn has Power. This Power is mine for locating the enemy. I search for that enemy which only Ysun the Great can show to me," she prayed.

This was the Power that drew many warriors to her. Even The Conqueror didn't possess this power to locate the enemy. Her Power had never failed her. For the first time, she doubted it. Every time she used her Power, it would turn her quickly in the direction of the enemy and the intensity of warmth she felt on her face and hands could tell her how great in number the enemy was. But now, she spun. The warmth was small, but it came from each direction. She stopped herself and sat down. This was not right. She grabbed a handful of dirt and rubbed it in her face to heighten her awareness.

"Speak straight so your words may go as sunlight into my heart," she prayed, then stood. She spoke her Power prayer again, but again she spun. She turned quicker and quicker until she grew faint.

"Ashoog," she whispered, thanking her Power. She knew not to question it. Her experience could mean only one thing, the enemy were few but they were all around. Wolf Rising was right. Now she would have to use all of her Power to determine where the Pale Eyes were fewest, because she had to lead her band somewhere and they were determined not to return to the bad place the Pale Eyes called a reservation. No, better to go on, all the way, to O'zho, the Happy Place, where her brother now was than to return to the reservation.

She prayed again, concentrating to slow down her spin. She concentrated on the warmth she felt, how it was different as she faced different directions. Finally, she felt the difference. They would have to travel south, the same direction her brother had followed. The possibility of meeting her brother excited her, but the possibility of leading her followers to their deaths frightened her.

As she walked down the hill she told herself there was no death, only a change of worlds. But even as she repeated it, it gave her no consolation.

•

Wolf Rising didn't like the idea of following a woman, even if she was The Conqueror's sister. The Conqueror was certainly the greatest of all the Indeh, but he was now gone. He watched him die and was powerless to prevent it. In Lozen, he saw enough of The Conqueror to make him sad that he was gone. Don't cry because he is gone, he told himself; smile because you knew him.

He knew all the stories about Lozen's skills as a warrior and her Power to locate the enemy, but she was still just a woman. A woman shouldn't lead a band. A man should. He should.

He knew he never would. He went his own way too often and spoke little. Other men heard him but didn't listen. He was always right when he spoke, but most of the warriors would hear one of the leaders repeat what he said and believe it was their words instead of his. When he was younger, Wolf Rising would try to make them understand he had said the words first, but few listened. Instead of trying to change his behavior, be more acceptable to more people, he withdrew into his own thoughts. This gave him a place, though. He was always the outlier or the scout. He faithfully kept watch; nothing got by him. He faithfully tracked enemies and found water and food and passes through the mountains. That was his place in life and he was content with it. But he was not happy with it.

Even women would have little to do with him. They would listen to his songs and stories and laugh but still go off with another. The only women he took to his bed were captives, but they gave him none of the comfort he sought and knew should be his.

Now Lozen called a council of all the warriors. He knew what this would be like. She had already decided what to do, where to go, but she would make the men think they had a say in such things. They should. All men should. But he knew Little Sister would follow her own heart and the others would follow her. He would, too. Where could he go otherwise? He didn't want to go away alone and he didn't want to go to the prison that was San Carlos. Even the reservation his Mescaleros had by the sacred Sierra Blanca was too much of a prison for him, unable to go and come as they pleased. He would live or die as a free man.

"There is one God looking down on us all," Lozen prayed after the warriors gathered and sat around the open fire. "We are all children of the one God. God is listening to me. The sun, the darkness, the winds are all listening to what we now say."

Then she described what her Power had shown her.

"This is as I told," Wolf Rising said. "The Pale Eyes are all around us."

"Lozen's Power has told this," Upsidedown said. He was the elder warrior here and was a little upset with Wolf Rising for usurping his right to speak first. "Has your Power said where we should go?"

She pointed with her nose to the south.

"We should not go south," Wolf Rising said.

Upsidedown glared at him again and mumbled, "You'll be back as a bear."

"Wolf Rising was with my brother and his words have importance here," Lozen said in a calm voice, looking at the newcomer. "We listen."

"Your brother rode south and all we found were Pale Eyes. Your brother went further south into Mexico and your brother met his death. These things just happened. The Pale Eyes are still there. We would be in great danger going south."

"What did your Power say?" Upsidedown asked Lozen.

"The Pale Eyes are in every direction," she repeated. "But we cannot stay here. Too close at Pine Springs is a large number of Pale Eyes soldiers and they pass by here frequently. If we do not long to return to reservations, we cannot go back to the west. My Power says the number is the least in the south. That way lies Rattlesnake Springs where my brother said he would meet us."

Wolf Rising hurled a twig into the fire. "Your brother is gone."

"So you say," she said. "I have not seen this. You say you have. Perhaps you do not know what you saw. I told my brother I would meet him at Rattlesnake Springs and I will keep that promise."

Give-Me-A-Horse rocked back and forth, sucking a little on his teeth. "And what if The Conqueror does not arrive?"

"What if only Pale Eyes soldiers wait at the springs?" Upside-down asked.

"If these things happen, we shall hold another council," she said.

"You are our leader. Lead," Upsidedown said loudly as he stood up. "Council's are good things for quiet times. They waste time in battle. If the enemy is all around us, we face battle soon. You lead. We follow."

"Enjuh," most of the group said at once, all of them getting to their feet. "This is a good thing."

"You will scout ahead for us?" Lozen asked Wolf Rising. "You've just come over the land."

"I will scout," he sighed.

154

CHAPTER 5
Lajitas

Graciela Salgado was a woman of many talents. Not only was she now Dutch Dave's only whore at his Mejor Que Nada saloon, she was mother to daughters Corazón and Alma, was the local curande-ra — a vital job when the nearest physician was more than 300 miles away in El Paso — an excellent cook, and a more than fair seamstress. She balanced all these tasks with ease, doing what needed to be done when it needed to be.

She had already served the Ranger a dinner of ham and biscuits and whiskey and brought the old scout his third beer. Now she re-turned with a neatly folded piece of leather clothing.

"You finished it already?" Ethan Allan Twobears said when Gracey placed the buckskin shirt on the table.

"Sí. I have a little time and it is an easy thing to do. You should try it on to make certain it fits properly, but I am sure it does."

Ethan started to unbutton the wool shirt he hated when Dutch, the bartender and owner, hollered over at him. "I slap don't need to see your birthday suit in this establishment. It needs ironing real bad. Take it out back."

Ethan gulped down his glass of beer, told Joaquin to finish eat-ing, and promised to be right back.

The evening was young, but very cold. A little early for these temperatures, Ethan thought, but it fit right into the rest of this year when it had snowed on the desert floor in early May, when it rained al-most every day through August, when the prickly pear and cactus had a second bloom in early October, when other wildflowers and the tall bluebonnets struggled but succeeded to make their own fall blooms.

With this north wind came not only cold weather, but crystal clear skies. As he looked up, he swore he could reach up and touch the stars that Coyote hung just out of reach to tease men.

He pulled off his woolen shirt, glad to be rid of the itchy fabric against his skin. The one shirt he loved, his old buckskin, he'd had to cut up for a breechclout last year when he crawled across the desert to save his friends. He'd worn that buckskin for so long. What was it? Ten years, at least. For the past five, he'd never taken it off. When he bathed, he bathed with the shirt on, washing it at the same time. Over the years that shirt molded to his body and became a second skin. It was soft and embracing. It was comforting. He tried living without it, but he couldn't. He wore cotton shirts and wool shirts, but neither felt right. Back when he wore a uniform, it didn't seem to matter which fabric he wore, but now it did. He was younger then and tolerated more things. After more than fifty years, he'd gotten very set in his ways.

So last month he rode into the high Chisos and killed some white-tail. The meat was always good, even though he seemed to have lost the taste for meat he once had. He didn't like killing things much either, but did when he had to. Not like when he was younger. His memory flashed back for just a moment to the battle of Gettysburg. How many men did he kill those couple of days? And for what? At least these deer he killed now would give him sustenance and clothing. He skinned the deer and tanned the hides himself, rubbing the brains into the skins until they were soft and pliable. He walked a couple of miles to a waterfall on the desert, a pour-off from the Chisos that cre-ated a secluded oasis, completely hidden from view. He gathered up a bundle of cattails and carried them out. He could have ridden his horse very close to the falls, but he enjoyed walking and didn't seem to do enough of it anymore. Besides, riding a horse would leave a clear trail to the falls but his mocassined feet wouldn't. He'd rather keep the place a secret from as many people as possible — not that many people were around in the desert anyway. Extracting the pollen from the cattails, he made up enough hoddentin to make the skins resist water after he rubbed the pollen into them. He'd wait to do that. The hoddentin was in a small bag in his jacal on his Terlingua hill and now that Gracey sewed the skins into a new shirt, he'd wear the shirt for a few days and get it soaked a few times, then he'd work the hoddentin into it and smoke it for a day. After maybe two years of dirt, sweat, and weather, the shirt would be what he wanted.

Right now, the shirt was stiff. He pulled it over his head and down across his tattoos. It fit perfectly, but it felt like metal. He didn't do as good a job tanning the hides as he should have, he thought. Probably got too impatient.

"I see Gracey did a good job," Joaquin said as Ethan sat back down at their table.

Gracey smiled and nodded her approval. Ethan gave her one of his gold coins, a couple months' worth of earnings for her, he guessed. "Gracias. But this is too much."

"Nope, it's not. It's not," Ethan told her, pushing her hand back when she tried to return the coin. "It's worth every penny to me. Every penny."

Dutch rolled his eyes at this. Gracey would now come to him with the coin and ask him to exchange it for American money, which he would. Then he would have to put it away like he always did when the old scout gave him one of those old Spanish coins with the hooked-nose fat man on it and then carry them on his once-a-year trip to San Antonio to convert the coins into real money for himself. And now that she had a little money, she would want a day or two off. Which he would give her. Times like this he wished Lizard Teats hadn't given up on whoring. His saloon lost too much money when he gave time off to his only whore. He consulted his railroad watch, wondering just where Lizard Teats was. Ingrid. Ingrid. He had to stop thinking of her by the nickname the ranch hands and soldiers gave her. She'd given up whoring but still shared his bed, and worked most evenings waiting on the tables in the saloon to help him out. It was seven-thirty and she should be here by now.

"Good to see other folks happy," Joaquin said, wiping up the red-eye gravy from the ham with his last piece of biscuit.

"When are you going to stop acting like a duck in the desert? At some point you've got to stop feeling sorry for yourself," Ethan said, sipping at a new beer.

"I'm not. It's just, well, why am I a Ranger if I can't be a Ranger?"

"You've been doing your job here. I don't recall hearing any complaints out of Fort Davis, certainly not from Austin. You can't do everything, you know. Not everything."

"Look, Captain Baylor chasing those Apaches all over along with the army was what rangering is all about," Joaquin said. "They were all around us most of the year. Rattlesnake Springs is just up from Fort Davis and look what the soldiers did there. Then the Rangers chased Victorio and what was left of his heathens into Mexico for the very last time. It was history, damn it, writ large, and I wasn't considered good enough to be a part of it. It may have been the defining moment of my generation in Texas, and I missed it because I'm not good enough."

Ethan waved over to Dutch, pointing at Joaquin. Dutch came over with a bottle of whiskey and a glass for himself, and sat down at the table.

"I see his lips're still stickin' out like a buggy seat. When's he gonna learn worryin' about it as useless as settin' a milk bucket under a bull?" Dutch asked, pouring the whiskey into his own glass and Joaquin's.

"Eh-yeah," Ethan said, as Joaquin pulled a glass toward him. "The lad doesn't understand that it's not always just about what he wants."

"This was important, damn it," Joaquin said, tossing the drink down his throat quickly, then raising the glass towards Dutch asking him to refill it.

"If you had to take the field against wild Indians or bandits, would you trust me to go with you?" Ethan asked.

"Certainly."

"Why?"

"Because I know what you're capable of doing."

"Eh-yeah. You've seen me in action. You've heard me tell stories. You've heard others tell stories. You know you can trust me with your life. Trust me. Baylor doesn't know you. You've been a Ranger now for just a year and, like it or not, you're stuck out in the middle of no place where nothing much happens. If you were Baylor and you had to mount a campaign against the fiercest Apache chief who ever depredated his way across Texas, would you take a young, inexperienced hand? He needs people riding with him he knows and knows he can trust. He just doesn't know you."

"And how am I supposed to get that experience? How do I get the captain to know who I am and that he can trust me if I'm not given the chance to prove myself? My God, man, they drove Victorio out of

Texas. That may be the last of hostile action ever again in this state."

"Mebbe so, but you think ol' George is happy with the way things turned about?" Dutch asked after drinking a little from his own glass. "He's prob'ly as pissed as you or more so. He and Grierson's boys ran Victorio to ground and the beaners just up and kicked them out of Mexico so they could get all the credit for rubbing the old chief out theirownselves. The Rangers and the army did all the work and the Mexicans get all the glory. You may think your situation is mighty pitiful, but no matter how big you are… and there ain't many bigger than George Baylor in this state… well, you still got to eat dirt sometimes. Like it or not."

Joaquin slammed his glass back on the table after downing his third drink. "That's all besides the point. How the hell can I prove myself if I don't ever get the chance? I didn't join the Texas Rangers to sit on my skinny ass and do nothing."

"I thought you joined the Rangers because your lady back home made you," Ethan said.

"Nobody makes me do anything, and you leave Rachel out of this. That's none of your business. And it doesn't have a damn thing to do with what we were talking about."

"Eh-yeah, but you're the one brought it up."

"I'm just not worth it. Not to Captain Baylor and probably not to my Rachel," Joaquin said.

"Bullshit! Look, nobody starts out big in life. You learn easy stuff and then you learn harder stuff. More difficult. You held your own at Calamity Creek last year. Work your way up. You're a baby ranger out here by your lonesome on this particular frontier. What you have to do is be the best damn ranger you can be where you are and with what you're given to do. Do that and people will notice. They'll notice."

"Now who's bullshitting who?" Joaquin said, quieter than before. He poured himself another drink, spilling a little on the table.

Ethan drank half of a new glass of beer. "You told me your lady said she would marry your sorry ass only if you completed three years in the Rangers. Why do you think she asked you to do that?

"I told you to leave her out of this," he snapped back.

"She's the whole God damn point as I see it," Ethan said. "If you want to sulk, go ahead. Sulk. I imagine that it was just this attitude that worried her just a little. For God knows what reason, she's probably in love with you but she's intelligent enough to know love ain't enough. It ain't enough. For a marriage to work you've got to be of one mind, that whole two-becoming-one thing, and as a woman in this day and age she needs you to be a man. Needs you to grow up. Needs you to put those sulking, childish ways behind you. Suck it up. She figures the Rangers will help you do that and she's probably right. Or was. This reaction seems like you're backsliding to me."

"Oh? And just how am I supposed to react? I mean so little, they've forgotten I'm even out here."

"Bullshit!"

Dutch grabbed the bottle off the table and stood up, shaking his head as he turn to walk back to his bar. "You two are getting' slap drunk and disgraceful."

Ethan raised his mug to Joaquin. "Hello, Drunk."

"Hello, Disgraceful," Joaquin responded, raising his own glass.

•

Ingrid flinched when she felt Karl's touch as he wrapped a blanket around her. The dress she put on that morning when the weather was clear but very hot now wasn't giving her much warmth as the cold cut her to the bone.

"It is well after dark and we should be getting back to town," Karl said. His hands lingered on her shoulders but she twisted away from them.

"I know," she said.

They walked down the hill carefully with only starlight to guide them. The back side of the hill wasn't as steep as the other side that looked down into what they had started calling Calamity Creek, now dry after a summer full of rainwater. Ingrid wouldn't take Karl's arm as they stepped around the small rocks, horsecripplers, and lechuguilla, but she was glad he was directly behind her and ready to catch her in case she lost her balance. She climbed up into his wagon.

Karl slapped the back of his draught horse, pulling the reins so the horse would turn the wagon back toward Lajitas. "You do not need to keep coming out here."

"I know," she said, pulling the blanket tighter against her. "Every morning I tell myself I won't, but then I do."

"It has been well over a year, and you do not owe these savages such dedication. You have visited this place every day since Ethan and I buried them."

"You mustn't've thought them savages to bury them and preach your Bible over them," she replied.

"We are all the children of God, even those who stray."

"Indeed," she said quietly.

"You come here, but you do not pray. You just sit in silence, looking over the rocks that mark where they are buried."

"I talk to them," she said, explaining herself to Karl for the first time in all these months of visiting here. "I want to know why they did it. I tell them I'm sorry that I caused their deaths."

"You did not. They made that decision to pursue you and to kill us all when we refused to turn you over to them. You cannot bear their deaths on your shoulders."

They rode for a while in silence, then Ingrid touched Karl's thigh. "Still, if I wasn't here, they'd still be alive. And those outlaws out by the Mule Ears, too. It was me they all were after. Me. And all I wanted was to be left alone."

Karl had a little difficulty concentrating. This was the first time Ingrid had touched him in more than two years. When he first came to Lajitas, she would not even let him approach. She fled. She would not listen to his pleas for her to repent her sins or his pleas for them to embrace each other again. Their love since they were children seemed as dead and buried as those Comanches on the hill behind them. She mellowed a little after she was rescued from John Ringo and his bandits and they had survived the Indian ambush. She stopped selling her body at the saloon. She refused to leave Dutch, but she did let Karl get near little by little.

When he found her by accident that day, out on the hill by Calamity Creek, looking over the graves, she let him speak to her. It was slow progress, but it was progress. And now she had touched him.

"You should feel lucky, you know," he told her. "We have both seen the hand of God. We have seen it with our own eyes, the eyes of true sinners. How many people on this earth go through their lives not knowing, doubting, wondering, believing, holding faith with something they have not seen with their own eyes. Remember the apostle Thomas? He did not see Christ rise from the dead and he doubted it ever took place, but a week later Christ came to the disciples and told Thomas to put his finger in his wounds, if he doubted. Thomas immediately believed, but Christ said, 'Blessed are those who have not seen and have believed.' We have seen!"

"I told you before not to preach to me."

"I am not," he said softly. "Truly I do not mean to preach. I am just illustrating a point so that you understand something. You feel that you are forsaken in the eyes of God and yet the opposite is true. God holds you in a favored place. He has shown Himself to you. You and I know, as few others do, just how real God is. He showed us this for a reason. Perhaps it was because we sinned as few others had—"

She laughed humorlessly. "Oh, yes. Few people go around humping each other like rabbits on the floor of a church. We're special, all right."

"Yes, we are. We sinned greatly but Romans says, 'God proves His love for us in that while we were still sinners Christ died for us.' And in First Corinthians it is even plainer: 'Christ died for our sins.'

"God gave us a true sign, Ingrid. His lightning struck the church and the church itself burned to the ground. And I saved the steeple and made certain it continued to serve as His church. He was showing us both His displeasure and His love at the same time. He wants so much for us to repent, to be embraced by His love again, that He showed Himself to us. You have to understand that part, Ingrid. It's wonderful."

"Wonderful is not a word I would have ever thought of using," she sighed.

"But it is! God exists! He cares! Don't you see how wonderful that is? This is not just something I believe or that we were taught or is from words in a book. He is real! He cares! Grasp this if you understand nothing else."

She was quiet for the remainder of the ride into Lajitas, but her thoughts raced. Perhaps Karl was right. Perhaps this was the way to have a terrible burden lifted from her soul. But she didn't know if she could repent. She didn't know how. She had done too much. How

162

could God forgive her the adultery, the fornication in His own church? The whoring she accepted. She was reminded of it everyday. How could she forgive herself? And how could she ever leave Dutch, the man who protected her and accepted her?

Karl drove the wagon to the rear of the Mejor Que Nada. Ingrid jumped down, removed the blanket and neatly folded it up and placed it behind the seat.

"If you love me," she said as she turned to go into the saloon. "If you love me, you'll destroy the steeple."

CHAPTER 6

The Lower San Antonio Road, near Hondo, Texas

Wyatt almost dozed off even though he held the reins of six hors-es pulling the pomegranate red Concord. This was the kind of routine work that bored him. The horses traveled this road so often they knew the way so he wasn't worried about catching a wink or two up in the boot. The last time his chin bounced off his chest, he sat bolt upright and chuckled a little, looking over at Sergeant Factor who he had been rubbing shoulders with him since San Antonio. Benjamin Factor wasn't used to stagecoach riding like Wyatt was. Benjamin sat with his right leg rigidly out in front of him to brace himself on the boot, both hands clutching his ten-gauge as if the shotgun would somehow secure him to the yawing coach. The knuckles on his brown hands were white, his eyes were wide open. He was as alert as Wyatt was lethargic.

Benjamin's eyes met Wyatt's. "Yah doin' okey? Yah not too tahrd t'run this hyah rig?"

"I'm fine, sergeant," Wyatt smiled at him. "Just remember what we discussed."

"Yassuh."

They passed through the small town of Hondo about an hour ago, but Wyatt didn't notice anything hard about it. They picked up no pas-sengers nor any shipments, so they and the passengers they had barely had time to slip to the outhouse before they were back on the road.

The hills were shallower now, the trees smaller, the brush thicker. Wyatt spied a stand of elms over the next hill with enough greenery surrounding them that he figured a creek passed by. Perfect spot, he thought, and forced himself wide awake.

Wyatt was correct. As the stage approached the elms, three men rushed from their cover, blocking the road and aiming pistols at the stage.

"Hold!" one of the men said. Wyatt pulled in the horses and stage slowed to a stop. The men had covered their faces with dirt and mud and dressed like ranch hands, their clothing and chaps covered with more dirt and dust to the point that the color of their clothes was undistinguishable. Unless you just happened to know one of them well, they would be very difficult to describe, he knew.

One of the men pointed his pistol directly at Benjamin. "Toss down the scattergun, nigger." Benjamin broke open the double-barrel, dumped the shells into the boot and placed the open shotgun on the floor.

"I said throw it down," the bandit said, glaring at him. Benjamin shrugged and dropped the weapon onto the road.

"Driver, if you've got a weapon, you'd better toss it along, too."

Wyatt shook his head no, holding up his arms so the man could see he had no sidearm. The other two outlaws stuck a pistol into each of the windows on each side of the coach, holding the five passengers at bay.

"Now throw down the boxes." The lead bandit ordered. Wyatt tossed down one of the treasure boxes.

The bandit motioned with his pistol. "All the boxes."

Wyatt pulled up the other tree green boxes and heaved each one to the ground.

"Now, git and don't be looking back," the chief outlaw ordered. Wyatt slapped the reins and the stage lurched forward. Once over the hill, Wyatt put the horses into a gallop.

"Damn you," Bart Dodge hollered up to Wyatt, his head sticking out from a window. As the stage bounced, he repeatedly struck the back of his head on the wooden frame. "You didn't do a blessed thing to stop that!"

"Better sit back, Bartholomew, we want to be as far ahead of those owlhoots as we can, so it's going to be a bumpy ride."

•

Brackettville

Jo-Jo, Maximo, and Michael Stephens were the only members of the troupe Doc would let wander around whatever town they were in. Tiny Alice and Earl, his wild man, would be too easily recognizable, so they had to stay close. Max rarely left, though. He preferred the company of his fellow show folk. He was also the boss canvasman, in charge of the tent and setting up for meals before and after the shows. Michael, the sword swallower, was a true gentleman and his roaming a town only helped bring out more people to the show. Jo-Jo couldn't be recognized out of her make-up. But Jasper, his fire-eater, was a belligerent drunk and Doc didn't dare strain the goodwill of any town they passed through so he kept Jasper close to the tent and wagons. Too often, righteous folks in a town would just gang up and deliver severe beatings to show folk just because they were show folk. Best to always be on their good side.

That's why Doc made his elixir so carefully, with just the right amounts of iron, quinine, strychnine, and ethanol. The ferrous sulfate helped with anemia, a common ailment out here. The quinine also helped with chills and fevers, more common symptoms. The strychnine, used in just the right amount, was a fine stimulant, like drinking several cups of coffee. And the 40 percent alcohol made everyone happy. The combination would make almost anyone feel good quickly and actually cure many minor woes. Doc never stayed in one town very long, so his personal guarantee that imbibers of his elixir would feel better quickly was always a safe guarantee.

The troupe never worked on Sundays and Doc had given them Monday off, too. It would be a nice break. One more show, then they would head on further west. He hadn't decided where just yet but he hoped he could convince the troupe to take a chance by trading a low income for possibly a very high return. This afternoon, he was content to eat dinner in the tent with Max, Jasper, Earl, and his occasional paramour, Tiny Alice. Michael and Jo-Jo had remained in town overnight. He guessed, correctly, that they were searching for bed companions or had found them.

Jo-Jo's companion was a plain, young girl she had seen watching her intently in Saturday's show. Just after noon on Sunday, Jo-Jo ambled down the boardwalk to the Sargent Hotel, hoping she might see the youngster in the lobby. Instead, she saw the girl on a bench outside.

Townspeople were either sleeping in from a rough Saturday night or still in church. The day was so still, the only sound was the windmill creaking behind the hotel.

"You look a little lonely, my lovely," Jo-Jo said to the girl.

Cynthia Laroch smiled as she looked up, holding Jo-Jo's eyes firmly with her own. "No. Not really. It's just there's nothing to do in this town unless you're a man and go drinking in the saloon."

"And it's such a dusty place," Jo-Jo said, sitting down next to Cynthia, brushing her skirt with her hands.

Cynthia continued to look directly into Jo-Jo's eyes, now just two feet from her. "Yes, it is. The cold and the wind only make it worse."

"You should get in out of this, then, and take a sponge bath in your room."

"Oh, that would be nice, but I have no room. I'll just sit here until the stage arrives tomorrow. The gentleman running the hotel said that when it gets dark I may sit in the lobby as long as I mind my manners and he wouldn't charge me and that he would look after me."

"I have a room, lovely," Jo-Jo said, standing abruptly, taking Cynthia by the hand. "Come with me. You shall have your bath."

First, Jo-Jo looked to make sure the hotel clerk was not in sight, then the two women walked up to her room.

Cynthia removed her bonnet and sat on the edge of the bed while Jo-Jo poured water from a pitcher into the enameled basin on the night stand. Jo-Jo pulled two long pins out her broad-brimmed straw hat, removed the hat, and shook out her hair. She ran her fingers through her hair to remove the tangles.

"Come, my lovely, lets get you refreshed," Jo-Jo said, unbuttoning Cynthia's blouse so quickly that the other woman scarcely noticed it was happening. She pushed the blouse off her shoulders, undid the ties of Cynthia's camisole and did the same. She dipped a silk handkerchief in the tepid water, squeezed it out, and ran it over Cynthia's back.

No one outside of her family had ever seen her bare before, Cynthia realized. And it was exciting. Certainly far more exciting than with her father or her brothers.

•

Wyatt would have normally pulled the stage up to the hotel, but the back portion of the building was ablaze. This was a common enough occurrence in the West that he didn't think of it as anything more than a minor inconvenience. The volunteer fire brigade was working on the fire with a pump wagon and it was already under control. It should be out soon. On the street, patrons of the hotel and curious citizens stood to watch the flames that were licking the sky just moments ago quickly wither under the onslaught of water from the pump. He drove the stage up the street to the Gilded Canary restaurant, then helped two of the passengers down from the coach.

"We'll be a while at the fort," he told them. "You can get a good meal here and wash up and relax a little until we're ready to get underway again. Normally, you could spend the night at the hotel and travel onward in the morning but as you can see, that's not possible on this trip. Mr. Snodgrass, he runs the Canary, might know of rooms available if you do want to spend the night."

The couple nodded their thanks and went inside.

Once they were gone, Bart spoke up. "I'm going to have a lot of explaining to do once we get to the fort. And you're going to have a lot of explaining to do to Wells Fargo, Mr. Earp. I know you have enjoyed the pleasure of occasional employment with our company over the years on special projects, but this irresponsible outing has ended all of that if I have any say in the matter, and as director of operations for the San Antonio District I have a considerable amount to say."

Wyatt turned without speaking and jumped up on the stage, driving it the few blocks to the fort. By the time the stage rattled up to the large, stone headquarters building, Colonel William Shafter was standing outside to greet it.

Shafter was a rotund man, unusual for a frontier soldier, and seemed tonight to be a happy one. Bart Dodge regretted that he was going to ruin the colonel's day but he knew where the blame would be placed: squarely on Mr. Wyatt Earp's shoulders and not his.

Before Wyatt had wrapped the reins around the brake, Bart was out of the coach, bounding up the steps to the headquarters' porch. The regular driver and guard were content to remain inside. Bart removed his hat and held it in his left hand as he extended his right to Shafter. "Colonel Shafter, it's good to meet with you again. I just wish it could be under better circumstances."

"You have a problem?" Shafter asked. "I've been in prime spirits for going on to a couple of days now. Victorio's dead and buried, most of his band has dispersed, and Colonel Grierson and his men are mopping up the Big Bend and north to Guadalupes, getting any redskins to hightail it from Texas and for good this time. Plus, for the first time in—"

"I'm sorry to interrupt, Colonel, but this is vitally important," Bart said, shaking his head. Wyatt and Benjamin had now joined him on the porch. "I am sorry to report that we have lost the third straight payroll shipment."

Shafter was confused. "Lost it? What are you jabbering about, man? That was the other thing I was trying to tell you I was thankful for. That this payroll made through."

"I'm sorry, Colonel. We made it but the payroll didn't. I had hoped this run would have been different. The highwaymen took all four boxes, just as before."

"Quit your jabbering about nonsense. The payroll was brought in two days ago. Every penny accounted for."

"What?" Bart said. He looked as if he would have toppled in a slight breeze. "It's already here?"

"Mr. Earp's younger brother carried it to me personally two days ago, yes," Shafter said. He reached out to shake Wyatt's hand. "Damn fine plan, too, even if I was kept in the dark. I recognize you, sergeant, but forgive me I can't recall your name."

"Benjamin Factor, suh."

Shafter shook his hand. "Any luck?"

"Yassuh," Benjamin said. "Th' man leadin' the bandits was Sar'nt Erny, suh. I know him sure."

Bart kept looking around first to Shafter, then to Wyatt, then to Benjamin, trying to decide who to ask. Finally, he turned back to Shafter. "I don't understand."

Shafter nodded to Wyatt.

"We figured we had to do more than just stop the robberies, we had to smoke the culprit into the open," Wyatt explained. "But we didn't want to lose the money. So while I was staying in your office, I removed the payroll from the strongboxes and Morgan stashed it all in some saddlebags and he just rode it on over to the fort without anyone suspecting anything. Then we ran the stage like normal. That's why I didn't want you heeled; I was afraid you'd put up a fight when the stage got held up. We had to let them come in and take the boxes. That's why I ran the horses as hard as I could from there because I knew once they got the boxes open they'd know they were filled with rocks."

"An', if Ah may, suh. Mistah Earp hyar figgered, an' rightly so, that nobody pays much 'tention to a darky anyways. One us allus looks like t'other t'most whites. We'd suspected the sar'nt. So Mistah Earp knows that Ah'll be recognizin' him, but he ain't like to recognize me. An' thas wha' happened."

"You took a great risk out there, sergeant," Bart said after a low whistle. "If the quartermaster had recognized you, you'd be dead. Along with the rest of us, probably."

"Yassuh, we knew th' risk. But, y'see, those of us here t'the fort, we'd also like to get paid some which we ain't in a coupla months."

Shafter turned and banged on the headquarters' door. A second lieutenant appeared almost immediately.

"Rolling, is Sergeant Erny on the post?" Shafter asked him.

"I believe he is off on a pass until tomorrow, sir." The lieutenant said. "I would expect him in sometime this evening, then, sir."

"When he arrives, have him escorted, under arms, to my office. Regardless of the time he arrives."

The lieutenant saluted. "Yes, sir."

"In the meantime, take a couple of men and search the quartermaster's office and his quarters," Shafter told him. "Thoroughly. We have reason to believe you may find a large cache of money in one of the them." The lieutenant saluted again and strode off.

"I know Sergeant Factor will testify against Sergeant Erny," Shafter said to Wyatt. "Will you stay until the court martial and do the same?"

Wyatt nodded. "It'll be my pleasure, as long as I recognize Erny as well when I see him. I don't believe that'll be a problem, though. I pay close attention to details. Would you have quarters for me here, Colonel? Seems the hotel has had a fire and I doubt they have any spare rooms."

"I did see the smoke," Shafter said. "Certainly. If you don't mind bunking with one of the unmarried junior officers. I hear the Bucket of

Blood always has a lively game of poker, plus there's a freak show in town that's highly entertaining. You might want to take that in."

The group shook hands all around. Shafter retreated into his office, Benjamin walked toward the stable to get his horse, Bart and Wyatt walked back to the stage.

"I assume Flocke's driver and messenger take over from here to continue the run?" Bart said.

"Unless you want to drive," Wyatt said. "I guess it's up to you."

Bart climbed onto the stage, unwrapping the reins. "I think I will drive for some distance. I haven't been on the complete run for some time now. It'll give me something different to do. You gentlemen come up on the box with me for a while so I don't get lonely."

The regular crew left the coach and climbed up, the messenger guard taking his place beside Bart while the driver sat cross-legged up top behind Bart. The guard retrieved his shotgun and pistol from the boot, handing the driver his own pistol.

"You did Wells Fargo a fine job, Wyatt, and I must apologize for not trusting you," Bart said.

"It's wise not to trust too many people out on this frontier," Wyatt said before Bart drove the stage back to town.

•

Cynthia rushed up to Doc, embraced him and launched into a crying fit. He was stunned by this. It wasn't often a strange woman would rush up and embrace a fat man with gray hair like himself. In fact, he thought as her chest heaved again his, it had never happened to him. He didn't know what to do. His arms fell loosely across her back, patting her back in what he hoped was a comforting way.

"I— I— I don't know where to turn," she said, barely able to catch her breath.

"What's wrong," he said flatly.

"My— my— my sister was in the hotel and there was— there was a fire—"

"We all saw the fire. Is your sister inside?"

"Yes," she cried. "Oh— yes— yes, she is. But the fire is out and I saw her body. She has burned up. She— she pushed me out of the room and told me to run when— when the fire began. We— we haven't seen each other in years. The first time— the first time I've seen her since she— she left home. I was so looking forward to— to seeing her once more. And now— And now, this. Oh, God, whatever shall I do?"

"Life gives us tribulations and we must deal with them," Doc said. "You should return home and get comfort from your family."

"No— no— I have no family. Not anymore. My mother— my mother died three years ago this September and my father—" Almost suddenly the tears stopped and her eyes grew cold. "My father just died. That's what I was coming to tell her, hoping she would take me in."

Doc still didn't know what to do. He had no known connection to this woman. Had she come to him because he was distinguished looking? Because he had stature and looked like he might be in charge? "Why have you come to me? How may I help you?"

"My sister worked for you," she said.

He pulled her away from his chest, holding her at arm's length. He recognized her as someone who had been in the show crowd on Saturday. "Who's your sister?"

"Etta," she said. "Etta Laroch. But you called her Jo-Jo."

Doc's hands dropped to his side. He turned to look at the still smoldering side of the Sargent Hotel and ran his fingers through his thick shock of gray hair. "You're telling me Jo-Jo died in that fire and you're her sister? Her name wasn't Etta. It was Madeline. Madeline, something, French, I think. Maybe Laroch, but definitely Madeline when I met her."

"Madeline— Madeline was her first name. All the family knew her as Etta because our mother's name was Madeline. I guess, I guess she just started using that. But now she's gone and I'm all alone with no one to turn to."

Doc was not a sentimental person and few of the show folk he ever met were, plus no one cared for Jo-Jo much. She was abrasive and kept to herself and, of course, her Sapphic ways were often a problem in the smaller towns they drove through. No one liked her much and he doubted she would be missed at all. He didn't take much to this sister of hers, either. She just spent the past few minutes crying on his shoulder but he felt coldness in the sobs. Must be a family thing, he thought.

She stood in front of him, fully a head shorter and frail. She kept her head bowed but looked up directly at him, like a tame critter lost in the wilderness. "What will I do? Where will I go?"

"You can travel with us for a while," he said finally, after mulling over whether he should make the offer not. "But we're not a charitable organization. At some point, you'll have to earn your keep if you want to stay."

Her head jerked up and a smile crossed her face. "Oh, that would be great. Perfect. And I'll work, I'll earn my keep like you say. I know what Jo-Jo did for you. She told me. She explained it all to me, about the make-up. I watched a show. All she did was sit in the chair and look mournful and I can do that. In the hairy make-up no one will know it's not her. No one will know me, will they?"

He would need another Jo-Jo, and this girl could certainly look as melancholy as his previous Jo-Jo could. He noticed she never mentioned her sister's name again. That made him wonder, but not for too long. He did need another Jo-Jo.

"Let me walk you to the wagons and introduce you around. Tiny Alice can show you how to apply the make-up. Do you have any of your personal things with you?" Doc said.

Cynthia did the best Jo-Jo look he'd ever seen. "No. Everything is gone."

CHAPTER 7
Lajitas

Dutch Dave was the first to see it that morning. Brother Karl's chapel was going up in flames. That didn't bother him too much, but he wanted to make certain the fire wouldn't spread down the mesa to town since Lajitas wasn't large enough to have a volunteer fire department. Luckily, it had been a wetter than normal summer so the sparse grasses weren't as dry as they could be.

Just like the morning last year when the chapel appeared on the mesa overnight, Dutch had just closed up his saloon and was heading to bed when he saw it.

"I smelled fire," Joaquin said, suddenly standing at Dutch's side. "What's going on?"

Dutch began walking up the short mesa. "I slap don't have a clue. Prob'ly be too much to ask for that the preacher was inside when it burned."

Joaquin walked along with Dutch, tucking his shirt into his trousers. He wasn't wearing his gun belt, but carried his pistol in his hand.

At the top of the mesa they saw Brother Karl standing near his wagon, watching the blaze.

"Who did this?" Joaquin asked.

"I did," Karl replied.

"The desert heat finally rattle your think box?" Dutch asked.

Karl moved close to the fire, picked up a stray board that had fallen away from the structure and quickly tossed it back into the main fire. "The Lord works in mysterious ways…"

"Why?" Joaquin asked, shoving his pistol into a trouser pocket.

"I was bidden," Karl said quietly.

"So the Lord called you to preachin' and the Lord's now tellin' you to git?" Dutch asked.

"I will never turned my back on God," Karl said emphatically. "This steeple was my church, but God is present whether I have an edifice or not. This was, after all, just wood and nails and glass and paint."

"OK," Joaquin said, walking over to Karl. "But why?"

The preacher stared into the fire with tears welling up in his eyes. "It is no longer necessary."

"Yeah, well, you'd best not let this fire get down the hill or you'll have hell to pay," Dutch said, turning to walk back down the mesa.

"We all have Hell to pay if we don't embrace the Lord," Karl said. Dutch waved a hand at him.

When Dutch got to his apartment behind the saloon he was surprised to see Ingrid up and dressed. She sat on the edge of their bed, staring out the lone window across the Río Grande. She didn't turn to greet him. In the early morning silence, they could hear the crackling of the fire even though it was a quarter-mile away. They could hear the wind rustling through the river cane. They could hear goats rummaging on the far bank of the river.

"He burned up the chapel didn't he?" Ingrid said, still staring ahead.

"You know somethin' about it?"

"How could I?"

"So how'd you know?"

"I asked him to do it, but I didn't think he would."

Dutch noticed that Ingrid had the valise she brought with her to Lajitas, packed and by her side. "And what's with you? Goin' someplace?"

"I need some time by myself, Dutch," she said, rising and walking over to him. She kissed him on his bald pate and took his hands in hers. "I just need time to think some things through."

"You're slap goin' off with that son of a bitch, ain't you?"

"No, I swear, Dutch. I'm not. Mrs. McGuirk is letting me stay in a room at their home and I'll do housework for her to earn my room and board. I just can't go on like I've been doing but I don't know what to do and I can't think it all through if I'm living with you and I couldn't if I was living with Karl either. I had a life, once, and I had dreams for what I wanted out of life. I haven't dreamed of those things in years, it seems, but now I think I'm starting to again. I want to be able to dream again."

Dutch reached over and grabbed her bag off the bed, handed it to Ingrid and held the door open. "Well, I think you're studyin' to be a half-wit, but you go ahead and dream on," he said. She moved to kiss him but the look on his face told her that would be a mistake. She took the bag and left, looking at the sand. Dutch slammed the door behind her. "Yeah, you go ahead and dream."

•

Salt Flats, South of the Guadalupe Mountains, Texas

The beast frightened Wolf Rising to the soles of his feet. This horse-ogre, this demon-mule, whatever it was, made a sound that resonated in the pit of his stomach. Larger than any horse he had even imagined, grotesque and misshapen, it strode off across the desert braying that terrible noise. His own horse whinnied and balked. He slid off his horse, caressing its neck in an attempt to calm both his mount and himself.

He dropped to the ground, holding the rope rein, and sat to collect his breath and his thoughts.

He examined his situation. He drank enough water, had enough mescal to eat, so he was rational. He didn't believe this was a vision. This was real. Perhaps this was some devil-horse the Pale Eyes brought with them? He didn't know and he didn't like not knowing. He rolled back onto his horse and rode as quickly as he could back to Lozen's camp. Maybe she could make sense of what he saw, but he doubted it.

The camp was two hours to the north, hidden in the saddle of two hills by a narrow creek that seeped into the ground at several places. Wolf Rising rode quickly.

In the camp, he saw Lozen placing a poultice on a warrior's leg and noticed another holding a damp rag to his bloodied head. They had been in a fight and he wasn't here.

"Pale Eyes?" Wolf Rising asked.

Lozen nodded once. "Soldiers. We were here and Upsidedown saw a black lion—"

"A black lion?" Wolf Rising said excitedly. "I saw a horse-ogre!"

"Upsidedown saw a black lion," she continued, ignoring his effort to outdo her tale. "And we followed it down the stream where the stream got wider. I saw the lion's lair and Upsidedown climbed up a cottonwood to see it closer. He told us to be ready, and we were, and he crawled out on a branch and the black lion crawled out on another branch. We saw this lion was different from all the other lions we've seen. It had black spots on its black fur. No one has ever seen anything like this animal before and we knew we must have it. The lion's muscles tensed and I warned Upsidedown and just when the lion leaped to the branch Upsidedown was on, he dropped to the water. The lion was angry but confused and we shot it. It dropped dead into the stream by Upsidedown, but we couldn't retrieve it because Pale Eye soldiers were nearby and they heard the shots and came over the hill."

"How many?" he asked.

She held up a full hand. "We fought for a while and killed or wounded three of the Pale Eyes, but they wounded two of our warriors. Caterpillar and Give-Me-A-Horse. The soldiers ran off but they took those warriors' horses with them. We came back here. Caterpillar and Give-Me-A-Horse are not seriously injured, but Caterpillar can't ride. We need more horses."

Wolf Rising squatted next to Give-Me-A-Horse who kept his eyes closed as he pressed the rag to the side of his head. "How bad?"

"Not bad," Give-Me-A-Horse said. "The bullet just cut my skin above my ear. I think the bleeding has stopped by now." He took the rag from his head and Lozen inspected the wound.

"The blood has stopped, but sit still," she said as she moved to the small fire and used a stick to remove a cup of boiling green mash. She set the pot down next to Give-Me-A-Horse and scooped some of the prickly pear poultice out of the cup with a smaller stick and smeared it on Give-Me-A-Horse's wound. He winced just a little at the heat. She tore up the rag he had been using, then wrapped it around his head to cover the wound.

"I wish to talk with you," Wolf Rising said then to Lozen. She rose and accompanied him up the creek bed.

"The Pale Eyes are from the camp to the east that I saw yesterday?" he asked her.

She nodded, "My Power says that is where they came from and

where they returned."

"I saw perhaps ten soldiers there, with horses," Wolf Rising said. "You are called the greatest of horse thieves, perhaps we can go alone and get the Pale Eyes' horses."

She was quiet for a while. She knew he had the proper skills to do as he said and she was confident of her own.

"We can do this," she said.

They walked back to the camp. She shed her skirt, standing in her breechclout and loose top. He touched the dragonfly around her neck. He handed his owl-feather turban and calico shirt to Give-Me-A-Horse. Lozen explained their plan and they ran off, each of them carrying long strips of rawhide.

The run was exhilarating, fast and smooth, along the creek bed then over two hills to get behind the Pale Eyes' camp. They sat on top of a hill overlooking the camp, an abandoned abode house with a corral made from a waist high adobe wall, and ate honey and wild onions while they waited for the sun to set. Wolf Rising saw no sign of the devil-horse and decided he would not mention it to Lozen again. He breathed in the scent of her deeply as they sat side by side. He was getting intoxicated by her nearness. Every time he thought up something clever to say to her, the Pale Eye soldiers below would bellow or laugh or snap orders and the moment would be gone. The soldiers rattled around getting food as twilight crept up. He hated their noise.

The sun set in a brief flood of orange. The shadows grew long and faint. The soldiers' noise grew muted, then ceased altogether. The glow from the bowl of a tobacco pipe showed Lozen and Wolf Rising where the lone sentry was.

Wolf Rising reached over and touched Lozen's naked thigh. "Inside or out?"

"You're more nimble, I'm stronger," she said. "You go in."

They moved quickly but silently down the hill, stopping at the far adobe wall. The horses inside shuffled around and blew just a little, but made no unusual noises that would draw the sentry's attention. Lozen gave Wolf Rising one end of the longest rawhide strip she had. She held onto the other end as he vaulted over the wall. Once inside, he tugged the rawhide tight and they sawed quietly through the adobe with it. It took a while, but finally they reached the ground. Wolf

Rising moved a few feet to the left and they repeated the process, creating two parallel cuts in the wall. From the inside, Wolf Rising slowly tipped the cut section of the wall toward Lozen who grabbed it and maneuvered it slowly to the ground. She tossed him more pieces of rawhide and he quickly formed nooses with them, dropped them over the horses' necks. The horses were beginning to get skittish now, so they would have to move fast. The two slid onto the backs of two of the twelve horses, each of them holding the nooses of five others, then galloped away.

The sentry fired at the noise, but his shot was far from any mark. The shot roused the other soldiers and soon they were firing at the fleeing horse thieves. One bullet grazed the eye of one horse, but Wolf Rising tugged at its noose and it kept running with him. Only one bullet struck anything, catching a horse in the flank just as they rode around the hill. Lozen dropped that horse's noose and they rode away into the night with eleven horses.

After a while, when they knew they were safely out of reach of the soldiers, Lozen and Wolf Rising slowed the horses to a walk. She laughed.

Wolf Rising nudged his horse next to Lozen's "You need a man. You need a man who is as good a horse thief as you are."

"You think you are this man?" she continued laughing. Wolf Rising knew Lozen's laughter was in delight at their successful escapade and not directed at him, but he was still hurt by it and didn't speak again.

•

Brackettville

The show must go on, Doc knew. He introduced Cynthia to the troupe who welcomed her without much comment. He explained to her that from this point on, she was Jo-Jo the Dog-Faced Girl and no one else. He explained about the canvas paintings that came from a shop in Gettysburg, Pennsylvania, and how they were all the same no matter where you went in the country because it was too expensive to make paintings with different names on them.

"What difference does a name make?" she had said with a shrug.

Doc knew that names were important. Although they could be changed at will, especially out here in the West, they defined who you were.

After all, he wasn't born Doctor Extraneous Hudspeth.

He was born Jacob Birnbaum in Buffalo, New York, and was satisfied until the age of 14 to become a cantor like his father, his grandfather, and his great-grandfather and several generations of Birnbaums before him. That was until he picked up a dime novel with a dramatic drawing of a bronco buster on the cover. From that moment on, all he wanted to do was break horses out in the Wild West before the West ceased to be wild.

He took every penny he had saved since his bar mitzvah and bought a train ticket to Fort Worth. He bought an outfit, tack and a good horse, and got a job. He was such a quick and enthusiastic learner that by his sixteenth birthday he was known across the area as Bronco Birnbaum, the best horse breaker in all of Texas.

On the cattle outfits where whites, coloreds, Mexicans, and even some Indians mingled, all that mattered was doing your job well and without complaint so his Jewishness made no difference.

But when he was nineteen, a particularly difficult horse slammed him into a corral fence gate and snapped his right leg. The leg was never right again and he was never able to ride a horse again without terrible pain. He found work doing rope tricks in a traveling circus. He learned quickly. He could do the Merry-Go-Round one and two-handed, the Neck Wrap, the Wedding Ring, Spoke Jumping, the Texas Skip, and the Butterfly all flawlessly. But even though he did these rather demanding tricks, the crowds never seemed to appreciate it. The audiences laughed at him expecting someone named Bronco Birnbaum doing rope tricks to be a comedian. After all, who ever heard of a Jewish cowboy? So he changed his name to Kid Lariat and succeeded for a little while longer.

He tired of doing the same thing for such little money, however. He bought a small wagon and just wandered through Texas and the New Mexico Territory, trying to discover what else he wanted to do. He even stayed for a while in an Apache village, entertaining the

Indians by performing a few basic magic tricks he'd learned back in Buffalo. He even took an Apache wife for that time, but he soon tired of the way they lived. It was too dirty and chaotic for him. But he cared enough for his wife that before he stole away he gave her a golden Cross of Lorraine s a keepsake. It was something a former woman friend had given Kid Lariat, not knowing he was Jewish. He cared for this Apache woman more than he cared for any of his women friends, but he needed order in his life, so he packed up and drove away.

In El Paso, he happened to see a medicine show and thought he could put together a better show. He'd seen sideshows back home, why not combine the two and take it on the road. It would certainly be unique. Of course, people weren't likely to buy a potion from Kid Lariat and they'd assume a Birnbaum was just out to cheat them. He needed a confidence-building name. He had to be a doctor, certainly, but who? As he traveled on with this idea in the back of his mind, he found an answer in Bandera. He met the sheriff, a Henry S. Hudspeth who was respected by everyone he came across. The man was stolid and upstanding, a pillar in the community. So he would appropriate his name and become Doc Hudspeth. But he needed a first-rate first name to go with it. And one evening he recalled a rabbi back in Buffalo calling him "extraneous." Although he never really knew what the word meant, it sounded quite grand, like something extra. So he became Doc Extraneous Hudspeth, bought a couple of wagons and a large tent, and mailed away to Gettysburg for a canvas bannerline.

It didn't take long to gather the folks he needed to portray the wonders on the canvases. Fire eating could be taught; you just needed nerves of steel and the ability not to gag on coal oil. A Jo-Jo could be created with some quality New York make-up. Dress the hairy creation up in the finest ball gowns to accentuate her malady. A regular fellow became a Wild Man by letting his hair and beard grow long and washing them in beer, not rinsing them, then teasing them without mercy. Then, of course, he had to develop a certain wild attitude, and know when to growl and leap at the audience. Usually when a pretty young woman passed near. Fat women were everywhere; just dress them in clothing that resembled a child's to create the illusion they were even larger than they were. Find a solidly built stevedore or longshoreman and dress him in animal skins and, there, you have the world's strongest man.

A bona fide sword swallower was difficult to find and in show business commanded top wages. Overcoming the natural gag reflex was something beyond what most people could do, but some could. He toured for a year before he found Michael, disgruntled at a circus that was just leaving Galveston.

Now, as Doc readied to bally on the platform, he looked over his troupe. He recognized that look the Wild Man and his new Jo-Jo exchanged. He'd been around intimate groups of show folks long enough to know the pairings were made quickly. Sometimes they led to trouble when jealousies appeared, but he was content his troupe had not presented him with any of those problems.

The old Jo-Jo preferred women but Tiny Alice did not practice the love of Lesbos and they were the only women in the troupe. Max didn't appear to like anything. Jasper was about average when it came to women, even if he was an abusive drunk. Seemed like he could always find some woman willing to be beaten up in order to be loved. Earl was a teetotaler but he was also a terrible womanizer. He didn't fancy Alice because of her size, which was fine by Doc since he didn't mind her size at all and Alice was convenient for him at times. Michael's tastes were universal. The age, religion, gender, or color of a potential partner didn't matter a whit to him, as long as the person was high class. He always said he would know if he were washed up in the show business if he ever woke up one morning next to another show person. Now came this new Jo-Jo into the mix and Doc saw immediately that she and Earl — a Wild Man in many ways — would pair off. He saw that it could mean trouble between Jasper and Earl, especially after Jasper had been drinking. It was something he would have to keep an eye on.

But now, the show must go on.

•

"Looky this one," a soldier said. "Wooo, doggies, now that's one little missy I certainly wouldn't be taking home to mother."

"Nah, sir," the other soldier said. "Why, I wouldn't do her with your tallywacker."

"Lord, it'd be like doing your own mount."

"Now, don't you be saying nothing bad about Ol' Dunny."

"Bad, hell, I think I'd rather do your ol' nag than this here dog-faced girly."

And the two soldiers laughed and slapped each other's backs.

Cynthia — now Jo-Jo — discovered sitting on the edge of the stage and taking the hoots and hollers of men wasn't difficult at all. She was able to tune them out easily. Sometimes she dreamed of living in a fine house with servants, like in the books she had read at home. Sometimes she dreamed of being the most famous Jo-Jo in the land, touring America and Europe, dining with kings and queens. Whenever she got too carried away with these glorious reveries, she recalled home and the pitiful look would return to her face.

When the show was over she didn't want to go directly back to her wagon and remove the make-up. Her hairy face was protecting her now and God help her if her brothers did show up and recognized her. What would they do? Unspeakable things, she knew. Alice had told her the make-up would stay on for days if she left it, but that the adhesive was so strong it might eventually damage her face. Right now, she didn't care.

"Excuse me, miss," a voice said from behind her.

She turned and saw one of the most handsome men she had ever seen, tall and steely-eyed.

"I don't think you're supposed to be backstage," she said quietly.

"It's OK," he said. "I won't take up much of your time. I was just wondering if you would like to accompany me to supper."

"I— I don't know," she said. The request was the last thing she expected a man to say to her. She didn't know what to do. "Let me ask Doc."

Doc had already walked over beside them, wondering what this towner was doing back of the stage. He was ready to yell his "Hey, Rube" if this man was out to cause trouble, but it wasn't something he ever liked doing. He tried to remember if he loaded his shotgun. He only had birdshot, but it was usually enough to cause troublemakers to back off, if needed. It would mean trouble getting out of town. At least this was their last show here.

"What's going on?" Doc asked.

Jo-Jo pulled him aside and said lowly, "This gentleman wants to take me to supper."

Doc stood back as if struck. He'd never heard of such a thing. But he couldn't find anything wrong with the proposal now that the shows were over here. "Well, if you wish to, that's fine. But you mustn't remove your make-up. We can't have him know you're a gaff and then tell the whole town. The word would spread. We can't afford that. If you go, you'll have to go as you are."

"I would prefer it," she said.

"We leave after breakfast," he told her. "Be here if you want to travel on with us."

She smiled, walked back, and held out her arm for the gentleman to take.

"I'll be happy to go with you," she said. "My name's Jo-Jo."

He patted her hand, leading her onto the street. "That's what the sign says. Mine's Wyatt Earp."

She thought she heard of the name before, but couldn't place where.

"Why don't you stay here by the tent and I'll get a rig and a supper from the Canary and we'll ride up into the hills and enjoy the supper by the setting sun," Wyatt told her. She looked downcast at the thought of not going to a real restaurant, something she'd never done before. He noticed and said, "I wouldn't want you to be the butt of all the jokes like you were in the show. We'll just go off by ourselves." She nodded agreement.

In no time, the couple was atop one of the tallest hills, looking toward the sunset. The lights and noise from the town were behind them.

"Thank you for asking me here," she said, looking up at him. He was nearly two heads taller than she was, and his sandy hair was framed by a deep blue sky and fluffy clouds beginning to glow yellow on the bottoms. She laughed a little, then said, "You have such a great background."

At first, he didn't know what she meant, then it came to him. It was first time he'd ever considered what life must be like for a short person, always looking up.

184

They reclined on a blanket, surrounded by creosote bushes, and ate the supper Wyatt brought.

"How long have you had this malady?" Wyatt finally asked, about halfway through their meal.

"Not long," she said. "Does it bother you?"

He took the drumstick from her hand and placed it on the plate, pulled her to him and kissed her. "Not really. It's certainly different. I've never had relations with anyone with a beard before."

In what seemed like only a moment, the two of them finished, smoothed out their clothing, and Wyatt helped Jo-Jo back into the buggy.

"Why don't you leave the show and come with me," Wyatt said.

"Where?"

"Tombstone," he replied. "It's in the Arizona Territory. There's a boom taking place thanks to the silver mines. You're so unusual that I'm certain many men would pay the highest dollar for your favors."

"What are you asking me to do? Sell myself to men?" she was genuinely appalled at the suggestion.

"I'm just a business manager," he said. "You would simply be providing a service and I would handle your affairs."

"And what would your wife say?" she asked, assuming that all well-to-do gentlemen had wives.

"I don't have a wife. I do have a business associate, like you would be."

"And how would she like you having another business associate along?"

"She does what I tell her."

Jo-Jo shook her head. "No— no, I couldn't possibly." But the thought intrigued her a little. The trouble was, she didn't know where this Tombstone was and it didn't sound like the sort of place she would care to be. It sounded too much like death. And she wasn't certain if this man would actually take care of her and protect her. And what would he do when he found out all of this uniqueness he talked about was faked.

"Well, it's up to you," he said, pulling the rig up next to the show tent. "But I'll have to stay around Fort Clark for a while waiting to testify in a court martial, then I think I'll be taking the leisurely way back, by stage, going through Fort Davis and catching the railroad at El Paso. If you change your mind, you can find me."

"I'll think on it," she said as he helped her down. "Thank you for the lovely supper."

CHAPTER 8

Along the Terlingua/Burgess Springs Road, Texas

The wagons stopped for the day. The brush country was several days away now, and the mountains were behind them. Ahead was a vast plain with mesas looming off to the east and west.

"I still think this is a waste of time," Jasper said, clunking around the impromptu camp, his peg leg kicking at small rocks.

"Everyone else agreed," Doc said. "Remember, I'm paying you regardless of whether we can gather a crowd. This will be a respite from our regular tour and, who knows, maybe we'll find the treasure."

Jasper stopped, crossing his arms across his chest. "Don't you think other people have looked for this long-lost treasure? Don't you think somebody else might have found it over all these years? Don't you think maybe, just maybe, it's all just one big windy? Some tale folks tell their kids before bedtime?"

"I think it's real," Doc said, chewing on some smoked meat. "I think the only problem will be if we can find it and whether it's accessible anymore. Could be it was buried long ago. But I heard about it from an Indian maiden I was close to, and she gave me details."

Jasper rolled his eyes and waved his hands. "An Indian maiden? Who are you now, Longfellow? Oh, Lord, save me." He strode away, looking for a cactus to water.

"He shudda have gone on wiff Michael," Max said. "Pay 'im no mind."

"If we do succeed, Michael will certainly regret his decision to leave the troupe," Doc said. "And if we do, Jasper will owe me an apology."

"I got no place else to go!" Jasper hollered. He buttoned up and returned to the wagons, wiping his hand on his trousers. "Michael can find work easy. I can't. This leg won't get me much. So I agreed to stay on, and only 'cause you said we'd still get paid. And if we somehow manage to find this treasure, sure I'll want my share. But you remember, if we don't find it, you're the one owes an apology. To me."

"Fair enough," Doc said. He washed down his supper with a bottle of warm beer.

"Just how detailed did this Indian princess really get?" Earl asked. "Maybe you should share some of that detail with us."

Doc gulped the last of his beer and returned the empty bottle to his wagon. "She wasn't too exact. She said her people knew of this cave and that it was high in the Chisos Mountains, and filled with conquistador booty. She sort of described a big square rock which was where to start looking, way up high. Might be difficult to get to. I expect it is."

"And there are towns out there?" Jo-Jo asked, pointing to the emptiness that spread out to the south.

"Well, that's a fact anyway," Doc said. "Two days away maybe. Couple of very small villages. Terlingua and Lajitas. Then it's along the river to Presidio. Even if we don't find any treasure I expect we'll do well in Presidio. I doubt they've ever seen a show anything like ours, ever."

After they finished eating and drinking a couple more beers, Max and Alice went to their respective wagons. The others sat on folding chairs next to Doc's wagon, not saying much.

"Where do you go in a place like this?" Jo-Jo asked.

"We're going south," Doc said.

"No— no, I mean, where do you go? Especially a woman?" she said.

Earl laughed and waved his arm out. "Anyplace you'd like."

"But it's so empty and all so open," she said. "And what about Indians? I'd be frightened to go off alone."

"Come on, we'll find you a spot and I'll protect you from any savages that might be lurking in sagebrush," Earl said, extending his hand to her.

Doc ran his fingers through his hair and shook his head just a little. Here it comes, he thought, noticing that Jasper was watching them just as intently as he was. Jasper drank another beer and rolled a cigarette. Doc was tired and wanted to go to sleep, but he thought he should stay up and keep an eye on Jasper.

Earl and Jo-Jo walked toward the mountains they had come down earlier in the day. A line of sage and sotol crowded the foothills and Earl indicated that Jo-Jo could squat behind them. "I'll look the other way, I promise, unless you yell for my assistance."

Jo-Jo did her business. After, as she walked toward Earl, the light from an almost full moon filled her face a soft blue.

He stepped in front of her and drew her to him. "I've been attracted to you since the first time I looked up from my cage and saw you standing in the crowd. You kept looking at Jo-Jo... well, the other Jo-Jo... and I was worried about that until we found out she was your sister, then I understood. And I've been meaning to tell you how sorry I am for your loss."

He didn't give her a chance to speak. He kissed her and she responded. "Now that Michael is gone, I have my own wagon, you know, me being the senior member of Doc's troupe after Alice. It's lonely in there all by myself. Maybe you can brighten it up."

She didn't say anything. She kissed him and put her arm around his back as they walked to his wagon.

Jasper glared at the couple, tossing the remains of his cigarette away.

"But anyway, you OK with this?" Doc asked him.

"Makes me no never mind," Jasper said, rising. "She's too damn skinny for me."

•

Lajitas

"What's he do all day?" Ethan asked Joaquin.

"Every time I notice, he's just sitting up there on the mesa by his wagon reading his Bible."

"And what's she do all day?"

"I never see her much. She comes down to the Catholic church at around noon and sits in there for about an hour then goes back up to the McGuirks."

Gracey brought them their suppers: ham and biscuits and whiskey for the Ranger, venison and beans and beer for the scout. She apologized to Joaquin about the lack of gravy, saying she didn't have the time to cook anything fresh today.

"You never see them together?" Ethan asked.

Joaquin shook his head no. "You?"

"Every evening. They go out to Calamity Creek."

"What on earth for?"

"Beats me," Ethan said, cutting a slice of meat with his own knife and sticking it in his mouth. "They've been doing it for months, I think. Months. They go out there and talk. They talk."

"Talk? That's all, just talk?"

"That's all."

"You think we should tell Dutch about all that?"

"I have."

"And what'd he say?"

"Not much," Ethan said. "Dutch doesn't like it but he knows there's nothing he can do. Nothing. I've never been certain how he feels about Lizard Teats. Never figured it out. Sometimes I think he doesn't care at all, others I think he might be in love with the little whore."

Joaquin folded a slice of ham into a biscuit. "She's not whorin' now."

"Nope, and I think that worries Dutch more. Afraid she might be getting religion and we know where that will lead."

"Straight to Brother Karl's arms. Maybe that'd be for the best. Get both of them out of here."

"I thought you liked Karl?" Ethan said, gulping some beer.

"I do," Joaquin replied. "But between him and Ingrid, they're upsetting everything. It's all people talk about. Dutch sulks about it. We're sittin' here worrying on them. They should just go off and work things out."

"Smart lad," Ethan said. "I agree."

Dutch was busy this evening, serving up drinks to a group of soldiers that were spending a couple of days in the area. Again he wished he had another whore, especially on days like this. Gracey was kept too busy. She didn't even have time to cook up supper tonight and with Ingrid no longer helping out with serving drinks and meals, Gracey and Dutch had to tend to those duties themselves. With Gracey going to her room out back so often, Dutch was becoming both waiter and bartender. He didn't like that at all.

Dutch had only six tables in the saloon and they were all full, forcing most of the soldiers to stand at the bar or lounge against walls. He looked over at the Ranger and scout, taking their leisure eating their suppers and taking up an entire six-top by themselves. And he knew they'd be here most of the evening taking up that space. At least Ethan would drink enough beers until the saloon closed to make it worth Dutch's while. But Joaquin left pretty early every night. He liked his sleep.

He looked over and saw Ethan had wolfed down his meal. He did appreciate the venison the scout brought in regularly, so he never charged him for that. Traded it out for food, but not for the beer. He'd go broke if he did that. "Ready?" he hollered over the noise to Ethan. The scout held up a hand and Dutch tossed him an air-tight of peaches.

Ethan opened the tin with his knife, spearing a peach slice. "Got a question for you. Just between you and me."

"What?" Joaquin said.

"Your name. I've heard you give four, maybe five or more different explanations on how you came to be called 'Joaquin.' I imagine it's about time to tell me the real story."

"One condition," the Ranger said. "I understand some about how Indians get their names… always a story behind it. You tell me yours, I'll tell you mine."

"You first," Ethan said. "Mine's the longer story."

"Another condition. You don't tell anyone."

"What difference does it make who knows?"

Joaquin drank the last of his whiskey and leaned forward. "I've been asked the same God damned question since I was old enough to talk. Got sick of it a long time ago. Now, when people ask, making something up keeps me from punching them in the nose."

Ethan laughed and nodded. "I won't even whisper it to a lizard."

"Well, it's the simplest story. I was born on the feast day of Saint Joachim, the father of the Virgin. The Spanish of the name is Joaquin and my mother liked that better, so I'm Joaquin. Your turn."

Ethan bit a portion of peach off his knife, sucking out the juice before munching up the fruit. "Only one other living person knows this and he's working behind that bar, so I'll ask the same confidentiality from you." Joaquin nodded and Ethan continued. "My real last name is Morys, M-O-R-Y-S. My father was a Welshman who married a Mic Mac woman. Only people who do that sort of thing back home are the French. Kind of a joke, really, that if you're French you have some Indian blood and if you're Indian you have some French blood. Lot of Indians in Vermont, more than most northern states. Got some Cayuga and Abnaki and Delaware, and Mic Mac. If you've got English blood or Scot or Irish or even Welsh, you're just expected to be better than that. They don't intermarry much. My father did and he was ostracized by just about everyone in town, even his own family. He put up with it for a while, but not long. He abandoned us a few months after I was born. My grandfather said it broke my mother's heart and she died in a couple of years and he raised me."

"And his name was Twobears?"

"Nope. Nothing like it. He gave me that name when I was about five years old and we were out berry picking. These two bear cubs decided I'd make a good playmate and they came romping over and I got so scared I screamed to my grandfather for help and climbed up a tree. He heard me hollering that they were going to eat me and came running over just when they started to climb up the tree behind me. He shooed them away and I came down. Never did see mama bear. So he named me The Kid Who Was So Afraid of Two Bear Cubs He Climbed a Tree. Two Bears for short. After that, he either called me Allan or Twobears. Only used Allan when he was pissed at something I'd done I wasn't supposed to. I never knew my real last name until I was about ten and he told me the whole story. When I went off to Dartmouth I just filled out the papers Ethan Allan Twobears."

"Where'd the Ethan come from?" Joaquin asked.

"Ethan Allen, the greatest hero Vermont has. Only one, I imagine; it's a small state. I'm not sure why I added it. I think my reasoning back then was that I wanted to keep Allan because that was the name my mother gave me. I knew I didn't want Morys or anything to do with my father. The Ethan... I don't know. I think I always felt like a second-class citizen, you know, always getting picked on by the whiter kids, and I imagine I thought that if I had a hero's name when I went off to school it would somehow make me stronger."

Dutch brought them new drinks and Ethan drank his quickly,

something he rarely did.

"Do me a favor?" Joaquin asked.

"Depends."

"I need to learn more," the Ranger said. "If I'm stuck out here for a while there's no sense for me to be wasting my days. I need to learn how to track."

"Eh-yeah, that's smart," Ethan said. "But you know a lot already even if you don't realize it. You herded cattle for some time, you had to learn some tracking skills. Searching for strays, hunting down cats or wolves. You know things."

"I guess I do, but I need to get specific. I need to learn more about tracking men and about tracking in the desert. This place is different than up in the Hill Country. Way different."

"How do you think it's different?"

Joaquin thought for a while. "The obvious, of course. It doesn't have any trees unless you get up into the mountains. The plants and critters are different. Mainly, though, I think it's that the desert is so damn unforgiving and so damn empty. Make a mistake out here and it's your last. If I lost my horse in the Hill Country, I could walk in a day's time at the most to some town. If I lose my horse out in that desert, I'm a dead man. Desert's got no pity."

"Eh-yeah, that's the smart way to think on it. Exactly. It's the thing you have to keep in mind all the time, especially when you're tracking. You have to be aware for yourself but you also have to be aware of what the other fellow might do because of that fact. Be aware. Where's water? Where's shade? Can he get to the mountains or the river? Does he know the desert or is he a tenderfoot? Anybody can figure out signs, but to be a good tracker you've got to learn to think like the one you're tracking."

"How do you do that?"

"Well, you've got to think, first of all. Don't make any assumptions. Learn what you can about the man, what his skills might be, what his fears are, what his needs are. Think it all out. The more you do it, the quicker you can do it."

Joaquin nodded. Ethan offered him a peach and the Ranger gladly ate it while Ethan drank the last of the juice from the can. "And you've to take care of yourself all this time," Ethan said. "There's an old Apache saying that goes, never pass up a chance to sit down or relieve yourself. Sage advice."

•

Ingrid stepped down from Karl's wagon in front of the McGuirk home.

"I don't think I'll be going out tomorrow," she told him. He nodded and smiled. "I think they're behind me now. You know, I've talked to God some the past couple of days. I guess that's praying. But when I talk to him there in the church, it's comforting. I don't feel that wrath anymore. I don't feel the shame anymore. I still feel lost, but the shame is over. I don't hate myself anymore."

Karl bent down and kissed her lightly. She didn't pull away. "Good night," he said and drove the wagon off, saying to himself: "The Lord is my shepherd; I shall not want. He maketh me to lie down in green pastures. He leadeth me beside the still waters. He restoreth my soul. He leadeth me in the paths of righteousness for his name'sake. Yea, though I walk through the valley of the shadow of death, I will fear no evil: For thou art with me; thy rod and thy staff, they comfort me. Thou preparest a table before me in the presence of mine enemies; thou annointest my head with oil. My cup runneth over."

•

Rattlesnake Springs, Texas

Lieutenant Mason Maxon bit a chaw off his tobacco plug and methodically chewed it into the cud he wished he could replace with a more civilized pipe, but Colonel Grierson forbid smoking at these outposts. The troops were supposed to be hidden and a light, no matter how small, could be seen for more than a mile in the desert. Maxon knew some of the senior non-coms didn't enforce this rule too rigidly, but all the officers he knew did. He certainly would. He believed in maintaining military discipline even in the field, even if it meant periodic inspections. He even required his men to bathe at least once every five days. After hours, they could relax a little, like tonight.

He sat on a rock against the wall of the low Sierra Diablos that overlooked Rattlesnake Springs. The plain to the east of the spring meant no one could approach it without being seen. He slid the braces off his undershirt and kicked the boots from his feet. Even well after dark, the weather was sweltering, a stark contrast to just a day ago when a cold wind blew through the camp. He'd never figure this Texas weather out, and this year had been even more unpredictable than most.

At least around Fort Davis the weather and the countryside were good for goats. He'd already started his own little Angora herd and hoped to build it up into a going concern by breeding his thoroughbred buck to mongrels.

The moonlight was bright enough to make moving around the rudimentary camp easy, but he still had to squint his small eyes to see who was standing in front of him. It was one of the two Seminole Negro Indian Scouts attached to his company. He was happy to have them. They were quiet, efficient, didn't get into any trouble, and knew their way around this Godforsaken country better than any white man ever would.

"Corporal?" Maxon said.

Pompey July stood more or less at attention. "We gots visitors, sir. At the base of the mountains acrost from the spring. East, maybe a mile maybe a mile and a half."

Maxon sat up and motioned for the black man to sit beside him on another boulder. "Have you seen them? Which way do you think they're moving, corporal?"

"Ain't seen them, just theys' sign," July said. "But theys ain't movin'. Been there all day. Theys sent a scout out, too, and he come over t'here and report back just like I'm doin' now."

Maxon chewed on his prodigious mustache while he thought, then spit toward a nearby yucca. "They have provisions?"

"Dried corn and mescal."

"How do you know?"

"Saw the corn scattered some on one side of the trail, saw some flies upon a small chunk of mescal on t'other side."

"How many?" Maxon asked.

The corporal scratched his chin. "Can't tell quite how manys, but more'n us. Apache. Maybe two dozen warriors and more, at least six women, a few childs. One of theys men is sickly."

Maxon shook his head. "How to you know one of the Apache is ill?"

"Because theys formed a travois to carry him on. I can't guess where they got the branches from, maybe from up the Guadalupes or down by Davis. The travois was drawn by a hoss blind in one eye."

"How in the world do you know that horse was half-blind?"

"Cause while all the other hosses, theys grazed upon both sides the trail, this one ate only what grew on one side the trail."

"How do you know it was a man injured?"

"Cause when they stopped on the trail, all the women gathered 'round him. Different size moccasin tracks."

"Apaches." Maxon said, amazed that July had gathered all this information without actually seeing anyone. The corporal's face was stolid but as unremarkable as any man's he had ever seen, betraying not an ounce of intelligence. "Will they attack?"

"My guess," July said. "But theys don't do't until just before dawn. That's what theys prefer. Depends how desperate theys is for water."

"Thank you, corporal. Get a good night's rest. Tell Private Remo to keep watch all night. Does he have a watch?"

"I don't guess so, sir."

"Give him this," Maxon said, handing over his biscuit watch with its heavy silver chain. "Tell him to wake the command at 4 a.m. Quietly. I'll pass the word to have everyone ready to do battle before first light."

The scout rose, saluted, and disappeared into the night.

•

Lozen's camp was up and ready to move.

"I still think this is a mistake. I've seen the Pale Eyes soldiers and your Power has told you they are behind the spring, we have enough water to move on. Why do this?" Wolf Rising asked.

"Beduiat," she said softly, afraid to say the name.

"Your brother is dead," Wolf Rising said, throwing his hand out flat in front of him for emphasis. "I saw this happen."

"He said he would meet me at Rattlesnake Springs near the full moon," she said. "I'll keep my part of that bargain. If he's not there, I'll know he has gone on before me."

Wolf Rising shook his head but readied for the battle. He dipped his finger into the paste made from the insects that stuck to the prickly pear and daubed it across his face in a long red stripe below his eyes. He touched his amulet, feeling the four-pointed star he had burned into the lightning-struck wood. After he helped Caterpillar onto his travois, Walking Stick gathered the women and children around him, singing softly. The warriors mounted their horses.

They moved quickly, not worried much about the sound they made until they got closer to the spring. Lozen sent half of the warriors to the north, half to the south. She hoped to catch the Pale Eyes still asleep. She didn't.

The moment the band moved within sight of the oozing spring, the Pale Eyes opened a withering fire. Her band returned the fire, but their bullets just flew randomly into the night. The dawn was barely breaking, so some light fell on the spring but the soldiers were in the shadow of the mountain. The rising sun would illuminate them soon, but not soon enough, Lozen knew. She saw two warriors fall, she didn't know which. She watched Wolf Rising jump from his rearing horse, kneel, and empty his rifle at a burst of flame that came from a Pale Eye rifle. He ran, holding his horse's rein, to behind a tall sage near the spring opening. He reloaded and waited for another burst of flame to tell him where to direct his bullets. Lozen yelled, "Ukashe!," urging her warriors to scatter and they did. She waited a few moments to survey the ground. As a line of light from the rising sun slid over the sand and rocks, she saw three of her men lying still. She called out to them. One moved a little. Under another fusillade from the rocks, she galloped her horse over to the wounded warrior and pulled Upsidedown up behind her.

"Always Ready and Corn Flower," he gasped, answering her question before she asked it. Always Ready was a good warrior and Corn Flower would be missed by his wife and three children.

Little Sister kicked her heels into her horse and followed the others away from Rattlesnake Spring for the last time.

CHAPTER 9
Lajitas

Joaquin retuned to Lajitas happy to have done something as a Texas Ranger even if it was only dealing with stolen goats. A goatherd from Paso Lajitas on the Mexican side of the Río Grande stole three nannies from his brother-in-law on the American side. When confronted, the Mexican goatherd admitted the theft but refused to let the Texas goatherd retrieve the nannies until Joaquin raised a shotgun to the man's belly — an internationally recognized form of extradition.

He wasn't prepared for what he saw when he rode to the center of town. In the empty lot next to Dutch Dave's Mejor Que Nada saloon was a large tent with a small platform out front and several garishly painted wagons parked behind.

A well-dressed man stood alone on the platform in front of paintings of several odd characters. He held a dark bottle in his hand, waving it about as he spoke. "To have good health, you must keep the bowels open. Too many people suffer constipation and too few realize that although the bowels move regularly every day, that movement may still be incomplete resulting in a literal poisoning of the blood."

Joaquin tied up his horse and joined the small crowd in front of the platform. He seemed to have gone through his adult life constipated and was more than a little interested in what this stranger had to say, especially if it was, indeed, a dangerous condition. Joaquin just thought it was inconvenient.

"That we manufacture within our own bodies poisons, just as deadly as are made in any chemical laboratory, has been documented by the French physician Dr. Bouchard. Before this, constipation was looked upon as the disagreeable cause of sick headaches, coated tongue, bad breath, lassitude, and the much-feared appendicitis. We now know that where there is not complete evacuation of the bowels there is soon an accumulation of putrefying food materials which, aided by the heat of the body, rapidly generates poisons. These are absorbed by the blood stream throughout the body. Pain in any part of the body is Nature's warning that something is grievously wrong. Otherwise the pain would not be present. If you have a dull ache in the region of the liver, danger is near. If you have sudden cramping of the limbs, danger is near. If you have frequent griping in the stomach, danger is near. If you have palpitations of the heart, danger is near. If you have tenderness in the small of your back, danger is near. If you have headaches, dizziness, irritations, weak spells, hot flushes, danger is near. There is no guess work or doubt about it, danger is near. Don't delay a single moment longer. Start at once to take my master herbal remedy, Doc Extraneous Hudspeth's Ever-Cure Elixir, that I hold here in my hand. It will promptly tone up your vital organs, drive out all poisons, and restore your entire system to a state of perfect efficiency."

"Might be good for what ails you," a voice said from behind Joaquin. He turned to see Ethan. The old scout almost always showed up at the saloon, but not usually until after dark. It was only late afternoon.

"Get lonely?" Joaquin asked as they walked away from the carnival atmosphere around the platform.

"Bored," Ethan said. "I didn't get much sleep last night. Been having a little trouble sleeping the past few days. I woke up early and did a few things around the jacal, but after a while I just got bored. It was either go hunting or come down and get drunk early and I didn't feel much like killing anything today."

"Maybe that elixir could help you sleep," Joaquin said.

"Eh-yeah, it probably could, probably could, but beer's much cheaper."

"Buy you one?"

"I knew there was something I liked about you," Ethan said, draping his arm over the Ranger's shoulders as they walked into the saloon.

They went up to the bar and Dutch immediately came over with a glass of whiskey for Joaquin and a mug of beer for Ethan.

"Not fair, you know," Dutch said, leaning on his side of the boards that stretched nearly the length of the room. Just coming in from the outside, the aroma from the whiskey barrels the planks rested on was potent. "We finally get rid of Karl's infernal chapel and now we get these show people. I'm slap out of patience with folks tryin' to ruin my business."

Joaquin hefted his shot glass up. "I don't think you have much to worry about. This is still cheaper than what that doc is peddling."

Dutch nodded. He reached under the counter and gave a letter to Joaquin. "This came in earlier for you from the Rangers at Fort Davis."

Joaquin thanked him and opened the envelope.

My dear Ranger Jaxon,

I have the duty to inform you that the broad U.S. Army presence in our region ordered by Col. Benjamin Grierson is being terminated over the next several weeks. With the recent death of the Apache renegade Victorio and many of his followers at Tres Castillos, Rep. Of Mexico, most of the hostile bands of Indians have been eliminated or driven from the State of Texas. Army scouts report only two hostile bands remain in the field. One is a band of Mescalero Apaches that were formerly a portion of Victorio's band. From their movements, Col. G. believes they are returning to their homelands near the Sierra Blanco in the New Mexico Territory. The other band is reported to be headed by Victorio's sister and is comprised of from between a dozen and twenty warriors, along with an undetermined number of women and children, of both Chiricahua and Mescalero Apaches. This group of hostiles has been traveling in a erratic manner and their ultimate goal cannot be determined. Sightings indicate this band remains within the Big Bend and the purview of Company E. At this time, no major operation is anticipated to counter this hostile band which scouts believe will cross the Rio Grande and beyond our purview. However, Capt. Baylor has ordered all Rangers in the region to be vigilant and to alert both landowners and the proper authorities.

Yours,

Sgt. R. K

Ranger Co. E, Fort Davis

Joaquin handed the letter to Ethan. "You think we'll see them near here?"

"Can't tell with Apache," the scout said, handing the letter to Dutch who waved it back to Joaquin. He'd already read it. "But I doubt it. Apache are mountain people. Out here, they've had strongholds in the Chisos and up around Davis but most of them are long gone. Sometimes I run into an old Mescalero and his woman up in the high Chisos, man calls himself Alsate. Can't be the original, of course, since he'd have to be maybe a couple hundred years old. Not the original. I don't know if the old man was named for the old chief or maybe descended from him or just appropriated the name. I mean, there's no other Mescalero around to challenge him on it, so he could get away with it. Apache change names often enough anyway. Something important happens, your friends start calling you by a new name. Break your leg, get a new name. Win all your fights, get a new name. That's how Victorio got his Chiricahua name. The Victorious One; he just never lost fights."

"Until this month," Joaquin said. He nodded with his head to their usual table and Ethan followed. They could hear the medicine show wrapping up outside as Doc talked townspeople into paying a little extra and stepping into the tent where oddities and wonders awaited them.

"Thank Grierson for that," Ethan said. "The man was brilliant. Has been for a long time. He made that spectacular raid through Mississippi to Baton Rouge during Grant's Vicksburg campaign during the war. When was it? Sixty-three? That helped break the Confederacy's back. Broke it. It wasn't regular Army tactics; more like Indian. I guess he got tired of chasing Apache all over and getting not much of anything for it. So he stopped chasing them and put small units in the field at as many waterholes they could find and just waited for the Apache to come to them. Just stopped chasing them.

"You see, Apache, they worry about what's behind them. They don't worry much about what's ahead. They've had generations of learning how to evade and run away. Grierson changed all that for them. Changed it. While they were looking over their shoulders for the pony soldiers, Grierson had the soldiers off their ponies lying in wait. Worked like a damn charm."

"They ain't withdrawin' all the cavalry?" Dutch said as he came over to the table. "You don't want your supper this early do you?"

Both of the other men said they would wait until their regular time, an hour or so after sundown.

"I imagine what'll happen is that they'll go back to their forts and march around in drills and go out on routine patrols and maybe guard a wagon or stage or two just to keep sharp. Things'll go pretty much back to normal. Be normal," Ethan said.

"If the Patchey are really gone, I wonder what that means up t'Fort Davis and Stockton, maybe even out to Clark?" Dutch said. "Won't be much of a reason to keep all those soldiers posted out here. Send 'em to Arizona or the Dakotas, mebbe? Damn. You have any idea how much of my business is from soldiers?"

"A lot," Joaquin said.

"Wow. Right on the nose," Dutch said.

Ethan hooked his thumb over his shoulder, aimed at the noise from the crowd exiting the show outside. "I guess you could mix up your own elixir and take to the road like those folks."

"That'll be the day," Dutch said, shaking his head. Some of the crowd came into the saloon so Dutch headed back to his bar. "The human brain starts working the moment you're born and never stops until someone starts trying to sell you something."

The Mejor Que Nada filled quickly. Maybe having a medicine show outside wasn't such a bad thing after all, Dutch thought. They gathered the crowd and he got to reap the benefits when they got thirsty. And add to that a Saturday night when many of the ranch hands came to town.

Dutch surveyed the crowd. Soldiers trying to shoulder their way to the bar, hands choosing up tables to settle in for a long evening of playing cards and drinking, townspeople looking for one or two nips before heading home, even a couple of strangers — he assumed they were with the show — came in.

Ethan rose and went to the bar where he was greeted by Dutch with new drinks for him and the Ranger. "Gracey woulda brought these over."

"I know, but I wanted to buy these soldiers a couple of rounds," Ethan said. Then, turning to face the soldiers, "You've got two rounds on me, men, my way of thanking you for the service you've done this year. Sterling job and my hat's off to you."

They didn't know what to make of this old man wearing an obviously new, stiff buckskin shirt, but they weren't about to pass up free drinks. Ethan tossed Dutch one of his gold coins and went back to his table with Joaquin.

"Excuse me, sir," Doc said to Dutch. "Doctor Hudspeth. And I am a man of great curiosity. I don't believe I've ever seen a coin like that before. Might I see it?"

Dutch shrugged and handed over the coin. "If you try to leave this place without returnin' it, your friends'll be carryin' you out in a box."

"Spanish?" Doc asked, turning the coin over in his fingers.

"Beats me," Dutch said. "Banks give me real money for it is all I know."

"How much?"

"Varies. I usually get $40 in Uvalde, $50 in San Antonio or El Paso."

"Interesting," Doc said, handing the coin back. "Very beautiful engraving on it. Where does that gentleman find them?"

Dutch stared at Doc for a moment, then at his two companions, both younger men with lean and hungry looks about them. He noticed one of them had a wooden leg. "Ask him yourself. I'm busy."

Doc touched the brim of his bowler, turned and said to his companions, "Wait here," then worked his way to Ethan's table.

"Doctor Extraneous Hudspeth," Doc introduced himself at the table, pulling out a chair.

"Did I invite you to sit?" Ethan snapped.

"Well, no, sir, no you did not. I didn't mean any insult. May I join you for a moment's conversation?"

"If it's a moment, you can handle it standing up," Ethan said, turning his beer mug around in his hands.

"That would be excellent, then," Doc said, standing up straight and pulling his smile tighter.

Ethan drank his beer down to the middle of the glass. "Parents didn't think much of you, did they?"

"Beg pardon?" Doc said.

"Extraneous," Ethan replied. "Hell of a name. I might've changed it myself."

"Well, I have tried to live up to it," Doc said. "Sometimes it's a burden but I've borne it. Helping people with my elixir helps me live up to it."

"Eh-yeah," Ethan said slowly. "You don't know more than a hog does about that ruffled shirt you're wearing, do you?"

"Beg pardon?"

Ethan waved his hand. "Nothing. Never mind. I don't mean to keep you here a moment longer than you need."

"Thank you, sir. I just had my curiosity piqued by that coin you tendered. I was wondering if it was Spanish? You see, I'm a coin collector—"

"I'll bet you are."

"—and that coin is missing from an almost perfect collection. Are you also a collector?"

"Do I look like a coin collector? A collector of anything?"

"Well, appearances may be deceiving…"

"Eh-yeah."

"Look, he just found it. OK? Now why don't you go back to your friends?" Joaquin said, stiffening in his chair. Ethan shot the Ranger an unappreciative look.

"Found it? Where might I ask?" Doc said.

"Out by Presidio," Ethan said, looking at Joaquin and not Doc. "Used to be a big fort there. Manned by conquistadores. Long time ago. Fort's mostly gone now. The fort's gone but every time the river floods some lost coins turn up. Whenever we have a big rain, I wander down and look in the mud and on the banks. Maybe five times of six I find one or two."

"Interesting," Doc said, doffing his hat to the men at the table. "Sorry to disturb you. I'm just a man of insatiable curiosity, is all."

"Eh-yeah," Ethan said.

•

"He finds them in the mud?" Earl asked as they sat around their communal eating table in the tent.

"What he said," Doc answered.

"You don't believe that, do you?" Earl said.

"Not for a moment, no," Doc said. "Maybe if we stay here long enough we can determine where he actually does find them."

"If you think I'm staying in this shit hole very long, you're crazy," Jasper said, throwing down his knife and fork. He rose and clopped out of the tent.

"Let me talk to him," Earl said, following the other man outside.

When he caught up with Jasper, he had to pull him by the back of the shirt to stop him. "Hold it. Hold it. Listen to me just a second."

"What?" Jasper spat.

"I'm with you," Earl said. "We don't need to stay here one second longer than we need to. I'm guessing this guy has the coins stashed away at his place. I mean, where would you hide something in this desert? Got it under his bed or in a pot in a cupboard. Something. We'll find out where, get it and split it up."

"Who's we?"

"Me, you. I'd want Jo-Jo along, just for company, you know, and Max. We might need the muscle."

"No Doc?"

"Doc's out. We don't need him. Just us."

"And since you and Jo-Jo are together, the two of you get one share. Fair?"

"Well... I don't think that is fair. We should all get an equal cut," Earl said.

"You're living together. Maybe you'll get married to the little bitch, I don't know. Don't care. But since you're together, if the two of you get equal shares, that means you get double and I don't like that. I don't think Max will either."

"OK, OK. Have it your way. I'm going back and see if Doc found out anything else. If you can, go on out and saddle me one of the horses and tie it to the back of my wagon. When the old guy leaves tonight, I'll follow him and see where he lives. Tomorrow, we can go on out and look around his place. Bet we find something."

Jasper searched Earl's face before agreeing. He wasn't certain he trusted Earl, but it did sound like a good plan.

206

•

They sat together on a blanket on the mesa, looking over the lights of the town now that the sun had gone down. Even though the moon wasn't full just yet — tomorrow, he thought — it was bright enough to cast gray shadows in the pale light. He had his arm around Ingrid's shoulder.

"Can you forgive me?" she asked.

"You have done nothing I should forgive you for," Karl said. "I love you now just as I loved you three years ago and just as I loved you ten years ago and just as I loved you the first time we met on Haupstrasse in front of the hardware store in Fredericksburg where our fathers happened to be that Saturday afternoon when we were so young. So long ago. God has forgiven you long ago. That is why Christ died on the cross: so we could be forgiven. He took all that burden on his shoulders. He took on the burden of all of our sins. The only person you need forgiveness from is yourself."

She nodded. "I know. I think I have. I'm not sure. How can I ever be sure? I think so. I don't blame myself for everything anymore. I want to have that life I always dreamed of before. I just want things to be normal. For once. Just be normal."

"Come away from the memories of this place and we can make a normal life," he said, pulling her closer. He looked down to her but she didn't look up.

"We couldn't go back home."

"No. But we can go where ever you want to go. Where do you want to go?"

She shrugged. "I don't know. A big city where I can be just one of many others. But you couldn't be a preacher anymore. I don't think I could deal with that level of hypocrisy."

"I am not a hypocrite," he said quickly. "But I understand how it might bear in on you. I do not have to preach the gospel to live the gospel. I can do many things and would be happy to work at any one of them to make you happy."

"A big city," she said.

"San Antonio? Galveston?"

"I think living by the sea would be nearly perfection," she said, finally looking up and him. He thought he detected the brief flicker of a smile. "It would be so different from here and so different from home. The sounds of the waves would be comforting."

"We will be married and we will make a wonderful home in Galveston, then. We will build it overlooking the sea and go to sleep every night listening to the surf on the rocks. When do you want to go?"

She saddened. "I don't know. I don't know how I can leave Dutch. He's been so very good to me. He was the only source of comfort and protection I felt for so long. I don't think I could tell him goodbye. I would feel badly sneaking away, but I couldn't face him. We would have to wait until he goes away for something. It's only a couple of months before he makes his regular trip into San Antonio. I can wait that long."

"Then so can I."

 **CHAPTER 10**
Terlingua

Ethan sat on the edge of the cliff facing east, waiting for the sun to set. It was one of the pleasures in his life, to sit on this cliff on top of his hill near Terlingua and absorb the mountain vista that filled almost all the southeastern horizon. Sometimes the setting sun reflected brilliant oranges and reds on the face of the Chisos. But not tonight. Tonight the mountains slipped into gray then purple. He was disappointed for only a few minutes. As the sky began to darken, a faint glow appeared in the clouds above the Chisos. He'd forgotten the moon would rise full tonight. The yellow glow brightened and almost suddenly a brilliant top edge of the moon rose just to the right of the center of the Chisos island on the desert sea. The moon floated upwards, the rabbit on its face peeking out from behind this small cloud, then that one. The black bodies of the clouds were outlined in luminescent silver, stretching out north and south and moving very slowly toward the west, toward Ethan and his small shack. Once the moon was fully up it dominated the dark grey sky with its radiance. The clouds stood out in wispy relief across the sky, paying homage to the great presence that filled the deep evening with light.

Damn, he thought suddenly, he was paying too much attention to the display in front of him and not enough to whatever was happening behind him, to whatever caused that little noise.

"Don't turn," a voice ordered. "I have a shotgun aimed at your back and I'll use it sure."

Ethan sat still, tensing his muscles in case he had to leap one way or the other. He knew he didn't want to go off the cliff; it was thirty feet and more to the ground with catclaw and mesquite dotting the cliff face. Everything in the desert either pricks, sticks or stings, he thought. The prickly, sticking stuff was in front of him; the stinger was behind him.

"Where's those golden coins you have?" a different voice said.

Ethan shook his head. Beer was clouding his judgment too often these days and it obvious had done so yesterday when he bought those soldiers a couple of rounds of drinks. So who was this behind him? He doubted it was any townspeople. Ranch hands? Maybe, but he didn't think any of them had seen the coin. That left soldiers and those show folk. He certainly didn't trust the show folk, but soldiers made more sense. And they'd know how to use deadly force. Would any of those actors and charlatans?

"We're waiting for an answer," the second voice said.

"I don't have any here," Ethan finally replied. "I find them sometimes out in the desert, out by Presidio, sometimes by the river. Spend a year or two out here yourself and you'll find a couple. You can get real wealthy that way."

"Don't be smart wiff us," a third voice said. Three of them, then. That would make a fight more difficult. Plus the shotgun counted for about a half-dozen more men all by itself. "Where is them coins?"

Ethan shrugged. He was poked in the back of the head by a piece of metal, the shotgun barrel. He heard someone whispering, a female voice. Not soldiers, then. He tried to remember if those paintings by the show tent depicted a woman. Probably, he decided.

"We don't have much patience," the first voice said.

Ethan rose slowly, his hands away from his sides to show he presented no threat.

"I told you not to turn around," the first voice yelled.

"Why not?" Ethan asked, turning around. Three men and one woman, a girl really. Two of the men he recognized from Dutch's place yesterday. The third man was short but built like Casa Grande peak itself. The peg-legged man held the shotgun, a long-barreled weapon that Ethan thought was an old goose gun.

The blonde-haired man, the one standing next to the girl, narrowed his eyes and his jaw muscles got visibly tense. "We're waiting."

"Waiting are you?" Ethan said. "Waiting are you? Well, go ahead and wait."

The man with the shotgun pulled the trigger and Ethan took a blast square in his chest. The impact knocked him over the cliff.

"You idiot!" Earl said to Jasper, hitting him on the back of the head as they all rushed to the cliff. Despite the glow of the full moon, they couldn't see anything below. Jasper leaned over and fired the second barrel. He reloaded quickly and fired again and again at where he thought the body would have fallen.

"He's not coming up from that," Jasper said, satisfied.

Earl pushed Jasper, who dropped the shotgun in the dust and fell backwards.

"You got no call to do that," Jasper said, struggling to his foot. After regaining his balance, he reached down for the shotgun then looked in his pockets for more shells. But he'd only brought four.

"Now we've got to search for it," Jo-Jo said, walking to the stone jacal. She held up a small lantern she had been carrying. "Someone give me a match."

Max fished a lucifer from a shirt pocket, struck it on a tooth and lit the lantern. They followed Jo-Jo into the shack.

It was only eight-by-eight-foot square, with a stone ledge on the west wall covered with bearskins. The door in the east wall had the only window. Jo-Jo found a lantern setting on a small shelf near the bed, lit that, and set her own light down on another shelf built into the wall near the door. The shelves were no more than long flat rocks sticking out of the rock walls.

"Tink it's gonna be in here?" Max asked, looking around.

"Got to be," Earl said. "If not, we'll wait till morning and rummage around outside. Maybe there's a well or something."

"Not going to be any damn well in this damn place... and you call me an idiot," Jasper snapped. Earl ignored him.

Jo-Jo overturned a wicker basket full of clothes and went through them. A pair of brown cotton trousers, a red flannel shirt, a light blue cotton shirt. Three pairs of white stockings. She didn't think the old man was the sort to wear stockings. When she felt of them, she guessed they were made of silk. She had never felt silk before but this smoothness felt like the word sounded.

Earl pulled the bearskins from the bed, four of them, three black and the top one brown. He felt along the stone bed, searching for an indentation or hole but found nothing. He kicked at the front of the bed to see if there was a door built in to it. Nothing. He pulled a box from near the bed, looked inside and found several tin cans of peaches and two large bottles of beer.

Max stood in the middle of the room, looking around and around but touching nothing.

Jo-Jo sat on the edge of the bed and she looked around. She looked up and smiled. She stood on the bed and reached into the sotol vegas that formed the roof of the shack. She'd seen a patch of white that didn't seem to belong and when she pushed aside two of the sotol stalks she saw the canvas bag and pulled it out.

The bag jingled as she pulled it down. When she spilled its contents on the bed, dozens of the gold coins fell out along with an engraved watch and a gold medal on a red-white-and-blue ribbon.

"A fortune!" Max said.

"How much?" Jo-Jo asked.

Earl ran his fingers through the coins, quickly counting them up. "Maybe $25,000, maybe $30,000 dollars if that bartender was right about how much he could get for them."

"Thirty would be perfect," Jasper said. "Makes for an even split."

"I don't get a share?" Jo-Jo said, looking at Earl.

"You're with him," Jasper said. "So you both get one share. We already agreed."

"You— you did?" she said, still looking at Earl.

"It's enough for both of us," Earl said, pushing the coins back into the bag.

"Then I keep the watch," she said. Earl shrugged and Jasper waved his hand.

"Prolly doesn't efen work," Max said.

She brought the watch to her ear but it wasn't ticking. She wound the stem as much as she could, listened again, and heard it tick with precision. She smiled. She opened the thick watch and beamed as a musical tune played. *Jeanie With The Light Brown Hair.* She knew that melody. She noticed the photograph crudely forced into the cover of the watch: a beautiful, light-haired woman cradling a child.

CHAPTER 11
Terlingua

When Ethan awoke in Hell a demon was sitting on his chest. His first rational thought was that the demon was smaller than he had imagined they would be. The pain, vertigo, and total disorientation made him vomit. At least he could turn his head to do so. The rest of his body seemed restrained in some fashion. He flailed around, trying to break free, but only suffered hundreds of small, painful wounds inflicted by other, unseen, demons.

His flailing frightened the demon, which leapt off Ethan's chest and bounded away. He felt the vibration. He forced his eyes to focus in the dim light. Funny, he thought, he imagined Hell would be a place of blazing light from the fiery furnaces. And he felt cold, not hot. The demon had remained close and Ethan saw it now for what it was — a jackrabbit. He kicked at it with his foot, but only felt more stabbing pain. His foot, he realized, was kicking into the branch of the mesquite shrub he was engulfed by. He tried to move more slowly this time, feeling the thorns stick him. He decided to stop and think through what was happening.

He'd been shot. He ran his hands over his chest and felt warm fluid, blood. He took a deep breath. No internal pain; a good sign. He'd fallen after being shot and must have landed in one of the mesquite bushes that managed to survive on the cliff face. Whenever he would wonder about a shrub or cactus growing from a cliff of bare rock or dirt, he recalled what his grandfather used to say about such things: "Life is persistent."

How far down the cliff was he? Three-quarters, he guessed. That's where the largest mesquite was. If he moved wrong he would fall the rest of the way. The fall wouldn't be fatal from there, only about ten feet, but he wasn't certain how badly he was wounded and a fall from any height might cause significant internal damage.

What time was it? How long had he been unconscious? He reached out slowly with his left hand, lightly touching a branch and following it back to the trunk of the mesquite. The cliff was behind him, so he was facing east. He strained his head back to see if he could find the moon. It didn't seem to be in the east or directly overhead, so it had been hours. But how long?

He shifted his weight and a sharp pain shot through his side. He felt to where the pain was, discovering a broken branch had jabbed through the flesh above his right hip. He lifted himself up just a little, enough to free himself from the branch, a move he knew could be fatal if he started to hemorrhage. Better to leave it alone until he could see, but he could barely stand the pain. The branch had to go.

Now what? Not much of a choice. He had to wait for daylight so he could see around him so he could move; he had to see how bad his wounds were. And he had to stay awake.

He'd fallen before…

He got drunk for the first time in his life on the day he received the letter from his sister-in-law telling him that Margaret and David had died of the influenza on their trip back to visit her family in Vermont. He didn't know what else to do. He want to go berserk, and did kick a dog in the middle of the parade ground, but he wasn't mean enough back then to carry through on a true rampage. So he got drunk. Dutch said the alcohol eventually helped you to forget. Dutch forgot to tell him that the magic only worked while you were drinking. Dutch also didn't tell him that whiskey tasted like coal oil. So he got drunk on beer. He had to drink a lot of beers.

The second day he got drunk, Lieutenant John Bullis walked by him on a street in town, and grabbed him by the arm. "Get aholt of yourself, man. Drinking never solved any problem and we've all lost ones we've cared for. Snap out of it. If you're on duty drunk I won't have any compunction at all in breaking you down a stripe or two."

Ethan just nodded and walked to his horse, climbed into the saddle and rode away. Maybe, he thought, I won't ever be on duty again.

He rode and rode, and the ride eventually sobered him up which angered him. If he'd just learn to drink whiskey, he could carry enough in his canteen to get him good and drunk whenever and wherever he wanted, but a person couldn't carry enough beer unless you were driving a wagon with a keg. He hadn't been paying any attention to where he was going, just in a northerly direction. Northeast. That way was Vermont and home. And Margaret and David. How could they be gone? Margaret was so full of life and David had been wriggling around in her arms in a way that told him his son would grow into an adventurous man. Perhaps it was all a mistake somehow. No, he didn't believe that. So why was he riding in that direction, even if it was 2,000 miles and more away?

The shadows were long and he knew he was going to need some shelter soon. He started to pay attention to where he was, in some foot-hills, the oaks getting more plentiful. He saw a couple of sheltering trees and rode for them, pulling up abruptly when he saw the hole.

The sinkhole was huge. He dismounted, tied his horse to one of the trees, and walked to the lip of the hole. He carefully went to the edge, looking over into the abyss. His eyes could make out a few features in the dark, but he didn't see any bottom. He saw a slope to one side but it disappeared into the darkness. Several cave swallows flitted around the opening.

Then the bats came, just a few at first, then more and more. He stood at the edge mesmerized. The bats gushed out of the hole — thousands and thousands of them — and flew directly toward him. He couldn't move. At the last moment, the column veered upwards and just over his head in a broad, gray wave. He heard their small peeping, caught fleeting glimpses of their ghostly bodies, even felt the wind from the flapping of their wings. He thought the bats would stop after a few minutes, but they kept coming. And coming. He turned to see where they going. As they flew off they looked like a thick column of smoke drifting to the darkening sky. Hawks apparently had been waiting in the nearby trees for they occasionally darted out from their cover and snatched a bat, then flew back. Here the bats are thinking they're going out to find things to eat only some of them get eaten, he thought. That's the way life was, he knew. You eat and you're eaten. Seemed like the only things that didn't eat to live were plants and trees. They're stuck in the ground and can't forage. They have to wait for a rain just to get a drink of water, but nothing survives on water alone. How do they get to be older than people ever get? His grand-father told him once that plants ate sunshine. That seemed strange, but maybe that's why trees were so pure and grand. They drink water from the heaven and eat pure sunlight. Trees shield us from manmade things, all the square boxes we make to live in and move ourselves in and put our stuff in, the boxes we make to sit on and eat off. Trees hide those boxes a little and remind us that nature is the dominant force, the beautiful force, in this world and not what men create. And the trees will outlast all our little boxes. And this he was seeing, these millions of bats flying by his head without even touching him, just fussing with their peeps, bathing him in their wingwind, how could any man improve on this? It was exhilarating.

He turned back from watching the swooping hawks and lost his balance. He grabbed at the edge but only managed to slow his fall a little. He fell some feet, hit the slope and rolled down it, plopping into a pile of bat guano.

He stood up quickly out of the guano and brushed himself off as well as he could. He looked up. The mouth of the hole was at least forty feet above him and the sky was darker now. Well, never in his life had he thought he would die in a bat hole. But death always came out of season. If only it didn't smell so bad, he might be able to sleep through the night and when daylight came figure some way to climb out of the hole. He doubted he'd get any sleep tonight.

Ethan was wrong. Stress from the past few days, lack of sleep, prodigious beer intakes all combined to strike him unconscious almost the moment he found dry ground to sit on. A rope striking him in the face eventually woke him.

"Stop your snorin', you half-breed son of a bitch, and mebbe I'll be kind enough to get you outta there," a voice hollered from above. It was Dutch.

Ethan stood up and held the end of the rope. "Where'd you come from?"

"Got worried when you didn't show last night and came lookin' for your sorry ass," Dutch said. "But you're slap wastin' breath, so tie that line around you and I'll see if your horse's got the fortitude to drag you to daylight."

Ethan did as he was told. He heard Dutch encouraging the horse on and Ethan slowly floated out of the sinkhole.

Dutch helped Ethan to his feet and untied the rope. "Havin' fun, are you?"

"Hell of a lot," Ethan replied. "That's the devil's own sinkhole. You wouldn't believe the bats that live in there. Thousands... millions."

Dutch waved his hand across his face. "Yeah, I would. Smells like you've been rollin' in bat shit. How in hell did you survive? The stench alone would have killed me."

"You ever smell a rose?" Ethan asked.

"You still drunk?"

"Sober as a scorpion."

Dutch untied the three ropes, coiled them and tied one to his saddle and one to Ethan's and handed one to Benjamin Factor. It was the first Ethan noticed the young scout and answered the unasked question that was in his mind: how did saloonkeeper Dutch manage to find him. Ethan gave Benjamin an informal salute and smiled.

"A rose, huh? I don't think so," Dutch said. "I was in San Antonio one time and this old man come up to me selling flowers and he says I should buy some for my wife. I tell him I didn't have no wife. He says buy some for my sweetie, and I tell him I didn't have no lady friend. So he tells me to buy a bunch to celebrate my luck. Listen, bub, I got more important things to worry about than gallivanting around sniffin' petunias. What's a rose smell like?"

"If you haven't smelled one, it's difficult to describe. It's subtle and haunting. It lingers in your memory. When I was down there, I kept remembering how roses smelled. Margaret always had this aroma of rose water about her."

"Well, whatever it smells like, you ain't it. I passed a small creek back there, let's get you and them clothes into it."

"Kin yah find yer way back without me, sarnt?" Benjamin asked.

Ethan walked over to shake his hand. "I can, soldier. Thanks for finding me."

"Tweren't diffcult," Benjamin said, jumping on his horse. "Yah mades enough tracks fer foah people."

Benjamin rode south while the other two rode west to the creek where Ethan stripped down and sat in a hole in the creek bed so that the water came up to his chest. He scrubbed his uniform shirt and trousers while Dutch, sitting on a nearby rock on the bank, brushed off Ethan's boots.

"I don't think that's all comin' off," he said, pointing to Ethan's large, elaborate chest tattoos. "Why you have that atrocity?"

"It's Mic Mac tattoos," Ethan said, taking a deep breath. "It protects me from harm."

"Doin' a hell of a job."

"It has," Ethan said. "I didn't die down in that hole, but I could have. I didn't die during the War, but I could have. I was shot twice and bayoneted once. I could have died at Remolino when I got stuck with a Kickapoo arrow, damn thing pinned both my legs together, but I didn't. Actually, Ben Factor's father, Debo, pulled me out of that mess. I'd say these tattoos have done exactly what my grandfather said they would do."

"The one on your shoulders protect you from back shooters?"

"That one I don't know if it would. I don't think it has any special powers; some woman talked me into getting it. It's Hawaiian. Got it when I was on liaison duty in the Sandwich Islands."

"You're telling me a windy. Can't be no place named after a sandwich."

"Earl of Sandwich," Ethan said. "That's the same guy they named sandwiches after."

"This guy and these islands all named for sandwiches?"

"No. They— Never mind that. These islands are out in the Pacific, way beyond California. Ruled by a mighty native king and some mighty pretty wahines."

"OK, you're losin' me."

"Great looking women there," Ethan said. "Very friendly, too. Nothing like we have in this country. Margaret knew where the Sandwich Islands were. I promised I'd take her there one day. I promised. "

He rose from the water, walked to the bank and carefully laid his clothes out on rocks to dry. He found his own rock and rolled back on it, letting the sun warm him, listening to the cicadas thrum.

"You know, Margaret was appalled when she first saw my tattoos. I tried to explain that they protect me, but in her refined society they were a sign of criminality and debauchery. Eh-yeah, she is… was a well-educated woman. Went to UVM."

"You're losin' me again. What in hell's a U-V-M?"

"Universitas Viridis Montis. Means the University of the Green

Mountains in Latin. Vermont is French for Green Mountains. So it's the University of Vermont."

"Geesh, why not just say it in English then, why fancy it all up? That's the trouble with you educated Easterners, always got to fancy things up."

"Eh-yeah, well, I'm certainly not too fancy. Not by her standards. She saw these tattoos and just recoiled. She rattled off some scientific book nonsense by some doctor. Lombroso? This doctor, she said, had clearly linked body markings and crime. It was an essential characteristic of primitive man, and of men who still live in the savage state, I think is what she said. Said the doctor said that. Savage."

"She thinkin' you still lived in that savage state?"

"Don't we? She never said as much, but I think she began to think so," Ethan said, closing his eyes, recalling her rose water again. "She thought after we got married I would take her away on all these travels, see all the exotic places I told her about. But all she ever saw was Brackettville. And me gone a lot of the time on patrols. Gone. I'd put my buckskins on and I could tell what she was thinking, that I was under it all still a redskin. Eh-yeah, I think by the time David was born she was getting disillusioned with savage ol' me and savage ol' Texas. I think if she hadn't died, we might have started to have some serious problems staying married."

…The first ray of sunlight that spiked over the Chisos woke Ethan immediately. He was sore to his bones. He could clearly see his surroundings now: the mesquite bush held him strong. It took him many minutes but he managed to roll to his left, getting new pricks with each inch he moved out of the thorny shrub and onto the cliff face. He stayed still for awhile, breathing deeply. He rolled onto his back and sat up. He was covered in bright red blood. New wounds. And dark blood was caked on his shirt and trousers. Yesterday's wounds. Still sitting, he slid down the cliff, going too fast for his liking but he had no choice.

Once on the desert floor, he got his small knife from his boot and slit his buckskin shirt open and peeled it back. He had at least a dozen small, puckered wounds on his chest, each wound haloed in caked blood. He took as deep a breath as he could. Still no pain in breathing.

From the size of the wounds, he guessed he'd been hit with bird shot. The small pellets had been slowed considerably by the stiff, new leather of his shirt. It might have saved his life, he thought.

He walked about a quarter of a mile to where he could easily walk back up the hill, then back to his jacal. He looked inside and saw what he expected. The place was torn apart and his valuables hidden in the rafters were gone. His gun belt and Remington had been tossed on the bed; his Spencer was by the door. He grabbed both. Back outside, he pulled his saddle from a lean-to shelter built on the back side of his shack and struggled with it over to his horse. The pain was slowing him down, but he managed to get the saddle up on the horse's back. He strapped on his gun belt, stowed the rifle in its scabbard, then pulled himself up. He rode to Lajitas.

Ethan rode into the village in mid afternoon. No one took particular notice of him as he rode to the Mejor Que Nada.

"Who put a spoke in your wheel?" Dutch said as Ethan walked inside, looking like he just survived a buffalo stampede.

"Gracey here?" Ethan asked.

"In back. Why?"

"I'm going to need a new shirt."

•

Brackettville

The court martial for Quartermaster Sergeant Paschal Erny, Private Charles Postlewaite, and Private Lawrence Rosenblatt was over. General Ord himself presided over a quick trial — all of three and a half hours. The board didn't even bother retiring to consider their verdict. Ord sentenced Postlewaite and Rosenblatt to 10 years at hard labor, Erny to 20. The general told Erny he would have preferred hanging him, but hadn't been able to find any regulation that would allow him to do that. It was still, they all knew, a life sentence for the 42-year-old quartermaster.

With the court martial over, Wyatt settled for playing poker at the Bucket of Blood saloon when he would rather be dealing faro in

Tombstone. One last hand, then he would retire early. It was now past midnight.

He missed his faro games and he missed his brothers. He didn't miss Mattie much. She was getting far too jugheaded and wring-tailed to suit him. He was glad he'd never married her. If he ever got married again, he'd make damn certain it was someone he was compatible with. Right now, he couldn't get Jo-Jo out of his mind. He was getting obsessed with that dog-faced girl. Go home to Mattie or try for another coupling or two — maybe more — with Jo-Jo? It was like holding aces in a two-handed game: the bet was obvious.

She said they were traveling toward the west, and that's the way he would go. The stage to Fort Davis, then another to El Paso, and linger a while at each town. Earn a little money, perhaps. See if Jo-Jo showed up. The idea of slipping over her sweaty, naked body with her thick whiskers tickling his cheeks made him smile.

CHAPTER 12

Wild Horse Draw, near Van Horn Wells, Texas

Lieutenant Maxon rode at the head of his column, glad to be returning to Fort Davis and end his 40-day-long patrol. He'd never been in the field that long before and neither had any of his men; the last two weeks they lived on hardtack and whatever game the scouts could shoot, usually jackrabbits. He was also glad to be returning with his troop intact. Only four men wounded in all that time, none seriously.

His orders had been clear: split up his half of H Troop of the 10th to guard four watering holes along the Sierra Diablos from the Guadalupes to Van Horn Wells then return after 40 days. His friend and fellow lieutenant John Bigelow was guarding the Van Horn area and south to Wild Rose with the other half of the understrength troop.

Appearing across the flat plain to the east was a sight he hoped he wouldn't see. One of the scouts was galloping toward the column.

Corporal July barely managed to rein in his mount, his horse colliding with Maxon's. "Them same Apaches, sir. Two miles behind me and heading our ways."

"They mean to engage us?"

"My guess. I spied theys real low on water. Plenty of food, but theys ain't drinking. Theys coming to get ours."

Meeting an enemy on an open plain was not good tactics, Maxon knew. He squirmed in his saddle, looking around. No high ground or cover within miles. If they ran, perhaps they could keep the Apaches behind them until they got into Wild Rose Pass. It would be a long ride and tough on their horses, but the only alternative he saw was to kill their mounts outright, dig in behind them and use them for cover. That was desperation.

"Sergeant, forward, at a gallop!" Maxon ordered. His first sergeant repeated the order and the troop raced to the southeast.

They all saw the dust rising from the desert plain about the same time, angling towards them. Maxon now had to decide whether it was worthwhile to order his men to draw carbines or concentrate on running. He hated to not be able to return fire, but reloading the trap door Springfields on a galloping horse was difficult at best. He wished for the older, repeating Spencers that Bigelow's troop had. He cursed Army administrators in Washington, sitting safely behind their desks, ordering the change to the Springfields to prevent panicking soldiers from wasting ammunition. Ammunition, after all, was expensive. He waved First Sergeant Shropshire to his side.

"Pick four of your best sharpshooters and position them on the east side of the column. Have them draw carbines and engage the hostiles as well as they are able without slowing down. Get them extra ammo from some of the others. Hold their fire until the hostiles get close enough for decent shots. You're in charge of the four and if at any time it appears you're in more danger than the column as a whole I want you to withdraw into the safety of the column, sheath carbines and ride like hell with the rest of us."

The first sergeant pulled his horse around in the middle of a salute. "Yes, sir!"

It seemed like only seconds before the Apaches reached the soldiers. Maxon couldn't tell how many warriors raced toward them since they were surrounded in much dust, but he guessed more than a dozen. In the last skirmish, his men must have killed several of their warriors and some were now likely to be guarding the women and children. That put the Apaches at a numerical disadvantage, but Maxon knew his men would still pay dearly if they fought them head on in the open. He guessed the Apaches riding toward them from the east were about a quarter-mile away.

"Sir!" Sergeant Kurney said to his right. Maxon turned and saw what Kurney was warning him about: another group of Apaches riding toward them from the west, perhaps a mile off. Eight to ten, he guessed.

"Ride like hell, sergeant," Maxon ordered, out of breath.

The Apaches in the east opened fire to no effect. The column continued galloping ahead and Shropshire's men held their fire for a couple more minutes then opened up. Two Apaches fell from their mounts, one grabbing for his horse as he went down, the other falling back with a thud Maxon heard even amid all the noise of the column's horses and his men's gear clanking. Maxon wished he could get his first sergeant's attention to send two of the sharpshooters to the west side of the column, but that was impossible now. The Apaches dropped to the off side of their horses as they approached closer and fired their rifles one-handed under their horses' necks. One of the troopers dropped off his mount; not one of the sharpshooters. Return fire dropped one of the Apache horses. Maxon considered dismounting his men for a brief moment but was determined he wouldn't be caught like Custer. This was a cavalry troop, damn it, and if his coloreds were to die it was going to be while mounted. The Apaches on the east side dropped back, trailing the column at a walk. The Apaches on the west began firing and one of the soldiers fell forward in his saddle, but not off it. Maxon heard return fire and twisted to see that Shropshire had led his four sharpshooters through the column as it flew forward. They were now on its west side. That man's going in for a medal if I survive long enough to write the citation, he thought. The sharpshooters fired another volley, turning the charging Apaches back. The west and east groups of hostiles gathered together as the cavalry troop rushed on. They split again, galloping to catch up with the soldiers.

The fight continued for several miles, longer than Maxon thought possible. They stopped and dismounted twice, letting the horses rest as long as they dared. When they rested and all the troopers shouldered their weapons, the Apaches withdrew to just beyond rifle range and waited until the soldiers remounted. Then the pursuit continued. He knew of two of his men definitely killed, two more wounded. He'd seen five Apaches unhorsed, seven of their horses killed or fatally wounded. And still the Apache came at them. They hit and they ran. They hit again and ran again. Again and again. Ten miles. Twelve miles. Maxon was thankful the Apaches were such terrible shots because he'd lost only five men now and at the outset of this fight he was worried that none of them would survive. His horse began gasping for breath. He heard one of the horses behind him stumble and out of the corner of his eye saw one of the troopers race back and pull the other trooper up behind him as the first man's horse struggled painfully in the desert dirt, failing repeatedly to get to its feet. Ahead, to the right, Maxon saw an outcropping of several large rocks and headed directly toward them. As he reached the rocks, he leaped from his horse, drawing his pistol. Other troopers gathered beside him.

"Kurney, get the troop dismounted and get a couple of men to hold the horses. Everyone else, draw carbines and fire at will!" Maxon shouted, gesturing with his pistol in the air.

He watched as the rest of the troop galloped to the rocks. The horse under one of the men — Private Tockes — stumbled and dropped to his front knees. The trooper spurred and hollered at his mount to get it up. Several Apaches were near enough to get good shots and one bullet found Tockes and one found his horse. As the bullet struck the horse, the horse jumped up but balked at moving forward. Maxon could see Tockes was bleeding from his side, the horse was bleeding from its neck. Maxon saw the sheer terror in the horse's eyes as Tockes spurred it. But the horse refused to move forward even as the Apaches got closer.

"Damn you!" Tockes said. "If you won't go that way, go this!" The trooper yanked the reins as hard as he could, turning his mount's head. The horse jumped again, and galloped directly into the five Apaches. Tockes fired his carbine but the shot missed. He tossed the rifle at one Apache, who ducked it, but Tockes drew his pistol and shot that Apache square in the face. He emptied his revolver, but the Apaches shot over and over until both the trooper and his mount fell together on the plain. Tockes had bought enough time for the remainder of the troop to get to the safety of the rocks. The image of the dead trooper still clinging to his dead mount, his boots still in the stirrups, would stay with Maxon forever as he told the story over and over again about the man he saw die a true cavalryman's death.

Maxon's dismounted troopers fired at the Apaches around Tockes' body. They didn't hit anyone, but the Apaches withdrew heading to the hills in the distant east.

•

Apache Camp, Hard Luck Canyon, Texas

"We need water," Upsidedown said softly to Lozen. She nodded. She knew. Three of her warriors were dead, along with seven horses. She bounded up, strode away from the band and said her prayer, all too quickly. She wasn't concentrating. She couldn't. She spun hurriedly. Still… her Power said to continue south.

"We can't afford another fight with the Pale Eyes," Upsidedown said when she returned. She nodded. She knew.

"Wolf," she said. "We must go where we know water will be. We must go to the long river. Scout ahead and find us a place that will be safe for us to camp. We need to rest for several suns, even a moon."

Wolf Rising scowled, but left immediately.

•

Lajitas

Gracey squeezed the last of the pellets from Ethan's chest; they had barely penetrated his skin. He was stretched out on Dutch's bed and Dutch and Joaquin looked on.

"You are one lucky hombre," Gracey said, washing his chest carefully with soap and water. She rinsed it as carefully.

Dutch shook his head. "Slap luckiest man I ever knew. Shoulda been dead a long, long time ago."

Gracey poured some whiskey onto a rag and rubbed that over Ethan's wounds. The scout wincing just a little. "I hate the smell of whiskey," he said.

"Who did this?" Joaquin asked.

Ethan scowled at him, noticing a little thrill in the voice. "Ready to play Ranger, are you?"

"Be serious," Joaquin said. "Tell us what happened and I swear to you I'll bring them to justice."

"Eh-yeah, well, you won't likely do it all by your lonesome. Was four of them. Four of them sneaked up behind me —"

"I find that hard as hell to believe," Dutch said. "I never saw anyone sneak up on you in your life, including a lizard."

"Happened," Ethan said. "I guess I'm just getting old. That edge is fading."

"You said four people attacked you. Who? Why?" Joaquin said.

Gracey broke open an aloe vera plant, working the pulp between her fingers then rubbed it onto Ethan's wounds. She handed him a clean, white nightshirt. "Put this on."

"Not likely. I won't sleep wrapped in a shroud."

"This will keep your wounds clean so I do not have to bind you up."

Ethan scowled again, grabbed the nightshirt and winced at the pain of moving too fast, then pulled the garment over his head and downward.

"Those four people?" Joaquin asked again.

"They were from that medicine freak show," Ethan said. "The big muscleman and the peg-legged man, another man and a woman. They wanted my gold coins. Got them, too."

Joaquin turned abruptly and left.

"Hold up!" Ethan called after him. Joaquin stopped and leaned back in by the door of Dutch's apartment. "Look, find out what you can but, promise me, don't go off by yourself. They're probably halfway to Presidio or Burgess Springs by now and they won't be difficult to track, but you're going to need help."

"You ain't goin' nowhere," Dutch said.

Gracey handed Ethan a glass half full of whiskey. "Dutch is right. You feel like you can now maybe, but you have lost much blood. You will tire easily. These wounds might get inflamed. You need to rest. And drink this."

He waved the drink away. "No whiskey."

"Hey, bub, this is my best stuff. Untainted Tennessee sippin' whiskey. Do you good."

"Drink it, you hard-headed son of a bitch," Joaquin said.

"I'll do it, if you promise not to go anyplace without me," Ethan said. Joaquin nodded and left. Ethan gulped down the whiskey, his face convulsing but he appreciated the warmth down to his stomach.

Joaquin stormed over to the gathered show wagons. The wind was kicking up the dust a little, but it offered no respite from the oppressive heat that had returned yesterday. The breeze felt hotter than the air. He felt the sweat gathering between his shoulder blades, on his forehead, and in his crotch. Doc and Tiny Alice were sitting on camp chairs, Doc shaking his head and mumbling while Alice sobbed softly between hiccups.

"What do you know about this?" Joaquin demanded.

"About what? About being ruined?" Doc said.

"I think you know."

"Sonny, don't be babbling to me when I'm facing ruination," Doc said. Alice touched Doc on his arm then rose and pulled herself up into the wagon.

"My friend has been robbed and almost killed, so I'm more concerned about that than whatever your problem is right about now," Joaquin said. "He said it was some of your people."

Doc looked up and waved him arm at the other wagons. "Anyway, that's something I don't doubt. I had my best man leave me before we came south, then I find out this morning that four others have fled the coop. Left me high and dry without so much as a goodbye." He stopped to catch his breath, afraid he was drifting off into a spiel. "Alice is all I have left, and all these empty wagons. How am I going to get these wagons anywhere? But anyway, the show is a true ruin now. It took me years to find the right people and build up the right sort of show that would entertain as well as help people out here on the frontier. Now all that time and hard work is gone."

"Where'd they go?"

"Stumps me," Doc said in a heavy sigh. "I guess I don't even care now. Makes no difference."

"Makes a difference to me. I aim to bring them to justice."

Doc chuckled just a little. "Good luck with that."

"Do you have idea where they might go?"

"Son, let me explain something to you," Doc said. "I doubt I even know these people's true names. I doubt I even know where they are truly from. I certainly have no inkling about their families or backgrounds. If any of these people were capable of learning a trade or willing to work hard at an honest living, they wouldn't have signed on with me. Anyway, each of them is probably running away from their own demons, real or imagined. I'm sorry for your friend, but I can't imagine how I can help."

Joaquin was quiet for a while, looking around, thinking. "If I find out you had anything to do with this, I'll nail your hide to this side of the river and stretch it over to the other."

"And just who are you to threaten me in this manner?"

"I'm a Texas Ranger, you snake oil salesman," Joaquin snapped.

"Kind of young for that."

Joaquin stepped over and kicked Doc off his folding wooden chair into the dust. As he walked back to Dutch's room, he felt something was out of place. He stopped in his tracks and looked around. Ethan had taught him to see in patterns first, to notice any disruption in patterns, then concentrate on the details. When he realized what it was, it was obvious. Too few horses in the big corral behind Tío José's small cantina. He walked over and without counting knew that four horses were missing, including two of his. He opened the small wooded shed by the moveable crosspieces in the fence that served as a gate and saw four saddles of the five usually kept there were missing. He was glad his own tack was in his room and Dutch kept his in the storage room behind the saloon. The group's tracks were obvious: they headed east.

He wanted to saddle up and ride after the bastards, but turned and went back to talk with Ethan.

"The Doc says he doesn't know a thing about what happened," Joaquin said. "But they've up and left him and stole four horses in the process. Two of 'em mine."

"Which way did they go?" Ethan asked.

Joaquin liked the fact that the scout assumed he knew the answer.

"East. They're head back to Burgess Springs, from there ¿quien sabe? I think I better get after them, they could be at a stage stop in two, three days."

Gracey shot Ethan a threatening look as he sat up in bed. "You need rest!"

"I can rest later," he said to her. To Joaquin, he said, "You can't go after four desperate people alone. These folks ain't amateurs. They hustle people for a living. They had no hesitation about pulling the trigger on me and the only reason I'm sitting here right now is because they were sloppy, didn't check their weaponry, and all that scattergun had in it was bird shot."

"We've been out-numbered before," Joaquin said.

"Eh-yeah, and look what happened. How did you get out of that mess?"

"I had a hand..."

"You certainly did. So did Dutch. I doubt I could have done it without your help, but that's my point. One of us alone can't take them down."

Joaquin removed his hat and wiped sweat from the band with two fingers then wiped his forehead with the back of his sleeve. "One of us alone can track them down."

"Eh-yeah, that should be easy. I doubt they have a clue about hiding their tracks. And I imagine they're just riding the road north. So, yeah, you can track them alone. Then what? No law to help you in Burgess Springs. You can't contact your Ranger pards any faster than you can ride to Fort Davis on your own. No talking wire down in these parts. These folks could be long gone by then."

"We can't just do nothing," Joaquin said anxiously.

Ethan took a deep breath, felt a sharp pain in his side, and settled back onto the bed. "Give me a good night's sleep. Tomorrow we'll head out after them. You up for a ride, Dutch?"

"Bet your sweet ass," Dutch said. "But you shouldn't be goin'."

"Gracey, did I break any bones? Have anything I might tear open riding?" Ethan asked.

She frowned. "No bones broke, just bruises. The small wounds will not harm you if you keep them clean until they heal over. The wound in your side, well, that is another matter. I sewed it up good and it should hold but if you go riding I cannot say. No sé."

"If you wrap me up real good, you think that would be OK?"

"No sé, no sé, no sé," Gracey said, frustrated.

"If I open it up, I'll head right back."

"No you will not. You're like the mule."

"I promise," he said.

"You need rest! Many days," she said.

"Everybody out. Gracey says I need rest and I'll get some. Be ready to go in the morning. I know a couple different shortcuts north and we can get way ahead of them," Ethan said. They turned to leave but he grabbed Gracey's arm and pulled her down to him and kissed her forehead. "I promise."

CHAPTER 13
Along the Terlingua/Burgess Springs Road

Jo-Jo didn't particularly want to kill Earl, but she saw no other way. The money could buy her a life of freedom, finally, but not if she had to share it with three others. She thought she found protection with the show. No one would recognize her as Jo-Jo the Dog-Faced Girl and that made her feel safe from her brothers who must be searching desperately for her. But they went and stole the gold coins and killed that old man so now she no longer had that protection.

The only protection she knew of was in Fort Davis, with the tall, handsome, cold-eyed man who was kind to her. He would protect her. At least until she could find a way to get far enough away where her brothers wouldn't follow. They had a farm to run now on their own so they might not follow her far or for very long. But she felt they were close by. They had to be. Wyatt would protect her until she could get thousands of miles away and this money would help her get there. Maybe she could even get more from Wyatt.

Killing Earl was easy enough. The two of them camped away from the others and in the middle of the night she picked up the largest rock she could lift and bashed his head in with one blow. It had been much quicker than with the old Jo-Jo. In that hotel room in Bracket-tville she had no rock, she had to use the empty chamberpot. She'd been asleep and the first blow stunned the woman. More quick blows and she was dazed. She groaned some, and that made her a little sorry, but the sadness quickly turned to anger when the old Jo-Jo just wouldn't die quickly enough. She didn't know how many times she hit her, but after a while her arm hurt. She thought the brass of the pot would have been strong enough to kill the other woman quickly, but she was wrong. So she had to smother her with a pillow, had to sit on the pillow to put her weight to work because she wasn't quite strong enough to hold the pillow down when the old Jo-Jo began flailing. But she finally died like she had to. How could she become Jo-Jo if the old Jo-Jo was still alive? Then she gathered up her things, some money the old Jo-Jo had in her purse, spilled the lamp's contents over the bed and curtains and set the room on fire. No one would ever know what actually happened to the old Jo-Jo. Now she was the new Jo-Jo, but the show was behind her now. For good. So she guessed she was Cynthia again, but for some reason she still thought of herself as Jo-Jo. She didn't particularly like being Cynthia…

That last morning Monpere came to her she just had enough. He and her three brothers had used her for years to satisfy their lusts. She tried to push him off her, but the old man had muscles like steel springs. She took him as she usually did, but this time her anger built to where she couldn't contain it. She looked around her bed and saw salvation in a pair of scissors on the bedside table. Without hesitation, she grabbed them and plunged them deeply into her father's neck. His warm blood flooded over her and she struggled to get out from under him. While he bled to death face down on her bed, she wiped herself clean with her bedspread and dressed. She knew she'd have to leave before the boys found out. They'd kill her or worse for this.

She packed what little she had in a carpet bag then went into the kitchen to see Mamere. Her brothers and their wives were already in the fields. She knew Mamere kept some money hidden away in a jar in one of the cupboards and she needed that money.

"Oh, my Lord, child! What have you done, child!" her mother wailed when she told her. Mamere rushed down the hallway to the bedroom to see for herself that Monpere was dead. When she returned, she slapped her daughter as hard as she could.

"You devil!" Mamere screamed, slapping her again.

"I need money to get away before they boys come home," she said.

"Money! You kill your own father and have the terrible gumption to demand money from me, child! What have you done!"

"Me? Why am I the fault? Why didn't you stop him all these years. And the boys, too. You knew. You let it happen. This is their fault and your fault but it isn't my fault. How could you let this happen to me? I couldn't take any more."

"That's what men do!" Mamere said, slapping her daughter again, sending her stumbling to the sink. "That's a woman's lot in

232

life."

She turned and opened the cupboard where she knew the money was. Her mother lunged, slamming the door on her fingers.

"No, child! You will not go anywhere and not with my money! You'll stay here and suffer the consequences and suffer you will!"

She fell back from Mamere's large frame, her hands catching her balance on the sink. When her hand touched a large butcher knife, she didn't even think about what she was doing. She grabbed the knife and lashed forward with it and slashed her mother's throat.

Mamere was shocked and dropped to her knees, grasping her throat with her hands. She tried to talk but only terrible noise came forth. After just a little while she fell back on her heels and slumped, dead, adding more blood to the Laroch farmhouse.

...She had the blood of her parents, of the old Jo-Jo, and now of Earl on her hands. And none of it her fault. If people would just leave her alone they would be alive and happy now. Well, they would be alive.

•

Max found Earl's body long after sunrise. He and Jasper figured Earl was getting some early-morning sugar so they didn't want to disturb him at first. But then they got worried that someone might have found the old man they killed by now and be after them, although they doubted that. It might be weeks, if ever, before they found that hermit's body so far from the town. But better safe than sorry.

Jasper pitched a fit when Max told him what happened. "That bitch. I haven't trusted her, not from the beginning. I doubt if she was even a sister to Jo-Jo."

"We're wasting time," Max said. "She mifet be some hours ahead ef us."

Jasper struggled to mount his horse. "You look for the gold?"

Max nodded. "Noffin. We gone bury Earl?"

"He made his bed, let him rot in it," Jasper said and spurred off.

Max followed.

●

Lajitas

"Sure you're up to this?" Dutch asked Ethan as the three of them rode out of town.

"Eh-yeah. I'll be fine."

"We should have started much earlier," Joaquin said.

"Patience is a virgin," Dutch said.

"So I over-slept," Ethan said. "Gracey said I needed the rest. It was just what I needed and I'm just fine now. Almost back to normal."

They followed the road east for a short while, then Ethan led them into the mountains north of the road.

"You know," Ethan said after a while, "I'm not even sure why I'm doing this. I can't take money with me when I die. I've never wanted riches, just peace and quiet."

"They were going to give you peace and quiet. They meant to kill you," Joaquin said.

"Eh-yeah. I suppose this is another lesson for you. If somebody tries to kill you, kill them back."

"We'll try to arrest them first. Remember that."

"Tell them," Dutch said.

●

Standing beside Karl's wagon on the mesa, Ingrid and Karl watched Dutch, Joaquin and Ethan ride out of town.

"We need to leave now," she said. He turned and hitched up his draught horse. "I want to be gone for a long time before they get back. I want to be on a train tomorrow."

He laughed as he fixed the straps. "That will not happen tomorrow. First we have to go to Fort Leaton. That may take us three days. Then we have to decide whether to wait for one of their ox trains going to Fort Davis and go with them or continue on to Presidio and wait for the stage to Fort Davis. That could be a week, perhaps even more. Then we have to wait on the San Antonio stage and it will be another several days before we get to the train depot."

"But we will go to Galveston?" she moaned. "As quickly as we can?"

"Then they went away quickly… fearful but overjoyed."

"Please, Karl," she said, touching his knee as he sat down in the wagon seat beside her.

"Good habits are difficult to break," he said, slapping the horse's backside with the reins.

•

Along the Río Grande between Lajitas and Alamito Creek

Wolf Rising didn't want to admit to himself that he was getting apprehensive going out on his own. Too many Pale Eye soldiers were around in places they shouldn't be. And he worried about seeing the devil-horse again. This year would go down in the annals of the People as the very worst in all of time. He didn't like being part of it.

He met the long river in a familiar place, many miles between the Pale Eye settlements. He relaxed for a while here, letting his pony drink and graze. The sound of the water rushing over the rocks in the shallow portion of the river here calmed him. He wished he could listen to that sound forever. Although he loved this spot, it was not a good place for the band to camp. It was too exposed. The nearby canyon offered little protection because it was too broad and it's mouth was also exposed to the road the Pale Eyes had created between their settlements. But for now, it was a good place to rest.

He woke when the sun began to burn his eyes. He hadn't meant to fall asleep. He walked into the shallow part of the river to splash water in his face. His pony snorted at him.

"I know," he said, walking to the horse. "We should be on our way." He mounted and rode along the river side of the road westward.

He didn't think he would meet any Pale Eyes along the road and he didn't. If he had, it would be a simple thing to get out of sight because the river grasses and cane would hide him. He had never traveled this portion of the river before so he carefully memorized it. He knew the area east of here up into the Chisos, but now the Pale Eyes soldiers occupied too much of the land for the band to travel safely.

As he rode on, the river traveled through a canyon formed by steep walls, so he had to follow the road for a while. He came to one inviting place, a narrow slit in the canyon wall forming its own little canyon. He dismounted and walked into the dark. The walls were steep and the floor twisted like a snake; bright sunlight mixed with the darkness here and there. It would be a good place to camp but had no water, unless the canyon led to the river. He trailed down the canyon as far as he could, having to scramble around drops and rocks that blocked the path. At one point he thought the canyon walls were closing together, but they didn't. But he reached a point where he could go no further without help; the drops were too steep. He turned around and walked out, remounted and rode on.

At the head of the large canyon, the river flowed by several strange rocks, tall and misshapen, and Wolf Rising thought they looked a little like demons. This area, too, was too exposed for a good camp even if he did feel comfortable around the balancing rocks, which he wasn't.

To the north he saw a broad canyon sweeping down from the mountains. He rode in. This was a good place, he thought. Much of it was hidden by hills and it wasn't far from the river and its water. He saw a deep cave on the face of one of the canyon walls and it looked like it could be accessed easily. Good shelter, if inconvenient. He would remember this place.

He continued riding along the road and was surprised by another strange looking rock looming over the desert. It, too, had a demon look about it but then he noticed its companion rock that looked like a giant turtle. A good sign. The rocks of the cliffs had been washed smooth and dozens of holes had been scooped out of their faces. As far as he could see, the cliffs were filled with these holes, each about the size of a curled up man. He rode a little up the canyon, not as broad as the one before but just as deep, heading up into the mountains. Before he had ridden too far in, he noticed the ground was wet. The damp soil gave way to a trickle of water that came from a small creek that was fed by a spring. The water flowed from the spring, down the canyon and disappeared into the ground before it got to the odd rocks. He tasted from the spring.

This was the place, he knew. It had sweet water. It was hidden from view. And it was guarded by a turtle god. He would camp here tonight. Tomorrow he would ride back to his shallow place on the river, then back to the band with his good news.

•

The Laroch Family Farm, Castroville, Texas

The Laroch brothers sat in rocking chairs on the expansive porch of the main farmhouse enjoying their after supper smokes. Henry Jun, the eldest, named after his father, lit his pipe and sucked on it three quick times, then a long one. Claude, the middle brother, already had his pipe lit. Teeny Henry, also named for his father, smoked a very large cigar.

"Ever wander where Cyndy go?" Claude asked.

"Not too much, but we've got beaucoup to tank her for," Teeny Henry replied, motioning with his cigar over fields that stretched as far as they could see, if it weren't so dark. "With Monpere and Mamere gone, this is all of it ours. Tout."

"Mais I miss her some," Henry Jun said. "Especially dose days when my wife's on the rag."

"Dat's a fact," Teeny Henry said. "But look at it dis way. Your oldest daughter be ready in a couple years."

They all nodded agreement and enjoyed the cool, night breeze.

CHAPTER 14
Along the Rio Grande

The morning dawned hot and so muggy that Ingrid couldn't seem to get enough air into her lungs. Her stomach was queasy this morning, but it settled down as quickly as it had before when she felt this way. It rained during the night, stopping just before she and Karl woke in the back of his wagon, and mists were rising from the Río Grande in delicate roils. They camped just past the big hill on the road, where the river was shallow. The sounds of the water falling across the rocks lulled them into a deep sleep the night before and the rain that fell gently for the two hours before dawn kept them deep asleep. Only when the rain ceased and birds started to greet the rising sun did they stir.

It was the first time Ingrid and Karl had ever slept together. They'd enjoy sex with each other many times over their years, but it was always surreptitious, hiding either from parents or her spouse. All they'd done last night was sleep, Karl holding her protectively in his massive arms all night long, both of them fully clothed.

Now he was gone, walking back down river looking for a private place to relieve himself, while she fried bacon in a skillet over the small campfire he built before he left. The sizzle of the bacon mingled with the burble of the water and the songs of orioles and cactus wrens as the sun rose just high enough to start burning off the mists. It was, she thought, the finest morning of her life.

When she heard someone behind her, she thought it was Karl returning even though he hadn't been gone very long, so she turned with a wide smile. Instead of Karl, she saw a frightening sight: a wild Indian crouching down, his knife drawn, a cap made of wild looking feathers, a stripe of deep red painted across his nose and under his eyes. He was close enough that she saw loathing in the black eyes. Her own eyes darted around quickly, hoping to see Karl but she didn't. She hoped he was unharmed. Two years ago, this situation would have panicked her. She would have frozen and screamed and acted like the sheltered, spoiled little girl she was. No more. Her hand was still on the handle of the iron skillet so she turned and threw the hot grease and bacon directly into the Indian's face. He screamed, dropping his knife as his hands went to his burning face. She tried to hit him on the side of his head, but the skillet struck one of his hands. As she pulled the skillet back to hit him again, he backed away quickly, turned and ran.

Karl came running to her side. "What happened? I heard a yell and I saw someone running away. Are you all right?"

"I'm OK," she said, hugging him around his waist. "An Indian was creeping up on me. Look, he had that knife in his hand. I don't know what he meant to do, but I was afraid he might have found you first. I threw the bacon at him."

"Bacon made him yell like that?"

She laughed through her nose, shaking her head. "The hot grease did."

"I think we should get down to Fort Leaton as quickly as we can," he said. "If that Indian has friends, we do not want to have to deal with them alone."

Karl checked to make certain his rifle was fully loaded and placed it on the wagon seat. He hitched up his horse as fast as he could and they drove off.

•

In the Mountains North of Terlingua

"Is that what I think it is?" Joaquin asked, trying to control his balking horse.

"Camel," Ethan confirmed, as the beast brayed at them for blocking the pass between two small mountains with candellila and lechuguilla dotting the buff-colored dirt.

"What in damnation is a camel doing out in the Big Bend country?" Dutch said. "This slap ain't Araby."

Their horses continued to resist going forward while the camel was in front of them, its unknown scent and sound confusing them, while the camel refused to move. "Used to be plenty around, before the war," Ethan said, dismounting. They followed his example as he grabbed his horse's bit and walked toward the great, russet, foul-smelling beast. "Jeff Davis himself had this idea when he was Secretary of War that the cavalry would be better off on camels than on horses, so the army conducted an experiment out on our desert for a while. Camels better than horses. Worked well, too. But then that war got in the way. The army just abandoned most of the camels to fend for themselves, and after the war nobody wanted to pick up where Davis left off since nobody wanted to champion an idea thought up by the president of the late Rebellion."

The three men pulled their mounts forward as the camel brayed louder but backed up.

"Had a friend, Polly Rodriguez, used to make money rounding up stray camels," Ethan said as the camel finally gave up and ran off.

"How'd this woman chase down camels?" Dutch asked as they remounted.

"Polly was a he. Policarpo. He was a camel herder back in the late '50s when the army was conducting that experiment, so he knew how to handle them. He got to know camels. After the war, the state of Texas had a pile of complaints from ranchers and travelers about running into camels, so they hired a couple people to round them up or kill them. Polly earned more money from Texas getting rid of camels than he ever did from the army for herding them."

"Hell of thing," Dutch said shaking his head.

"They smell something terrible, sulfur kinda," Joaquin said.

"They taste OK," Ethan said. "A little like prairie dog cooked over buffalo chips."

Joaquin scowled. "How far ahead do you think they are?"

"Good question. I've been thinking I should probably scout around and see what I can see," Ethan said. "If I do that, I think it's best for the two of you to continue through this pass and on to the road. Go to the road. It's a couple miles ahead. You'll see it when you get through the pass. We could go up over those mountains and get to Burgess Springs ahead of them, assuming they're on the road, but I don't see any reason to do that. It's a rough climb for the horses. Too rough. We'll catch them soon enough."

"Then what do you want to go off for?" Dutch asked.

240

Ethan chewed on the inside of his lip and nodded to the north. "Two things. Mainly, I want to make certain they are on the road. If they're in the mountains we'd be wasting a lot of time trying to head them off before they reached Burgess Springs. I don't think they are. They're city people. They'll stay to roads. But I want to be sure. Plus… I don't know how to explain it… but the camel made me a little leery. It's got my hackles raised, and I'm worried we may not be alone. No evidence for that, I'm just uneasy. I want to look around."

"You shouldn't be off alone," Dutch said.

"I'm fine," Ethan said.

"But don't you try to take them by yourself if you run into them," Joaquin said.

"That goes for the two of you, too," he said, turning to the west. "I'll see you after sundown. Make a big fire but don't sleep around it."

●

Along the Terlingua/Burgess Springs Road

"Jo-Jo has to be in Fort Davis by now," Jasper said as they stopped to swill water from their canteens. "We stole some worthless nags."

"Hosses can't go all dey long and neifer can we," Max said. "You ride 'em too hard."

"Don't tell me how to ride a God damned horse!"

"I wassn. Jest some facks mebbe you forget. You doan ride much."

"I know how to ride a God damned horse!"

Max shrugged. Arguing with Jasper was always a lost cause and he never did. Life was too short for arguing. Do or don't do. Lead, follow or get out of the way. He always did. He also always followed. Less arguing both ways.

Jasper was still furious with Earl for letting Jo-Jo steal all their gold. If she had taken up with him instead of Earl, like she should have, she would still be here and so would the money. If she got on a stage at Burgess Springs or Fort Davis they might never track her down. Their only hope was knowing that the stage ran only once every twelve days through Burgess Springs and a different line serviced Fort Davis only once a week. Burgess Springs was too small a place to hide in, barely a village, and Fort Davis wasn't very large either. If they could catch some good luck for a change and if they weren't more than a day behind her, they could catch up with the new Jo-Jo and turn her into the Dead Dog-Faced Girl.

•

Lozen's Camp, in the Mountains North of Terlingua

Wolf Rising rode directly into the camp, nearly fell off his pony, and scrambled across the dirt to Lozen's feet and passed out. When she turned him over, she saw how the burned skin was peeling back from his face. She moved quickly, asking for her medicine bag and some of the rawhide food bags and water. They had so little water, but she had no choice but to use some of it now. She prayed to Controller of Water yesterday before they slept and he had provided some needed rain. But not enough.

She lifted the small rawhide bag of honey and slowly poured some of it over his burned face. As she spread it delicately with her fingers, Wolf Rising woke and grimaced with pain but said nothing. She opened another bag, broke off a small piece of peyote root and placed it in his mouth. "Eat this," she said. Her voice was soft and comforting to Wolf and he found himself wishing through the pain that she would speak this way to him in a more intimate situation.

Upsidedown and a few others stood over them, watching their leader work.

"His face is like the madrone tree now," Upsidedown said. "Like the bark peeling away to reveal the naked tree underneath. Wolf Rising is dead now; Madrone is born this day."

"Enjuh," several of his companions said quietly. "This is correct."

Lozen removed a prickly pear cactus pad from another bag, placed it on a flat rock then mashed it with another rock. With a twist-

242

ing motion, she ground the pad into a pulp. She mixed in a little honey with her fingers then carefully spread the poultice over the warrior's face — the face of Madrone as his fellow warriors had renamed him. It was a cruel name, she knew, but appropriate. He and the band would remember this event forever through his name.

The peyote calmed Madrone and lifted the pain. He fell asleep. Upsidedown and Rabbit carried the burned warrior near the fire, as Lozen asked them to. Upsidedown found a sage, stood over the fire, and dropped the branches and leaves in while Lozen fanned the smoke to cover Madrone's face.

"Rabbit, do we have enough corn for tulpai?" she asked.

He checked one of the bags, surprised at her question. Lozen didn't allow tulpai when the band was moving and she didn't like her warriors drinking it even in a permanent camp. "Enough."

"Will you make some?" Lozen asked. "Not for us. Madrone will need much to drink tomorrow. It will help him heal."

"We're staying here and not moving to the river?" Upsidedown asked.

"We stay until Madrone can ride easily. We now have five wounded warriors. We need to rest and give their wounds time to heal. Two days, perhaps three. This is a sheltered place and enough rain fell last night to get us through those days. We have enough food and perhaps Upsidedown can find us meat."

"Will we get some of the tulpai?" Rabbit asked, knowing the answer.

"Only the wounded," she said. She turned and looked at the warriors gathered around her. "Only the wounded."

•

Fort Davis, Texas

Wyatt looked up from the card table to see what the commotion was by the front door. A woman — a girl, really, small and frightened looking — just walked into the saloon carrying a small carpet bag. No one could recall a woman other than one of the saloon girls ever coming into the place before. Certainly no respectable woman. She ignored the calls of the men as she looked around the room. Wyatt was already back to his poker hand when she walked up and touched his shoulder. He was immediately aggravated, looked up and began to tell her to go away when he recognized her. It was Jo-Jo.

"You shaved," he said, playing his cards.

"Can I speak to you?" she asked.

"Wait outside until I finish this hand," he replied. "You shouldn't be in here."

She left immediately. He shook his head.

"Your daughter come to fetch daddy back home to mother and the other children," one of the soldiers at the table said.

Wyatt tossed two cards on the table with contempt, quickly picking up two other cards the dealer dealt him. "I'm not married and I've never had any children, unless your mother was one of those whores I diddled in a buffalo camp some years back."

The soldier made a move for his pistol, but another soldier sitting next to him put a hand on his arm, stopping him. "You better remember who that is," the friend said.

"I ain't afraid of no Wyatt Earp," the first soldier said.

Wyatt made a large bet, casually tossing coins into the pot. "Yeah, you are but not because of who I am. It's because of who you are, a sniveling coward without the balls to call."

"You think so, eh?" the soldier said, throwing coins into the pot. "Let's see what you have, big mouth."

The soldier turned over a pair of queens; Wyatt held up three deuces and pulled the money toward him.

"I'll see you later," the soldier said, standing so abruptly he knocked over his chair.

"Careful, I might be the last person you see," Wyatt said to the soldier. He picked up his winnings and put them in his coat pocket and addressed the table, "I'll be back, but right now I have something personal to deal with."

Jo-Jo was standing to the right of the door and he caught a glimpse of her as he left the saloon. He turned, took her elbow and escorted her down the street.

"I'm glad to see you, but why did you shave?"

"Oh, I didn't" she said, smiling. "That was just stuck on with

244

glue. I was just pretending."

He was sorry to hear that; her beard was what made her exotic. Now she was just another frail young woman, the kind he'd seen far too often over the years. She was small and plain, good enough for another night or two, but he knew he'd never take her with him to El Paso and certainly not back to Tombstone. "My hotel," he said, nodding at the two-story building he stopped in front of. The evening breeze in this mountain city had a serious chill to it and he noticed her shivering without a coat or jacket. "Join me?"

"Of course," she said.

He stopped for a moment and held her at arm's length. "Just how old are you?"

"Seventeen," she said. "I'll be eighteen next month."

He escorted her inside, thinking she had looked more mature with the beard and seemed more outgoing. Now she was as shy as a child, almost fearful. Well, maybe just one more night but no more. He had a fast rule never to sleep with anyone who had more problems than he did, and he felt her problems went very deep.

CHAPTER 15

In the mountains north of Terlingua

Ethan spent the night on his stomach, watching the Apache camp
from the top of a hill. He didn't like the idea of Apache anywhere near
him, especially hostile ones like these. He saw quickly their leader
was a woman. The only woman who led a band that he knew of was
Lozen, Victorio's sister. This was not a good thing. He studied her for
a while as she moved confidently among the men, nothing like the
way Apache women acted. She was tall for a woman and muscular.
The long fringe on her clothing gave her a considerable beauty as she
moved, accentuating every action. The sun was behind him so he felt
easy about using his small spyglass and looking through it he noticed
something that intrigued him. Lozen wore a gold pendant around her
neck. It was a Cross of Lorraine, something he hadn't seen since he
lived in Vermont. The double bars on the cross made it distinctive, the
top one shorter than the other. This was the symbol of Joan d'Arc, the
Maid of Orleans, the only other woman warrior he ever heard of. How
could this woman have gotten that cross, he wondered. Taken it off a
dead immigrant? From a soldier she killed? Or had someone given it
to her. It reminded him of his home near Lake Memphramagog and
he didn't want this Apache to have it. He wanted the two worlds to
remain separate.

He studied the camp, counting six injured warriors. One was
burned and they paid him considerably more attention, cleaning his
face and putting some sort of poultice on it every hour or so. Like
most Apache he had seen, the burned one didn't make a sound even
though he had to be in great pain. Apache loved to hear the painful
moans and screams from their enemies but were trained from birth
never to allow their enemies to hear their own screams or moans. He
didn't feel even a little pity for the burned man and hoped he was in
terrible pain. He was certain the Apache deserved it.

He knew what the Apache were capable of. On one patrol, he'd
come upon the bodies of a rancher and his wife who had been tortured

to death. The man was buried up to his neck in the dirt so he could watch as they took turns assaulting his wife and when they'd had enough of that fun they tied her to a tree and skinned her alive. Slowly, he imagined. Then they disemboweled her. He'd been told how this was done: slowly, pulling the entrails out carefully and placing them on the ground for the victim to see. If ants were around, so much the better because they would then march up the bowels to the body and eat away there. The husband wouldn't be able to look away because his eyelids would have been sliced off. The Apache would then take to a nearby location and watch the buzzards gather to feast on the woman and the soft parts of the man's exposed head — the eyes first, then the cheeks and tongue. By then they would both be dead and the Apache would be bored and ride off. Ethan hadn't been able to get rid of that woman's imagined screams in five years. No, he didn't like Apache being nearby and, no, he had no pity for the burned warrior.

He was on a hill where he expected the band's outlier should be. Perhaps one of the wounded was their regular scout, perhaps even the burned one, and no one thought to place someone else out to guard the camp. They were probably confident they were isolated enough not to worry about such things.

Not too long after dawn his stomach growled and he realized before long his horse might make a noise that could be heard in the camp, so he slid back from the hill's edge, mounted, and quietly rode off.

In a couple of hours he joined Dutch and Joaquin riding north on the trail to Burgess Springs. Only then did he pause to tear off some jerky he had in his shirt pocket and wash it down with water.

"What'd you find?" he asked Joaquin.

"They split up," the Ranger said. "You could tell from the tracks where they camped the first night out. One of them rode off but the others followed after some hours. I'm guessing there was no honor among these thieves and one of them made off with the gold leaving the others behind."

"Eh-yeah. Which one?"

Joaquin was confused. How could he know which one? He shrugged.

"It's good you saw their camp and could tell newer tracks over an ᴊder set, but you didn't pay enough attention. One of them is buzzard bait, behind a small hill away from the main camp."

"Which one?" Joaquin asked.

"He was picked over rather well by the time I saw him, but it had to be the man they called Earl. The remaining tracks were made by the peg-legged man and the big fellow. The big fellow's tracks are deeper than any of the others and he walks funny, side-to-side like he's waddling instead of front-to-back like most folks walk," Ethan said. "And if you looked, you'd see the other set of tracks, the ones that left earlier, were smaller and not as deeper and they were slick. Not made by boots. Made by moccasins or slippers."

"The woman stole the money and hightailed it?" Joaquin said. "She kill the other guy, too?"

"That's what it looked like to me," Ethan said. "I think the two of them sought privacy behind the hill and in the middle of the night she did him in. Stabbed him or hit him with a rock. She didn't shoot him because that would have roused the other two and they would have been on her quickly. She has at least a six-hour head start on them."

"And us," Dutch said.

"Eh-yeah. But where can they go? We'll catch up."

Joaquin drank a little from his canteen. "That little, pitiful look-ing girl with the hairy face and arms, she did this?"

"Oh, yeah," Ethan said, nodding.

•

Fort Davis

Years of being a gambler and a lawman taught Wyatt two things: never trust anyone who wasn't a blood relative and sleep lightly. The skills served him well as he woke to a faint noise in the hotel room. He didn't move, but raised his eyelids just enough to see what was hap-pening.

Jo-Jo was illuminated in the early morning light, fully dressed, removing his wallet from his inside coat pocket. She tip-toed to her bag, put the wallet in, and walked toward the door. Before her hand touched the door handle, Wyatt grabbed her from behind and threw her onto the bed. He jumped over, straddling her, and slapped her as hard as he could, which, he knew, was very hard indeed. Her nose started to bleed and he knew she would have a purple eye before too long.

"Not even a kiss good-bye?" he said. She heaved up violent sobs. He stepped off her, standing at the foot of the bed, still naked, and picked up her carpet bag. He opened it, removing his wallet, then dumped the contents on the bed. Jo-Jo rose, making a half-hearted attempt to reach the door but Wyatt caught her, pinning both her wrists together in his left hand, forcing her to her knees.

"What else you have?" he said, sorting through the items scattered on the bed. He didn't find much: a change of clothing and undergarments and a canvas bag. The bag wasn't tied tightly so he opened it without letting go of Jo-Jo who was squirming more now.

"That's mine!" she said as he spilled the gold coins onto the sheets.

He sorted through the coins with his free hand, picking one up to feel its weight, then did some quick calculations. "I'd say this cache was worth $36,000. Where'd you come by it?"

She squirmed harder and screamed at him, "It's mine! Not yours!"

"It may not be mine, but I'll give ten-to-one it's not yours either," Wyatt said, twisting her arms to hurt her enough to get her to stop squirming. "Where did you get it?"

"None of your business," she spat.

"Where?"

"My mother gave it me before I left home."

"Where?"

"I found it."

"Where?"

"It's none of your business, now leave me alone!"

Wyatt threw her as hard as he could into the far corner of the room. She hit her head with a distinct thud. Stunned for a moment, she sat still as he drew on a pair of trousers. He picked up a small pistol from beneath his coat, sticking it in his waistband.

"I'm going to give you a break," he said, stuffing her clothing back in the valise and tossing it at her. "I won't turn you in and you leave town."

"My money," she pouted, still on the floor.

"Not your money," he said, pulling her up.

"Where will I go? What will I do?"

"Like I give a shit," he said, opening the door and throwing her out into the hallway.

•

That's what being nice got her, she thought, as she mounted her horse. She could have killed Wyatt like the others, but he'd been so nice to her that she thought she would be able to creep out of his room without him noticing. He seemed sound asleep. He had a large knife on the table with his gun belt. It would have been easy. But no, she had to be nice and now her money was gone and her protection, too. She couldn't go back to Jasper and Max; she couldn't go back home. The boys would still be searching for her, she was certain. She had to go far, far away to be safe and she need money to do that.

She felt the man they killed in Terlingua probably had more coins stashed away, but Jasper had been too impatient. So they settled for the bag of coins. She bet he had more buried somewhere in or around the shack. It was a gamble, she thought, but maybe no one found the body yet and she could sneak back and look around. If she found more coins, she was saved. If not, well, she could find Doc who was probably still in Lajitas and convince him Earl and the others forced her to go with them. She could convince Doc. Then she could become Jo-Jo again and disappear with the show if she had to. But she didn't think she would have to.

But Jasper and Max would be on her trail, perhaps even close to Fort Davis now. She rode to the livery stable.

"Excuse me," she asked a man pounding on a horseshoe over a smithy.

The short, older man looked up. "M'am?"

"Is there another way to get to Terlingua other than the road that goes through Burgess Springs?"

He pumped his bellows to keep the fire hot and thought for a moment. "Kinda," he said. He pointed with his hammer to the west. "See that road? It goes on out a ways from town then goes south a ways. Comes up maybe twenty miles west a Burgess, then cuts back southeast and meets up with the same road maybe another twenty miles or so south. Not used much. You wouldn't be going that ways all alone would you?"

"Oh, my, no," she said. "My three brothers and I are traveling together. One of them had some trouble in Burgess Springs the last time we were through there and we'd prefer to avoid the place if we could. Thank you, very much."

She headed her horse west.

•

"Sheriff around?" Wyatt asked the man shuffling papers around a desk in the sheriff's office.

"No, señor," the man said. "Gone to San Antonio with two prisoners."

"You're a deputy?"

"No, señor. He took one deputy with him, the sheriff, and the other is working the night shift." He stood up and held his hand for Wyatt to shake. "My name is Josiah Guerrero. I'm a constable."

"Pleased to meet you," Wyatt said, shaking his hand.

"My jurisdiction is in the Chihuahua section of town," Josiah explained, waving his hand. "But the sheriff lets me use the same office and use the same jail. How may I be of service, señor?"

"Wyatt Earp," he said, tossing the canvas bag on the desk.

"I've heard of you, señor," Josiah said, curious about what had jingled so loudly when the bag hit the desk.

"A woman attempted to rob me this morning," Wyatt explained. "Because we'd had a personal relationship, I let her go advising her to leave town. But I also found this bag among her belongings. I'm certain she stole those coins from some other unsuspecting soul."

Josiah dumped the coins on the desktop. They were large and, if he was any judge, of high quality gold but he'd never seen anything like them before.

"I think you'll find about $15,000 worth of gold there, constable," Wyatt said.

"A fortune. What do you want me to do with this?" he said, scooping the coins back into the bag.

"Lost and found. If someone comes in telling you a young woman robbed him, you'll be a hero by being able to give him back his money. Part of it, anyway. I'm certain she spent some of whatever she stole and I've taken a portion for my troubles and by way of reward."

"But what if no one comes in with such a story?"

"I believe it's customary for the finder to keep any unclaimed items," Wyatt said, smiling. "I've turned it over to the proper authority, so my conscious is clear. As far as I'm concerned, you've just found it. I'm on my way west on tomorrow's stage and don't want to be bothered with paperwork and a possible trial over this."

Wyatt touched the brim of his hat and left. Josiah couldn't open the office safe fast enough to get the bag in it.

As Wyatt walked to his hotel, he was stopped by a man with a wooden leg.

"You," the man said, pushing him back.

Wyatt slapped the man's hand from his coat lapel. "You'll not touch me again. Now get out of my way."

"Not before you answer my question. Bartender at the saloon says he saw you leave last night with a young woman. The hotel proprietor said you escorted a young woman to your room. I aim to find her. Now you can tell me where she is."

Wyatt took a step forward, but the peg-legged man pulled a pistol from under his coat and shoved it into Wyatt's gut. It was, Wyatt knew, the classic mistake of someone who didn't fight with pistols. If the man had stuck the pistol into Wyatt's stomach and pulled the trigger, Wyatt could have done nothing, but the man didn't fire and Wyatt knew he could slap the pistol out of the way, or turn away, before the man could pull the trigger. Especially since he hadn't cocked it yet. This man was a talker. Wyatt wasn't. Wyatt slapped the pistol aside with one hand and with his other drew his own pistol and quickly buffaloed his assailant, knocking him to the street.

"Hey!" another man, a very large man built like a block of granite, said as he walked over.

Wyatt pointed his pistol at the man's head. "You related to this turd?"

The big man shook his head no, slowly.

"Pick him up and carry him to the jail for me," Wyatt ordered. The big man did as he was told.

Josiah was startled to see the men walk in, wondering what Wyatt was doing.

"Got a client for a cell," Wyatt told Josiah. The constable rushed to open the door that led back to the two jail cells. Wyatt waved at the big man to put the peg-legged man down on a cot, then motioned for the big man to leave.

"Come back and get your friend tomorrow. That meet with your approval, constable?" Wyatt said.

"Sí, señor," Josiah said. "A charge?"

"Assault, but not a very effective one," Wyatt said, escorting the big man out of the sheriff's office.

"What's your name?" Wyatt asked him.

"Maximo," the big man said.

"I want the both you gone from Fort Davis as soon as you get your friend out of jail. You understand?"

"I hear you," Max said.

CHAPTER 16
Fort Davis

Joaquin was confused. "She went back? "

"What the blacksmith told me," Dutch replied. They arrived in town late in the night and slept near the stable, using the south wall as a windbreak. The rising sun had warmed them and woke them. Dutch was getting tired of sleeping on the ground, and alone. He wanted a soft bed and a soft woman. He thought he could get both in Fort Davis, but now that didn't appear likely. "Said she asked about a different route back south. Said she told him she was traveling with her brothers."

"You think the show folk caught up with her?" Ethan asked.

"Got me," Dutch said. "But he did say he watched her ride out on the west road alone yesterday. This blacksmith, he sees everything goes on in this end of town from his open door."

Ethan shook his head. "She's got a guilty conscience that's bothering her and she's headed to Lajitas to give back the money and apologize for killing me."

"You slap don't believe that for a second," Dutch said.

"Nope."

"Well, then?" Joaquin asked.

"I don't have any theories," Ethan laughed. "You?"

Joaquin tossed his saddle across his horse's back, cinching it down. "I'm going over to Company E headquarters and get up a posse. We'll track them all down."

"You want someone else to get all the credit?" Ethan said. "Look, if it were up to me, I'd never be after them in the first place. Yes, they shot me, but I survived. I'm not concerned about the money. This seems like a waste of time to me."

"Like you've got more pressin' business elsewhere," Dutch said. "If you weren't up here with us, you'd be passed out in your jacal after drinkin' all night. You drink so much when you sweat you're a fire hazard. Only time you have a sobering experience is when I close the

254

saloon. Hell, you drink so much every time you mount your horse we can hear you sloshing. I figure we're slap saving your life by dragging you along on our little quest."

Dutch and Ethan saddled their horses.

"OK," Ethan said. "We'll get Joaquin his big arrests, but don't go off and get a bunch of Rangers. They'll only get in the way. Besides, there's only three of them left. I imagine we can handle those three."

Joaquin nodded his agreement and they rode out of town.

"Now we just have to avoid the Apache along the way," Ethan said.

"What Patcheys?" Dutch asked.

"One's I saw a couple days ago. They're in the mountains between Burgess Springs and Terlingua. Heading for the river it looked like."

"That girl could be heading straight into them," Joaquin said.

"Maybe she can use her girlish charm on them," Ethan said.

•

Jasper had the worst headache he ever experienced. He vaguely remembered waking up in a jail cell, wondering why he was there, then passing out again. This happened several times during the night. In the morning, a deputy gave him beans wrapped in a tortilla for breakfast and cold coffee that tasted like it had been made the day before. When he tried to ask the deputy what was going on, his head hurt so badly that he couldn't form any words before the deputy left the cell room. Now the deputy was back, and he could see Max standing in the main office behind him.

"If you behave yourself, you can go now," Deputy Blair Pittman said.

"How come I'm the one in jail when he was the one who hit me?" Jasper said, walking slowly to the cell door. Each step he took sent a stabbing pain through his temple.

"You were disturbing the peace," Pittman said, his hand holding the cell key. "And consider yourself lucky. That was Wyatt Earp. You could be dead now."

"The Wyatt Earp?" Jasper said. He'd heard plenty of stories about the lawman in his travels. "I thought he was in Kansas?"

"Not anymore, I guess. Constable said he was leaving on the west-bound stage today. If I were you, I'd go the opposite direction."

"He stole my money and my woman," Jasper said.

"He didn't have any woman with him and I seriously doubt Deacon Earp stole any of your money, as if you ever had any. And even if he did, my mama didn't raise no fool; I'm not about to confront no Wyatt Earp. So consider yourself lucky. Now, I don't want any more trouble in town. Behave?"

Jasper nodded and the deputy opened the door. He and Max walked toward the saloon.

"You find out anything?" Jasper asked.

"Jo-Jo's not wiff him," Max said. "I axed 'round. Stableman says she leff yesterday. Went on the west road."

"Well, we'd best get after her, then," Jasper said, shaking his head and regretting it the moment he did. He was afraid he was going to have this headache forever.

•

When Wyatt pulled himself up into the stage he saw a familiar face and smiled, touching his hat. "Constable."

"Oh, no more, señor. I resigned this morning."

"Going west?"

"Sí," Josiah said. "I was born and raised in Fort Davis and thought perhaps I would see more of the world. I'm going to California. They say a man can make his fortune out there."

"Takes money to make money," Wyatt said, withdrawing two cigars from his breast pocket, handing one to Josiah.

"Sí, I have heard that. Are you traveling to California?"

"I'll board the train west when we get to El Paso, but I'll disembark at Tucson," Wyatt said.

"At least I'll have the pleasure of your company until then," Josiah said, lighting Wyatt's cigar then his.

"Indeed," Wyatt said. "And when we're on the train perhaps we can relax the time away with a friendly game of cards."

"That would be nice, señor."

Wyatt drew on his cigar and smiled. "Nice indeed."

•

"Major, we've been back just a day now," Lieutenant Mason Maxon said, cursing himself silently for whining.

Major Anson Mills sighed and sipped from his steaming cup of coffee. His orderly made the best coffee he'd ever had. Those colored cooks sure knew their way around food and a coffee pot; too bad they tried to be soldiers, too. "Welcome to the army, lieutenant."

"Sir, begging your pardon, but my men need more rest than this to go back out," Maxon said, firmer this time. "Certainly we have other companies. Lieutenant Davis hasn't been out in some time, nor has Captain Keyes."

"Davis is being coddled by his father-in-law, you know that," Mills snapped. "We'd have hell to pay to Grierson if anything happened to Davis— "

"You know the colonel's not like that."

"You back-talking me, lieutenant?"

"No, sir." Maxon replied, cursing himself silently again. "It's just the strain of 40 days in the field and only one day's rest. It's been a strain on all my men, which is why I'm asking for consideration, sir."

"I think your blue-coated jungle-bunnies are used to it," Mills said. "I doubt they do much out there, anyway. These patrols are like holidays to them; they don't like being cooped up on a post. Not a post up in the mountains. They like the heat, lieutenant. Prefer it. They like the wide open spaces."

"Are you saying you're sending us back out so soon because they're colored troops?" Maxon blurted out.

Mills stood up from his desk and leaned on it with both fists. Maxon stared down onto the major's bald spot and watched his scraggly beard jumping up and down while he talked like a goat chewing on an old shoe. "It's a shit detail to be certain," Mills said. "And I will not send white troops out on a shit detail when I have niggers. They want to be cavalrymen, let them be cavalrymen and that means keeping their asses in the saddle. Now carry out your orders, lieutenant."

"Yes, sir," Maxon said, made a smart about face and left the major's office. He walked quickly across the parade ground, away from the row of whitewashed houses that made up the officers' quarters to the long enlisted barracks.

Without knocking, which was the military custom, Maxon entered his first sergeant's room and sat down, slapping his gloves against his thigh in disgust.

"Sir?" Shropshire asked, startled.

"The company leaves after breakfast tomorrow," Maxon said. "Apache have been sighted in the mountains north of Terlingua and Lajitas and headed south. Our agreement with the government of Mexico obliges us to prevent them from crossing the Río Grande. We, sergeant, have been chosen for this… this patrol."

"But, sir, we've only just— "

"You don't have to tell me, Shelvin," Maxon said, the first time he could remember ever calling an enlisted man by his Christian name. "Get the men ready for a month's absence. But I want a wagon full of provisions and ammunition this time. Double provisions, damn it." Maxon withdrew a wallet from his inside jacket pocket, taking out several dollars. "And get a case of whiskey from the sutler's."

"My boys'll be ready to ride come morning," Shropshire said.

•

Presidio, Texas

Karl sold his wagon and draught horse. The money was more than enough to buy them tickets on the stage north, then the stage to San Antonio and on by rail to Galveston as he had promised. They walked through blowing dust to the one-room adobe hotel and got them two rooms.

"You have been very quiet today," Karl said as they sat in the lobby. "What is wrong?"

She laughed that single, dry, sarcastic laugh of hers and rolled her eyes. "What have you got?"

"Ingrid," he said, taking her hands in his. "Do not be like this."

"I'm sorry," she said. "It's one of things you'll have to learn to put up with if you want me back. I'm not the same Ingrid."

"I know. I love you both."

That made her laugh genuinely and he felt her relax. She let go of his hands and sat back in her chair. "I think now I'm worried about Dutch. I don't feel like I've treated him well by running away as soon as I could. I feel guilty. I feel like I should have faced him. He deserves to know face-to-face."

"You could not do it," he said.

"You're right; I couldn't. I couldn't even bear to see his face again. I don't think it'll mean much to him. He's certainly had many other women before me, he had many other women while I lived with him, and he'll have many others after. But, still, I feel ashamed about running away. That's what I've always done before, all my life. When I felt bad at home when we were children, I'd run away to you. When I felt bad at home after I was married, I ran away to you. When we were caught by God in that church, I ran away here. And now, I'm running away again."

Karl was quiet for a long time, but continued to stare into her eyes. "No, this time it is different. You are not running away from something. You are running toward something. We are running toward the same thing together. We are running toward our future. You no longer have to worry about the past, and you no longer have to worry about the present. The past is past. I will care for your present. You and I together will shape our future."

She sighed and looked down at her hands. "That's not all. I should have told you this before, but I couldn't find the words. I'm pregnant."

"I know," he said, still staring into her eyes. "Your loose dresses may have disguised your condition for some people, but I have known you too well not to notice. When I touched your stomach as we slept the other night I was certain. It is Dutch's."

"How could you know? Even Dutch doesn't."

"You have not sold yourself in more than a year and you have not slept with anyone but Dutch, so this must be his child," he said, taking her hands and shaking them, getting her to look him in the eyes. "It will be our child. It will always be our child and I love it as our child."

She smiled and kissed him, feeling content.

CHAPTER 17

In the mountains north of Terlingua

Catching her was easy; confining her was more difficult. On the second day out from Fort Davis they found her curled up under a large mesquite, wrapped in the only blanket she had, shivering so hard they heard her teeth chatter. She hadn't planned on the desert being this cold. Seeing her so cold brought to Ethan's mind that back home this was the Hunter's Moon, soon to be the Beaver's Moon. It would have snowed by now, that first fall of virgin snow that seemed to purify all things. That first snow was so untainted he hated to walk in it for fear of desecrating it.

Dutch held her horse as they walked up on her. They expected her to run, but she could barely stand when they pulled her out from under the bush.

"You're under arrest," Joaquin said. Ethan doubted the girl understood a word the Ranger said. He untied a blanket from behind his saddle and wrapped it around her, then built a fire using mesquite branches. He looked around and found a small leatherstem, snapping off a branch then breaking that up into much smaller pieces. He poured water from his canteen into a small pot, tossed in the leatherstem and waited for the pot to boil. When it did, he poured some of the tea into a cup and gave it to the still shivering girl. She drank it down in one gulp, made a face, then asked for more. She sipped at he second cup.

"What's your name, child?" Dutch asked.

"Jo-Jo," she said. "Cynthia. No. Jo-Jo."

"Make up your mind," Dutch said.

"Jo-Jo," she said firmly and tossed the hot tea toward Ethan. The scout dodged the hot water enough so that it fell on his shoulder but before he could move toward her, she jumped up. Before she could run, Dutch and Joaquin grabbed her. She fought hard. She kicked and hit and bit and kicked some more. "Leave me alone! Leave me alone!"

Ethan got his lariat, but the girl was flailing around so much he had trouble grabbing either of her arms. Finally, he roped her feet and tied them tightly together, then managed to tie her wrists together but not before she had hit them all several times.

"Wildcat," Ethan said to Dutch. "You break her and put her to work and she'll earn you top dollar."

"Thinkin' the same thing," Dutch said, rubbing his chin where she had kicked him.

"She's going to jail," Joaquin said firmly. She still wriggled on the ground, trying to loosen her bonds but Ethan had tied them too well. "Where's my friend's money?"

"Leave me alone!"

"Listen to me," Joaquin said, trying to stop her squirming. She wouldn't. "Listen to me! You're young and a woman. The judge will go very easy on you, may not even send you to prison at all, if you just return the gold."

"He stole it!" she hollered. "He stole everything. Now leave me alone!"

Ethan went to her horse and looked into her empty saddlebags, then searched through her moth-eaten carpet bag. He shrugged at Dutch who then ran his hands over her body, checking up under her skirt and then feeling her chest.

"Nothing," Dutch said.

"She's either telling the truth or she buried it someplace," Ethan said.

"Who stole the money?" Joaquin asked her.

"Leave me alone! Leave me alone. Leave me…" Finally, she stopped struggling and was still. Ethan tossed the blankets over her. She was crying now.

"Who has the gold?" Joaquin asked quietly.

"Wyatt Earp," she sobbed.

Joaquin's head snapped back. "Wyatt Earp? The Kansas lawman Wyatt Earp? What—"

She nodded. "He took it from me. If you want it, go get it from him."

"Where were you going? After him?" Joaquin asked.

"I don't know where he went and I don't care," she said. Her sobs got fewer and she looked at Ethan directly for the first time and gasped. "You're dead!"

"Last time I looked, I'd say you were wrong," he laughed. "Your friend didn't use a man-sized load in his scattergun. And where are your friends?"

"They're not my friends," she said, snapping her head back and forth several times. "They got me into this. It's their fault. I just wanted to be let alone."

"Who's fault was Earl?" Ethan asked.

She glared at him, a lone tear rolling down her cheek. "Earl's own fault. Some wild man he was."

"I think your friends may be coming after you to get that gold you stole from them that you stole from me. Too bad Earp stole it from you," Ethan said, smiling.

"That's your problem, not mine," she said.

Joaquin pulled her up and Ethan untied her feet.

"If you kick again, you'll be riding across your saddle instead of in it. Your choice," Ethan told her. She nodded. They hoisted her onto her horse and tied her hands to her saddlehorn. Ethan then dropped a loop around her neck and fastened the end of the rope to a leather strap holding her saddlebags behind the cantle.

"What if my horse falls or rears or runs wild?" she said. "I could be strangled."

"Best make sure you ride easy," Dutch said.

They rode north all day, making good time back toward Fort Davis. Ethan rode two miles ahead of them, expecting to run into the girl's two friends but he never saw them. Perhaps they knew Jo-Jo or Cynthia or whatever her name actually was no longer had the money.

•

"Were loss," Max said, halting his horse. He'd seen the same peak before, earlier in the day. They had been riding in a wide circle to their left. Earlier they reached a point on the indistinct road where it looked as if the road might be forking and Jasper insisted the deeper route was the correct one. But it had looked like a dry creek bed so Max, and that's what it was. Now they couldn't find the seldom-traveled road again.

The night had been cold and one blanket each hadn't been enough. They slept spooned together with both blankets wrapped around them, their body heat and the blankets warming them enough. And now, past mid-day, the sweat was pouring out of them. Jasper drank up all his water by noon and begged Max for some of his. Max reluctantly agreed, but had to fight to prevent Jasper from drinking it all. In the desert, water was more precious than gold. Max knew this; Jasper did not.

Max looked at the sun dropping toward the horizon. "Norf is this way. We should go norf."

"Jo-Jo went south," Jasper said. He rubbed his neck with his hands and licked his lips. "We have to go south to get that gold back."

"Why would she go souf?" Max asked. "I doan tink she hass the gold no more."

"I don't know why she's going south, but she's got to have the gold. Where else would it be?"

"We die of thirst befoah we fine her," Max said. "We go norf, maybe we fine water, maybe we fine Fore Davis."

"We're going south, damn it!" Jasper said, spurring his horse onward.

They rode for about an hour in hills that all looked alike to them. Rocky hills with some lechuguilla and ocotillo, but not even much of those. Neither of their horses liked the route any better than Max did; they walked slowly and had to be urged on often. Suddenly both horses bolted forward.

Jasper turned to Max. "They smell water!"

The horses were moving too quickly to stop them from running over one small hill into the Apache camp.

●

Upsidedown and two other warriors jumped up and pulled the two Pale Eyes down from their horses. The horses continued on to a small trickle of water falling from a rock and lapped at it.

With rifles pointed at their noses, the Pale Eyes stopped struggling. Rabbit searched them and removed the pistol from the one with the wooden leg had. The big one had no firearm. Lozen walked up and looked the captives over. She had never seen a man with a wooden leg before and she had never seen a man as big as the other. The large Pale Eye was two heads taller than she was and at least three times as wide. His shoulders and his chest and his waist and his thighs lined up straight, all the same size. She guessed it would take every warrior in camp to hold this one down, if they could.

Upsidedown kicked at the wooden leg. He'd seen one before, on a trapper who lived near the reservation. He wouldn't mind having this as a trophy. How many warriors had three legs? "What do we do with them?"

"I don't know now," Lozen said. She pointed with her chin toward the large Pale Eye. "Can you bind this one so he won't get loose?"

"I think we have enough rawhide. If we wet the bonds, when they shrink they'll get tighter and that will help."

"Strip them down," she said. "If they have no clothing or shoes they won't be able to run very far if they do get loose."

They motioned for the Pale Eyes to stand, and they did. Two women then took off the men's clothing. The big man tried to push his woman away, but Rabbit's rifle in his face again made him compliant.

Jasper stood naked, his wooden leg strapped on above his left knee. Upsidedown motioned for Jasper to remove the leg. Jasper sat and unstrapped the leg, handing it to Upsidedown who smiled.

"Look at this," Rabbit said to Lozen. She looked to see the big Pale Eye's underclothing. It was a made of a spotted lion's fur. It had short legs that he wore like drawers and a single strap that lopped from front to back over the left side of his bulging chest muscles.

"Ask Madrone to come here," she said to Maiden Fern. In a moment, Madrone was standing beside her, his face still raw and peeling but, he said, the pain was gone and poison had not set in. He was ready to ride whenever they were.

"You speak the Pale Eyes tongue," she said to him.

"Some," he replied, noticing for the first time the two strange men just beyond her, a one-legged man sitting naked on the desert and the biggest man he ever saw standing by the fist wearing an animal fur like a shaman would.

"Why is this man wearing an animal's skin?" she asked him.

"You shaman?" Madrone asked the big man.

"I am shamed, yes," the big man said.

"No," Madrone said. "You. You shaman? Medicine man?"

The big man shook his head no and struck a pose, his arms up beside his head pulling his biceps into steel knots. "Maximo the World's Strongest Man!"

"I believe," Madrone said. He explained this to Lozen.

"How strong is he?" she asked. Madrone explained this to the big man. The big man held his hand out for Rabbit's rifle but Rabbit pulled it away quickly.

"Unloaded it and give it to him, but stand back," Lozen said. Rabbit did as he was asked.

The big man grabbed the barrel of the rifle with one hand near the muzzle and the other near the stock. He quickly dropped to one knee and after much grunting, bent the barrel downward. He handed it back as the gathered band shouted their approval.

"My rifle," Rabbit moaned.

"Take the one off his saddle," Lozen said. "He won't need it. I think it's newer than yours was."

"We work in a traveling show," the one-legged man said to Madrone. "We perform amazing feats."

"Feet?" Madrone asked. "I don't understand."

"Feats," the one-legged man said. He waved his hands in the air, as if he were describing smoke. "Big medicine. Magic."

"What magic?" Madrone asked.

"You've seen some of Max's magic," the one-legged man said. "Max is stronger than any Indian. Stronger than any Indian horse. Max is stronger than these rocks around us."

"And you?" Madrone asked.

"I can eat fire!"

Madrone explained this to Lozen. Her eyebrows rose in disbelief. A man stronger than horses or rocks and another who could eat fire. This would have to be seen. "Is the animal skin his source of power?"

Madrone asked the big man who shook his head no. She wasn't certain this was so. Shamans drew great power from their costumes and the fetishes they carried with them and on them. She asked Maiden Fern to remove the animal skin from the big man, then handed the skin to Rabbit.

"Put this on and see if you can bend that rifle barrel back," she said.

Rabbit put the skin on, but it was big enough for three men of his size. He let it drape over his shoulder and the other warriors laughed at him. He grabbed one of the rawhide strips and tied the skin tightly around his waist. But try as he might, he could not bend the barrel.

"I need no skin. I am Maximo." The big man, now naked, grabbed the rifle from Rabbit and struggled to bend the barrel back. It remained misshapen, but it was bent back toward its original form. The band shouted their approval again.

Lozen motioned for the big man to sit and asked the warriors to keep their rifles trained carefully on him. She motioned for the one-legged man to rise and he did with Upsidedown's help. "Sit him on the rock so everyone may see," she said. The Pale Eye hopped to a large rock and sat on it. She asked Maiden Fern to bring over a stick from the fire.

"Show us how he eats fire," Lozen told Madrone as Maiden Fern gave the burning stick to the one-legged man.

The man took the stick and placed the burning end in his mouth. The fire didn't harm him. He repeated this three times and finally closed his mouth on the stick and removed it with the fire extinguished. He had, Lozen acknowledged, eaten the fire.

"Set him on fire and see if he can eat that," Madrone said to Lozen.

"No," she said. "You know my feeling about torture. My brother wouldn't allow it and I will not. If we have to kill them, we will, but we will not torture them."

"What do we do with them?" Madrone asked.

"Bind them and we will take them with us," Lozen said. "They will amuse us for awhile."

•

The past few days had caught up with Ethan. He could barely

keep his eyes open as the sun set on their camp.

"I'm sorry, guys, but I just can't stay awake," he said. "You're going to have to pull guard duty on our little hellion tonight."

"I think we can manage," Joaquin said.

"Split it up. You take four hours, let Dutch take four."

"Sounds good," Joaquin said. "I'm wide awake now. I'll take the first watch. You catch some sleep, Dutch, and I'll wake you up."

Dutch nodded.

"But be careful," Ethan said. "She's not the little girl she seems. She's killed one person we know of and bamboozled those professional bamboozlers. Don't let her bamboozle you."

"I been handling women all my life," Dutch said. "Women were the last thing God made and he must've done it on a Saturday mornin' 'cause his handiwork behaves like it was done by someone with a severe hangover."

Later, during Dutch's watch, Jo-Jo stirred, struggling at first against the ropes that bound her hands and feet.

He leaned over and whispered in her ear. "Mind yourself. Go back to sleep."

"I have to go," she whispered back.

"You slap ain't goin' anyplace," Dutch said.

"No. I have to go."

Women, he thought, were always a problem just because they were women. He could just let her soil herself — it's what Ethan would do — but then he'd have to spend the next three hours smelling it. He reached over and yanked her to her feet. "You do exactly as I say and keep quiet or I'll break those skinny legs of yours and you won't be running off anyplace."

She nodded. Dutch untied her feet and led her away from the camp, behind a small hill. She lifted her skirts and squatted.

Dutch couldn't hear her doing any business, so he leaned over her and whispered, "Best get'r done quick or we're goin' back whether you're finished or— "

Jo-Jo found the perfect size rock, holding it solidly in her hands and swung around hard as Dutch leaned over. He moaned an obscenity but fell back and she hit him again and again until he stopped moving. She found his knife and, holding the handle between her feet, leaned forward and cut off the rope around her wrists. She walked as quietly as she knew how to the horses and pulled herself up on hers without bothering to saddle it. That would make too much noise. She disappeared into the night.

CHAPTER 18
In the mountains north of Terlingua

It was nearly noon and all Ethan was able to do all morning was sit by the body. He knew this bag of meat and bones and blood was not his friend — his friend had gone on — yet he couldn't move, couldn't speak.

When Margaret and David died in Vermont, he had a chance to go to the northeast but by the time he would have arrived their bodies would have been in the ground and visiting a grave was not the same as seeing his wife and son. It was much worse. He would rather have the memory of them alive than have the memory of their grave. He learned that when his grandfather died. He was nineteen and home from Dartmouth for the summer and was relaxing at their camp by the lake while his grandfather was out fishing just before dawn, his favorite time. Ethan sat by the campfire, waiting to prepare the fish for breakfast. When the sun shined across the lake, it cast his grandfather's canoe in deep silhouette, a sight so familiar to Ethan that it was like the face of a landmark cliff. Usually his grandfather would paddle in with first light and they would watch the sunrise together, but this day the canoe lazed around in the sheltered cove. Once the sun was fully up, Ethan got concerned and hollered out across the water, something he knew his grandfather would chide him for, scaring all the fish. But he heard no answer. The figure of his grandfather did not move. Ethan shed his clothing and swam out to the canoe and even before he reached it he knew the truth: his grandfather was dead. When Ethan touched him, the body slumped forward. Ethan held the gunwale of the canoe and swam it to shore, pulling his grandfather's body onto the beach.

He never knew how his grandfather had died. The doctor said it was just old age, and maybe that was it. Maybe the old man had just worn out, but Ethan couldn't imagine this man so full of life ever wearing out. But he had gone on. That day his soul felt frigid, worried that he would never see his grandfather again. The old man told him of

Kluskap's promise more than once, usually in an attempt to get him to behave.

"Those who do not act as they should must remember there is a place of Darkness Forever," his grandfather said of the myth of the Great Power who made the world. "Those who do not act as they should will forever have to hunt their game in darkness. There will be be no sun for them."

Ethan never paid much attention to the other portion of the story, the part where Kluskap warned the people to always behave, even when the white men came. "Do not worry," Kluskap said. "I will come. I will raise you from the burial mounds. I will call you down from the crotch of the trees. I will call you down from the scaffolds of the air, to go north with me, to live where no white person shall ever come." And the last part was what frightened him since he was part white. When he died would he not be able to finally be with his grandfather? Would he be barred from this safe place? It sounded like it.

That first mistake, of seeing his grandfather's dead body, was one he couldn't avoid. The second one he could have, but didn't. He went to the small funeral attended by a few of his grandfather's friends. They carried the body, wrapped in blankets with the face covered by a basket decorated with quills, into the mountains and found a tall tree then raised the body to a fork in the tree. Ethan knew the procedure. In time, the body would dry out and be preserved, then lowered into a family burial mound. He visited the tree again and again. And now some of the strongest memories he had of his grandfather were of the old man's body sprawled on the beach and of the tree cradling the blanket-wrapped remains. The body and the resting place were not his grandfather, but now they shared his memory. If he could never see his grandfather again, his memory was all he would ever have and it was tainted with death. He refused to do it with Margaret and David. They had to live on unadulterated. He was thankful he never had to see their bodies, and refused to ever see their graves.

Now his friend had gone on. His best friend. One of the only friends he'd ever had in his life, and his dead body was before him. They hadn't touched it. The legs were askew, the arms outstretched, one side of the head crushed with the earth beside it dark with blood. It was an image he wouldn't be able to get out of his mind and damn that girl to hell for giving it to him.

Joaquin touched his shoulder. "We should bury him."

"He never smelled a rose," Ethan said, standing.

Joaquin waited for more, but the scout was silent again for a while. Ethan finally turned and walked away back toward their camp.

"We have to bury him," Joaquin said.

Ethan shook his head, grabbed his saddle and walked to his horse. "You'll have to do that. I can't."

"Where are you going?"

"After her. Trail's getting cold."

"You promised me you wouldn't harm her."

"Oh, I won't," he said, settling into the saddle. "If I come close to her I'll kill her and killing would be too good for her. I'll leave you a clear trail. You bury the body and find me as soon as you can. I'll find her."

•

Jasper was glad the Indians let him put his trousers back on. Max was wearing only his leopardskin. In his trouser pocket were two small rubber bladders full of coal oil, the ones he used in his act. He could palm one into his mouth at the appropriate time and really give these heathens a show. Swallowing fire was easy. All you had to do was overcome your fear of fire, then exhale as strongly as you could when the fire approached your mouth. And if you closed your mouth completely, the fire would die from lack of air. Just keep a lot of saliva on your tongue and in your mouth when you did it. But the bladders gave him that little extra that always drew gasps of excitement from the rubes. After taking the small cork from the bladder, you put the bladder under your tongue and when you brought the fire near your mouth you squeezed down on the bladder shooting out a fine stream of coal oil. The fire ignited the coal oil and created a bright, blazing stream of fire away from you. With practice, you could even light other torches doing this. He couldn't do that with the savages because he had to use small sticks instead of his torches that were already soaked in coal oil to make them ignite instantaneously. But he was certain breathing fire would impress them enough.

He'd heard tales about magicians suckering in wild Indians with their acts in order to stay alive. That's what he and Max had to do now. Keep the heathens entertained until they could find a way to escape or they were rescued, although he couldn't think of a soul who would bother rescuing them.

•

Ethan hadn't gone more than four miles when he stopped and dismounted. The hills gave way here to an expanse of the desert and he sat on the last hill, pulling his Bowie knife from its sheath on his gunbelt. He methodically cut off his hair, finishing the job by pouring water over his head and scraping the knife blade across his scalp to get his head smooth. When he remounted, he looped the stampede string of his hat around his pistol butt, letting the sun warm his now bald head.

He saw two sets of tracks at the base of the hill. One was obviously the Apache band, almost too many to count. He guessed at least two dozen ponies, two warriors being carried on travois, several women and children walking. Jo-Jo's tracks crossed over them, more recent, going in a similar direction. He decided to follow the Apache.

By sundown, the Apache made camp on the far side of a hill. Still no outlier. He tied his horse to a creosote and slowly crept up a nearby hill to look down on the camp.

He half expected to see Jo-Jo in the camp, but she wasn't there. The two other show folk were. The Apache had tied each of the strongman's arms to a rope, fastening the other end of each to a horse. They hollered as one of them, the one with the burned face, slapped the horses with a switch to get them moving in opposite directions. The strongman held firm. It was something he might even be able to do, Ethan thought. The horses didn't start moving until the strongman had already pulled the ropes taut. They couldn't get up any momentum. At some point, the strongman's endurance would give way to the horses', but until then he appeared very strong. The Apache shouted their approval and the leader ordered the strongman released. Ethan noticed the leader was a woman — Lozen — so this had to be the same band he'd seen before. He doubted whether any more dangerous band of Apache could be loose on the land than this one now that Victorio was dead.

The peg-legged man had lost his peg leg. He hopped around on one leg, helped by the burned-face Apache. A woman brought the one-legged man several burning sticks. He stuck the first two slowly in his mouth, extinguishing each one. The third stick exploded as he brought it near, a tongue of fire bursting from the man's mouth. The Apache howled first with fear then delight at this. Then the man was allowed to hop back to his friend's side and they were given some water and a little food. Ethan wondered how they liked the hoosh.

•

Joaquin found Ethan in the morning. He didn't comment on the scout's new bald pate, figuring it was some Indian custom he wasn't familiar with. "You find her?"

"Nope," Ethan said. "Found the Apache, though. Laid up all night watching their camp. They left earlier, heading due south. The girl is wandering more or less in the same direction, but more southwest."

"We have to reach her before she runs into the Indians."

"Too late for her friends," Ethan said, walking his horse. "Apache have the strongman and the peg-legged man. Course, the peg-legged man doesn't have his leg anymore so he's not going to run away."

"They haven't killed them?"

"Not yet. I think they're the after-supper entertainment."

"Entertainment? They torturing those men?"

"No, not at all," Ethan said. "They're putting on a little show for the Apache. Peg-leg was breathing fire and strongman was holding off horses pulling him in opposite directions. At some point it could turn into torture once they get bored with the same show every evening."

They rode off to the southwest. Ethan was wishing he could sleep. He hadn't slept at all the night before and wondered now whether he would be able to tonight. This had happened before, when Margaret and David died, and he didn't sleep for days. It took alcohol to turn off his brain and let him sleep, even if fitfully. And all last night his mind was racing, thinking about Margaret when it was his friend who had died. Something suddenly hit him and sent a shiver up his spine. It was Mic Mac custom never to speak the names of dead loved ones once they had gone on. He could only refer to his grandfather or to his friend, never even thinking of them by their names, but he had no trouble thinking or saying the names Margaret and David. Was that because he had never seen their bodies while he had seen the others? He didn't know, but it bothered him considerably.

"We should do something about those men before things do turn bad," Joaquin said.

"Why?"

"They're white men. They shouldn't be left to savages."

"I see."

"I didn't mean it like that."

"Sure you did," Ethan said. "You just happen to know me. If you didn't know me, I'd be a savage, too, or worse, a half-breed savage, good for nothing in either culture. All because you know me. You don't know any of those Apache. Could be some decent folk among them, but we don't know because we don't know them. Since they're different, they can be savages."

"I read about what Apache do to whites and I've heard you tell similar tales," Joaquin said.

"They're not Quakers," Ethan said, nodding. "They can be brutal and laugh about it. But I saw white soldiers do the same during the war and they were doing it to other whites just because of where they happened to be born. Seems like one group of people always has to have another group of people they can look down on. Gives 'em an excuse to get their meanness out. Be like me or you're a savage, the whites say. Be like me or you're not even a human being, the Apache say. Tell me the difference."

The rode on in silence for a while. Finally, Joaquin said, "You always have this Indian thing going on in your head, but you've made your living cutting them down."

"Eh-yeah," Ethan said. "And before that I made my living cutting down trees and I adore trees. Closest I come to having a religion. But people need shelter and trees are the quickest, cheapest source where I'm from. Trees are everywhere. Out here where trees are scarce, people use the earth. They make homes out of adobe mud. Back home, the company I worked for didn't clear out whole areas, though, we picked and chose individual trees, planted new trees, left clearings for more trees to grow. Harvesting. My grandfather taught me to thank each tree for its gift of life before I cut it down assuring that its gift would provide people with shelter and give them life. It's no different from raising cattle or hogs or chickens. No different from raising corn or onions or beans."

"Killing Indians isn't quite the same, though, is it?"

"Nope. But there's good Indians and bad Indians, just like there's good whites and bad, good black folk and bad ones. Chinese, too. It's the same thing since the beginning of time: one group conflicts with another. The strong survive. The weak must change or die. Whites now dominate this country and the Indians better learn to become more like them. When they kill innocent people, I have no trouble at all killing them."

"Even their innocent ones?"

"There are no innocent people," Ethan said.

•

After what Madrone told her about finding a good camp near the river, Lozen prayed to her power. Her hands tingled a little when she faced northeast and more when she faced south. She attributed the stronger feeling in the south to the Pale Eyes settlements along the long river. But Madrone said this camp was away from those settlements and looked like sacred ground. She asked the band to follow her there.

•

"There she is," Joaquin said, pointing to a moving shadow he guessed to be a little more than a mile away. He thought Ethan would have spotted her before he did.

The scout looked up, startled from the reveries he knew were serving him no purpose. "Eh-yeah," he said, but kept his horse to the walk they'd been in all day.

"Well, let's go get her," Joaquin said.

"No rush," Ethan said. "The Apache are too close and we can't afford to attract their attention. We wouldn't stand a chance against a couple dozen of them, especially not this band."

"What's so special with this group?" Joaquin asked through gritted teeth.

"Lozen. It's her band. Victorio's sister and just as capable as he was. I'm guessing she may even have some stragglers from the Mexican dust-up that finally got him. I'm not about to tangle with them."

"Look, she's seen us," Joaquin said.

"Eh-yeah. Looks like she's moving west now. Let's get a little closer, but we've got to be careful. I don't aim to come riding over some hill and find Apache on the other side. I imagine that's what happened to those two show folk they have."

Joaquin stopped to guzzle some water from his canteen even though he wasn't very thirsty.

While they still had daylight, they followed Jo-Jo across the desert, always at a distance. Every now and then Ethan would ride off, saying he was trying to locate the Apache. Once they knew where the hostiles were, he said, they'd be able to grab Jo-Jo without much danger. In the meantime, they followed her. But she always saw them and changed her direction more than once. Judging from the general direction they were traveling in, Joaquin guessed they would cross the Lajitas/Presidio road the next day. If she crossed the Río Grande Joaquin couldn't legally follow, but he doubted that imaginary border was going to stop Ethan.

CHAPTER 19
Presidio

Lieutenant Maxon led his troop from Fort Davis to Presidio, the safest, easiest way to get to the Río Grande. The city had only one hotel and it wasn't large enough to accommodate their numbers, but they wouldn't have been allowed to stay in it anyway. So they camped just east of the city at Fort Leaton, the private trading post with its thick walls. Maxon paid for a beef and the cocineros at the fort barbecued it up just perfectly for his men, ladling on a variety of fresh vegetables from carrots to onions to cabbage.

His orders were to patrol for thirty days a rectangular-shaped area from Fort Davis to Presidio to Terlingua back to Fort Davis and to capture or destroy any hostile Apache bands. The desert hills in that rectangle were an uninhabited land, a land so harsh the Apaches would only pass through it. Maxon had his orders, but they didn't specify how he was to carry them out. He knew his men deserved better than they had gotten and he was going to give it to them. The good part of the plan was that he could actually defend his tactics if he had to. He knew the Apache band that had been sighted would be a roving band and wouldn't stay long in the land the Mexicans called el desploblado. They'd be heading for the river. No sense in him rummaging around that terrible desert looking for hostiles who weren't likely to be found. He'd just patrol the river road and wait for them to come down out of the hills. He'd separate the troop as before, into smaller squads, and they'd just ride the river for the next month. He'd rotate a couple of the squads into Presidio and Lajitas every few days. He aimed to make this the safest, most comfortable patrol they'd ever been out on.

He kept First Sergeant Shropshire and a few men in Presidio. He sent Sergeant Faulkner and his squad to Alamito Creek; Sergeant Kurney to the hoo-doos around the big hill; and Sergeant McCoun to Lajitas. He would lead Sergeant Clayborn and his squad to ride the road between the hoo-doos and Alamito.

•

"You need to get some sleep, for Christ's sake," Joaquin said. "Been three nights now. We need to just nab that girl and go back to Fort Davis, put you up in the hotel and let you sleep sound knowing she's in custody."

"She's not what's keeping me awake," Ethan said.

"And what? Thinking about Dutch? Blaming yourself for him being on watch instead of you?"

Ethan stood up in his stirrups to make certain Jo-Jo was still in his sights. They had dropped below her earlier in the day and had almost reached the Presidio road. She saw them and headed back north, then turned west. The chase had gone on this way for several days, always staying close enough to see her and she them but never capturing her. "Actually, I hadn't even thought about that. I made the right decision at the time, given my condition. He should have been more vigilant. I warned him. I always told him women would be the death of him, but I thought it would be some jealous husband shooting him dead when he was about eighty years old and too pooped to run."

"Then what?"

"I keep thinking about my wife and son. It's what always seems to happen when I've been sober for a while. You'd think by now I'd be able to deal with it, but I guess not. I imagine the problem is that I never said good-bye. Never said good-bye properly. It eats at me. I'll tell you something else, too, I don't imagine I ever deserved a woman like Margaret. She was educated and had class and me, I was just a savage."

"Wait a minute," Joaquin said. "Don't tell me you're still brooding over what I said a couple days ago. I told you— "

"It's not what you said," Ethan said. "That's what she called me. Called me a savage the first time she saw my tattoos. I think white folks all think the same thing. Only two kinds of folks in the world: folks with tattoos and folks afraid of folks with tattoos. Only time folks didn't react badly was when I was in the Sandwich Islands. It's not scandalous like here to have men go about bare-chested and lots of them have tattoos. The only reason they ever looked twice at me was because they didn't see too many whites with tattoos. And I am, all things considered, a very white looking son of a bitch."

"She must have just been startled, is all," Joaquin said.

"Eh-yeah," Ethan said. "But the look in her eyes whenever she saw them never went away. In the back of her mind she must have thought she'd made a terrible mistake."

"If that's what she thought then she didn't have the class you think she had."

"Eh-yeah. I thought the same thing. Even wondered why she came out west if she had all that education and class. This place ain't much like Vermont, you know. Cold versus heat, trees versus no trees, clover versus sparse grass, snow blizzards versus dust storms, lakes and rivers and brooks versus a few wet-weather creeks and one long boring river, Canuk versus Greaser, civilization versus the frontier. She always said it was the money. Some combine up in the northeast scoured the Kingdom looking for school marms for Texas and the territories west and paid them a rather hefty bounty when they signed up. Helped a little that they were told the ratio of men to women was wonderfully in their favor. If they couldn't find a husband out here, they were destined from birth to be old maids. And, of course, all the men were handsome and wealthy."

"Aren't we all?" Joaquin said. They both laughed and trotted toward the last place they had seen Jo-Jo.

•

The camp was everything Madrone said it was. It was secluded; it was protected from the wind; a creek flowed through it; the river was not far away; all the holes in the rocks would have given the place a sacred feel even if a giant rock turtle and rock ogre weren't guarding the pathway into the canyon. If only Pale Eyes didn't live near here, it would make the perfect permanent camp, Lozen felt.

A semi-permanent camp was being set up. The women found enough huisache and tamarisk along the river to make wickiups from the branches. Sage gathered from canyon would make a sweat lodge for the wounded warriors. They could relax here for a long time, then cross the long river whenever they wanted to or needed to.

She sent Madrone off on a scout of the surrounding land. He was finally at full strength and she trusted no one else, except perhaps for Upsidedown, to scout as well as he could. Even burned, the much younger Madrone had more stamina than Upsidedown. With Pale Eyes settlements only a couple of suns' ride upriver or downriver, daily scouting would become the most important job in the camp.

Madrone rode in before she expected him, leading a captive.

"I found this Pale Eye not far away," Madrone sat, leaping down from his pony and pulling the woman off hers in nearly one motion. The woman fell to the ground and screamed with pain, but Madrone placed his foot on the back of her neck to keep her face down in the dirt. "I looked for some distance, not too far, but saw no other Pale Eyes with her."

"What is she doing out here alone?" Lozen asked. Madrone let the woman rise, telling her what Lozen asked.

"Leave me alone!" the girl hollered. "I haven't done anything to you! Leave me alone!"

"She won't say," Madrone told Lozen.

The big man rushed over to them, the one-legged man hopping behind him. The one-legged man fell only once; he was getting better at hopping. "Jo-Jo," the one-legged man said.

"I think the woman was looking for these men or got separated from them," Madrone told Lozen. In English he asked the one-legged man, "You know this woman?"

"Damn right we do. She stole our gold and killed our friend but now she'll get what she deserves."

The woman crumpled to the dirt and covered her face, sobbing. Madrone thought the one-legged man was about to kick her, but stopped at the last moment. That would have been funny, Madrone thought.

"Is she also special?" Lozen asked. "Does she have a talent that will amuse us?"

Madrone asked the woman if she could do magic like her two friends.

"No, no no! I'm just a girl who's lost! I'm not who these men think I am. I've done nothing! Leave me alone!"

"The woman has no talent to amuse us," Madrone says. "Let me have her to avenge what was done to my face."

"Was it this woman?" Lozen asked.

"No, but she is a Pale Eye like the one who did. I will torture ten Pale Eye women in vengeance for my face and I will start with this one."

"I will not allow torture," Lozen reminded him. "If you wish to have her as your wife, you may. If you wish to kill her, you may. You will not torture her."

Madrone pushed the one-legged man over and kicked the woman for him. The big man moved toward Madrone, but stopped when Madrone looked him squarely in the eyes. The big man sat next to the woman and petted her like he might a dog.

Madrone turned to Lozen. "I will have my vengeance. You should not deny this to me. Look at my face! Look! If this had happened to you, you would want vengeance. What if this happened to your brother? I'm not asking to torture her for our amusement. I'm asking to torture her for vengeance. I need to hear her screams. I will now forever be Madrone. Wolf Rising, the man who sneaked up on a wolf and strangled him before he could rise, is now dead. The man people knew for that feat is dead. Madrone stands in his place. And people remember Madrone as a victim and not a conqueror of wolves. I don't wish to end my days always thought of as a victim. Her screams will remind our people Madrone is not a victim. Only through vengeance will Madrone not be a victim. You must allow me this."

Lozen looked at the three Pale Eyes on the ground before her, pitiful looking, even the big one now. She looked at Madrone, forcing her eyes to examine every crease and wrinkle and splotch and strange coloring on his face. She tried to imagine the pain he had endured. He had been a valuable friend to her brother and now to her. She had known him most of her life. He seemed pitiful too, now, and a warrior shouldn't seem pitiful.

"I will pray on this," she told him.

•

Ethan and Joaquin camped on the side of the road, some distance west of where they had seen the Apache camp. Earlier they looked down on the hostiles, seeing the show people, including Jo-Jo. Joaquin wanted Ethan to try to sneak in and get the woman out, but Ethan would have none of it. It was far too dangerous. Joaquin suggested he wait until dark. He'd crept into an Indian camp before under darkness and succeeded. That was a Comanche camp, could it be any more difficult in an Apache camp? Ethan insisted it was.

Before they finished rolling out bedrolls, a squad of cavalry rode up and Joaquin invited them to spend the night.

"Mason Maxon," the lieutenant said, dismounting to shake their hands. "You don't mind camping with coloreds?"

"Lieutenant, I served several years with Bullis and I spent much of my time in Texas guiding the Fourth and the Tenth. I got no qualms about black folk."

"Good," Maxon said, motioning for his men to dismount. "I'm getting very impatient with people who do."

"You're in the wrong place to expect any different," Ethan said.

"Suppose you're right. How many years did you serve?"

"All together, counting the war, fifteen years or so. Left as a first sergeant in the Scout Service."

"You don't look Indian," Maxon said.

"Half," Ethan said, smiling wide. "You don't mind camping with a half-breed do you?"

"No," Maxon laughed. "Be happy to." The lieutenant explained he had half a troop of cavalry scattered along the road.

"Well, we're mighty glad to see you boys," Joaquin said, introducing himself to the lieutenant. He told him about the Apache camp in the canyon and that they were holding three white captives, three whites who the State of Texas wanted for robbery and attempted murder and murder.

Maxon didn't want to hear that. He was hoping for an uneventful month and now that was ruined just a few days into the thirty. "How many?"

"Two dozen, mas o menos," Joaquin said. "I think we should storm their camp right now."

"No," Ethan said quickly.

"No? We've got the men now. We don't have to worry about being outnumbered. Those three people deserve our help, even if we just toss them in prison afterwards," Joaquin said.

"No," Ethan said. "It'll be dark soon. Dark. We don't want to go stumbling around after dark. They're all likely to get away and we'll be lucky if we don't shoot ourselves up in the process. Wait for daylight tomorrow. They're not going anyplace. You saw the camp, they just set up like they're going to stay a while. They're staying."

"I think this gentleman is correct," Maxon said.

"No offense, lieutenant, but I'm no gentleman. And, yes, I am correct."

Most of the soldiers bedded down right after their supper. Two of them played cards by candlelight. Joaquin, Ethan and Maxon sat talking. Maxon looked at his watch when they heard the first scream. It was nine-thirty.

"Did you hear that?" Joaquin said.

"Clearly," Ethan replied.

"We going to do anything? They're torturing that woman," Joaquin said, standing up and looking in the direction the scream came from. More screams floated down the canyon.

"What would expect me to do?" Ethan said, his arms wrapped around his knees. "Go charging into an Apache camp after dark and outnumbered?"

"We can't just sit here," he said. "Maybe could distract them and save that woman."

Maxon took a long pull on his pipe. "It's too late for her and her friends. It was this afternoon. They were dead the moment they were captured. We go charging in, the Apache will just kill them all sooner than they might have otherwise."

"If we can't stop them from killing her, surely we can stop them from torturing her. If we did fire on their camp and they did kill the woman wouldn't that be more merciful than having her die some terrible death?" Joaquin said. The screams were louder and more frequent now, rousing all the soldiers.

"You said this woman and her friend were wanted for murder? And other crimes?" Maxon said. "Why should I risk a single one of my men in a hopeless cause?"

"Because it's your job," Joaquin spat.

"Yours, too, for that matter," Maxon said. "I'll do my job as I see fit. You're free to do yours as you wish."

Joaquin wanted to rush toward the screams immediately, but he knew he would do so alone. He kicked a rock and stomped around the camp. He came back to Ethan's side and sat back down. "What are they doing to her?"

"Imagine the worst," Ethan said. "When you have, it's worse than that."

"Will they rape her? Cut her open?"

"The raping comes first," Ethan said. "Probably the first screams you heard. The beginning. When she thought that was over, another warrior raped her then another. If a warrior's wife happens to be along, the wife might hit her with rocks or a stick to let her know she doesn't appreciate her husband taking a white woman. I imagine that's where they are now. Once those screams stop she'll think it's over, but they'll start in on something else. Slice her up some, maybe skin her alive."

"But not quickly," Maxon added. "Just a little at a time and if she passes out, they wait a bit and rouse her with water then continue."

"When does it end?" Joaquin said, barely able to speak.

"Apache are experts at this sort of thing," Ethan said as they heard a scream, more terrible than any that had gone before. "They can make it last all night."

CHAPTER 20
Woman Hollering Creek

They heard the screaming all through the night. The soldiers whispered to themselves about it after Sergeant Clayborn asked Lieutenant Maxon if they were going into action and Maxon said not until morning and that they should get some sleep. But no one slept.

The screams were sometimes whimpers, sometimes blood-curdling. With each dreadful shriek, they all thought it would surely be the last one. How could a girl survive whatever caused her to scream like that? Certainly this scream had to be her final breath. But it wasn't. Somehow she had just enough life for another appalling squeal. They thought one of the screams would never end, it just carried on and on, building in a horrific crescendo. Then, just as the sun dawned, the screaming mercifully ended.

Ethan had already made coffee and offered some to Joaquin when the Ranger walked over to the fire.

"You did this on purpose," Joaquin said. "You drove her into the savages to be massacred, to be butchered."

"Eh-yeah," he replied, handing Joaquin a cup and pouring some coffee. "I could have killed that woman for what she did, but it wouldn't have been enough. Not enough. I couldn't have tortured her myself as much as I might have liked to. The Apache could. That screaming was justice being done."

"How are you ever going to sleep again? I'll hear that woman's screams all my life and so will you," Joaquin said.

Ethan sipped his coffee. "Nope. I can go to sleep in peace now listening to that woman hollering."

The soldiers broke camp, saddled their mounts and stood by them waiting for orders. Maxon turned to Ethan.

"Will you scout the canyon first? If we're going in we need to know the lay of the land and how many warriors and how well armed," Maxon asked.

"Eh-yeah," Ethan said, finishing his coffee. "Don't do anything rash until I get back."

●

"Your Power is right," Madrone told Lozen as he rode back into camp. "Many Pale Eyes soldiers at the mouth of the canyon. I have seen more that way along the road and more that way. Riders left early this morning from this group and now all the soldiers are gathering here."

Her Power frightened her this morning and she was certain it was punishment for allowing Madrone to torture the white woman. Her brother taught her torture was wrong and she believed it, but Madrone convinced her that just this once would be a good thing. And it was for him. She could see his stature rise in the eyes of the other warriors throughout the night. But what benefited him did not benefit all of them. Now her Power told her Pale Eyes soldiers were very near; it told her more soldiers were almost everywhere around them. They could no longer cross the river. They could not go into the mountains in the east. They could not go to the mountains in the north. They could only go west, back to the reservation they fled many moons ago. This saddened her and made her feel less of a leader. But the Pale Eyes were too numerous. They were everywhere. She asked the band to break up the camp and follow her back to the reservation.

"What do we do with them?" Upsidedown asked, indicating the two Pale Eye men.

"They've amused us enough," she said, stepping over the flayed body of the woman that ants were now feasting on. "Kill them or let them go. I don't care."

"They're not worth a bullet," Upsidedown said. He walked to the two men. "Ukashe," he ordered but they didn't understand. "Ukashe!" he repeated. This time motioning with his hands for them to go. The Pale Eyes looked at each other, looked back at Upsidedown, looked at Lozen, then walked toward the mouth of the canyon, the big man helping the one-legged man.

●

Ethan went north on the road, then over the mountain that formed one of the canyon walls. He was a half-mile away when he first saw the Apache band moving up the canyon and into the western mountain. He rode closer to see who was riding with them. He didn't see any of the show people.

He rode along the ridge watching the hostiles maneuver their ponies up the steep slope to his left. Their leader turned and saw him. He recognized Lozen and held his hand up to make certain he got her attention, then he blew her a kiss. He knew she wouldn't understand. What he wanted to do was ride down and talk to her, ask her about her pendant and who gave it to her or who she took it off. He hadn't seen one in decades and never saw one very far from home. He wondered if she even knew what a Cross of Lorraine was but doubted it.

He turned and returned to the soldiers at the mouth of the canyon. Maxon and several troopers were standing beside the large, oddly shaped rocks that guarded the canyon. His men were aiming rifles and hollering.

"Thas the biggest damn Injin I ever did see," one of the privates said.

"Funny lookin' Injins, though," another said.

They were on the verge of shooting at the approaching vision of one man hopping on one leg while another man — a huge man wearing an animal loincloth — helped him. The big man waved his free arm and was yelling at them not to shoot.

"Hold your fire," Joaquin said, still mounted. "They're white men."

The soldiers weren't certain this young Ranger knew what he was talking about, but they were going to wait for their lieutenant to give the order to fire anyway, and that order never came.

"What about the Apaches?" Maxon asked Ethan.

The scout dismounted and drank from his canteen before answering. "They went up the hill on the west wall of the canyon. Looks to me like they've got their tails stuck between their legs."

"They're not heading toward the river?" Maxon asked.

"If you ask me, they're heading to New Mexico. The Mescalero Reservation ain't half as bad as any of the others, nowhere near as bad as San Carlos. These Apache know they're not going south. If they thought they could, they would have come straight at us and blown right through. River's not far. Not far at all; they could maybe make it. Settlement north and west. You horse soldiers riding all over the desert between the Guadalupes and the Chisos and the Chinatis. I imagine they're off to visit relatives at Mescalero."

"I'm inclined to believe you," Maxon said. "But just to make certain, I'll keep my troop scattered along the road blocking any access to the river until our time's up. Then we'll go home, too. I think we've seen the last of hostiles in Texas. This state's just getting too civilized for them."

"Sounds like a plan," Ethan said, taking another drink.

The two show people, both filthy, stumbled up to the soldiers.

Joaquin rode to them. "What about the woman?"

The big man shook his head lowly. The one-legged man replied softly, "It was the most horrible thing I've ever seen. You hear the stories, you know, but this was worse than anything. She killed Earl and maybe even killed our old Jo-Jo, but I don't know that she deserved what she suffered."

"You're both under arrest," Joaquin said.

"Tank you," Maximo, the World's Strongest Man, said.

CHAPTER 21
Lajitas

Ethan and Joaquin sat at their usual table, Joaquin sipping his whiskey and Ethan sipping coffee. Gracey was running the bar at the Mejor Que Nada, but she insisted it was only temporary. She didn't want to run a bar, she didn't want to spend her time serving alcohol and being responsible for money. She was a whore. She liked being a whore. She wanted to be a whore.

Ethan told her she couldn't be a whore forever, but she said she would as long as she could. Then she might run a whorehouse. But she wouldn't ever run a saloon or café. She wanted to serve only one item. Anything else was too complicated. He told her someone had to run the saloon and she suggested he do it. Dutch had no heirs, so for all practical purposes the saloon would go to whoever wanted it.

It seemed to them that the Doc from the medicine show might have made a good proprietor, but he was gone by the time they returned from upriver. Gracey said Doc aimed to sell his spare wagons to the Burgesses at Fort Leaton. Said Doc was going to put his fat lady friend on a train and send her home to Georgia and he was going to seek a long lost love out in New Mexico or Arizona if he could find her. Said this love was an Indian maiden, of all things. Tío José had no interested in running the saloon in addition to his café because he liked to go to sleep when it got dark and wake when it got light and not the other way around. The McGuirks wanted nothing to do with the wages of sin.

Joaquin sat at the table sorting through the mail Gracey gave him. A few newspapers, this quarter's bible of wanted men from Ranger Headquarters, and a scented note from his beloved Rachel. He put that in his vest pocket to open later in private when he could enjoy it. He savored her elaborate penmanship, picturing her laboring over every letter in every word to give it just the right flourish.

"When do you leave?" Ethan asked.

"Haven't decided yet," Joaquin said, glancing at the newspapers.

"My sergeant said as long as I'm in Fort Davis and ready for duty on the New Year, he'll be a happy man. I think I'll take a week off and celebrate Christmas with Rachel and her family in San Antone, then head back west."

"Family Christmases are a good thing," Ethan said. "We'll miss you around here."

"Don't be too down in the mouth. I'll be down here often enough. The Rangers decided it wasn't such a good idea to have just one man here and there, better to consolidate the force in various locations and patrol out."

"It's one big county. They should break it up into several small ones. Hell, even if they split it in two each half'd still be larger than some New England states."

Joaquin nodded his agreement and continued scanning the newspapers. "Gracey's right, you know. You should take over this place."

"What do I know about running a saloon?" Ethan said.

"People pay you money for products, you put it aside, you buy new product, it gets delivered and you sell it and the process starts all over again. Just one big circle. You just have to be quick enough to grab some of the cash as it goes by."

"I don't need the money. I don't need the aggravation."

"But you need something to do," Joaquin said. "Look, I appreciate you continuing to help me learn how to track, but pretty soon I'll have learned all I can. Then what? You stopped drinking, and that's a good thing, but now you've got a lot more conscious hours to fill. What are you going to do with them?"

"Eh-yeah, that's a good point. Hadn't thought much about that. Hadn't given it much thought at all. But I'm not sure this is a good place for me to be spending that free time. A drunk running a bar?"

"Afraid you'll fall off the wagon? I don't think you will. You said you stopped because that's what Dutch wanted you to do and I can't picture you dishonoring that memory. Even if you did go back to drinking, you'd be no worse off than you were before."

"I don't know…"

"Look, you already left that shack in Terlingua and moved here. You're changing your life. Take the next step."

"I'd have to find another whore," Ethan said. "One's not

enough."

"Probably," Joaquin said, then snorted through his nose. "But I know one woman you won't get to whore anymore."

"What's that?"

Joaquin folded up the *San Antonio Express* and showed it to Ethan, pointing to an item on the society page.

Ingrid Jarrel and Karl Weichkopf, a couple from far West Texas, were united in the bonds of Holy Matrimony at San Fernando Cathedral at about noon this past Saturday. At 8 o'clock in the evening, a bouncing boy weighing nine and a half pounds, was born to the blooming bride of less than ten hours. The loving couple, and the son they have given the cumbersome appellation of Ethan David Joaquin Weichkopf, plans to live in Galveston.

"I'll be a cross-eyed snail herder." Ethan said.

"See," Joaquin said. "You're already talking like a saloon owner."

Book Three
SECOND COFFEE CREEK

Fall 1881

CHAPTER 1

South Rim of the Chisos Mountains

"That's twice you've saved my life now," Texas Ranger Joaquin Jaxon said, his hands trembling as he buttoned up his trousers then tucked in his shirt.

Ethan Allan Twobears sat cross-legged beside the body, examining the cuts across his own arms and chest. He ran the edges of his hands over the cuts to wipe away as much blood as he could. He didn't like the animal's blood mixing with his own. "Eh-yeah." His remark was echoed in the distance by a falcon and he looked in the direction of the sound but couldn't see the bird of prey.

"And twice you've done it with a knife," Joaquin said, staring at the old scout who seemed just as calm now as he was a few minutes ago when they rose from their bedrolls into the chilly September morning. He was grateful for the respite from the desert heat up here near the tops of the mountains, but he knew that the sun would blister them with heat by midday — just not the blast furnace heat of a few miles away that started in April and was relentless until November.

"Eh-yeah," Ethan said, cleaning his knife blade by shoving it into the dirt several times. He'd resharpen it when they returned to Lajitas. "But I wouldn't recommend killing a catamount with a knife. Especially not one this large. Not this big."

Joaquin broke some branches to build the fire up enough so they could have some breakfast and coffee. His hands still shook. "Felt like a freight train when he hit me. If I'd been any nearer that cliff, you'd been figuring out some way to get down there and pick up the pieces about now."

"Long drop," Ethan said. "Most of the Chisos is like that. I imagine this was some old volcano that collapsed or maybe it was just a mountain that wanted to be a volcano but never quite made it. Sides are pretty steep up here above the basin. You go over and you've got time enough to say the Lord's Prayer on the way down before you smash to pieces. Long way down. I know of one or two cliff faces that have ledges, but not many. And even if you stopped on one of them, you'd play hell getting back up. Or down safely."

"Why'd he hit me instead of you?"

"You're — what? — five-foot-six or seven and don't have an ounce of fat on you. I stand six-foot-three and I've gotten a little rounder in my old age. So you're smaller. Plus you were squatting down and I imagine to this big cat you just looked like an easy breakfast."

"Couldn't help that," Joaquin said. "My early morning bowel movement is the only time I can grunt all day. Been plagued by constipation since I took up working cattle. Probably all that time in the saddle, y'know, during the day. Then I'm too packed in at night but by morning I guess it loosens up and I wake up cramping to go."

Ethan laughed and nodded. "Quite a sight to see when that cat struck."

"I'm glad I could amuse you," Joaquin said, cooking some bacon in a pan.

"Only wound you got was on your bottom. How're you going to explain those long scratches to your lady Rachel?"

"It'll heal by the time she sees it," he snapped.

"Eh-yeah. Heal up into a couple nice scars. And your wedding night will happen before the year's out. Right?"

"Bit more," Joaquin said, forking out the strips of bacon onto a rock heated by the adjacent fire. He dropped two tortillas into the bacon grease and warmed them up. "Our plan is to have the wedding on the day after New Year's Day, like a new beginning for us."

"She'll be glad to find out you're going to be around instead of chewed up by a wild beast and becoming catamount shit in the woods."

"You want some of this or not?" Joaquin said, motioning with the frying pan.

Ethan rose to his feet in one motion and stepped over as his friend dropped the greasy, warm tortillas on the rock next to the bacon. He picked up one of the tortillas and filled it with several pieces of bacon, rolled it up and bit in. "You're gonna make Rachel a wonderful wife. Good breakfast."

"Mmm," Joaquin replied with a scowl. "Too bad you haven't

learned how to make a decent pot of coffee yet. Tastes like diluted bear grease."

"You're the one who forgot to bring enough grounds for two mornings. I never drank coffee in my life until last fall so cut me some slack," Ethan said. He wiped his mouth with his shirt sleeve, gulped down some of the coffee and grimaced with just how bad it was. He went back to the mountain lion and gutted it, tossing the entrails over the cliff. He roped its hind legs together and strung the big cat up on a tree limb so it could bleed out.

"You taking that lion back?" Joaquin asked.

Ethan rubbed his hands and forearms with dirt to clean them, poured some water over his hands and dried them on his trouser legs. "Pretty good eating and a lot of him."

"Never had the pleasure."

"Gracey'll do him up proud."

"He'll be a hefty load to carry back down. We should have ridden the horses up here."

"Nope. Walking does a man good. Slows you down, lets you feel nature, gets your blood flowing. Since the beginning of time that's what men did: walk. That's what we're made for. Besides, if we'd brought horses up here that catamount would've gotten one of them."

Joaquin poured the remaining coffee on the fire, putting it out in a gush of smoke. "Better a horse than me."

"Well, he might have gone for you anyway. I imagine that lily-white bottom looked downright scrumptious to him."

Joaquin rolled the remaining bacon into his own tortilla, scooped it into the remaining grease, then handed the pan to Ethan to clean. "I shudder to think what might have happened if you didn't have that knife in your boot."

"Eh-yeah," Ethan said, scrubbing the pan with dirt. "All our guns were by the bedrolls, including my big knife. If I didn't have this small one in my boot you'd have been shredded by the time I got to my rifle. Just shredded. That was a bitch, though, 'cause that cat just didn't want to die. I must have stabbed and slashed him more'n a dozen times, and he slashed me some, too, before he finally gave up."

"Didn't think he was going to give up," Joaquin said. "Y'all were rolling all over the place and he was screeching and I heard you say a cuss word or two in the process and all I could see was that lion's claws and teeth and your knife. Don't know how you did it."

"You just have to be pissed off enough. The cat started off hungry, then he got confused, then he got to fighting. By that time, I was so angry I imagine I could have killed him with my bare hands."

"Angry at what?"

Ethan rolled up his blanket and slicker and tied them together, slinging the roll across one shoulder. "Well. Two things if you must know. Biggest thing was that I was pissed he was making me kill him. Can't reason with a wild animal. Not with a wild animal in survival mode. It comes down to him or you. You can't negotiate a truce. Kill him quick before he does you. And why? Because he's behaving the way God made him. He's a wild animal. He's your basic carnivore; he kills other animals to eat. That's not good or bad, just what is. Well, he paid the ultimate price for just being what he was. Like those Comanche, remember? They were just being wild Indians, just like God made 'em. And they paid for it. I made 'em pay for it. Having to do that, to those Comanche or to that cat, really pisses me off."

"And what's the other thing?" Joaquin asked, kicking dirt over the still smoldering fire.

"You."

"Pissed at me because the lion attacked me?"

"No," Ethan said. He walked over to the lion's body and lifted it off the tree branch, tied its front legs together then shouldered the body, adjusting himself a couple of times under the weight. "I was pissed at you because you were standing there with your panties around your ankles watching me wrestle with a catamount. Just watching. Your rifle wasn't that far away, y'know."

Joaquin shook his head and looked away. "Jesus. I never even thought. I was so caught up in what was happening, the idea of going for my gun never occurred to me. Jesus, I'm sorry. I should have. Damn. Damn."

"Don't beat yourself up over it. Happens," Ethan said. "Let's go back down this other way. There's a spring and small creek near a big boot-looking rock that I'd like to soak in for a while. It's one of the things you need to remember, though, when shit like this happens is when you need to get as calm as you've ever been in your life."

"But I thought you need that blood pumping to give you an edge."

"You do when you're in the thick of it like I was. Otherwise, you got to get yourself calm and do it quick and think about what to do."

"And I thought I had everything all figured out," Joaquin said, walking beside Ethan, carrying both of their rifles.

"You're doing well. Just try to keep making new mistakes. That's how you learn. You keep making the same mistakes, well, that's how you die out here. You die."

They walked for a couple hours, more sluggish than Ethan would have liked, but the weight of the lion slowed him down considerably. He was glad to throw it on the ground when they got to Boot Spring.

"Maybe we should spend the night here instead of going all the way back today," Joaquin said, pulling his boots off to soak his feet in the spring. "We never did see a deer yesterday, nor today for that matter. Bet they come down to this spring, though."

Ethan removed his own boots but instead of sitting on a log like Joaquin, he stepped into the creek and lay down in it, letting the cold water wash over him, numbing the throbbing pain of his claw cuts. "I'm tempted, but I think we should get back so I can have Gracey look at these wounds and clean them out properly. Wash 'em out with some whiskey."

"She always seems to be doctoring you up, doesn't she?" Joaquin said. "Maybe you just ought to marry her so you always have a good curandera around when you need one 'cause you're always in need of one."

Ethan laughed and nodded. "You could be right. Maybe I'm carrying a torch for her and this is just my way of getting her to pay attention to me."

"Pretty extreme if you ask me."

"Eh-yeah. I don't think any woman is worth getting clawed up over. But even without these cuts we should go back today. I don't know about leaving the horses alone for another day. Still Apache in these mountains, y'know."

"So you say, but I've never seen them."

"Not unless they want to be seen," Ethan said. "Alsate doesn't have a large band up here. They're almost like ghosts. You don't see them unless they want to be seen. Ghosts."

"Mescaleros?"

Ethan struggled out of the creek bed and pulled on his boots over his wet feet. In the deep shade, as soaked as he was, he shivered. In a few minutes, though, he knew they'd be in open sun and he would dry quickly. He nodded to Joaquin who put on his boots and grabbed their rifles. Ethan shouldered the lion again and they walked off. "¿Quién sabe? Maybe they were at one time, but they've been off on their own so long I don't know the Mescalero claim them anymore."

They walked through the thick forest until it gave way to brush, giving them a clear view of the desert that stretched out as far as they could see, interrupted only by more mountains in the distance. Soon they'd lose sight of the desert and be heading towards the Chisos basin again. "You know," Joaquin said after a while. "I'll never forget this. Once, I'd never forget. Twice, I don't even know how to repay you."

"We'll think of something."

CHAPTER 2
Southern Pacific Railroad Work Camp, west of Burgess Springs, Texas

A Canadian cold front pushed high winds ahead of it. The front at this time of year in this part of Texas would drop temperatures by at least three, perhaps even four degrees—just enough to bring the heat below 100. The winds were already ferocious with the frustration of not being able to expend some of their energy in wide temperature swings and as they dropped off the Davis Mountains and fell south, they picked up velocity. And they picked up dust.

Dust was about all that moved in daylight hours here anyway. Desert critters hid away until the sun went down. Desert plants grew far apart, sipping as much moisture as they could out of their exclusive, broad plot of dirt. In between the plants, the dirt dried out, the winds blasted the dirt into smaller and smaller particles until what remained were several layers of dust. Dust that would be relocated by winds such as this.

The winds grabbed up the dust and cast it before them, creating a tan curtain that moved like an angry slap across the landscape.

One of the convict workers looked up and saw the curtain rushing at them and hollered, "Dust storm!" The workers dropped their aggies, shovels, sledges, and lever bars and as quickly as their chains would allow, hobbled off to seek shelter behind the engine and tool car. The guards were already there, dismounted and covering their horses' noses with wet handkerchiefs. The guards carried no pistols; their rifles and shotguns were on thick leather straps slung around their shoulders so no freedom-minded convict could take them; and they kept their horses between them and the workers. The storm hit, turning the world brown, trying to bury the men alive.

Benjamin Factor lay on the infirmary cot in pain; the convict hospital steward hid under the cot as the sides of the tent began flapping. Ben knew what was coming, he'd been tasting the dust for a long time, and managed to soak a blood-stained towel in a bucket of water and cover his face with it. He wanted to turn on his right side to be away from where the wind was blowing from, but the pain was too great to roll over onto the crushed hip so he curled up as best he could and covered up further with a sheet. When the storm hit, it blew one of the tent pegs out of the ground, exposing a corner to the elements that rushed in with a fury. The storm behaved like a wounded animal, howling and thrashing about, looking for something to vent its anger and confusion on. Having no weapon, Ben did as he would have in the wild when such an animal was near: he hid and prayed.

The storm distracted Ben from the pain, but then his right foot itched. It itched almost as brutally as the storm sounded. This was, he knew, impossible because he no longer had a right foot. He lost that in the accident that crushed his hip. The steward amputated the foot not four hours ago and Ben believed it was still in a slop bucket somewhere in the tent… or it was. Perhaps now the disembodied foot was dancing across the desert until it got stuck in an ocotillo. The thought of his foot imbedding itself on the thick thorns of ocotillo stalks made Ben wince in pain. The itchiness was gone now. Then the imaginary pain gave way quickly to the real pain on his hip and he thought he heard the storm chuckling at his situation. Boze, the steward, said he would heal, that he would walk again, but only with difficulty and only with a crutch. When the steward said the foot was too damaged to save, Ben at first thought he would carve himself another foot out of a cottonwood root — cottonwood was very light but relatively strong and easy to carve — but that was before he knew about the harm to his hip. It wasn't crushed exactly, but that's the way he thought about it. Boze said it felt as if it was broken in several places, parts of bone sheared off was how he put it, and while it would all heal up it would never function properly again. So if he had no full use of his hip, why bother with making a foot? It'd be pretty but serve no useful purpose.

Ben heard the steward — a man twice his own 30 years — coughing under the cot. "Takes as short a breaths as y'can," Ben said as loudly as he could, unsure if the orderly could hear him. "Jest doan pass out."

"Ah'm the doc hyar," the deep voice of the steward replied.

Ben had no interest in arguing the point, no interest in arguing any point, not much interest in anything right now. Not since the trial.

The wind picked up a little, died a little, then picked up again.

Ben tried to recapture that one moment in the trial when he thought, for that one second, he might go free. It was an exhilarating moment, one dashed to pieces in the very next moment, but that first moment was glorious. He almost seized the feeling, but remembering Judge Joe E. Taliaferro's words dashed the emotion because he knew the words that followed.

"It is a terrible crime and a terrible shirking of the responsibility a husband bears towards his wife, to engage in brutality with little or no cause," the judge began when he pronounced Ben's sentence. "And it is a terrible thing for a brother, who has proven himself over and over to be the finest sort of gentleman a man of his race could hope to become, a man who has served his flag proudly, to have to sit idly by and witness such brutality visited with such regularity upon his younger sister. I say to this court that is a fearsome burden to bear, and we can only imagine the emotionally wrenching suffering that Mr. Benjamin Factor standing here before us must have endured for so many months. Who among us would not have done as Mr. Factor has done, and smitten his unruly brother-in-law into Kingdom Come? Who among us would not and still be thought of as decent gentlemen? That is why I am inclined to be lenient in this case." That was the moment. That's when Ben imagined the next words out of the judge's mouth would set him free. Instead, he heard, "But, gentlemen, this is a nation of laws and laws must be obeyed otherwise chaos ensues. Mr. Factor should have sought legal recourse for the wrongs his heinous brother-in-law was inflicting on his frail sister. At the very least, he should have spirited his sister away from this beast and provided a divorce.

"But Mr. Benjamin Factor did not follow the law. He ignored the law. He grasped the law into his own hands and acted as judge, jury and executioner. The law cannot allow this. I will not allow this in my court.

"Mr. Factor, you have committed a murder. The normal punishment for this crime is to be hanged by your neck until you are dead, but I am inclined toward leniency because of the extenuating circumstances surrounding your crime. And if you were a white man, sir, I would be sorely tempted to declare you guilty of nothing more than justifiable homicide. However, you must also serve as an example to those of your race, to demonstrate that this is the United States of

America, sir, and you will not take to the law of the jungle nor to the law of the red man. It is, therefore, my ruling that you serve twenty years at hard labor as the Texas State Prison Board shall determine."

The gavel sounded, the judge rose, and Ben was yanked out of the courtroom by his chains.

He was disappointed by the judge's ruling, but he wasn't angered by it. He had no regrets about beating Adam Hepzibah to death out by the dump north of The Camp near Fort Clark.

Ben and all his brothers warned their sister Dolly about Adam. They knew the man as a shirker and a drunkard, but Dolly professed her undying love for Adam, telling her brothers that the love of a good woman would change him. All of them much older than Dolly, her brothers knew love could start a marriage but couldn't make it last. You needed respect and shared values and a kindredness of spirit that went beyond love to make a marriage survive and thrive. It took, they knew, work from both the parties and they knew Adam did not like to work at anything. He found the answer for all problems in the bottom of a bottle of whiskey. His only joy in life was in getting to that bottle's bottom.

At first, the Factors tried to lead Adam down the proper path. Then they resorted to threats. Then they gave up. How many times had Dolly sought refuge in the middle of the night in one of their shacks only to return to Adam the next morning? You could put up with that behavior only so long. If the woman didn't care enough about herself to save herself, what could they do?

Ben was closest in age to Dolly and every time he knew Adam had beaten his sister, he became angrier and angrier until the day he watched it happen. Dolly dropped something on the ground as she and Adam walked through The Camp. Ben never saw what it was, but it was apparently important to Adam. Adam grabbed Dolly and swung her around to hit her, but in the violent pull on her left arm, the arm broke. Ben heard the bone snap. He saw the elbow turn in an obscene direction. He watched his sister drop to the ground in pain. So Sergeant Benjamin Factor, U.S. Army Scout Service, band of Seminole Negroes, ran up to Adam Hepzibah, a private citizen in the band of Seminole Negroes, grabbed his left arm and snapped it in two.

When the man howled that Ben had done him wrong, that it

wasn't fair for a man larger than he to do such a thing to him, Ben lost all control. Adam was sitting on the ground, rocking back and forth while holding his arm and whining in pain. Ben kicked Adam again and again, until the other man fell backwards. Then Ben kept kicking him until his brothers pulled him away, leaving the bloody mess that was Adam Hepzibah in the dirt.

After conferring with Lieutenant John L. Bullis, the scouts' commander, Colonel William R. Shafter decided to turn Ben over to the civilian authority in Kinney County since it was a civilian who was murdered and the killing took place off the post. They felt they were doing one of Bullis' favorite sergeants a good turn by giving him over to the county, knowing the army would send the soldier to a firing squad without a thought.

As the dust storm subsided, Ben took in several deep breaths, trying to ignore the pain in his hip. The big convict steward pulled himself up from under the cot, surveying the wind damage, angry that Ben wouldn't be able to help him find lost items or tidy up. As a steward, a man of many years, and the only white inmate in the work camp, he was used to certain privileges. The guards would have the other inmates cleaning up the work site, so he'd get no help at all.

For all that had happened to him in the past few months, Ben still didn't feel sorry for himself. He gave Adam Hepzibah what he deserved, and now he would get what he deserved. He was willing to pay that price. If only his sister didn't hate him, he would be a happy man—crushed hip, missing foot, and incarceration be damned.

 **CHAPTER 3**
El Paso, Texas

He was on an unfamiliar, uncomfortable path. He knew he should be happy to leave all the troubles so many miles behind him, but it was a new life ahead and he'd have to be careful. He stepped toward the stagecoach, handing his bulging saddlebags, portmanteau, and rifle to the messenger who was loading passengers' luggage in the rear boot.

"Y'all got a permission slip from your mommy to git on this hyah stage, kid?" the man said.

"My mom's been dead and gone a lot a years now and I'm old enough to drive this stage not just ride in it," Henry McCarty snapped.

"Kid's got spunk," the messenger guard said to the wizened driver. He spit a large, dark stream of tobacco and saliva into the street. "I hate spunk."

The driver took a step closer, scratched behind his left ear, and looked directly into Henry's face. "Stop pickin' on the boy, Ernie. Looks to me like he's gone through some tribulations. That true, kid?"

Henry nodded yes.

"Looks t'me like you lost someone dear," the driver said.

Henry nodded yes, thinking he'd lost the one person closest to him in all the world: himself.

The driver opened the stage door, picking up a short two-step from inside and placing it on the ground to help passengers board. "How far y'all goin'?"

"Fort Davis," Henry said.

"Family there?"

Henry shook his head no. "I'm headin' to a place south of there. Hope to work up a sweat at Milton Faver's ranch on the Cibolo."

The driver whistled. "Lord, kid, that's a long way off in bad country."

"It's all I know," Henry said, shrugging his shoulders. "All I've ever done is tend horses and cattle."

"Well, Don Milton's sure got a passel of 'em," the driver said, extending his arm so the short young man would have support as he climbed into the stage. He noticed the boy's hands were even smaller, almost dainty like a lady's. The hands didn't look like those of a cow puncher. "Thousands of cattle and more sheep and goats. Good man, though, Don Milton. Don't know him personal, y'understand, but I hear from all accounts he's a stalwart fella."

Henry jumped into the coach. "I used to work for a stalwart man. Treated me the best. But he's gone now, too. All my pals are gone, too."

"I'm sure it'll all work out," the driver said, latching the door. "You're a young lad with a long life in front a you, so just keep a positive outlook and things'll all work out.

Yeah, Henry thought, settling in on the stage seat. Yeah, he'd had a positive attitude all his life and it got him out of more than a few scrapes in Brooklyn and Indiana and Kansas and Colorado and Texas and Arizona and New Mexico, but now, he realized, that attitude was all self-centered and that attitude was also what caused all the problems he'd dealt with the past few years.

As the stage lurched forward into the Eastern expanse of dust that seemed more a part of New Mexico than Texas, Henry wondered if that attitude was why people kept giving him breaks regardless of what he did. Oh, he knew the senoritas found him handsome and nearly everyone was charmed by his lopsided, buck-toothed smile, but maybe it was just that positive attitude he kept about him. He chuckled a little, thinking about Sheriff Harvey Whitehill. Henry fell in with the Sombrero Jack gang and his first real crime was stealing several pounds of butter from a rancher. He was caught almost immediately, but ol' Harv, he just released him after Henry promised to behave from then on. Why, Harv even got him a job washing dishes at the Star Hotel. Harv was disappointed when Henry only smiled and shrugged after being caught stealing clothes from a celestial laundry, and that time Harv locked him up. But Henry just scampered up a chimney and escaped. He had a knack for that, escaping from jails. Why, there was the time he was jailed for stealing Army horses from in front of a Fort Grant saloon and didn't he escape from that one, too. Once he got to New Mexico he fell in with Jess Evans and they stole ponies off the

Mescalero Reservation. Yeah, he was so smooth he could steal horses from Indians. Too bad he wouldn't be able to tell that story anymore. Then he broke one of his pals out of the jail in San Elizario. Jails were like cake, he chuckled again. They looked substantial but there really wasn't much to them. Even armed guards at the Lincoln jail couldn't hold him in. Then Juan Largo helped him get out of all the troubles. Why, didn't the governor promise Henry a pardon and didn't the damned county attorney renege on it, so why shouldn't Juan Largo help him out? They were pals. Didn't they get handy with a runnin' iron more than a few times together? Before he got religion and got that star on his vest? Sure, pals were deeper than stars. Didn't Juan Largo make sure the coroner's jury was all friends? Didn't Alejandro appreciate his jokes and free beef and wasn't Alejandro the J.P.? Yeah, with a sheriff and a justice of the peace and the whole coroner's jury and witnesses like the man who figured he was going to be your father-in-law, why, you could pull anything off, including dying. And didn't he die? Why, it was in all the papers, so he must be dead.

A bump in the road rattled Henry out of his reverie. He laughed, removed his hat to push it back into shape, and rubbed his now sore head. He looked across at the elderly woman traveling with a younger man and smiled broadly. "Hope you're faring well, m'am, that was a rough patch for sure."

She smiled back at him. "Yes, thank you, young man. I'm well. I've traveled by wagon and stage for many decades and always bring my cushion with me to soften the rough spells. And I've got quite the good balance, so I don't sway to and fro."

"I'm afraid I'm so small that's all I seem to do, sway," Henry said.

"My name's Matilda Cline and this is my son Ferdinand," the woman said, tapping sweat from her forehead with a lacy handkerchief. "We're on our way to Fort Davis where my son will establish a newspaper for Presidio County." Her son gave a perfunctory smile and nodded, looking at Henry directly for the first time.

"Pleased to meet you," Ferdinand said, extending his hand.

Henry shook it and told the man his name.

"You look vaguely familiar," Ferdinand said. "Did you live in the El Paso region? Perhaps I've seen you around the town as I was the star reporter for the *Mesilla Valley Independent*."

"Gee, I don't think we've met. I'm not from El Paso. I'm from... Arizona and traveling south for a job in the Big Bend."

"Didn't know there were many jobs out in that region," Ferdinand said. "Except for the army and saloons. You don't seem like you'd fit in at either."

Henry touched the brim of his hat. "He-he. No, I'd be a puddin' foot as a soldier. And I don't paint my nose when I go into a saloon, but I've frequented my share of card games in 'em. I must say that, yeah, I love the cards. But I'm headin' south to work for Milton Faver's ranch. At least I hope to. I understand he has a wide spread down there and always needs good hands."

"Can't say as I picture you riding the range, either," Ferdinand said. "And as a journalist, I'm a pretty fine judge of character."

"Guess you missed this one, mister," Henry said. "I've pushed cattle since I was a boy. Only job I know. I don't count cards as a job 'cause that's too much fun."

Ferdinand smiled and was quiet, but continued to stare at Henry.

"I'm certain you would excel at whatever endeavor you attempted," Matilda said, reaching over to pat Henry on the knee. He grinned wide at the touch.

"He-he. Whatever I do always seems to work out just fine," he nodded.

•

Cibolo Creek Ranch near the Chinati Mountains, Texas

A week later, Henry rode up to the headquarters building of the Faver ranch, an imposing adobe structure with rounded turrets rising on the corners and small gun slits cut into the walls. This, he thought, was a man determined to succeed in the heart of hostile Indian country. What would the hostiles be here, he wondered, Comanches, Apaches, Yaquis? Apaches, he decided, since the Comanches were off on a reservation up in the Nations and the Mexicans had pretty much wiped out the Yaquis. He dismounted and tied his horse to a railing by the main entrance. The horse and saddle were both old and nearly worn out, but it was all he could afford to buy in Fort Davis. He knew if he signed on here, the ranch would provide him with much better mounts and saddlery.

"You lost, muchaco?" a vaquero asked him just as he entered the courtyard.

"I'm looking for Mr. Faver. Looking for a job."

"Does Don Milton know you?"

"No, señor, but I'm an experienced hand and heard he was hiring."

"Sí. Wait here."

Henry dropped his leather portmanteau and rifle next to the wall and stood by them, propping himself up against the wall with his left foot. He whistled a tune, taking in all that he could see.

The ranch was a busy place. Herders and hands came and went, some men with hides, women carrying laundry and ollas of what he assumed were water. The ollas were being carefully packed on straw in an ox cart. Does this man sell bottles of water? Henry wondered. Who would be stupid enough to buy bottled water? The vaquero returned with a viejo. The old one looked like a farmer, with canvas trousers, sandals, and a peon's white shirt with too long sleeves held in place with purple garters. He wore a small straw sombrero and his brown face was almost completely hidden by a long white beard that fell to below his waist.

"I'm Milton Faver," the viejo said. "Mi segundo, Jim Juan, says you're seeking a position here. Our cattle are not so good for a good year but not so bad for a bad year, so I have a job or two. What do you do?"

Henry snapped his foot off the wall. His eyes lit up and he smiled the grin that made people instantly like him. "I'm a good hand, sir. I've punched cattle in Colorado, Arizona and New Mexico. I've run cattle into Sonora and into Chihuahua. Hablo español."

"You don't appear old enough to have this much experience," Faver said smiling, his head tilted down to shade his eyes under the sombrero's brim.

"I'll be 22 in November," Henry said. "I do look young for my age, he-he. I've worked as a hand since I was 14, sir. Sé caballos y ganado."

"La reata," Faver said to his segundo. Faver took the man's lariat and handed it to Henry. "Rope something."

Henry dropped the coils of the rawhide lasso, holding the honda in his right hand, made one spin to get the loop the size he wanted, and tossed it with gentleness and accuracy onto the neck of a large olla perched on a woman's shoulder. He yanked the lariat and the clay olla flew from the woman directly into Henry's hands. He bobbled the jar, spilling some of its contents over his clothes. It wasn't water. It smelled sweet.

Faver laughed, motioning for the woman to come over and re-trieve the jug. Henry scooped some of the thick liquid up with a finger and tasted it.

"Peach brandy," Faver said. "Best in all the southwest. I have an orchard and I love the brandy we can make from the fruit. Others love it, too. We sell to a great many places. Do you favor brandy?"

"No, sir, I'm not a drinking man," Henry said. "But I must say this is mighty tasty. Might develop a taste for this."

"Jim Juan, show this lad to the bunkhouse and get him a bath. Get his clothes washed out. Tomorrow, get one of the hands to show him where the cattle and sheep are—"

"I'm not a sheep man, Mr. Faver."

"No, I'm certain you're not. But you will need to know the pas-tures we have and what we have grazing on them. That will take you a couple of days. After that, I will send you and another man down to the river to make some deliveries so you can get a feel for this land. Presidio, Fort Leaton, Lajitas. You'll find it similar to New Mexico but still quite different. You have a horse and tack?"

"Yeah, I do," he said, grinning again. "He's got a lot of fiddle hair, though, not worth much to run cattle from."

"We have one of the best remudas in Texas and you'll have your pick. After the more senior hands, of course."

"Of course. Thank you, sir." Henry tasted more of the brandy from his shirt as he followed the segundo.

CHAPTER 2
Galveston, Texas

Ingrid Weischopf walked barefooted on the beach alongside her husband, twirling her lacey parasol lazily on her shoulder. She carried their shoes in a brightly decorated canvas bag. Her husband Karl carried their son Edjie. They had called him that since his birth a little more than a year ago, deriving it from the initials of his Christian names—Ethan, David, and Joaquin.

This was their regular routine on Sundays after church, weather permitting. Ingrid packed a sumptuous picnic, complete with wine and a sweet cake, which they ate sitting on a blanket spread out next to their carriage. They would then walk off the dinner with a slow stroll at least a mile down the beach and back to the carriage. They also followed the same ritual on holidays when Karl closed his bank.

They walked north, back to their carriage, nodding at other folks on the beach, occasionally dodging children who ran from the waves to a family blanket with some story to tell or a shell to show off. A few of the adults were dressed in swimming outfits, but most were dressed as the Weischopfs, in their Sunday finest. In deference to the heat, Karl left his suit coat in the carriage and had rolled up his shirt sleeves to his elbows, but his paisley cravat remained firmly knotted at the starched collar around his neck. He hummed to Edjie as they walked. Ahead of them, perhaps a quarter-mile away, loomed a green and gold balloon, at least 200 feet tall with a large woven basket attached to it.

"I think we should celebrate," Ingrid said.

"And what should we celebrate?" Karl said, knowing the answer but wanting to hear the words again from another person.

"Your election to the Texas State Senate," she humored him.

Karl shifted Edjie from his arm to behind his neck, holding onto the boy's legs and his son grabbed onto his father's hair and giggled. "And how should we celebrate?"

"We should soar into the sky," she said with delight. "We've seen the balloon pilot take passengers up for a fee, and we should do it. It'll be grand looking out over the Gulf of Mexico as if we were a family of seagulls taking wing."

"But perhaps that would not be proper since the special election was held only because Senator Smith drowned in that very Gulf not a month ago."

"Luscious Abel Smith lived a long and prosperous life. He made his fortune from the sea and as a sailor I'm sure he would have thought passing at sea was the perfect way to go. And we can pay him homage from the clouds. It'd be a proper way to appreciate him."

They walked a little without saying anything more, a sign to Ingrid that Karl had agreed with her. She smiled.

"You have come a very long way," he said to her, jiggling his son a little on his shoulders to keep him amused. "Since Edjie was born, you always manage to put everything in the most positive light. Two years ago, the outlook you had was the precise opposite. You always saw the darkest side of things. You have indeed seen the light and that makes me love you more than ever, if that is possible."

She touched his arm lightly. "How can I not be positive with two such adorable people to love and who love me?"

Karl dropped softly to his knees, pulling Edjie over his head and setting him on the sand. His son balanced himself at first with his hands, then stood awkwardly and toddled off, falling into the sand with almost every step and laughing each time. Karl held his wife's hand and pulled her down to him, kissing her. They sat for a few moments, watching Edjie play in the waves that rushed in to tickle his feet before escaping back into the Gulf. The boy couldn't figure out why the water wouldn't stay put when he reached over to grab it. Bored with his game, Edjie stumbled back to his parents, reaching his arms out to his father. Karl picked the boy up, flipped him upsidedown once, then plopped him in the crook of an arm. They walked to the balloon.

They stopped in front of the ornately painted sign beside the balloon that read: "Travelin' Jones Will Take You On The Journey Of A Lifetime. Only $10."

"That is expensive," Karl said.

"Perhaps they won't charge a full fare for Edjie," Ingrid said. "And even if they do, we can afford it, Senator."

"Hush," Karl said. "I have not even stepped foot in the capitol yet."

A tall, handsome man in his middle forties stepped around the basket, doffed his top hat to Ingrid and waved it at his balloon.

"Might I escort you into the sky?" he said.

Karl put Edjie down and Ingrid knelt down to hold him lightly. Karl removed three $10 bills from his wallet and gave them to Travelin' Jones.

"Your lovely child may accompany us without remuneration," Jones said, handing one of the bills back.

"We Weischopfs pay our way, even the tiny ones," Karl smiled, refusing the currency.

"As you wish, sir," Jones said. "And in return we shall perhaps stay aloft some time longer than the usual." Jones opened a door in the basket and they all got in. "Hold your son dear to you, sir, and there will be no danger."

Jones disconnected the hose that fed coal gas into the balloon envelope from the city main, stepped into the basket himself and latched the gate behind him.

The coal gas in the envelope caused the balloon to strain at its tether. Travelin' Jones untied the rope and, using a small winch, slowly fed the tether out, allowing the balloon to rise into the air. The Gulf breeze was light and blew the balloon slightly away from the beach.

"Oh, my," Ingrid said. "I've never been this high in my life."

"Nor I," Karl said.

"And yet we shall go even higher," Jones pronounced. "We shall go higher than the vast majority of people in the entire Galveston and Harrisburg area have ever been in their lives. Now we are at two hundred feet."

"Can we see our home from here?" Ingrid asked.

Jones let out a little more of the tether. "Where might that be, madam? The higher we go, the further we shall see."

"Almost at the end of Mechanic Street. A large, gray stone building," Karl said.

"I know it well, sir," Jones said with a flourish, pointing to the northwest. "It is one of the sights I always point out, that along with the other fine homes, whenever I take passenger aloft from this vantage point."

"Oh, I see it, Karl. I see it," Ingrid said. "Look, Edjie, you can see home way off there. See?" Edjie was busy looking at birds squawking and flying by. Karl held his son at his waist, hugging the boy to him, but stood close enough so that the boy could see over the edge of the basket. Karl looked out to the sea that stretched to infinity below them, the gray waters almost still today. He never tired of watching the Gulf. He always saw the Hand of God in it. And now he was just a little closer to God and this made him feel very small and humbled, something other wealthy bankers, and senators, seldom felt. He hoped he could always feel this way.

Their journey lasted just long enough and they descended; Travelin' Jones cranking the winch to wind up the tether. Below them was a large crowd, the size that always gathered whenever he took passengers up. He knew from experience that perhaps a fifth of them would have the means to also want to soar with him.

"I trust you have enjoyed our sojourn in the sky," Jones said as the basket touched down. He unlatched the gate and the Weischopfs stepped out. Edjie reached out to try to grab the balloon and take it with him. When he grabbed only air, he started to cry.

"I think someone needs a nap," Ingrid said.

Karl shook Travelin' Jones' hand, balancing his whining son in his other arm. "We each enjoyed it tremendously. It was indeed the journey of a lifetime. Thank you."

•

Travelin' Jones always charged a premium for his sunset rides, $20 per passenger, and always had takers. On July Fourth and New Year's Eve he charged $25 for each because the city fire department always set off fireworks just after the sun went down. He usually flew no higher than 500 feet. He could take his balloon higher, but he had learned anything beyond that point tended to make the landlubbers ill. But even at that height, his passengers got to look down on the fireworks display, giving them a story they would tell to the end of their days. As he descended for the final time on this Sunday he saw a sight that turned his stomach: soldiers. Soldiers in blue uniforms.

"Good day to you, sir," one of the soldiers said, striding up to Jones and offering his hand. Jones ignored it.

"What can I do for you?" Jones asked, latching the basket behind him, shifting his weight a little so he could feel the weight of his Schofield hidden in the small of his back by his coat. He didn't expect trouble, but whenever he saw blue bellies he felt a little more comfortable knowing he was armed.

"Major Zachariah Jones," the officer introduced himself. "Army Bureau of Topographical Engineers."

Hearing the man's name turned Jones' stomach. He hoped he wasn't related to this damn Yankee. "And?"

"Well, sir, your country has a proposition for you. A rather lucrative one."

Jones immediately thought, It's not my country unless you're talking about Texas, but said nothing.

"We know you served in the late War with the rebels—"

"The Confederate State of America," Jones huffed. "You've waited 15 years to bring me to Yankee justice?"

"You misunderstand my intentions, sir," the major said. "We know you piloted the famous silk dress balloon in the Carolinas and given the precarious nature of that device it must have been a heroic act indeed. You have proven aeronautical skills and you've honed those skills at fairs and exhibitions in the years since the War. And we need your skill and your balloon, in Texas, and Washington will compensate you very well for both."

"What's this all about?"

"We are in the process of completing what we hope will become the most accurate survey of the Texas border in history, Mr. Jones," the major said. He pulled a map from a leather case and unrolled it against the wicker basket of the balloon, his finger tracing the Río Grande. "Much of this river is barely charted. The land has been virtually uninhabited forever. Our hope is to use modern technology to remedy that lack of knowledge. Our regular surveyors are even now mapping out the western and eastern portions of the river, where the land is relatively flat, but where the Río Grande makes its big bend from flowing southerly to northerly the land is mountainous. There we will use balloons. Our goal is this: to send balloons aloft from the American side of the river with the pilot, a surveyor, and a photographer in each balloon. The surveyor will make his usual measurements while the photographer will record each segment on plates. Once we take those together, we will have an absolute portrait of our border with Mexico."

Jones whistled, his eyes widening. "Sounds like a preposterous undertaking."

"It's ambitious but far from preposterous," the major replied. "We have divided the river in the Big Bend area into segments and we are hiring aeronauts for each segment and they will all go aloft simultaneously. Our primary obstacles are the four canyons in the area: Colorado, Santa Helena, Mariscal, and Boquillas. From Presidio to Colorado Canyon we will tether a balloon to a boat and float downriver. You're probably familiar with this practice, as I believe it was done in the war."

"I am. But those were boats along the coast; I'll bet this won't work on the river in those canyons."

"No, sir, the rocks and currents are too unpredictable. What we will do then is send a couple of wagons as close to the canyon rims as we can reach safely and each balloon will be tethered to a wagon. If the balloon rises high enough, we could get a commanding view of the river in the canyon. Even this will probably not be too easy. The area around Santa Helena and Mariscal canyons are our primary concern because previous surveying parties report they are not only remote but exceptionally steep, and this is where we want our most experienced balloonist to go. We're estimating we will need half a dozen balloons for three months to complete the project."

"How many balloons do you have committed now?" Jones asked, intrigued by the possibility of flying over uncharted country.

"We have five. Three have come from the Navy, the remaining two are citizen pilots like yourself. Quite frankly, Mr. Jones, none of them has your level of expertise."

"So you would want me to scramble around those bad canyons?"

"Exactly. You'll have considerable help," the major explained. "You'll have several wagons and a platoon of our best men."

"And how will I get my balloon aloft? Hot air?"

"I believe you used turpentine-soaked pine tree knots to fuel your hot air balloons during the War," the major said. Jones nodded. "That was given much thought and hot air was the initial consideration, but after investigating the region thoroughly we decided there aren't enough good-burning trees to provide fuel for a sufficient time. And of course we're hundreds of miles from a city gas main. So we've decided to use gas generators."

Jones whistled again, smiling this time. He'd always wanted to see one of the legendary Thaddeus Lowe's devices in action, creating inflammable air to power a balloon. It was one of the Yankees' biggest advantages when it came to balloons because they didn't have to rely on hot air like the poorer Confederacy did. They could use hydrogen. Wherever and whenever they wanted. "And how many Yankee dollars do I get for providing this service?"

"Can you keep the amount confidential?" the major said. Jones nodded. "We're paying each of the other balloonists $3,000 for three months work with $1,000 per month, pro rated, beyond that if additional time is necessary. Since you would be working in our most difficult segment, we're willing to pay you $4,000 for three months and $1,500 per month after if needed. But we recognize that sometimes personal jealousies can develop, especially among aeronauts, so we would request that you keep the extra amount confidential."

The pay was considerable. Jones could make more in three months than he usually made all year. And he would be back in action, after a fashion, getting that adrenaline rush he had during the War. He'd become a pilot just because no one else had the nerve to get into the fragile device when it was delivered by John Randolph Bryan, at the time the Confederacy's only aeronaut and a reluctant one at that. Balloon Bryan taught him the basics, which were simple enough, and he was thrilled every time he flew. Yankees fired at him with rifles and cannon to little effect. The cannons couldn't aim as high as he flew and even rifled balls lost their accuracy before they reached his altitude. The few that managed to pierce his envelope didn't do much damage because of the way his balloon was made. Southern ladies from across the country donated their best gowns to the cause, and they were sewn together to form the envelope, a veritable Joseph's coat of many colors with ornate, flowery patterns, squares, and plaids in blues and greens and crimsons and ebonies. The strong stitching binding each dress to its neighbor prevented any significant tears in the fabric if it was pierced. The result was an ugly, glorious balloon that Jones named the Gazelle. But it was lost to the Maratanza, a Yankee gunboat during the siege of Charleston back in '63. The balloon had been going aloft tethered to the Confederate gunboat Teaser and when the Yankees captured that, they found the Gazelle, destroying the last of Southern women's finery. And Jones went back to the infantry. But those few months that Jones piloted the balloon were the most exhilarating of his life. And now he might be able to recapture a little of that feeling out on the frontier. It would be lucrative. It would be an adventure. He stuck out his hand. "You have a deal, major. When do we start?"

"Soon. I'll have a messenger deliver railway tickets for you and your balloon to San Antonio where you will meet up with the remainder of your unit. I'll meet you there and we'll caravan by wagons to Fort Davis then south into the Big Bend."

CHAPTER 5
Apache Camp, Chisos Mountains Basin

The cloud hugged the inside of the basin, obscuring the rest of the camp, teasing Alsate who stood at the top of a small hill whirling his tzi-ditindi ferociously over his head. The sounding wood made a noise like the gush of a rain-laden wind. The wood was made from a prized piece of lightning-struck pine with lightning bolts carved and painted into both sides; it was about the length of his forearm and as thin as the soles on his moccasins. His arm was tired but still he threw the twisted rawhide cord forward and whipped it back over his head, over and over, listening to the rumble he created, praying for the rain they needed, hoping to convince the cloud he stood in the midst of that it should release its life-giving moisture. After a half-hour, all he did was raise the ire of his warriors.

"You've disturbed our sleep, Old Man," Owl Eyes said. Four Fingers and Lame Coyote were by his side.

Alsate's face drooped as the cloud began to lift with the morning sun. "You should not be asleep with the sunrise."

"We had a long and prosperous evening," the younger man said. "We arrived back not long ago. We have mutton and whiskey and a couple of horses. You should be singing our praises."

Alsate waved a hand at Owl Eyes, a man of twenty-five summers who acted as leader of this small band even though Alsate was chief and had been chief twice as long as Owl Eyes had lived. "The raids are a mistake."

"You say this and you say this, but are not providing for our band. We are. We are Indeh and Indeh have always taken what we wanted from the Mexicans. You have forgotten this in your old age."

Alsate strode up to Owl Eyes, almost touching his nose with his own. He spoke through gritted teeth. "The snake loses its skin. The egg hatches and the birdling grows into a falcon and soars in the heavens and grows old and then becomes a meal for the fox. I was not born with gray hair and arroyos in my face. Things change. If we are to survive, we must change. Cochise is dead many winters ago. Victorio is dead last summer. Our cousins are on the reservation in New Mexico. Nana and Geronimo, are on the reservation in Arizona. Few children have been born to us the past two summers. We have few wives, fewer children. We are the last band of Chishi Indeh left in the world and we number barely one hundred. If you continue these raids, the Mexicans will catch you and kill you or the Texicans will do so. We have seen more and more of the Pale Eyes near our stronghold. Their villages grow."

"Old Man, you are becoming an old woman."

Alsate sighed and walked to his lodge. He could not control the younger warriors, yet the band still respected him enough to keep him as their leader. But they followed Owl Eyes.

"We must have peace with the Nacoya and the Pale Eyes," he told his woman, Little Moccasins, as he slumped down on the floor. She was the only woman he ever had and she had stood by his side through nearly forty summers. She bore him three sons and two daughters and they were gone to the Happy Place now. "We must learn to live with them, perhaps even among them. This will not happen as long as the young men keep raiding."

"I know," she said, combing his long hair. "I know."

"Why do they not know?"

"They are young."

"Was I not young?"

"Yes, you were just as young and foolish. I loved that young and foolish man and I love this old and wise man."

"But we could raid in those days. The raids were more profitable than now, exciting, and we could escape safely to these mountains time after time. No escape is safe today. The young men stay close to their lodges and their women and do not walk the ridges like I do. I see the Pale Eyes every day. I recall a time when I didn't know what one looked like. But now I see them and their soldiers. And for how much longer can we challenge the Nacoya? We are piling up rocks that are bound to fall down on our heads."

"You are chief, do something about this. You have always done so in the past."

"I am chief, but they do not follow me. I am a man with seventy summers. They look to the young men who give them presents and excitement."

"You can do anything they can and more. You have experience. You have the wisdom they lack."

"I wish you were correct," he said, shaking his head. "But if I am to remain chief, I must be their leader. Otherwise, I do not belong here."

"Come to bed," Little Moccasins said.

"Now? It's not even mid-day."

"What else do you have to do?"

●

The Presidio, San Carlos, Chihuahua, Mexico

Capitan Ulysses Lerdo kicked the chair that was in his way as he marched to the desk in his small office. If his desk weren't so massive, he would have kicked that, too. Last night, Apaches raided farms outside the village, stealing some sheep and some goats and two horses and a small cask of sotol, and one of his men broke a leg when his horse fell on it while they were chasing the red devils, and he himself broke a tooth by clenching his jaw too tightly in his anger when the Apaches laughed at him after they crossed the river.

The tooth—what was left of it—was sore and ached with pain that sometimes shot up the side of his face to his eye. Now a new officer was reporting for duty.

His orderly escorted the lieutenant in, righting the chair for the new officer to sit in.

"Panocha?" Lerdo asked.

"She is gathering her things and is coming, mi capitán."

"Bueno. When she arrives, bring her to me immediately."

"Sí," the orderly said, saluted smartly, turned on his heel and left. He left the door open so the breeze would blow through the office.

"Lieutenant Arnulfo Díaz y Paredes," the new officer said. He placed a leather satchel on the floor next to the chair and handed a sealed letter to his new captain. Lerdo saw through the veil of dust that had settled over the soldier to notice polished leather and brass and that the fabric of his uniform was new and creased. "The letter is from General Díaz and is for your eyes only."

"Indeed," Lerdo said. He removed his uniform blouse, draping it over his chair. His shirt was already soaked and stained with sweat even though noon was a couple hours away. He ran his fingers through his unruly spade beard and poured himself a cup of French bourbon, the only thing he liked the French for. "Sit."

The lieutenant sat stiff as a board on the old chair, watching his commandant slowly sip from his cup then slowly remove a small knife from a drawer in the desk then slowly open the letter. No wonder the man never got anything done, Arnulfo thought. He moves too slowly.

Lerdo unfolded the letter. He read the usual formalities, he read an introduction to his new lieutenant— a man with great potential, according to the general. It was the final paragraph that made him clench his jaw and send new pain across the side of his face: "The Apache continue to raid unabated. These incursions must stop. If you cannot do this before the New Year, I will place Lieutenant Díaz y Paredes in your position as Captain of Fiscales in San Carlos."

Lerdo crumpled the letter and tossed it directly at the lieutenant who did not flinch. "Do you know what's in that letter?"

"I do not," the lieutenant replied. "But my uncle did brief me on the situation here before I left Chihuahua City. He said my job was to help you capture or kill the Apache raiders."

"Your uncle," Lerdo said, rubbing his cheek. "Of course. Your uncle."

The orderly interrupted with a knock on the open door as a slender woman walked in. Her hair was gray at her temples, her skin dried from the desert, but she was a strikingly handsome woman for her age.

"Panocha. Querida," Lerdo said as she walked to his side. His arm found her waist and he hugged her without standing up. "I have broken a tooth."

"You have much pain?" she asked. He nodded yes. "Open your mouth." She moved a finger around his gums, pulling away his cheek a little, seeing the broken molar on the lower left side of his jaw. The lieutenant meanwhile had pulled a book from his satchel and sat quietly reading while the curandera treated the captain.

She poured a little of the bourbon from Lerdo's cup into her palm and with a small splinter of wood mixed in some powder to make a greenish paste. She scooped up some of the paste, nodded for Lerdo to open his mouth again, and rubbed the paste into the broken tooth. Lerdo winced.

"This will dull the pain but the tooth cannot be saved. You must have it removed and I cannot do that. I do not have the strength. Serna, the barber, has the tools and the strength. But do not have him do this until late in the evening. You will be in much pain for many hours. If you wish to work today, do not have the tooth pulled until later."

"Muy amable, but what do I do until then?"

"The herbs will help. And this." She reached into her bag and removed a portion of an empty pistol cartridge. The case had been cut back and edges filed smooth. She nodded for Lerdo to open his mouth again then slid the case over the broken tooth. She had guessed the correct caliber, and it fit snugly. "This will keep stray items from going inside the tooth. But you must have it pulled."

He squeezed her buttocks as she turned. "Panocha, you are beautiful."

"Sí," she said, rolling her eyes. "Visit Serna before you come home. I'll give you another potion to help you sleep then."

As she left, the lieutenant closed his book and recited an old saying, "If your tooth hurts you, pull it out."

Lerdo wanted to smack the young lieutenant on his ass, and would have if the man's uncle weren't a general. The adage had nothing to do with teeth; it meant that it was up to you to solve your own problems. The lieutenant clearly knew what was in the letter. So Lerdo snapped, "From the hand to the mouth, the pudding is lost."

The lieutenant didn't appear to know that his captain meant him a clear threat: that nothing was certain.

Lerdo stood, grabbing up the book the lieutenant had placed on his desk. *The Illiad.*

"I find Homer quite exhilarating and instructive," Arnulfo said, standing when his captain did.

Lerdo waved the book around. "These children's tales will not help you in this place."

"I would respectfully beg to differ, sir. Do you know Homer?"

"What is my name, lieutenant?"

"Captain Lerdo," Arnulfo answered, confused.

"My whole name?"

"Ahhh… Captain Ulysses Lerdo."

"Yes, and with a name like that don't you think I know Homer? My mother would read passages from that book to put me to sleep as a child. I read it myself before I was fourteen. I've found nothing I could apply to this hell hole in it."

"But, sir, I have seen the Chisos Mountains where the Apache retreat to. Is it not like a fortress city? Has this battle not been waged for years and years?"

Lerdo laughed and shook his head in wonder at the ignorance of his new officer. "Yes, I imagine those mountains do resemble a fortress in some ways, but do you think we'd ever besiege it? Lieutenant, we have a dozen men and our job is to patrol the border and seize contraband. We may keep half of what we seize, but so little passes across that it is almost meaningless. Our main job has become to protect the villages near here, San Carlos and San Vicente, Paso Lajitas, and Boquillas, and Ojo Caliente from bandits and Apaches. Now think for once, lieutenant, where is that fortress city?"

"Ahhh… Texas, sir."

Lerdo nodded. "Texas. And as much as everyone in Mexico would wish otherwise, Texas is now part of the United States. We are not raiding into another country and besieging a mountain stronghold. Now go find Sergeant García and tell him you will be the new officer in charge on the night watch."

Arnulfo grabbed his satchel, saluted, and left. He forgot his *Illiad* on Lerdo's desk.

Lerdo returned to his chair and slumped in it, rubbing his cheek again. The pain was gone and his jaw was just sore now. His fingers touched the silver cover of *The Illiad*. He wondered how much of this old book he recalled. He flipped through its pages, his eyes falling on one line: "But Odysseus had his bag of tricks."

CHAPTER 6
Lajitas

The saloon cleaned up and the day's receipts locked away, Ethan stripped his clothes off and rolled into his bed, pulling the threadbare quilt over him to cover his head. He moved a little back and forth to tuck himself in. His only thought was relief that Gracey agreed to open the Mejor Que Nada for him in the afternoon so he could sleep in. He hadn't had a good night's sleep in days. She'd given him a powder to help him sleep. It was nice having a cook-waitress-whore who was also a curandera. The powder relaxed him and the second his head touched his pillow, his eyelids bounced closed. Then the first rooster crowed. Another answered. From the sound, they were across the river. He knew what was next. The roosters on the American side began to crow. In moments, dogs on both sides barked. Crowing and barking. Then the hens squawked. Goats bawled. Hell, he thought, at any moment I'll hear the God damned crack of dawn. He pulled the pillow over his head. That dulled the sounds until his muscles relaxed, the pillow dropped away, and the noises pulled him back into consciousness.

"Shut up!" he bellowed. His admonition only made matters worse when the dogs answered him.

He threw the pillow against the lone window in his room, snapping back the quilt. He jumped out of bed and strode to the door, opening it to the darkness. The sun would be fully up in perhaps a half-hour. He knew why his friend hated those roosters so much. When your bedtime was the same as when they started their day, you needed to be young or exhausted to sleep through the racket. Well, exhausted apparently didn't work, either. Nor drugs.

He was groggy from the lack of sleep and Gracey's powder, but walked purposefully out the door. No one else stirred, but they would soon. He walked to the river bluff, down it, then to the crossing, splashing across the Río Grande in four long strides. Up the bank on the other side, unfriendly stones under his feet forced him to realize he hadn't put on any boots. Or clothing. He didn't care as long as he could avoid stepping into a lechuguilla. He walked to the sound of the chickens, flung open a gate and reached for the first rooster, snapping its neck with a quick flick of his wrist. He opened the coop, left the yard and walked to where he heard the second rooster, repeating what he'd done a moment before. The dogs still barked somewhere. He'd bring a shotgun and shut them up tomorrow. He turned and splashed back across the river, vaguely hearing someone yelling behind him. He returned to his room, wrapped himself in his quilt, and fell asleep before his legs were even in the bed.

His dream was paradise. He dreamed of Mahealani and her house on the cliff overlooking a waterfall and a bay in the Sandwich Islands where he spent many a balmy day and evening. In the dream, the humidity wrapped around him like a comforter. They lazed on straw mats watching the surf, dipping their fingers in poi and pork. They had no cares, no needs beyond each other. The rest of the world did not exist, only the grass and the trees and the rocks and the surf and the fragrance of the orchids. He felt as if he were evaporating into the humidity and doing so felt right; he would rise to the sky blended with Mahealani and return as the early morning mist.

A pounding on his door startled him awake. The light streaming in the window told him it was late morning, well before he told Gracey to get him up. His mouth was dry. For a fleeting moment, he dropped back into the paradise of his dream, rising up over the island, but another knock on the door brought him back.

He lost his balance trying to get to the door too quickly. He grabbed the door and flung it open. "This better be good."

Joaquin took a couple steps backwards. Ethan saw his Ranger friend standing next to Lionicio Castillo, a goatherd from Paso Lajitas across the river. A few steps behind them — failing in an attempt to look casual and disinterested — stood Armando Baeza, Lionicio's cousin, a goatherd who lived on the American side.

"Put on some trousers," Joaquin ordered. "That birthday suit's too wrinkled for decent folks."

Ethan scowled, turned and slammed the door behind him. As he pulled on his trousers, then his boots, he recalled his friend, the former saloonkeeper, telling him almost those same words about his birthday suit. Where did this snot-nosed pretender get off quoting his only true friend?

"What?" Ethan said, flinging the door open again. He grew a little angrier when he saw the smirk on Joaquin's face.

"Señor Castillo says you killed his rooster and ran off his hens this morning," the Ranger said.

"Eh-yeah? What does he know?"

"Well, he saw you."

"How? It was dark."

"So you were there?"

"I heard the damn roosters when I went to bed. It was dark."

"Just before dawn, he says he saw a crazy naked man running from his chicken coop to the river. His rooster was killed and his hens let loose. He says it was you."

"How's he know this?"

"You were bare-assed."

"He recognized my ass?"

"He recognized that tattoo across your back. You're the only man anyone's ever seen around here with tattoos. Big ones, too. I'd say that makes you pretty damn recognizable."

"So what? Life's too short to worry about a missing hens. And those chickens were in Mexico. Out of your jurisdiction, isn't it? Not in your jurisdiction."

"Technically. But he recalls last year when I went across and shoved a shotgun in his gut to bring back some nannies he'd stolen from his cousin here. Remember? He says if I can cross the river to do that, I can make you pay for killing his rooster and running off his hens. Says the nearest Mexican law is twenty miles away in San Carlos and they don't care much about Paso."

"He's probably got all the damn hens back by now."

"Some, señor. The dogs have made a meal of some before I can get them herded back into my place," Lionicio said.

"Jesus," Ethan sighed. "All I was trying to do was get a good-night's sleep."

"You won't do it by killing the roosters, you know," Joaquin said. "I've seen it when chickens lose a rooster one of the hens steps up to take his place. At least the part about being the boss. Makes just as much noise. You've got to find a better way."

"Maybe I'll just kill them all. Kill-them-all."

"It's a grave international crime," Joaquin said.

"You think this is funny, do you?" Ethan snorted deeply, cleared his throat, and spit a wad of green phlegm at the dirt by the Ranger's boots.

"The picture of you running bare across the river to assassinate this man's rooster? Absolutely. You've fallen a long way from sneaking into a Comanche camp or carving up a wild mountain lion."

"Getting old," Ethan said. He searched in his pockets, finding some coins and paper money. He handed Joaquin a five-dollar bill and four silver dollars. "This should be more than enough. Basta?"

"Sí. Sí, señor," Lionicio said as Joaquin handed him the money.

"Just don't ever come into my establishment again. Never. Comprende? You neither, you son of a bitch."

"What have I done?" Armando said, surprised. He was one of the Mejor Que Nada's best regular customers.

"You're related to this son of a bitch and you've got chickens, too. Get rid of your chickens and you can come back. Dogs, too. And your goats while you're at it."

Lionicio smiled to reveal a single tooth in his mouth, then bowed a little. "Señor, I am sorry my chickens keep you from sleep."

"Don't repent," Ethan said and went back inside, hoping he could return to paradise. "Stop sinning. If you can't make this racket stop, I'll just kill the both of you."

•

Joaquin sat at the bar, eating a pork stew Gracey had cooked earlier in the day. He scooped up a large spoonful of meat, onions, carrots, potatoes, and apples, savoring every chew.

"Best I've ever had in my whole life," he told Ethan.

"Eh-yeah. When she's got the spare time, she's the best cook I've ever known. Ever. We've had the potatoes and apples in the cellar for months now, but somehow she knows how to make it all tasty."

"Only way it could be better was if it was beef instead of pork. But I'm not complaining."

"We're supposed to get a few beeves in here soon and when we do I can stop buying hogs from Tío José and get you some real meat."

Joaquin scooped up more food from the large wooden bowl. "That woman is wasting her talents being a whore."

"No she's not," Ethan said, pouring the Ranger another finger of whiskey in his glass.

"I wouldn't know, I guess."

Ethan smiled wide. "I would."

"I'm glad to see you're in a better mood tonight," Joaquin said. "You were pure surly this noon."

"Well, you know, surly to bed, surly to rise."

"You gotta do something about that."

"Eh-yeah. I know, but I don't know what. I made two big mistakes last year. I should have never moved down to Lajitas and I should have never taken over this saloon. Never."

Joaquin gulped down the last of whiskey. "So why did you?"

"The top of that hill in Terlingua was a lonely place to be once I stopped getting drunk," Ethan said as he poured Joaquin more whiskey. "And you're responsible for getting me in the saloon. You talked me into it. And now the old saloonkeep is gone and you're spending more time out of town and once you're married who knows if you'll even be a Ranger anymore. I liked philosophizing with Brother Karl, but he's gone, too. Nobody left."

"Gracey's still here. You could settle down and get married."

"Marry a whore? My moral standards wouldn't let me do something like that."

"You know, most of the time I can never tell whether you're serious or not."

"Eh-yeah," Ethan said. "Me, too."

Joaquin sipped at his third glass of whiskey, doubting whether he should but the doubt was short-lived. "So…?"

"I really don't know," Ethan said. He pulled up a stool to sit on, resting his arms on the board that served as the bar. "A man has to have sleep. And I'd like a little peace of mind, too. At least up in Terlingua my nearest neighbor was about a mile away. Quiet. And the Mejor Que Nada gives me something to do, but riches do me no good. I can't take them to Heaven with me. I already give all the profits away, mostly to Gracey and her little girls. What I need to do is either convince Gracey to take it over or sell it to somebody. God knows who. Who? I don't like the commitment to this place, worrying about inventory and getting the doors open and closed and serving up folks like you and those soldiers over there every day of the damn week. Why would I do this? Why? I need to just pack up and get the hell out. Out."

"If you are all gone, Lajitas will not have any heroes left," Gracey said as she retrieved a bottle of the cheaper whiskey from behind the bar to pour more for the soldiers.

"We weren't heroes. We were just a bunch of drunks hanging around a saloon who went out sometimes and killed people who needed to be killed, then came back to the saloon to drink some more."

"Maybe you are right. But where would you go?" she said as she walked away. Joaquin nodded, indicating he had the same question.

Ethan rested his chin on his hands, the aroma from the empty whiskey barrels supporting the bar board filling his nostrils. He looked up at Joaquin. "Paradise or home. One or the other."

"What's at home? Still have family back in Vermont?"

"Not after Margaret and David died," he said, sitting up straight. "When my grandfather died that was essentially the end of the line, so to speak, for my family. I suppose my father was still alive back then someplace but I didn't know where and I didn't care. It'd been a lot of years since I'd even heard of him. I'm sure he's dead, too, by now."

"So home's out."

"Well, I don't know. I think about Vermont a lot. More so in recent years for some reason. Maybe just homesick. Homesick because this desert is so completely different than Lake Memphremagog and the forests where I grew up. But the forests are where magic takes place. The deeper the forest, the stronger the encounter and we have some deep forests back home. The forest is fluid and changes itself and those in it. All things are possible in the forest. It's special because of the trees. They live in our world but their feet reach in to the underworld and their arms reach into the sky."

"And what's this 'paradise'?"

Ethan closed his eyes and sighed. "Sandwich Islands."

"You've mentioned it before. Someplace out in the Pacific

Ocean, right?"

"Eh-yeah. I was on liaison duty for nearly a year with the Army some years back. Long before I got married, thank God. That's even more different from this desert than Vermont. Tropical. Swaying palm trees; swaying naked maidens. Everyone seemed happy there wherever I went. 'Course they didn't have much reason not to be happy. When I got there, it was in October, right when this big four-month religious holiday begins. Almost nobody works. They just have parties, couple as much as they can, and play sporting games. All dedicated to Lono, their god of fertility." He laughed. "One of the games you'd never even believe."

"Try me."

"I don't know if I can describe it." Ethan slid off the stool and started gesturing as he spoke. "First, try to picture this. Ever been to the ocean?"

Joaquin shook his head no.

"Well, you've been to a lake."

"Yes, I have," the Ranger said, nodding firmly, his head aching a little as he moved it.

"OK. Picture yourself sitting on a bank above the lake but you can't see the other side. It's just all water as far as you can see. Water. Then picture a storm brewing up. The storm kicks up some high waves."

"I think I can see the waves."

"Higher than you've ever seen. Maybe as tall as two or three men standing on each other's shoulders. That surf keeps rolling in, nonstop. Lots of foam in the waves. Now picture men, some naked and some with just a small loin cloth, dozens of men lying on ironing boards and paddling themselves out into those waves."

Joaquin's eyes narrowed; he pursed his lips, cocked his head. "You just lost me. What do ironing boards have to do with anything?"

"It's the only way I can describe the boards if you haven't seen them. They're like long planks with a pointed end, kinda like an ironing board, about as wide."

"How long?"

"All sizes. Some tall, some short, some in between. Tallest are taller than a man."

"And these big waves don't capsize them?"

"No. Picture a piece of driftwood floating on waves. Same thing. Too low to be tipped over."

Joaquin laughed. "As long as they don't stand up."

"Well... that's exactly what they do."

"Huh?"

"They get way out into the waves and wait for a wave they like and they turn around toward the beach and let the wave pick them up like that piece of driftwood and then they jump up on the board and balance themselves and ride the front edge of the wave in. Surf keeps pushing them ahead of the wave. Pushes them ahead."

"They stand up and ride this huge wave in to shore?"

"Pretty much."

"Oh, Christ. You must think I'm drunker than I really am. I've heard some windies before, but if I believed this I woudn't have enough brains to grease a skillet."

"I guess you wouldn't believe it then if I told you some of these guys were so good that they could guide the board anyplace they wanted it to go, including inside the wave."

"Inside the wave... ?"

"Eh-yeah. They wait for that wave to start breaking, you know where that big wave starts falling over and it kinda creates a big tunnel, well, they ride into the tunnel. Inside that tube."

Joaquin slapped his palm on the bar and laughed uncontrollably. Ethan scowled and grabbed Joaquin's whiskey glass, wiped it out, and placed it on a shelf behind him. The three soldiers who had been quietly drinking and playing cards around a corner table looked over at the noise. Joaquin couldn't stop laughing. In a few moments he developed hiccups that pained his chest every time one snapped at his diaphragm.

Ethan gave him a beer. "Sip this real slowly." Joaquin did, the sips interrupted by a lone hiccup and a few more laughs. Finally, he calmed down but his cheeks were sore from the laughing.

"I've heard lots of fantastic tales in my life, but people putting their lives aside for four months just to fornicate and ride waves in the ocean on ironing boards is an amazing tale."

"True, though," Ethan said quietly, hurt that his friend didn't believe him.

"Look, I've heard of people living on the moon, too,"

"Eh-yeah. I read a book once that speculated people did. Or some kinda people."

"Seems like there'd be a lot of open range up there," Joaquin said, on the verge of laughing again.

"Eh-yeah, but how would you get there?"

"Be an awfully tall ladder wouldn't it?"

•

The saloon was closed. Gracey had mopped the floor, Ethan cleaned the glasses and plates, then wiped down the bar. He untied his apron, walked over to Gracey and handed it to her.

"I think it needs to be cleaned," he said. "Aren't you doing laundry later today?"

"Sí, I will wash it. Do you have anything else?"

"No. But. Um, sit down a minute."

Gracey had never seen such a serious look in Ethan's eyes. "What is wrong?"

"I have to leave," he said, exhaling a tremendous amount of air. "This saloon is not my life. I'm not comfortable here. It's making me crazy and keeping me from sleeping and I just don't care about it. It reminds me too much about— about…"

"Dutch," she said, nodding her head.

"Eh-yeah. I miss seeing his face every day. When I walk in that door, I should see it. I won't anymore. I can't stay here any longer. I know you said you didn't want to run this place, but you have to. You love Corazón and Alma, don't you?"

"Sí. You know this. They are my heart and my soul."

"Then you want what's best for them. Growing up with their mother being a whore—"

"I am not ashamed of being a whore," she said quickly.

"I know, I know. I love you for that. But you have more to offer your children than that legacy. Take over the Mejor Que Nada. The nearest place to get spirits is down a 70-mile bad road in Presidio. This place has a corner on that business. It makes more money than any place around except for the McGuirks' store. Take that money for your daughters. When they are grown, the three of you can escape to San Antonio or Ciudad Chihuahua, anywhere. They can have a good future. It's not against the law to be comfortable."

"I do not know if I can do this."

"You must. I'm leaving, whatever you decide. He would want you to have his saloon. You stood by him a very long time. It's your right. You've earned it."

"I do not know if I can do it. I am a woman. I am a woman alone."

"You can. You must."

"When will you go?"

Ethan shook his head slowly. "I don't know. First I have to decide where to go, then I'll leave."

"I will do this only when you leave. If you stay in Lajitas, I will not take the Mejor Que Nada over. I will after you have gone. Where will you go?"

"Paradise or home," he said, pushing back his chair. He was exhausted. "Paradise or home."

CHAPTER 7

On the Presidio Road, south of Fort Davis

After camping for the night beside newly laid railway tracks, the wagon train split up. Some of the wagons headed west toward El Paso, and would turn south around Van Horn Wells. Some of the wagons headed toward Burgess Springs, and would turn south some 80 miles east of there. The wagons carrying Travelin' Jones' balloon, the gas generator, and supplies kept moving south. Thirty mounted soldiers followed the wagons. Four scouts from Fort Clark were already ahead of them over the horizon.

Major Zachariah Jones rode in the lead wagon with Travelin' Jones. The aeronaut hated to admit it, but after all the time they'd spent together in the past couple of weeks he actually liked the Yankee surveyor.

The major drove the wagon, something he liked to do from time to time. It broke the monotonous motion of rocking to and fro in the saddle and he got to engage in conversation that helped pass the miles quicker. The heavily-laden wagons moved slowly.

"What's that you've got?" the major asked Jones.

"Picked it up near the tracks this morning. I don't know why I paid any attention to it; it's nigh on to the same as nearly all these here rocks. Seemed out of place, though. Balloon Bryan trained me to be carefully observant and I've always practiced that and I've seen over the miles that most of these small, dark rocks have a white underbelly. Maybe you know why that is. I can't imagine."

"Never noticed. I don't gaze at rocks much."

"Well, look around when we stop next and you'll see what I'm speaking of. This here rock stood out to me this morning because it was bellyside up. So I just picked her up and found some scribbling on it."

"Somebody wrote on a rock out in the desert?"

"Seems so. Looks like they painstakingly cut into the rock with a sharp stone, maybe a knife. It's not ink nor paint."

"So, what is the inscription?"

"Says here, 'Circular thoughts ramble in my mind dodging all the bubbles and with them all the troubles that sneak in to plague my happy ignorance.'"

The major flicked the reins across the backs of the four mules pulling their wagon. "Now what in blue blazes do you suppose that means?"

"I'm baffled," Jones said. "I would think anyone going to all the trouble of scratching something in a rock with a stone would be carving something of great import, at least his name and a date. This is doggerel."

"People sometimes do strange things. If you don't mind me bringing it up, it always seemed to me that silk-dress balloon was a strange thing."

"You ever see the Gazelle, major?"

"I was too young to serve in the War. But when I was given charge of this project I talked to many officers who did see it."

"It was born of necessity. The Confederacy didn't have the supplies and money you Federals had. We understood the balloons could give us a significant edge in battles and we wanted to put as many up as we could. You had the wherewithal but never did it much."

"Internal squabblings. Jealousies. Military politics. From what I gather, no one took balloons very seriously in Washington."

"We did," Jones said. "We knew by rigging a telegraph wire from the balloon to the ground we could direct artillery fire far more accurately than had ever been done before. We could see units' movements. I spied cavalry hidden in the woods one time and that enabled the infantry to prepare for them. We just didn't have the materials. We had to rely on hot air to get us aloft. That's how you blue bellies won the war. Not because you were better soldiers or had better generals. Hell, ol' Abe Lincoln himself wanted Robert E. Lee to head up your Federal army and when he kept with the south Abe had to settle for a pack of ignorant jackasses or self-inflated dandies or—

"I'm sorry, major. I can get carried away."

"No offense, Mr. Jones," the major laughed. "Although a brother and three cousins did serve, I didn't so I have been the spared the visceral hatred that seems to stay with those who did serve. On both sides."

Jones nodded agreement. "Be a long time before it all settles down, I would imagine. I'll tell you a little secret about that silk-dress balloon, though. It weren't all dresses."

"No?"

"No, not even most of it. What happened was we needed the fabric and we did use some dresses that had been donated to the cause, but mostly it was dress material we had. Now I wasn't present when they crafted the balloon, but I saw the result. And it was glorious. Most of it was various lengths from bolts of silk that might have otherwise been made into dresses. Southern ladies suffered in not having any new dresses for some time, but they didn't clean out their armoires just for us."

Jones turned the inscribed rock over in his hands once, then tossed it behind him into the wagon. He wanted to figure out what it meant, but he'd do that later, smoking a pipeful or two by the campfire tonight. "What's this Big Bend country like, major?"

"I'm mostly mystified. I've read reports and I've looked over what few maps we have, usually field maps drawn by inexperienced officers. I've spoken with Lieutenant Bullis over at Fort Clark extensively about what I might expect and he wasn't too encouraging. You?"

"Never been south of San Antone," Jones said. "Who's this Bullis?"

"Commander of the Seminole Negro Indian Scouts. Those are four of his men up ahead of us keeping us safe and finding us water. He's crossed nearly every mile of this uninhabitable countryside, from San Felipe del Río to El Paso, on both sides of the Río Grande."

"And what did he say to discourage you?"

"Wasn't that he discouraged me, exactly. Just that what he did say wasn't of much help, except the part that we'd be on our own in a very hostile place and when he talks about a hostile place he's not speaking of Indians. He's talking about the land itself. Says that everything you'll find in the rest of the world can be found jumbled all together right in the Big Bend. You've got rivers and mountains and deserts and forests and playas and hot springs and arroyos and dried-up lakes and lava flows and waterfalls and canyons and valleys and broad expanses of grass and broad expanses of nothing but sand and stones. You can't plan for a place like that. You can't take enough supplies because you'd have to take everything. At least we can get resupplied to a limited degree from some settlements out there like Presidio where we're headed now and Fort Leaton which is nearby there. Big livestock operation at Cibolo Springs. Small village at Lajitas. But if we need anything at all for your balloon other than the spare parts we're carrying, we'll have to get it from San Antonio and that won't be quick."

"You think we can accomplish our mission in three months?"

"I'd certainly be surprised if that were the case," the major said.

•

Southern Pacific Railroad Work Camp

He finished his breakfast of boiled bacon and sour corn bread, thinking it wouldn't have been half bad if breakfast wasn't exactly the same thing day after day after day.

Ben was getting good at moving around on the crutch he'd made for himself. He found the long mulberry branch on the ground, near the infirmary tent. It was relatively straight and strong and forked at one end. Over a few days, he cut the two arms down, then carved a more gentle curve between them. He stripped the bark from the branch and trimmed the long end until he got the crutch to just his size. He asked for a tattered saddle blanket about to be thrown away and, to his grateful surprise, was allowed to keep it. He cut the blanket into strips, layering them into the curve at the top of the crutch, wet strips of rawhide and tied the soft blanket pieces on. He covered that with a piece of leather cut from part of an old satchel and tied that in place with wet rawhide as well. The crutch was as comfortable as he could expect.

He wasn't fast. His hip didn't function properly and he had no right foot, but by balancing on the crutch and moving his good leg forward, he could move smoothly. What amused him was that he could move quicker than the other convicts, hobbled as they were by the leg chains that were never taken off outside the camp house. And he didn't have a chunk of heavy iron rubbing sores into his ankles. Ankle.

Right now he was moving toward the guard captain.

"Ketch in," hollered Boss Leonard Slipher from his gray horse, balancing his shotgun on his broad shoulder. The inmate workers shuffled off to their posts, swinging hammers and moving rails and timbers.

"Boss," Ben said.

Slipher looked down with gray eyes set too close together at the crippled man who spoke to him. He moved his horse just enough to knock Ben out of balance. Ben clenched his teeth but didn't fall; he was getting good at using the crutch.

"Boss, Ah's hopin' to get some work," Ben said, moving back.

"What t'hell can you do? We fixin' to send you off t'Huntsville."

"Ah can drive the meal cart jes' fine," Ben said. "Ah could dish up vittles. What Ah cain't do is sit 'round all the day long an' do nothin'"

"Oh, you cain't?"

"Prufuh not to, Boss. Ah'd like to keep busy, help out. If Ah do what Ah cin, mebbe you get another hand out to work."

"Tell you what," Slipher said. "You go to the canteen and tell 'em you can drive the Johnnie wagon around. You can put out the slop buckets in the mornin' and pick 'em up oncet work's over. Then you help out in the hospital tent. Boze prolly got a few things you can do in thar."

"Thank ya, Boss. 'Preciate it," Ben said, and went to hospital tent.

Boze, the large, white inmate steward shook his head slowly when Ben told him Slipher said he could do work there. "Cain't git me no able-bodied man I got's to git you. Jumped-up Crimminey sakes, I cain't ketch no breaks no way no how. Now what am I suppose to do with you anyways?"

Ben shrugged.

"Well, you cain't carry things, that's fer sure," the orderly said. He looked around the tent and had an idea. "You can stand, though, cain't you?"

Ben nodded. Boze walked over to a table on which was the body of one of the convicts that had been brought in earlier in the morning.

"You can be our cadaver steward," Boze laughed. "All's you has to do is stand right up at the table an' wash down the bodies when theys come in, then you sews them up in that sheet of canvas underneath him. Then we'll dump the bodies in the bog 'round hyar or we'll dig us a hole oncet we move too far from the bog. You doan have to worry 'bout that part. You jes' strip 'em down and clean 'em up and sew 'em up."

"Ah can handle that," Ben said.

CHAPTER 8
Lajitas

The Mejor Que Nada was packed. Soldiers, ranch hands, farmers, miners, and a couple of travelers occupied every chair in the place; they stood around the six tables; they leaned against the walls and on the bar. This was more people than Ethan had ever seen in the place at one time. But what struck him most was the number of newspapers people were waving around. He was certain no place in the Big Bend ever saw that many newspapers in one place at one time before. The bar's patrons waved the papers, thumped them with the backs of their hands, pointed at them with their fingers, crumpled them up and flung them with disgust against the walls.

It was only six o'clock according to his old friend's railroad watch, and this had been going on for at least an hour, soon after he opened his doors. He sold more whiskey than he ever had, but less beer. The patrons seemed determined to get drunk as quickly as possible, slamming the shots down their throats and hollering for more. But Gracey hadn't made a dollar yet, and didn't look like she would. Everyone wanted to just talk and argue.

Ethan had been kept so busy, he didn't really pay attention to what was going on. At one point, filling a beer glass full of rye whiskey at the request of a soldier at the bar, this bothered him. He usually had to know everything that was going on around him. Usually, he was so attentive to his surroundings he knew if an ant farted two miles away — at least that's what his friend the old bartender used to tell people. He wondered if the job was sapping that curiosity out of him. Being confined was doing it, he decided. He was not meant to live within four walls and under a roof; the walls separated him from the real world.

He motioned for Gracey to watch the bar and he stepped outside. He sat cross-legged beside the door, happy to relieve the fatigue from his feet. The sun was still high and warmed his face. It was hot inside, too, but out here he could feel the warm breeze and feel the sun and hear the doves and if he tried to block all the noises from inside the bar he could hear the Río Grande.

The rushing of the water reminded him of the waterfall in the Waimea Valley...

"Why me?" Ethan asked Mahealani Keakuhaupio. She had told him her first name meant "heavenly moon" and he thought he'd never met anyone so appropriately named. She was young and round and ripe. Her black eyes were like the night sky. They had finished making love under an overhang on a cliff that faced the waterfall. The noise was loud but calming and the sight of the falling water mesmerizing in the late afternoon sunlight; the water pooled at the base of the water-fall before running off to the coast no more than forty rods away, he guessed. Several people laughed and splashed about in the pool far below them. He'd been on the island less than a week, met Mahealani just yesterday and now she had guided him away from the top of the cliff where the luau was being held by King David in honor of the Americans. The islands were now the most important stop for ships traveling across the Pacific—Ethan was surprised at the forest of masts in the harbor when he'd arrived—and the king was determined to court favor with both the Americans and the British. The country had even gone so far as to create a national flag that combined elements from the Stars and Stripes and the Union Jack in an attempt to win over the two seagoing powers.

But politics had been the furthest thing from Ethan's mind. Once he and Mahealani got to the overhang, she untied her ti skirt, lifted several strands of orchid leis off her breasts, and pulled him to her.

She traced his lips with her little finger. "Why you? Because you needed it. You needed to smile."

"And did I?"

"You still are," she laughed.

They stood and dressed. "Pali?," he said, waving a hand at the cliff. This place was paradise. He'd never seen any place so lush, so alive. He never met people so full of life.

"Pali," she repeated. He was learning her language quicker than most foreigners. She'd been taught by missionaries and became the king's official interpreter thanks to her father's influence. Her father taught David Kalakaua the lua, how to be a warrior and how to be a king from the time he was a child and still wielded great influence in the court. That's how they met, she interpreting for the king, he for the ambassador. Too few foreigners even tried to learn her language, a language she thought the most beautiful in the world, certainly more beautiful that the harshness of English.

"Kai?" he said.

"The sea," she nodded.

He pointed out to sea where several men stood on boards riding the surf to the beach. "I've never imagined such a thing before. What's it called?"

"He'enalu. Wave sliding," she said, shaking her head. "But the word doesn't describe it. It has a hidden meaning. Is hidden the right word in English? A second meaning. A deeper meaning, that the person who does this becomes liquid, becomes the motion of the foam."

"I can't imagine such a thing is even possible. How long does it take to learn?"

"I don't know. The alii, royalty, are taught this from the time they are children."

He nodded in recognition. "Kinap. Power."

"Kinap?"

"A Mic Mac word. It's also difficult to define, but essentially it means power, the life force that's in all things. We would say that a man who can do this, who becomes liquid, has increased his power."

She smiled just as they heard screams from above them. Ethan's head snapped upwards and he saw a body falling toward him. He took a step forward to the edge and as the body flew by he reached out and grabbed an arm. The jolt nearly pulled him over with the falling person, but he had braced himself well and with one motion was able to swing the person up onto the ledge. The man embraced Ethan's feet, mumbling something, then stood up. His body was covered in small cuts and would be heavily bruised soon, but he was otherwise unharmed. The man was barreled-chested with powerful forearms and a deeply tanned skin. He had the broad nose and thick lips of his fellow Polynesians but sported large, black and curly mutton chop whiskers that reminded Ethan of a general from the War.

"King Kalakaua!" Mahealani said. "What happened?"

"I was too excited by the men in the waves and stepped too close to the edge of the cliff and when someone called my name and I turned to see what it was they wanted, my foot slipped and then I fell and hit the face of the cliff and your friend saved my life by snatching me out of the air like a warrior will catch a dragonfly," the king replied in Hawaiian. Mahealani translated quickly for Ethan.

"Don't do it no more," Ethan said, smiling. She translated this as "Thank you," then told Ethan no one, especially not haoles, ordered the king to do or not to do anything.

Several people from the party scrambled down the narrow path to the overhang. The queen rushed to her husband, then looked to Ethan.

"That was a magnificent thing you did," Mahealani translated to Ethan. He bowed a little to her.

"You'll get a promotion out of this," Ambassador Pierce said, shaking his hand.

The king walked over to one of his entourage and removed a strand of flowers— hundreds of orange petals strung together and intertwined with green leaves—from the man's neck and placed it around Ethan's.

"Thanks, king," Ethan said, bowing his head.

As they all walked back to the top of the cliff behind King Kalakaua, Ethan asked Mahealani, "What am I supposed to do with these? They're beautiful, but I'm not a flowery kind of guy. Would you like them?"

"Oh, no, you need to keep them and wear them all the time. It's a great honor the king has given you. Only high chiefs wear the ilima and maile leis."

…The two soldiers approaching pulled Ethan back to the present. He knew them: Corporal Engelhart and Private Burns. They'd been coming in the Mejor Que Nada for a couple of years now but he didn't know their first names. Didn't need to. They stopped a few feet from him when Burns pushed Engelhart.

"If you don't unnerstand it was because he was a foreigner, you got nothin' under your hat but hair," Burns said.

"Being from annuder land got nothing to do wid it," Engelhart responded as he pushed Burns back.

"Everthin' to do wid it. You think he'd a done it if he'd been a real American?"

"Booth vas a real American. And what you tink makes a real American anyvays?"

They stood now just above Ethan, not noticing him.

"Naw, you ignorant heine, Booth was a Southerner and that meant he was no American," Burns said. "Only someone born here makes an American."

"I have a paper says I'm an American. And I outrank you, too."

"Aw, a piece of paper don't amount to shit unless you're gonna wipe with it."

"I tink was because he was a lawyer," Engelhart said, shaking his head. "Cannot trust lawyers here or anywhere."

"Trust 'im if he were an American lawyer."

"Vat turnip wagon you get off from? Good ting all Americans not as stupid as you."

"Yaw, well, I say pack up all you foreigners and ship 'em back to where you come from."

Engelhart laughed. "OK. We go. Then who goes? Vas your fadder born here? Your mudder? How far back before your family comes here from annuder land? I tink only Apaches maybe been here long enough to stake claim."

"Whaw, you're an Injun lover now? I think that's downright traitorous, and you a corporal and all. And my parents may have come over from Scotland but me and my brothers and sisters were all born here, right in Providence, and you can't say that, and I figure the same for this assassin Geetoo... Guytoe... hell, I can't even pronounce his damn name."

"Hey," Ethan said, getting their attention as he stood up. "What's going on?"

Burns' eyes got wide as he tipped his hat back to wipe his forehead with his arm. "Yaw don't know? What rock you been livin' under? President's dead. Kilt by a foreigner."

"A lawyer," Engelhart corrected.

It was Ethan's turn for his eyes to get wide.

Engelhart pushed a newspaper into Ethan's hands. "Stupid half-a-breed. If you read, there is all the news."

The soldiers went inside and Ethan read a portion of story in the *New York Herald*, wondering where they got a copy of a New York paper.

PRESIDENT DIES!

President James A. Garfield of Ohio was pronounced dead yesterday after lingering for more than two months, the result of a cruel murderer's shot fired in embitterment this past summer. Physicians attending the President counseled that this beloved War Hero died as a result of severe infections and internal hemorrhaging resulting from the bullet fired by Mr. Charles J. Guiteau, an attorney, at a Washington railway station on the 2nd of July. Witnesses reported that Mr. Guiteau, since described by officials as a mental imbecile from Chicago who believed the President had denied him a consular posting, screamed as he fired the shot, "Stick that up your bung hole! I am a Stalwart of the Stalwarts!" Garfield served as President barely four months before being struck down.

Over the next few weeks after what proved to be the fatal shot was fired, surgeons tried valiantly but failed to locate the bullet in the President's back. Even Mr. Alexander Graham Bell attempted to assist the surgeons by inventing a metal detector. Unfortunately for the president, the bullet was imbedded so deeply in his body that Mr. Bell's metal detector could not pinpoint it.

At 2:15 P.M. today, the 20th of September, Vice President Chester A. Arthur was sworn in as the twenty-first President of the United States of America.

Born in Fairfield, Vermont, the son of a Baptist minister, President Arthur most recently served as Customs Collector in New York City before being sent by the voters of our great land to Washington with President Garfield.

"Men may die, but the fabric of our free institutions remain unshaken. No higher or more assuring proof could exist of the strength and permanence of popular government than the fact that though the chosen of the people be struck down his constitutional successor is peacefully installed without shock or strain except the sorrow which mourns the bereavement," President Arthur intoned in his first address to our saddened nation.

"Summoned to these high duties and responsibilities and profoundly conscious of their magnitude and gravity, I assume the trust imposed by the Constitution, relying for aid on divine guidance and the virtue, patriotism, and intelligence of the American people."

President Garfield served as a Major General of volunteers and served in order to preserve and protect the Union and to free the Negroes from slavery. Abolition of slavery was President Garfield's life work and his dedication to this cause was evidenced in a passage we repeat here from his Inaugural Address on March 4 this year, a passage which we believe the President would gratefully appreciate us reminding his fellow citizens thereof:

"The elevation of the Negro race from slavery to the full rights of citizenship is the most important political change we have known since the adoption of the Constitution of 1787. NO thoughtful man can fail to appreciate its beneficent effect upon our institutions and people. It has freed us from the perpetual danger of war and dissolution. It has added immensely to the moral and industrial forces of our people. It has liberated the master as well as the slave from a relation which wronged and enfeebled both. It has surrendered to their own guardianship the manhood of more than 5,000,000 people, and has opened to each one of them a career of freedom and usefulness. It has given new inspiration to the power of self-help in both races by making labor more honorable to the one and more necessary to the other. The influence of this force will grow greater and bear richer fruit with the coming years.

"No doubt this great change has caused serious disturbance to our Southern communities. This is to be deplored, though it was perhaps unavoidable. But those who resisted the change should remember that under our institutions there was no middle ground for the negro race between slavery and equal citizenship. There can be no permanent disfranchised peasantry in the United States. Freedom can never yield its fullness of blessings so long as the law or its administration places the smallest obstacle in the pathway of any virtuous citizen."

Ethan was interrupted by a slap on his back. He turned to see Joaquin.

"What do you think?" the Ranger asked as they walked inside.

"I don't think much, therefore I might not be."

"I swear sometimes talkin' to you is like talkin' to a pack mule. What's your opinion about what happened?"

"I can't believe a fellow Vermonter is President of these United States," Ethan said. "Never thought such a thing was possible."

"What kind of president do you think he'll make?"

"Beats me. I don't know him. Never heard of him. But you can rest assured he won't be like people might think. Vermonters are fiercely independent as a race. One thing he will be and that's his own man."

"Paper I read said he was a stooge for Boss Conkling and his Stalwarts in New York."

Ethan poured his best Tennessee whiskey in a glass for Joaquin and handed it to him from behind the bar. "I'd say that newspaper you read and Boss Conkling, whoever he is, are in for a great surprise if they believe that."

"I know you're a hard-headed son-of-a-bitch, but does that mean all Vermonters are, too?"

"Eh-yeah," Ethan said. "Like Texans in a lot of ways. You have to remember that Texas and Vermont are the only two states that used to be independent republics. When that happens, you get used to thinking your own way and the rest of the country be damned. Attitude gets handed down through the generations."

"Vermont was its own country? Like Texas? Never heard of that."

"Why would you? It's not like we're an important place or anything. I'll bet you can't find a Texas school kid who even knows where it is. But it was independent way earlier than Texas was. Fourteenth state."

"Hell, I don't even know where it is. Since you've spoken about Canada, I've assumed it's way up in the north, someplace near New York, but I don't even really know where New York is, except that it's far away and not much like Texas."

"Eh-yeah. Travel northeast from here and go maybe 2,000 miles and you'll run right into it. Nothing much like Texas at all. Not much, anyway. It has forests and lakes and clear, cold brooks and the best apples you've ever eaten and the best maple syrup you can imagine and true and constant citizens."

Joaquin sipped his whiskey, turning around to face the rest of the room, taking in all the noise. He rested his elbows behind him, on the bar. "All the times I hear you speak about Vermont I wonder why you don't go back."

"I get homesick," Ethan said, opening two whiskey bottles and handing them to Gracey. "But I realized a while back that I'm homesick for the Vermont I grew up in. With my grandfather. He loved his routines and I think that's what I loved the most. Following him around on those routines. If the weather was good, we got up early and went fishing on the lake for breakfast. If the weather was cold, we went out and chopped wood to bring in for the woodbin he kept just inside the door of his cabin, put some older wood in the stove and he'd make this drink by warming up milk and putting in shavings from a large block of chocolate he kept wrapped up in the pantry. Good chocolate. When it was raining, he always made the biggest breakfasts of eggs and potatoes and ham and flapjacks and syrup and we'd eat sitting at his small writing table by the front window instead of at the dining table and just watch the rain over the lake. Mon ami, those were magical moments, mi amigo. Magical. That's what I'm homesick for. If I went back and didn't have that, I don't know if I could stand it."

"Go back and create your own magical moments."

"Now there's the philosophizing I miss now that Brother Karl is gone," Ethan smiled, slapping Joaquin on his back.

The Ranger turned back around, holding up his glass for a refill.

"This may be too personal, but is that why you married your wife? Because she was a Vermonter and you were homesick?"

Ethan cleaned out a few glasses before he replied. "You may be partially right. I know that's what made me seek her out. It may have been even more so for her because that was the first time she'd ever been away from home. And why else would she have married someone twice her age?" He hesitated some more. "I think that homesickness and her belief that I was going to take her off to all these exotic lands she'd read about and I told her about."

"Those Sandwich Isles you've spoke of?"

"Eh-yeah. I think she thought we might go back and visit the king in his palace. I saved his life once. King David."

Joaquin shook his head as he sipped his whiskey. "Is that your life's mission? To save people's lives?"

"It was just blind luck. I happened to be the right person in the right place at the right time is all. The right one. I don't recall ever saving anyone's life in the Ottoman Empire, though."

"Now where in hell is that?"

"Right on the edge of Europe and Asia. I was a translator for an American consular official to the Sultan Murad for about a year. Believe it or not, I had quarters in the Topkapi Palace, where the harem girls were kept. Same job in the Sandwich Islands. I've always had a talent for languages and learn 'em pretty quickly. Unfortunately, I tend to forget 'em pretty quickly, too."

"I know you can speak Spanish and some Apache. What else?"

"Well, in order of how good I am, at one point I could speak English, French, Latin, German, Mic Mac, Spanish, Mescalero, Greek, Kiowa, Kickapoo, and Hawaiian."

"Hawaiian?"

"What they speak in the Sandwich Islands. Beautiful sounding, but I found it the most difficult to learn because they make up one word sometimes by putting other words together. I grew up speaking French along with English because half our lake was in Canada and most of our relatives spoke French as their first or second language and their first was Mic Mac. Learned German at Dartmouth because I was becoming an engineer and a lot of those math and physics texts were in German. Margaret knew French. That became our intimate language. A way for us to keep secrets. Maybe because I spoke French so well and was graduated from a college, she thought I was more sophisticated than I actually am. And unless you know, I don't look much like a red savage. She thought I was classier than I am."

"Now there's a classy guy," Joaquin said, pointing at a man who had just walked in.

The man dressed in a red and burgundy striped hip-length coat over a gold brocade waistcoat and black and brown striped trousers. He wore an emerald tie fastened over a green striped white shirt. A flat-topped, short-brimmed hat perched on his bald head. A banjo was slung over one shoulder on an embroidered strap and a guitar was slung on the opposite shoulder on a flower-carved leather strap. He walked directly to Ethan.

"Might you be the proprietor?" the man asked.

"So far," Ethan said, extending the man his hand. "Ethan."

The man seemed surprised Ethan would want to shake his hand. He smiled a wide smile, his white teeth overpowering his walnut face. "William George Washington Russell. But they call me the Sunrise Kid."

They shook hands and Ethan smiled back. "I can see why they do. What can I get you?"

"A beer would sate my thirst nicely, nicely," Sunrise said. "I, sir, am a traveling minstrel on my way to seek my fortune in California."

"You're not on the most direct route," Joaquin said.

"I know that, sir, nor the quickest. My aim is to see every nook and cranny of our great land before I reach its end at the Pacific. I've been on my way nigh onto fifteen years now. I was wondering if I might entertain your customers. I work just for donations. You wouldn't be out a penny for your kindness."

"Place could use some livening up," Ethan said, handing him a beer. "Play for tips and two beers a night. How's that?"

Sunrise sipped at the beer, found it to his liking and then down the remainder of the glass in a couple of gulps. "Sterling, sir."

Sunrise hopped up to sit on the bar. He removed his hat and placed it next to him, taking a metal sign from his coat pocket that read, "TIPS," and placed it so that it stuck up out of the hat. He swung the banjo around and began playing. The music brought immediate silence to the room. None of the regulars had ever heard music in the Mejor Que Nada before. Sunrise's fingers moved in delicate and precise banjo rolls over the strings and the music flowed out, surrounding the gloom in the bar and forcing it to surrender. A few of the men clapped hands to the music, some tapped on the tables, some shouted encouragement. After a few minutes, he changed tunes and began singing *Oh! Susanna,* then went right into *Dixie* to a few jeers and much applause. His baritone filled the room as easily as the banjo. He had everyone's attention. He played three more songs, ending with an instrumental similar to the one he started with. The room applauded loudly and many of the men stomped their feet as well. A few walked over and dropped coins into the hat.

"You keep dis man," Corporal Engelhart said, dropping an entire dollar in the hat after rubbing Sunrise's head. "He makes me happy."

Sunrise jumped off the bar and counted up his earnings: $4.07. He smiled that broad grin. "Your crowd always this good?"

"Not out in this God forsaken place," Ethan replied. "I think everybody came in because they heard about the president dying and they just wanted the comfort of other people around. Nobody wanted to be alone. Different when Lincoln was shot. Everybody then was in shock. That had never happened before. Now? I don't know. The mood's different. We're not at war, the economy seems to be good, railroads are being built, people are moving around the land. Optimism in the air. With Lincoln everybody seemed pessimistic. This crowd may last another day. After that, we'll be back to normal."

"And what, prithee, is normal?"

"Good night will be a dozen people. A bad night and you'll be singing to me and Gracey."

"Ah, the beautiful bar maiden," Sunrise said, just as Gracey walked over.

Ethan took an armful of empty bottles from her. "Not so much a maiden."

Sunrise dipped his head in greeting, took her hand and kissed it, introducing himself. He walked off holding his second beer.

"I have just met the man I will marry," Gracey announced to Ethan and Joaquin.

"Him? You don't know him at all," Ethan said.

"I know all I need to know. He is a gentleman and he brings joy to people. I like his laugh." She turned to Ethan and patted him on the cheek before walking away with another bottle. "You never laugh."

CHAPTER 9

Cibolo Creek Ranch, between Presidio and Lajitas

"I'm, I'm in the wagon; you're in the s-s-saddle. Can you handle that?" Stuttering Tom said.

Henry McCarty did a quick jig in front of the bunkhouse. "He-he, three beeves? I can handle three beeves as easy as hoppin' over a caterpillar."

"Two b-b-beeves. One's ahhhh m-m-milk cow."

"Lord I hope you don't drive as slow as you talk," Henry said. "I'm hopped up to see this countryside."

Some of the other hands were gathered around, waiting to get their assignments for the week from Santiago Juan Sanchez, Faver's segundo for his cattle operations, but Jim Juan hadn't arrived yet.

"Plumb hate to see you go, kid," Singleton laughed. "I was hoping we could get better acquainted, if you know what I mean. Ain't he just the daintiest feller you ever saw, boys?"

"With them teeth he could eat pumpkins through a picket fence, but come the big drive, he'll keep your bedroll warm of a cold Kansas night," Flyspeck Jack said.

Cold Neck George reached out to pinch Henry on the cheek. "If ol' Stutterin' gits to 'im afore we cin, the kid might git spoilt. I doan think Stutterin' cin stop oncet he gits a-goin'."

Henry grabbed one of Cold Neck's fingers and snapped it back, driving the larger man to his knees. At the moment his knees struck the dirt, Henry had a pistol barrel covering the man's left eye. Henry smiled and cocked an eyebrow up. "The way through a man's heart is through his underwear. If I cock this hammer, you'll be chomping through mine if I give the say-so. He-he."

"You hold on," Singleton said. Like all of the others except for Cold Neck, his hand was on the butt of his pistol.

Henry stood back, laughed again, spun his ivory-handled Colt's Lightning on his finger and dropped it neatly into its holster. "This isn't my first hoedown. I'm a right happy man until I'm riled, then I turn into a wildcat. I killed my first man four years ago in the town of Bonito in the Arizona Territory because he tried to cheat me at cards. I've put twenty other men under the sagebrush since then and I'm just twenty-one. I'm turning twenty-two in a couple months so I'm thinkin' I could use another dead man before then, so if anyone has any more funny idears, well, step right up and try me."

"You muchachos don't get paid for standing around like old ladies after church," Jim Juan said, walking up and hitting Cold Neck hard enough on the back of his head to knock his hat a dozen feet in front of him. He turned to Henry. "Has Tom told you where you will be traveling?"

Henry nodded. "Presidio, Leaton, Lajitas, just like Mr. Faver said."

"Don Milton," the segundo corrected him. He handed Tom a list, reciting from it. "Four jugs of the brandy, six bushels of carrots, two bushels of peaches, two bushels of pears, and the four quilts are for Spencer's Store in Presidio. Four jugs of our brandy, four bushels of peaches and two bushels of pears are for Johnny Burgess at Fort Leaton. Two jugs of the brandy, two cases of canned peaches, one case of tinned peaches shipped down from San Antonio, two bushels of fresh peaches, two bushels of pears, and the cattle are for the Mejor Que Nada cantina in Lajitas. I do not know who runs the cantina now, but he will pay for what was ordered. Do not lose the cattle."

Henry shook his head. "He-he. I couldn't lose cattle in a dust storm or a snow storm."

•

Presidio

As they were leaving Presidio, Henry's brag was tested. The dust rolled in while the cattle bawled. Henry stood next to his horse, covering its nose and eyes with a wet neckerchief. Tom stood between the two horses of his team, holding their reins as tightly as he could and humming to them. The men bent their heads down to use the horses' necks to block the sand being blasted at them. They walked as steadily as they could but slowly. The stormed lasted barely two minutes.

Henry laughed at the dust covering Stuttering Tom. "Made you into a gingerbread man."

"You're the sah-same," Tom said. "B-b-better c-c-catch those c-c-cattle."

Henry was already back in the saddle and spotted the cattle immediately. The three of them grouped together just a hundred yards away, still bawling. He rode over, waved his lariat, whooped and hollered, and got them back to behind the wagon. Only then did he pour more water on his neckerchief from his canteen and wipe off his face and dig dust out of his ears.

"Good to be alive, he-he," Henry said to Tom. He spurred his horse around the wagon, galloping ahead a few yards then, spying a clump of prickly pear, he dropped over the side of his saddle and snatched up a wrinkled purple fruit from one of the pads. He turned his mount, galloping up to Tom then slowing to a walk. He vaulted off, fed the tuna to his horse and jumped back up after showing the palm of his hands to Tom. "Look-ee there. No stickers. I'm about as slick as snot on a greased eel." Tom just shook his head.

Yeah, it was good to be alive, Henry thought as he rode back behind the wagon, occasionally saying a few words to the cattle to let them know he was still around.

They think they got me up in Sumner, buried like an outlaw with my feet to the west, but they ain't got me yet, not by a long shot, he thought. He was thankful his pal Juan Largo thought up the scheme and he was thankful Segura and Milnor and Silva and Lucero and Lorenzo, and Antonio all went along with it. Just a simple lie. And Pete, of course. Couldn't have pulled it off without Pete. He missed all his pals. Most of them were dead, dead, and dead. Mostly, though, he missed Juan Largo because Tall John was still alive. They'd ridden a lot of trails together. They were so inseparable for a while that everyone they knew took to calling them "the long and the short of it." But that wasn't fair. He wasn't so short as much as Juan Largo was so tall. That's how his pal got his nickname, after all. Their other nicknames didn't make much sense to Henry. He'd heard folks call them "Big Casino and Little Casino," but while Henry loved to gamble, Juan Largo didn't much like to. Always said he had a difficult time risking any of his hard-earned money. But what was money for if not to have fun with? If you go broke, you just go get more. His pal figured it was time to get married and get a job, and that just about ended their friendship right there. But the plan saved him, as long as he stayed out of New Mexico forever. Well, all the people he wanted dead were dead, dead, and dead now, so he didn't care about New Mexico anymore. The United States had plenty of states he could ride through. And there was always old Mexico. He didn't worry. He figured he had a long life in front of him—and even if he didn't he was sure going to enjoy the ride while it lasted.

•

Lajitas

The old man they delivered the remainder of the goods to at the Mejor Que Nada seemed an unhappy soul, scowling at them, almost blaming them for delivering stuff he had ordered himself. He made them unload it all, but then offered them a beer. Henry declined the beer and as soon as he did, Tom asked if he could have it. The old man smiled and said, "Why not?"

The saloon was crowded with people and that always made Henry nervous. He just didn't like crowds, especially crowds that had been drinking. But saloons were where the card games were. Tom drank his first beer then disappeared in the back with a chubby Mexican woman. Henry's eyes burned from cigar, cigarette and pipe smoke. That was a common feature of saloons, but he never got used to it and this place seemed to have less ventilation than most. Here he was nearing middle age at twenty-two and he'd never taken to smoking or drinking or whoring and couldn't think up a good reason why he hadn't. Pete used to tell him it was good that he didn't have those vices because they were bad for his health, but his health wasn't a thing he ever worried about. He figured he'd be shot to death or hung or stomped into the ground during a stampede before any drinking or smoking could ever kill him. Was it because his brother Joe took to opium and whores and rigged games? You'd go crazy trying to figure out stuff like that.

The saloon was too crowded. He'd never get into a game of cards with so many people sitting at all the tables with people standing behind the chairs, waiting to take a position if anyone left.

He stepped back outside, glad to have the fresh air.

A man dressed in what were once white trousers and a shirt came up to him, touching his small-brimmed sombrero. "Señor, por favor. May I please ask of you a favor?" The man's shirt was at least two sizes too large for his frame. He wore a vest that had been patched too many times.

"¿Qué?" Henry asked him.

"My name is Armando Baeza and I live not far from here," he said, pointing to a bluff on the far side of the road. "If you would be so kind, would you go into the cantina and buy me two bottles of mescal?"

"No dinero?"

"It is not that. It is that the owner of the cantina has banished me. But this is the only place where I can obtain good liquor of any kind. I have the money. And I will be happy to buy you a bottle as well for your kindness."

"That's generous. I'll do it. What are you banished for?"

"My chickens make too much noise and the owner of the cantina cannot sleep during the day."

"He-he, but that's what chickens do. How can you quiet a chicken?"

Armando shrugged and scowled. "I do not know a way."

"Mescal, you say?"

"Yes. It is brewed by a family across the river in the old ways and it is quite good. You should try some."

"No. No. That's not for me. That stuff will make you go blind."

Armando counted out three dollars into Henry's palm. That seemed to be far too much money, Henry thought, and said so.

"You can buy whatever you would like," Armando said. "Buy that first. Use the remainder to buy me as many bottles of the mescal as you can. It will keep, and then I do not have to come back and depend on the kindness of strangers too often."

Henry nodded, shuffling the coins in his hands.

"Oh, and get a bucket of beer for my goat," Armando said just as

Henry turned to go inside.

"Your goat?"

"Sí. I hate to drink alone and now the goat must have it or he gets very mean."

"He-he, a beer-drinkin' goat," Henry said. He returned quickly, carrying several bottles. He handed six to Armando and kept one.

"I think I'll try some of this peach brandy. Seems like it will be good to sip while playing cards. Do you play cards, Armando?"

"Oh, yes, yes. I love playing cards but I cannot find many people to play with me. Sometimes my cousin, sometimes my wife humors me. But if I win money from my wife, who am I taking it from? Just myself. There is little fun in that."

"That's why I'll never have a wife," Henry said. "Let's go to your place and play a few hands." Leading his horse, he followed Armando across the road, over the bluff and west by about a quarter-mile. To the left of Armando's jacal was a large chicken coop, its wooden slates broken and almost falling apart. The chickens clucked in a contented way. To the right of the jacal was a fenced-in pen for goats, several of them bleating. One billie with a broken horn slammed against the fence gate as if to get Armando's attention as they walked by.

"You wait and you will get your beer," Armando told the goat, tapping one of the bottles on the top of the gate. The goat bleated.

Inside, Armando put the bottles on a shelf and placed two roughly made ceramic cups on the table, pouring a third of one of the mescal bottles into one of them. Just when Henry got ready to pull out a chair and sit down, Armando told him to come back outside for a moment. He carried the bucket of beer with him, walking directly to the obnoxious goat. The goat raised his head in anticipation and Armando placed the small pail on the ground. The goat lapped up the beer as quickly as he could.

Henry shook his head. "A beer-drinkin' goat," Henry said. "I never saw such a thing."

"My wife does not drink and when I come home and want to drink I do not like to drink alone, so I taught my lead goat how to drink with me. He has a taste for the beer. He does not like much of anything else, so he is a cheap drunk and that is a good thing."

"He-he. I never heard of such a thing." He was tempted to see if the goat liked peach brandy, but the bottle was too expensive to waste on a goat. "What's his name?"

"He has no name."

"A beer drinkin' goat deserves to have a name."

"What is your name?"

"Henry."

"Then I shall name him Henry," Armando said, and they went back inside. This time, Armando's wife was there. "I have decided to name the big goat Henry in honor of my friend. Now I am going to play some cards and drink some mescal."

His wife wiped her hands on a towel and nodded. "Then I shall stay with my cousin this night."

Armando dismissed her with a wave of his hand and the two men sat down at the lone table in the shack. Henry handed Armando a deck of cards he pulled from inside his waistcoat, asking him to shuffle while he uncorked his brandy.

After an hour, Henry was $3 behind. He didn't realize how much alcohol he was consuming because the brandy tasted almost like candy to him. He got up once to relieve himself in the yard and was so dizzy he almost fell down. He laughed it off. He didn't think losing $3 to this goatherd was funny, though. Armando had finished off the second bottle of mescal and kept shaking his head as if to keep himself awake. His speech and motions slowed down. That's when Henry saw him deal himself a card off the bottom of the deck. He'd been in more than enough card games to know to watch a stranger dealing and he thought he had caught Armando cheating a couple of other times but hadn't been sure. This time he was certain. Henry reached out and pulled all of the coins on the table toward him.

"What... ?" Armando said, his head wobbling as it rose to look up at Henry.

"I warn you, where I come from I'm a dangerous man. And I don't take to card cheats."

"Oh, I would never cheat..."

Henry stood, knocking his chair over behind him. He shoved the coins into his pockets. "I saw you, you snake in the cactus. You're tellin' mighty big lies for such a short feller, and all that on top of cheatin' me."

Armando pushed back his chair, almost lost his balance, and stumbled back against the wall. His hand went up and pulled down a large butcher knife. "You put the money back, cabrone."

"He-he," Henry sang. "Si no me matas a mi. You te mato a ti. If you don't kill me, I'll surely kill thee."

Armando lashed out with the knife, but he was too far away. Henry pulled his revolver and shot the goatherd squarely between the eyes.

CHAPTER 10

The San Carlos Presidio

Lerdo's sweat was almost unbearable. It soaked completely through his shirt, it flowed into the palms of his hands, it poured down his forehead enough to keep him nearly blinded no matter how often he blinked or rubbed his eyes, it trickled into his beard, it filled his socks so much he could feel the clamminess between his toes when he took a step, it flowed down his ass and stomach and settled in his crotch. He couldn't keep his tongue out of the empty socket in his mouth and he swore that his gums were sweating.

He stormed out of his office to sit in the horse-watering trough by the front porch. He dunked his head into the water, rubbing the water into his thick head of hair as deeply as he could. He stood up, stepped out of the trough, and walked to his rocking chair on the porch. He sat down after wrapping a wet handkerchief around his forehead. Sergeant García saw this and when he walked by the trough he dipped his hat in the water and placed it back on his head while walking up the porch steps.

"Do you think they have ice in Mexico City?" he asked his top sergeant. "I saw ice one time in New Orleans in the middle of August. They keep it in a big warehouse in large blocks. They cut off what they want to cool their drinks and keep their meat fresh."

"Except for frost in the winter, I have never seen ice," García said.

Lerdo stretched his hand toward the olla tied to the porch roof. García retrieved it for the captain, who took a long drink before handing it back. "I dream of ice."

"I dream of women with big breasts."

"I used to, before this heat came. It has no mercy."

García nodded. "But what can you do? The gringos have all the cold places."

Lerdo nodded back. "The gringos can have ice in the summer and we have ice in the winter. So we both have ice. Life is fair, is it not?"

García shrugged. "Life is what is, jefe."

"Alsate is cool right now, sitting in the shade of a big tree at the top of his mountain," Lerdo said, feeling his shirt sleeves. They were nearly dry and it was only a couple of hours past breakfast. "Why didn't the Spaniards build this city at the top of a mountain?"

García shrugged again. He had no answers to these kinds of questions his captain liked to ask. He was just a sergeant. His job was to pass orders along and see they were obeyed and when his men complained he made certain his captain never heard those complaints.

"Sergeant, do you know of anyone Alsate trusts that we could use to take a message to him?"

García removed his hat, rubbing his forehead. He pursed his lips and scratched his broad nose. He looked far to the west.

"I know of perhaps two men. One lives in Lajitas, the other in the Lajitas across the river. They are goatherds and cousins and have traded with Alsate's band many times. I do not know how much Alsate trusts them."

"Who is the Mexican?"

"Lionicio Castillo," the sergeant replied. "He raises chickens and goats in Paso Lajitas."

"How well do you know him?"

"I have met him only twice or perhaps three times. He is the brother of my wife's cousin's husband. I know him to see him."

"Do you think he will take a message to Alsate if we ask him?"

"I think that for money, this man will do anything."

"How much is a lot of money for this man?"

García carefully screwed his hat back on. "I cannot say. A hundred pesos? This seems like a lot."

"I have that much here. Come inside."

They went in to Lerdo's office where the captain took a key and opened a small lock box in a drawer in his desk. He removed twenty pesos."

"Go to Señor Castillo and give him ten pesos and tell him that his country needs him to be of service and that we need him to deliver a message to Alsate."

"What kind of a message? I know he will ask. A good message, he might pass along. A bad message, he would fear Alsate would kill him on the spot."

"A message of peace," Lerdo said, leaning back in his chair, his wet trousers making him uncomfortable. "We need to end our conflict and I will do so the only way I know how. I need for you to find this man now and bring him to me."

"I will do so. But, you have given me ten more pesos than you said to give to him."

"For your trouble, sargento. I am feeling either generous or desperate, and either way works in your favor."

"Sí, jefe."

•

Apache Camp, Chisos Mountains Basin

Alsate returned to his wickiup after throwing up into a ditch. When he tried to eat something his stomach rejected it, going into the convulsion that drove him outside. He hadn't slept well, either.

Little Moccasins finished wrapping a lock of her hair in a piece of buckskin she had decorated with blue and yellow beads. Alsate took it from her and tied it to the top of his lance, just below the obsidian head. He had similar locks of hair, one from each of their five children, already tied to the lance between strands of horsehair, but hers stood out, gleaming white below the black lance head. He handed her the lance and got dressed. He put on his ceremonial buckskin shirt that she had painted light blue for him. She also painted the four-pointed star in white across the chest with six other smaller stars around it. Fringe hung in twisted, long strands from the arms and along the bottom that reached to his shins. He pulled on his knee-high moccasins, also painted blue. Finally, he placed his red fox fur turban on his head. The turban was decorated with golden eagle feathers and silver coins that Little Moccasins polished. She handed him back his lance and he went outside. She stayed in the lodge to pray.

The young men gathered around the morning cookfire, laughing and bragging.

Alsate walked up to within an arm's length of Owl Eyes and although he spoke to all the warriors, his eyes stayed fixed on Owl Eyes. "Yusn gave us this land through our forefathers. It has come to us. It was our land before the Pale Eyes and the Nacoya came. It is still our land. Yusn had me born to be an Alsate. The name was my father's and his father's and his father's and his father's, back as far as when we fought the Spanish. The name is one so old we no longer know its meaning. This is an honor I hope to live up to. I am chief of the Chishi, but now the number of the Chishi is small. Perhaps I am the last chief. Only Yusn knows this. I do know I will die as chief of the Chishi. This band is my life, as it has been the life of all Alsates before me. The welfare of this band is more important to me than anything else in our world. For this reason, I, as chief, cannot have the band follow anyone but their chief."

Without hesitation, Alsate drove the head of his lance into Owl Eye's sternum.

Owl Eyes dropped to his knees with the same look of astonishment on his face as all the other band members. Frothy blood gushed from the wound in spurts. He fell to his side.

Alsate waited a minute, then pulled his lance from the dead man's chest. "If anyone wishes to challenge my leadership, let him do so now. I will either lead this band or I will die as its chief. I am happy to do either one this day."

•

The San Carlos Presidio

A day later, Sergeant García brought Lionicio Castillo before Captain Lerdo. Lionicio stood in front of the large desk, hat in hand, looking at the floor of faded, broken tiles.

"You know Alsate?" Lerdo asked.

Lionicio continued to stare at the floor.

"Do you know Alsate? You will not be punished for knowing this Apache, but I must know if you can speak with him."

"I have spoken with him, capitán," Lionicio said in a voice barely above a whisper.

"Good. You must take this message to him. Tell him that I, Capitan Ulysses Lerdo, wish for the animosities between our peoples to cease. It harms us both. Tell him I am willing to sign a treaty with him and that if he signs this treaty of peace between his band and our village, I will see to it that four times a year he may have ample supplies of food and some trade goods for his people. In return, his people must never raid our village or any other village on the southern border of the river again. He must promise this and we will promise this. If he agrees, he should come to San Carlos and we will sign the treaty and have a fiesta to celebrate the good fortune of both our peoples. When you return, I will pay you another ninety pesos."

Lionicio looked at Lerdo for the first time, seeing a large man but one younger than he had pictured. "I do not know what Alsate will say to this."

"Your job is to deliver the message. I think the old man must be as tired of these raids as we are. Raids are things of the past. Why endanger the lives of his warriors for less than what I am willing to give him peacefully? Deliver the message."

"I will go now."

Lerdo and García followed Lionicio outside and watched him slide onto his burro and ride away on the road to the river.

"Has Chihuahua City finally listened to your pleas, jefe?" Garcia said. "We often do not have enough for the command, as small as it is. You have promised much more than we have ever gotten."

Lerdo removed his uniform blouse and draped it over his shoulder for the walk to his Panocha's jacale. "That's what I promised."

CHAPTER 11
Lajitas

Ethan stood on the bluff above the river watching a typical October thunderstorm roll in from the west. He was intending to open the saloon, but as soon as the creosote and sage filled his nostrils he knew rain was coming. The thunder with the storm was low but hard, vibrating the ground. He watched the sky above him turn deep blue with the onrushing gray of the clouds sweeping a curtain of rain under them. The storm moved quickly and it would have been on top of him before he could get shelter except that it turned south just above the shallow river crossing a couple hundred feet upriver. The storm threw thick mist in his direction, but no raindrops. The drops—large, heavy drops—fell nearby with a noise that masked everything else, creating holes in the water and in the dirt as it passed over the river. The aromas the rain kicked up were almost overpowering.

He inhaled it deeply. As quickly as the storm rushed in, it had gone on, drenching Paso Lajitas. Good, he thought, maybe it'll drown some chickens and dogs.

"Did you sleep well?" Gracey asked him when he opened up the front door. Her apartment was in the rear of the building and had a connecting door to the saloon so she could conduct her main business. His apartment was also in the back, but had only one door that opened toward the river.

"Eh-yeah. I don't know what was in that mixture you gave me, but it knocked me right out. Flat out. My eyes are still a little twitchy from it, I think."

"Do not use too much of it or use it too often," she cautioned him. "If you do, you will not be able to sleep without it."

Then he noticed the Sunrise Kid stroll from Gracey's apartment. He was barefoot, wearing only his trousers with one side of his braces over one shoulder and the other drooping below his waist. He scratched behind his ear, walking to the bar. "Celebratory snort?"

Ethan scowled but nodded approval, then snatched a broom from beside the door and began sweeping out the saloon. "A married whore is ridiculous," he mumbled to himself. It was unusual to have business just after opening so he wasn't paying any attention when he swept some dirt directly onto the boots of three men standing just outside.

"I'd watch that, I were you," the square-jawed man in the middle said.

"Sorry," Ethan said with a shrug. "Wasn't paying attention."

"Where's this Ethan Allan Twobears? He's supposed to work here. That you?"

"Eh-yeah." No one had ever coming looking for him before. He grabbed the broom handle tighter, wondered if he could get to the shotgun behind the bar before any of these men shot him down and decided he couldn't. He looked them over quickly. The man who spoke had a star on his rain-soaked shirt and carried a pistol butt forward on each hip over well-worn chaps. The other two were younger men, each carrying a rifle. Deputies, he guessed. "Whadya want?"

"You're under arrest," the sheriff said. He motioned to one of the deputies who stepped forward and shackled Ethan's wrists.

"When the Lord poured in your brains, some angel must've jostled his arm because you didn't get near your fair share. No brains at all. Just what is it you think I've done?"

"I'm arresting you for the murder of Armando Baeza."

The goatherd had been killed two weeks ago but the shooting had been a mystery. At first everyone in Lajitas thought Armando's cousin Lionicio had done it because Armando had stolen goats from across the river and everyone knew Armando's younger wife was in bed with Lionicio whenever they could steal time from their spouses, but Lionicio was occupied with Teresa Baeza during the murder, and Lionicio's neighbors knew it so they both had alibis.

"He did not murder anyone," Gracey said, putting herself between Ethan and the deputy who shackled him.

"Well, we'll just let a jury decide on that. I've got motive, I've got threats, and I've got eyewitnesses," the sheriff said. "Now you step aside."

"Where are you taking him?"

"You come visit him in my juzgado up in Fort Davis. But do it fast because we tend to have quick trials for murders up there.

368

Gracey's face went blank, the corners of her mouth quivering. "What do I do?"

"You and Sunrise run the saloon. You can run a bar, can't you?"

"Surely can," the Sunrise Kid said.

"Try not to steal too much. I'll be back as soon as I can," Ethan said as they led him out of the door. "Soon as I can."

•

Fort Davis

Joaquin felt guilty. If he hadn't left for Fort Davis at daybreak, two hours before Baeza's body was discovered by his wife, he would have been the one investigating the killing and if he had been investigating he didn't know who he would have arrested but he surely knew who he would not have arrested. He knew Ethan well enough to know that the man could be deadly but was no murderer. He could kill easily, but only if his own life or someone's else's was at stake. If he had been the one to investigate the murder, his friend wouldn't be here in jail.

Ethan popped off his bunk when he saw Joaquin come into the sheriff's office. The Ranger had a few words with the sheriff then walked back to the cages. Ethan stood with his forehead resting against the bars, his wrists on a crossbar. "Took you long enough."

"I just saw your name on the report Pittman filed with Company E. I couldn't believe it. I thought maybe you'd dropped off the wagon and went off and killed more chickens. I couldn't believe it when I saw the charge."

"You do know I didn't do it."

"Of course I know."

"Then tell the sheriff to release me."

"I'll tell him what I know, but now that the charge has been filed he can't just let you go. He has to hold you for trial. And the judge refused bail."

"Eh-yeah. He said I was a flight risk. He's right about that. Let me out and I'll sprout wings and fly away."

"You would probably disappear."

"Eh-yeah, damn straight I would. I should have left this place a few weeks back. Should have been gone already. I just couldn't make up my mind where to go."

"I don't see how they can convict you. Pittman's got witnesses, but no eyeball witnesses who saw you do it. Just Baeza's wife who puts you there that night."

"I was never there. I've never been at his place."

"She said it was you."

"She's lying or mistaken. She's a stupid, lying adulteress, and hard of hearing and hard of seeing, too. She wouldn't know me if I stood up in front of her and bit off her nose."

Joaquin leaned back to rest against the wall. He was furiously trying to think of something encouraging to tell his friend.

"I won't stay in jail," Ethan said quietly. "I'd die in a lock-up."

"You won't have to. The trial is in a couple of days. I'll be there. I'll ride back to Lajitas with you when it's all over and we'll laugh about it all the way."

"I haven't laughed in years."

Joaquin nodded and walked over to the sheriff's desk. Sheriff Blair Pittman was slowly sipping his third cup of coffee.

"I want to be on the list to testify at the trial," the Ranger said.

"You see something?" the sheriff asked.

"I wasn't there. I should have been, but I wasn't. If I were, that man would never be in this jail. I know he didn't do this."

"How's that?

"I know him. He's saved my life twice and he's saved the lives of three other people in this county and saved the life of a king and that's just the ones I know about. You get to know a man over a couple of years of being around him nearly everyday and I know this man. He wouldn't kill anyone without a good reason and if he did kill someone, he'd be the first to explain that reason to you."

Pittman took a longer drink. He was not impressed by this man who was as young as his oldest boy. Rangers weren't particular who they signed up and it was all up to the company commander. But a sheriff had to stand before the people and be chosen just as he was last year rising up after eleven years as a deputy and three as chief deputy.

He knew who was more likely to be right in a criminal case like this. It wasn't this boy. Let the Rangers fight Indians, let the peace officers enforce the law. No Indians left to fight, fine, let them disband the Rangers. Too much like that damned State Police force anyway to suit him—carpetbaggers and galvanized Yankees not worth a bucket of warm piss. He didn't see the Rangers much differently.

"They played cards and Baeza pulled a knife out. Your half-breed friend was probably cheating. His life was threatened and he did the only thing he knows how to do. He killed him. He'd threatened to do it before. In front of witnesses, and I think threatened him in front of you."

"Sheriff, he says a lot of things when he's angry. We all do. You ever gone days without sleeping? Really riles the blood up, doesn't it? And besides, would he go off to play cards with a man he wanted to kill?"

"Mebbe that was a ruse to get alone with him so he could kill him."

"He was running a saloon, for God's sake. He didn't have time to go off and play card games. Besides, I've never known him to play cards."

"That saloon was packed full of people. Even his own whore said he was in and out all night, who knows how long he could have stayed gone. It was so busy, no one would have noticed."

"I think they'd notice if they weren't getting drinks."

"I take it this whore did that when he wasn't around. Doubled as a waitress."

Joaquin shook his head. Pittman had his mind made up. "You said you had witnesses, but it's all just say-so. Nobody really saw anything."

"This man's cousin from acrost the río, Castillo. He said your friend killed all his chickens and dogs and was going to kill Baeza's, too, but you stopped him. That's when your friend threatened to kill both Castillo and Baeza."

"Ethan killed two of the man's roosters and let his chickens loose. He didn't kill any dogs. And I didn't stop him from doing anything. He just told them to shut their livestock up and went to bed."

"You know any way to shut livestock up short of killing them?"

Pittman said, putting his cup down and leaning over his desk. "The half-breed's off his mental reservation."

"I can testify Castillo is lying, and a jury will believe me long before they'll believe him."

"Mebbe so, but Baeza's wife saw the man."

"I don't think so."

"Says she did. Castillo told me she did and when I asked her she said it was the saloonkeeper."

"I still don't think so."

"Well, we'll just let a jury decide all that."

•

The trial was short and bitter. Judge Joe E. Taliaferro would let Joaquin testify only about the confrontation Ethan had with Castillo and Baeza after he'd killed Lionicio's roosters. He had to acknowledge the threat Ethan made. The judge refused to allow Joaquin to testify about Ethan's character, saying it had no bearing on the facts of the case before the court. Ethan's denials on the witness stand seemed pathetic, even to Joaquin. Ethan just said he didn't know what had happened, that he hadn't been at Baeza's that night, and that he couldn't prove it. Sheriff Pittman read a statement he said came from Gracey Salgado saying that Ethan came and went out of the saloon all that evening. He read similar statements from three soldiers and a ranch hand that worked for the esteemed Don Milton Faver. Teresa Baeza testified she saw Ethan with Armando that night as they sat down to play cards and drink. Ethan could only counter that he liked to go outside for a breath of fresh air because the saloon was too crowded and noisy and filled with smoke. And no one on the jury believed for a moment that a saloonkeeper would leave a crowded saloon, especially for those reasons.

The district attorney summed up the case well, pointing to Ethan's actions in killing livestock, pointing to his threats, pointing to the testimony of Baeza's wife that Ethan was the last person to see her husband alive, pointing out the man's volatile temperament, the man's history of being a drunkard, pointing out the scattered cards and the knife by the dead man's hand. The jury took less than half an hour to convict Ethan.

The judge considered himself a lenient and liberal man when he passed the sentence of twenty years at hard labor as the State Prison Board shall determine. "It is the opinion of this court that it cannot be ascertained with absolute certainty how this argument over cards began, nor can it be ascertained with any certainty which of the participants in this fatal night instigated the argument that culminated in the death of Señor Armando Baeza. It is only that remnant of uncertainty that saves you from the gallows, Mr. Twobears."

Besides, the Southern Pacific Railroad Company paid him a bounty of $50 for each prisoner the judge added to its work camp.

CHAPTER 12
Apache Camp, Chisos Mountains Basin

Alsate rejoiced seeing the red sky when he rose from a sound night's sleep. His experience told him that usually meant bad weather and that was what they desperately needed. It hadn't rained here since July. The camp was stirring; morning cook fires crackled to life under the care of several of the women. The crimson seemed to hang in the sky longer than normal, then faded quickly into orange to gold to a pale yellow that yielded to a hazy blue telling Alsate that moisture was in the air. Not enough, though, to form the early morning fog that often filled the basin. He wondered for the first time in his seventy summers where that red came from and where it went.

The camp had been quiet since he killed the upstart Owl Eyes. When warriors passed by him, they averted their eyes. Others would speak to him only if he spoke first and then they would respond politely with a voice so low as to almost mumble. No one wanted to speak what was on his mind. They were all—Alsate included—waiting for something else to happen.

In mid-morning, Lionicio Castillo rode his mule into the camp, leading a pack mule. His unannounced arrival shocked Alsate. No one was guarding the paths into the mountains. He cursed himself silently for neglecting his duties; this was the sort of thing he had left to Owl Eyes.

"Why do you come here?" Alsate asked the man in Spanish before he could dismount.

"May I speak a while?" he asked. Alsate nodded and Lionicio slipped off the mule and followed Alsate to a corner of the camp that overlooked the desert to the west through a giant V shaped by the sides of the mountains coming together.

Alsate sat cross-legged, facing the west, tilting his head back a little. "Why do you come here?"

"I bring a message from Capitan Ulysses Lerdo in San Carlos," Lionicio said. Alsate motioned for him to sit beside him and he did.

"You know that the fields surrounding San Carlos are the best farm land for many days' ride all around, and you know that many cattle grow strong on the grassy plains around the river that flows into the big river. But your people have raided these fields and these cattle too much and the San Carlos people are worried that with the drought we have suffered this year they will have great pains surviving another growing season if your people continue their raids. Capitan Lerdo wants an end to these raids and he has a proposal that is mutually beneficial to your people and to his."

Alsate disliked Lionicio more than most Nacoya, more than most Pale Eyes, because the man was a liar and a cheat and could not be trusted, but as the goatherd explained the proposal, Alsate had to make an effort to contain his happiness. Here was, at last, if he could believe Lionicio, a way for them to end the eternal hostilities and perhaps forge new friendships. It was a legacy Alsate desperately wanted to leave his people.

"How do I know you speak the truth?" Alsate said after a while.

"Capitan Lerdo asked that I give you this message. Nothing more. I do not care one way or the other if you continue to raid or if his soldiers continue to kill your warriors. He cares. I think you care. He proposes a treaty between the two peoples, a treaty that does not involve governments. He knows those treaties are often not kept. He wants a treaty between Alsate and himself. He knows that treaty will be honored. He proposes a celebration in honor of this treaty at the next full moon. You will see then just how true his words are."

Alsate rose in one motion and walked toward the heart of the camp, Lionicio trying to keep up. Alsate handed the reins of the mule to Lionicio. "Tell Lerdo we will hold council on this matter and decide. Tell Lerdo I want to do this, but I do not know if I will."

Lionicio pulled himself into his saddle. Motioning to the other mule, he said, "This is a present from the San Carlos people to Alsate's people to show their good faith." He rode away, leaving the pack mule.

As some of the women unpacked the onions and cantaloupe and sweet potatoes, the warriors gathered around Alsate who told them of the Nacoya offer. He was glad to hear them finally express a strong opinion on something, but he was distressed that their opinion was counter to his own.

"We have time before the full moon," he said. "We should pray on this."

•

In the Foothills of the Mesa de Anguila, East of Lajitas

Three wagons were lined up side by side by side. One was a regular army supply wagon, its canvas top pulled back to reveal four barrels of iron filings and ten carboys of sulfuric acid. The other two wagons were square, enclosed wooden boxes, each painted with "Lowe's Gas Generator" on the side. One hose ran from each gas generator into a smaller box placed on the ground with another hose attached to this smaller box that ran to the neck of the balloon. Travelin' Jones disconnected the hose to his balloon. After four hours, the envelope was fully inflated, straining against the lines held by soldiers. "Major, I insist that you accompany myself and our photographer on this first flight."

"I didn't join the army to be a bird," Major Jones said, shaking his head.

"I can assure you the balloon is perfectly safe. You may not wish to ascend another time, but this first impression is vitally important to your mission. You need to scrutinize the lay of the land to determine where the wagons can and cannot go. You might trust to my expert observations, but nothing serves like seeing things with your own eyes."

"Safe?"

"I have never had an accident," Travelin' said, holding open the gate of the basket. Raymond Ballheim, the photographer from San Antonio, stepped in, moving to the back. "We never had a balloon accident during the entire War and that was when we were being shot at. Always without result. The same was true for Federal balloons. Ascending into the heavens in my balloon, sir, is safer than riding on your stallion across this ground."

Major Jones scowled but stepped into the basket. As Travelin' latched the gate closed, the major moved to the side, looked ahead and grabbed onto the lip of the basket with each hand in a death grip. "What if the soldiers release the lines? What if the cable snaps?"

"The soldiers are supposed to release their lines. But the cable is strong and tested to be so. Such a cable break won't happen, but were it to then we should just float away on the gentle breezes."

"What if the balloon springs a leak?"

"Such won't happen, but were it to we should just gradually float back to the earth."

"What if the fabric of the envelope suffers a massive tear and the gas is suddenly released?"

"I've never heard of such a thing happening, major. Even during the war, I had several balls pierce the envelope and the balloon remained aloft. The fabric is sewn so that if a rupture does occur it's halted by a seam." He paused and reached into a small sack, pulling out a rock and gave it to Major Jones. "You'd be wise to heed the words of the wise man who wrote these words."

The major turned over the rock, one of several Travelin' had found when they were further north, and read aloud: "'When the rains of life/mat down your hair/don't despair/lift up your face/and drown a little.' Why do you keep these things?"

"They amuse me. I hope we find more. Now, relax, major and enjoy the beautiful view."

Travelin' indicated for the soldiers to release their lines, he then turned the handle on the winch on the floor of the basket feeding out cable through the hole in the bottom. The balloon slowly rose. He stopped at 200 feet to let his passengers get acclimated to the view and the possibilities of what they might be able to see at even higher altitudes.

"Jumpin' Jehosaphat," the major said, still bent over and holding onto the basket rim. "Look at that. This surveying can work from a balloon!"

"You had doubts?" Ballheim said.

"One never knows," the major said.

"Now you can understand why I wanted you to see this at least once," Travelin' said. "Besides, you will have to decide where we can take the wagons. The canyon is just a couple of miles to our south and we should be able to see its rim at a higher altitude. We should be able to plot a course from Lajitas to the top of this mesa and along by the canyon until it ends near San Vicente." He winched out more cable and the balloon rose again not stopping until Travelin' estimated they were near 2,000 feet.

"Oh, my God," Ballheim said.

"Lord," Travelin' moaned.

"Shit," the major spat, pounding his fists on the basket lip, the first time he'd let go of it.

What they saw was the top of the Mesa de Anguila stretching for several miles to the east of them, and the rim of Santa Helena Canyon just to the south of them, and the village of Lajitas a couple of miles to the west of them. They could see a way to get wagons and mounted soldiers up onto the mesa from Lajitas, but what then? All they could see were crevasses and steep hills and cracks in the ground, everything was wrinkled and folded and twisted.

"No wagon could possibly traverse that," Major Jones said.

"I always thought the word "mesa" meant "table" and I always thought tables were flat," Ballheim said. "That mesa is anything but flat."

Travelin' held a long field glass to his right eye, looking as far as he could. "I hope you have a contingency plan, major."

"Mules could make it," Major Jones said.

"Indeed, but they'd travel ten miles to cover one. And just imagine all the water we'd have to carry for us and the mules," Travelin' said. "And without the generator, how would we get the balloon aloft?"

"You Johnny Rebs used hot air during the war. Could this balloon be made to rise on hot air?"

"It can," Travelin' said. "But where would you get the firewood? Do you see any trees out there?"

The major shook his head. "No, but we could go to the Chisos, cut as much pine as we would need, and pack it in on the mules."

"You're speaking of a major endeavor, major," Travelin' said.

Major Jones moved carefully around the basket, straining to take in as much of the area as he could. "A boat? Balloons were tethered to boats during the war. We could float through the canyon and the balloon would be guided by the boat."

"Could work, but from what little we've seen and been told, the walls of that canyon are sheer. A thousand feet to fifteen hundred feet is the estimate. The boat wouldn't be able to stop. Seven, eight miles through the canyon? Imagine if a boat capsized; you'd have a very long swim out if you could do it. And even if a boat could make it through, it would be moving too quickly for the photographer or surveyor to do their jobs from the balloon. Have you even heard of a boat surviving a trip through that canyon?"

The major slowly shook his head, sighing. "What else do you suggest, Mr. Jones?"

"I think we need to think it all out, Major Jones," Travelin' said, winching in the cable, pulling the balloon down.

•

Southern Pacific Railroad Work Camp, West of Burgess Springs

"New man, hunh?" Boss Slipher said, not looking up from his noon meal of beans and fried possum.

"Ethan Allan Twobears. Sent to us from Presidio County authorities for the murder of a man in Lajitas," said the guard.

Slipher expected to see an Indian when he looked up so he was surprised to see a man who looked as white as he was. Tall, well-muscled, but gray. The muscles would serve him well on the work crew but Slipher worried that the convict's age would take a quick toll laboring in the brutal heat. "Y'all know me?"

Ethan shook his head no.

"Then why are y'all eyeballing me like that? Y'all don't know any manners I be glad to let Big Black Dick teach y'all some." Slipher wiped his mouth on the sleeve of his shirt, stood, and picked up a long wooden stick with leather straps attached. The stick was painted black. Ethan thought the leather had been dyed black to match but quickly realized the coloring was dried blood.

"Y'all missed dinner, but normally we have three meals a day here. All our convicts are well fed," Slipher said, caressing the bat in his hand. "And y'all, like them, are gonna see lots of hard work, from can see to can't. If y'all begin to shirk, I won't spare Big Black Dick here for I find that in the convict business the judicious use of leather is just as important as feeding to get an honest day's work outta y'all. Now, I'm not sure why y'all were sent hyar, prolly just 'cause Fort Davis be so close to our camp. Usually, y'see, the niggers go to the fields and the whites to the mines or lumber camps and the redskins to the railroad."

"Perhaps I should be sent to the lumber camp, then, because I've got extensive experience as a timberjack," Ethan said.

Slipher slammed the butt end of his bat into Ethan's stomach, doubling him over.

"Y'all need to learn that y'all don't speak less spoken to. When you want to speak, you raise your hand. I see y'all're 'bout half redskin, so y'all can forget about cuttin' trees."

Ethan raised his hands, the chains rattling as he did so.

"Speak, half-breed," Slipher said, smiling.

"When may I see the warden?"

"Ain't no warden on the work gangs. I'm the captain in charge and I'm the one y'all answer to. And in case y'all're thinkin' about complainin' to the Texas Prison Board inspector when he comes through, well, the last convict we had complain to an inspector suffered a long series of unfortunate events. I believe his hip was smashed and his right foot had to be amputated. All accidents, of course."

"Of course," Ethan said.

Slipher rammed the bat into Ethan's stomach again, then on the back of his neck when he doubled over, knocking him to his knees. "I see we may have troubles educatin' y'all. But we'll get 'er done." He waved for the guard to remove Ethan from his tent and put him to work.

Ethan was given an aggie—a long, heavy hoe used to break ground with every stroke. He was put on a squad with twenty other men, mostly Apache and some Kickapoo and two Cherokee. The crew used their aggies to chop up the soil, thin out the plants, and level the ground as a bed for the rails. Chinese crews toted and placed ties on the prepared beds. Other Chinese used large levers to maneuver rails into position so they could be nailed to the ties. Coloreds wielded the

380

hammers and spikes. The work was slow and harsh. When the sun started to set, the Chinese left to go to their tents about a mile away from the camp while the convicts trudged to their tents. Inside the tents—one tent serving fifty convicts—guards removed their shackles and the men sat on their cots waiting for their supper. The shackles had torn at Ethan's ankles.

"Yah nevah get used t'it," a convict at the adjacent cot said to Ethan, showing him his own ankles covered with sores and calluses and scabs and fresh blood. "Th'iron's too heavy for folks t'wear all the day. But we do, nonetheless. Fella found a rock with scribblins on it and that sums up our lot. Rock said, 'Every horse/thinks/his own pack/is the heaviest.' We think we be havin' it bad, but nother fella he be workin' out here with no foot."

Ethan showed the other man a small rock of his own, one he'd picked up earlier in the day. One side was almost pure white, the other dark gray. On the white side was an inscription. When the other man said he couldn't read, Ethan read it for him: "You cannot know what lies ahead/or behind as death conquers all/unless you live life while you can."

"I found me one them rocks like a week back," said one of the other men. "I don't recall zackly but twere sumthin' 'bout waitin' under a willow tree searching for a love. I know couple more been found, too."

"Who writes them? And why on rocks?"

"Dunno. Always seem to be on these here rocks with the desert varnish on 'em. Breaks up the day when you find one. Keeps your head occupied so you ain't thinkin' of the rotten work you're sufferin'."

"Chow!" one of the convicts called. The men lined up to file out of tent. As they left the tent, another convict gave them a tin plate and cup full of water. They continued in single file to the rear of a wagon where another convict filled their plates with pork, boiled corn, and bread. Then they filed back into the tent to eat, rest as well as they could, sleep until dawn.

As Ethan held up his plate for food at the rear gate of the Johnnie wagon, one of the two men on the wagon said, "Sar'nt?"

He looked up. "Ben?"

Ben shook his head slowly as he dished up the food. "What you doing here, sar'nt?"

"Long story. You?"

"Sad one."

"Hey, y'all stop that jawin' and keep the line movin'," one of the guards hollered. "Other folks get to eat, too, y'know."

"Oncet I finish up, Ah'll come over to your tent," Ben told Ethan. "Ah'll be drivin' the wagon for the slop buckets. If ya volunteer to handle 'em from your tent, ya can ride on out a ways with me to dump 'em. We ketch up then."

Ethan gobbled down his meal, not realizing just how hungry he was.

The latrine consisted of four one-gallon buckets lined up behind each tent. Ethan didn't have to volunteer to dispose of the buckets' contents; as the newest man in the tent he was told the duty was his until a newer convict arrived. Ben drove his wagon around and Ethan set his tent's four buckets against the others in the wagon bed. The stench was seriously bad and Ethan was disappointed at how quickly he got used to it. As the last tent on the run, Ethan would accompany Ben to the dumping ground.

"Spose to rotate around, get a different tent be last each day," Ben told him as they drove off. A mounted guard followed, his shot-gun held behind the saddle horn.

"Why in hell are you here, Ben?" Ethan asked.

"Kilt my brother-in-law. Kilt him good and dead and good riddance to his sorry ass."

"Adam?"

"That's the one."

"What happened?"

"Kicked 'im to death and glad of it. Ah was tired him abusing my sister."

"But you're in prison now."

"That's true, but Adam, he don't harm my sister no more. But why you here?"

"Convicted of murdering a man in Lajitas."

"Did you do it?"

"Hell, no. No I didn't. Barely knew the man."

"Know who did?"

"Not a clue, Ben, not a clue. If I were a sporting gentleman, I'd bet on the man's cousin but the cousin was far away and can prove it. You know how small a place Lajitas is. If somebody were going to kill somebody, everybody would pretty much know who. We'd know. But nobody knows. I've got a friend who is a Texas Ranger and he's promised me to find out. I hope he does."

"Could take years do that," Ben said as he stopped the wagon at the edge of a smelly bog.

Ethan jumped off the wagon seat, opened the back gate and picked up the first two buckets. "Eh-yeah." He dumped all the buckets in the bog, found the mop behind the seat and swabbed out the back of the wagon.

"You don't belong here, sar'nt," Ben said as they rode back to the camp.

"Eh-yeah. But here I am."

"We need to figure a way for you to get out."

"Eh-yeah. Figure it out."

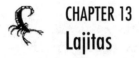

CHAPTER 13
Lajitas

The Sunrise Kid beamed a broad smile at Joaquin when the Ranger entered the Mejor Que Nada, but Joaquin was in no mood to smile. He understood the Sunrise Kid didn't really know any of the people in Lajitas so he had no emotional ties to them, and he understood Sunrise hadn't planned for Ethan to be carted off by the sheriff and sent to a prison work gang, and he understood Sunrise couldn't have known he'd marry the woman who inherited the saloon that provided him with a living that was probably beyond his expectations. He understood all of that. But he still resented the Sunrise Kid anyway.

"What may I serve you?" Sunrise said.

"Tennessee whiskey," Joaquin replied. Sunrise poured a glass and slid it across the board to the Ranger. "Where's Gracey? I need to talk to her."

"In the back."

"Working?"

"I would deem it a little premature in the day for that, sir," Sunrise said, still smiling. "I believe she's settling her little girls in for the evening and will bring in a pot of stew for evening vittles, of which you may enjoy a bowl without compensation, if you've a mind."

"She makes good stew. I'll take you up on that." He walked across the empty room to the table he and Ethan favored when Dutch ran the bar. He missed the saloonkeep's bad attitude and bad jokes.

When Gracey came into the saloon, she put the stew pot under the bar and, at Sunrise's direction, ladled up a bowl for Joaquin and carried it to him.

"Sit down," he said. "And thanks for the stew. Pork?"

"Sí," she said. "I used the last of the apples in it. Put in some peaches, too."

"Ethan would've liked that."

"Sí," she nodded slowly. "I was thinking of him so I put the peaches in. I have not tried that before. It is good, no?"

He chewed up a spoonful. "It is good, yes."

"You miss Ethan."

"I do. He taught me how to track and how to survive. More. I don't how to put it into words, but he taught me more. He was more than a friend."

"You were simpático," she told him.

He ate more stew and nodded.

"He is a strong man. He will survive. He will always survive."

Joaquin laughed and lifted his whiskey glass in a toast. "You should know. You keep bringing him back to life."

"This is something I must always do, if I can. I owe him my daughters."

"Corazon and Alma?"

"Si. They are his children."

He sat quietly for a full minute. She sat back and smiled at him.

"How do you know? Not to be brash but you've been with many men."

"Sí. Hundreds. But a woman knows these things. I planned it that way. I have ways not to get children and I have ways to get children. I wanted children with Ethan because he has strong blood and I want my daughters to be strong women who will marry well in a big city and his blood will lead to the success of my children and their children and their children. I come from nothing, señor. My family is large and they have nothing and we would always have nothing. I wanted to break that. I am more than willing to lie with men for money in order to make my purse fat and that money will help my daughters. As will his strong blood."

"He doesn't know."

"Oh, no, and you must not tell him," she said, reaching over and touching the back of his hand. "Por favor, señor. No. If he knew he would feel an obligation to them and he must not. He must be free. That is his nature. And knowing their father will not help Corazon and Alma. If they knew and he knew, this would not help them be better. It would harm them. He has a strong heart, but is a lost soul."

"Do you love him?"

"Oh, no," she shook her head over and over. "No. I have loved only one man in my life."

"Dutch?"

"Sí."

Joaquin ate the remainder of his stew while Gracey sat in silence. Finally, he said, "I'm trying to save Ethan. He couldn't murder anyone."

"I think you are incorrect. He could. He is sudden."

"No. I think if he did, he would admit it and explain it. He says he didn't and I believe him."

"I believe him as well," she said.

"Then who did?"

"¿Quién sabe? No one saw."

"I know, but we know everyone who lives here and everyone who visits here. I think we would have an idea. Ethan thought Castillo did it, but the man has a tight alibi. So my guess is that it was an outsider."

"Many people were here that night who I never saw before. Many soldiers, some ranch hands, a traveler or two perhaps. I cannot remember."

"You know how soldiers and ranch hands behave when they're here. Did any of them seem different to you? Not act the way you'd expect?"

Gracey put her elbows on the table, then her head in her hands. After a little while she rubbed her face. She looked up. "There was this kid… "

"A boy?"

She shook her head no. "A grown man but a kid. Delicate. He had buck teeth and came in with Tom from Don Milton's ranch. Tom is shy and cute and has… nevermind that. They brought the cattle and fruit and brandy. I have never seen this kid before and he did not say his name. Tom did not say his name. But he came in and left quickly. Then he came back and bought several bottles of whiskey and a bottle of brandy and some beer and left again."

"All that for one kid?"

She shrugged. "This is what he bought."

"Sounds like he was going to a party."

•

The next morning he rode to the Baeza farm and found Teresa Baeza scattering dried corn for her chickens. He identified himself and she said she knew who he was.

"I need more information about your husband's murder," he said.

"I told the sheriff everything I know," she said, not looking up from her chore.

"I don't think so. I don't think you saw Ethan here that night."

"Sí, the gringo."

"A gringo. Not that gringo."

"Gringos all look alike."

"Tall or short, old or young?"

"He was taller than me or Armando, but we are very short, so how can I say. I did not see his face. I left when they came in. I knew he was a gringo by his speech. They spoke in Spanish and in English and his Spanish was worse than Armando's English."

"What was his name?"

She looked at him for the first time, exasperated. "We were never introduced, señor. I left because when Armando is drinking he gets mean and hits me. I do not like that, so I left."

"To lay with his own cousin."

"Sí. Lionicio is kind to me. Armando knows. Lucinda, my cousin who is Lionicio's wife, she knows, too. They do not care. We think perhaps they are with each other, too. I would not do this, perhaps, but as I said, Armando gets mean, like his goat."

"He had a goat who was a mean drunk?"

"Armando never has many visitors, and he does not like to drink alone, so when he wishes to get drunk he also gives beer to his goat."

"A beer-drinking goat?"

"Sí, that way he does not have to drink alone because I will not drink with him. That night, he named the goat."

"He named his goat?"

"Sí, after all these years of drinking with the goat he had never given it a name. That night he did," she said, slowing down as she realized she was telling the Ranger too much. Lionicio told her just to identify the saloon keeper and that would be the last anyone would ask her questions about that night. Now she said too much, but had to explain further. "He named it after the gringo."

"My God, woman, what name?"

"Enrique."

"Henry," Joaquin said, spun on his boot heel and left.

•

Cibolo Creek Ranch

"It's a two-holer, come on in and sit a spell," Don Milton said to Joaquin from behind the outhouse door. Jim Juan had shown Joaquin where the ranch owner was after the Ranger insisted on speaking to him immediately. Perhaps Don Milton's hands gave their patrón privacy at times like this, but Joaquin was impatient so he opened the door and sat down next to Don Milton. He had already introduced himself through the door.

"How can I help the Staaaate of Texas?" Faver said.

"I'm trying to locate someone named Henry who works for you."

"Popular name. We haaave lots of Henrys around here. We got tall Henrys, short Henrys, fat Hennnrys, skinny Henrys. Hell, we've even got an albino Henry."

"I believe he's just recently signed on. Young kid."

"Yeaaaaah, Henry McCarty. Hard worker. Likes to laugh. He steeeeeal some cattle?"

"Not that I know of. Why would you say that?"

"Seems the type. Has a little too much fun, if you mighhht know what I mean. Told me he was from Arizona, but he spoke Mexican more like from West Texas or New Mexico. Hard worker, though, puuuuuls his own freight. What do you want him for?"

"I think he may have been involved in Armando Baeza's murder."

"Ahhhhhh. I thought the law caught the man who did it. That Twobears?"

"He's the one convicted, but I don't think he did it. Henry was with Armando the night he was killed and I need to ask him what he knows about that."

Faver ripped a few pages from an old newspaper, wiped, pulled up his trousers, then reached to the floor and picked up an old 1860 Colt that had been converted to fire cartridges and tucked that into the front of his trousers, smoothing his long white beard over it. He stomped his feet and they left the outhouse.

Faver sent a boy to find his segundo and before they'd taken four more steps Jim Juan walked up. "Sí, patrón?"

"Where's Henry working today?" Faver asked.

"Not working. He works the night watch on the south forty this week so he is sleeping in the bunkhouse."

"Take Mr. Jaxon over there, por favor."

"This way, señor," Jim Juan said.

Two bunkhouses were located outside the walls of the main hacienda, along with several other shacks. Jim Juan pointed to one of them, turned and left Joaquin alone.

Henry wasn't asleep. He was playing cards with two other ranch hands on one of the beds. Henry sat crosslegged at one end of the bed, another man sat in the same fashion at the other end while a third man, as young as Henry but taller, sat on the floor at the middle of the bed. Two other beds were occupied with men snoring up a racket. Joaquin knew immediately which one was Henry from Gracey's description: a kid with buck teeth. He had a guileless smile, baby blue eyes, and a relaxed attitude that would make most people instantly like him. Joaquin didn't.

"New hand?" the Mexican opposite Henry asked Joaquin in a deep voice.

"Just visiting," Joaquin said.

"Jump in," Henry invited.

Joaquin shook his head. "I think I'll just watch for a bit. You like playing cards?"

"Do I like playing cards? He-he, mister, all work and no play makes Jack a dull lay. Why, playin' cards, it's the most fun thing in life, especially when you're good at it like me. I'm beatin' these pals of mine outta a month's wages so far."

"If I weren't watchin' this kid here like a damn hawk, I'd swear he must be cheatin' he's won so much. Not just today. All the live-long time," said the man on the floor, tossing his cards on the bed in disgust. "I never seem to catch me no cards, but he does all the live-long day."

"Not the cards, pal, just how you play 'em," Henry said. "Never cheated in my life. Never had to. I hate cheats. Cheats should all be shot dead, dead and dead."

"Armando cheat?" Joaquin asked casually.

"Not even good at it—" Henry stopped and looked up from his cards. "Say, just who did you say you are?"

"I didn't," Joaquin said. He pulled aside his vest to display the star on his shirt. The other two men moved quickly out of the way, Henry stayed seated on the bed. "That why you gunned him? Because he was cheating or because he was cheating badly?"

Henry slowly rose from the bed as Joaquin backed away a little. The Ranger noticed a bird's head revolver sticking out of the left side of the waist band of the kid's trousers, butt forward. Henry stood with a hip cocked out, the fingers of his right hand tickling the ivory handle of his pistol.

"Cara de beato, uñas de gato," the Mexican said to Joaquin who nodded agreement.

"I heard they caught the man killed ol' Armando," Henry said.

"Wrong man," Joaquin said.

"Who says so?" Henry said, his fingers continuing to dance on the pistol butt.

"Actually, you did, just a moment ago and these men heard you. And they seem like honest men so they'll say so in court."

"Ain't a hoosegow built that can keep me penned up. Never has, never well, he-he."

"So this ain't your first baile?"

Henry laughed harder. "The fires I've started can't be put out by anyone." As his hand began to close around his pistol, Joaquin raised his and shot the kid in the chest. Henry dropped to the floor in a sitting position, his legs directly out in from of him, his arms hanging down at his sides. He looked down at the blood rushing out to cover his white shirt and looked at Joaquin with hurt in his eyes.

"The laugh's on me this time," Henry said, coughing but unable to move.

"The man convicted for your crime taught me a lot of things. One of them was if you're going to shoot, shoot. Don't talk."

"Your friend doesn't sound like any fun at—" and Henry slumped forward, dead.

The Mexican crossed himself, the tall man moved to leave the bunkhouse, and the two sleeping hands roused from their cots demanding to know what in hell was going on. Joaquin grabbed the tall man's arm and motioned for him to sit at a small table, then motioned the Mexican over as well.

"I'm going to get some pen and paper and I'm going to write down what just happened and you two are going to sign it, witnessing to the truth of it all," Joaquin told them.

"Neither of us can read nor write," the tall man said.

"I'll write it, you make your mark. I'll have Don Milton witness your marks. He can read the statement to you after I write it so you can be sure what I wrote."

CHAPTER 14
Galveston

Edjie reached out to his father as Karl came through the door. Karl took his son from Ingrid's arms, kissed his wife, lifted Edjie above his head a couple of times and rubbed his nose on his son's.

"Been a good boy?" Karl asked.

"Pretty much," Ingrid answered. "He's getting to be hard to keep up with. He'll be running me—us—in circles in no time."

Karl gave Edjie back to Ingrid so he could remove his coat. He took a large envelope out of a coat pocket, folded the coat neatly and placed it on the back of a chair. "The Lord works in mysterious ways, His wonders to perform."

"Karl..."

"I think you will agree when you hear what is in this letter," he said. They sat on a large, flower-print sofa in their living room. "This letter is from Joaquin. He has proven Ethan innocent and has enclosed all the documentation necessary to present to the governor in order to get a full pardon for him. And listen to this part: 'I know you will use your considerable influence with the governor to effect this pardon, but if you need further re-enforcements I would urge you to contact King David Kalakaua who we read was visiting this month in Texas. Ethan saved the king's life some years ago and I'm certain the king will be delighted to be able to return a favor.' Can you believe that?"

"That's who we're having supper with tonight at the Tremont along with the governor, isn't it? King of the Sandwich Islands?"

"The very same. If the capitol hadn't burned down a week ago, they'd all be in Austin instead of here. We should have a pardon before the cigars are passed around."

Governor Oran Roberts—who was known to pardon people at the drop of a hat to save the state money on maintaining the prison—actually signed a letter of intent to pardon Ethan Allan Twobears for the murder of Armando Baeza before dinner was served. Once King David was told what had happened, he couldn't stop urging the governor to act immediately. His voice rose as he told everyone how Ethan had plucked him out of the air, saving him from a devastating fall. He left out no details. He told of the luau and explained what a luau was. He told of the Makahiki festival and how his people celebrated for many weeks. He told of wave sliding and the love of the surf and now the governor understood why the king preferred to stay at the lower class Beach Hotel than at the grand Tremont for the Beach was directly on the seashore and the sounds of the waves could be heard all the time, reminding the king of home. He told of Ethan having relations with the king's young cousin on a ledge below the luau, and how thankful he was they had finished before he fell. The women blushed, fanned themselves, and giggled.

"I will go to your prison to release my savior personally," the king declared.

"That gesture will not be necessary," the governor said, clasping the king around the shoulders. "Senator Weischopf tells me he is not in prison, just at a work farm so he's been treated well. My aides will draw up the formal pardon tomorrow, but in the meantime my letter'll be forwarded to the Texas Rangers to gain your friend's immediate release. He's in a remote location, Your Highness, and this letter will reach the proper authorities before we could ever get there in person. I will instruct the Rangers to conduct this Mr. Twobears to your quarters at the Beach and he should be here within a fortnight."

"The king's itinerary forces us to travel westward in two days," an aide told the governor.

"Ahhh, well, perhaps we can have him meet with you along the way. You're traveling by train through El Paso to San Diego are you not?"

"That is correct," the aide replied.

"Our schedule is strict in order to sail on the appointed ship," the king said. He turned to his aide and said, "Tonight, you will draw up papers under my seal that the governor can have delivered to his Rangers who will deliver it to Sergeant Ethan so that he will be given passage on a ship of his choosing to visit us for as long as he wishes. My cousin has longed for his return."

"I'll see to it that your letter is delivered with my pardon, Your Highness," the Governor Roberts said. They shook hands.

The governor took Karl aside. "Excellent job, senator. This news should have us in all the papers from here to New York and San Francisco and back again. And it seems that you now wield considerable influence with the king here and I've got a huge herd of cattle that I'll bet he could use to start an entire new industry over there in them islands. Could put their entire country on a pay-as-you-go basis. You could put in a good word for me."

"I will be happy to, sir," Karl said.

Ingrid walked up and put her arm through her husband's. "A lot of politicking going on tonight."

"That is what politicians do. I cannot describe how good I feel to be able to help Ethan."

"Yes," she said, putting her head on his shoulder. "But I've always wondered why he never liked me."

"We spoke of that once. He said, 'She reminds me too much of me.' I thought that was rather philosophical but I was never certain just what he meant by it."

"I do. You remember that hymn we used to sing in church, 'I once was lost but now I'm found'? That's the way I feel. I was lost and you found me and I found myself. I think Ethan's the same, only in reverse. "

"It has been a long time since you quoted Scripture," he said, kissing her.

"Don't exaggerate, senator. It's not Scripture, just a hymn."

"The words of the Lord nonetheless."

●

Southern Pacific Work Camp

Ethan figured he had two broken ribs. His left eye was swollen and bloodied. He had welts on both sides of his neck from the leather strips on Slipher's heavy black bat. He coughed up enough blood to worry the gang boss that he might have serious internal injuries, so Slipher had two convicts drag Ethan to the infirmary tent where Boze was now inspecting his injuries. The blood was from biting his own cheek inside his mouth so he could convince Slipher he was more seriously injured than he was.

"Worked ya ovah mighty good," Boze said. "Doan know why'n't they jes finish ya off. I gets ya back to walkin' and they put ya right back on the line. Ya won't make it more'n anutha week, mebbe less'n that."

"Wonderful bedside manner you have, doc," Ethan wheezed.

"Hush and get yo'self some sleep. Be only peace ya get. Drink this hyar and ya'll go off."

He sipped at the laudanum and set his head back on the cot, letting the room twirl around him. Before he passed out, he thought, Ben better be right about this. He would hate to have picked the fight for nothing.

When Ethan woke it was night. He took only short breaths because the broken ribs stabbed at him. His eye ached and he couldn't see out of it. He lifted his head and looked around the tent. A single candle burned on a camp table next to his cot. In the dim light he could see another convict on the cot next to his and Ben in a chair between the two, working on something in his hands.

He reached over easily and touched Ben's thigh. Ben sat upright, placed the stone and lone metal tool in his lap, and looked over. "How ya feel?"

"Is that a joke?" Ethan said.

"Keep ya voice down some," Ben whispered.

"Afraid to wake up your other patient?"

"He's not wakin' up. Some kinda shock after some kinda stroke is what Boze says. He be havin' a day or two. Three tops. We not even feedin' him. Ol' man anyhow."

"Too bad."

"Foah him, not foah you. That's why Ah had to git ya in here. Onliest way was to get ya pounded up good. He be your ticket out."

"How's that?"

"One of ma jobs, I clean up the dead bodies and sew 'em up in a bag and they gets dumped where we dump the slop. Ah figger we can substitute you for him when he passes. Ya get dumped. Water's shallow, so ya cuts yer ways out and run oft. Guards come in, see him in your cot, figger he's you. Work foah couple days. Gets ya a heads start."

"What'll they do to you when they find out?"

"Sar'nt, they cain't do no more to me. Ah'm 'bout as busted up a man cin git."

"They can kill you for it. Kill you."

"Sho they cin, but Ah figgered they'd kill me for murderin' my brother-in-law anyways. This way Ah gots a few more days outta life and Ah gits to help someone needin' help."

"I'll come back and get you."

Ben laughed quietly. "Naw, Ah ain't no good for nothin' no more. Ah'm crippled up and Ah'd only slow ya down in yer escapin'. Ah deserve to be here, sar'nt. You don't. Return the favor on somebody else ya git the chance."

"You have my word."

"Good 'nuff for me," Ben said, picking up his tool and scratching words into the rock.

"What're you doing?" Ethan asked.

Ben finished a final word and handed the rock to Ethan who tried to bring the words into focus but failed, asking Ben to read it.

"A firefly flickers/in the coal black murk/scattering small light/out over the fields/out through the cactus/a faint friend/in the dark-ness."

"You're the one been writing poems on rocks?" Ethan said. "Found some?"

"Eh-yeah. Saw one and when I did I asked around and a couple other convicts said they'd seen some, too. How many have you done? What for?"

"Somethin' t'pass the time when Ah'm just sittin' 'round. Ah get these thoughts and have to set 'em free. Ah put 'em out in the desert, other folks find 'em and they carry off a small piece of me with them whether they want to or not. Prolly wouldn't pay me no nevermind face to face."

"Hell of a way to publish your work," Ethan said, and dropped back to sleep before he heard Ben reply, "More perm'nt than paper."

Ethan had hoped the old man on the cot next to him would have survived a couple more days so his own wounds would heal better, but the convict died later that night. Ethan was still sore and ached, and could barely breathe. They carried out their plan as quickly as they could, a seriously wounded man and a cripple moving a dead body from the long table in back to Ethan's cot. Ethan had a sharp butcher knife with him as Ben laid a heavy stone at his waist and sewed him into the canvas. Ben told him he would drop off a change of clothes as he drove back from the bog.

Ethan's only problem was staying awake in the canvas bag as he lay on the table all day waiting for the slop wagon to leave just before sunset. If he slept and snored, anyone passing by would know he wasn't a dead body. Of course, if he'd been found out, he might become a dead body quickly. So he waited the way his grandfather taught him: he sent his mind away, recalling a Mic Mac poem...

A long time ago
A woman came from a far place
Her hair was fair and her feet were covered in leaves.
When she walked through the woods
She sang, "I am lonesome. So lonesome."

From another far away place
Came a wild man who heard her.
She saw him but was afraid
For he was covered with the rainbow.
She ran and he pursued her.
He chased her to the foot of a greathouse mountain
Where they married and had a child.

The first words Margaret ever said to him were, "What a fine looking man." Could he ever forget those words? Could any man? He'd introduced himself to her, cap in hand, saying that a friend told him she was from Vermont. So was he, he said, and that's when she said, "What a fine looking man." Not, "How do you do?" Not, "Pleased to meet you." Not even, "Where from?" Just, "What a fine looking man."

He was tall and lean with wiry muscles, with the smooth, confident gait of a man totally in charge of himself and responsible for the wellbeing of others. He'd just returned from two weeks in the field the day before so he was exceptionally tanned. She was his opposite: as white as a person could be, with light green eyes and blonde hair and the most beautiful woman he had ever seen. She was nearly a foot shorter than he was, but so delicate that he always worried a strong breeze would break her in two.

He helped her clean up the one-room school house and walked her home every night for a week, until he was sent back out on a patrol.

"Why did you come out here?" he asked her on the second day.

She wrinkled her nose. "It seemed ever the perfect idea at the time. I was just graduated from UVM and I had no beaus and no prospects. I wanted to travel. I was always wanting to see what was on the other side of the hill, even if it were just another hill. A gentleman from New York came to college a week before Easter the year I graduated and gave a presentation to the girl's dormitory about jobs in the Wild West. Oh, he made it sound ever so romantic and lovely. All the men were stalwart and true. Crops drew rain with ease. We would be compensated well for teaching children and all of our travel expenses would be paid by the community which hired us on. And I remember he lowered his voice when he said this as if to draw us in on a conspiracy, he said that we should find husbands more easily in the Wild West because the population comprised far more men than women."

"How could you resist?"

She laughed, exposing deep dimples in her cheeks he hadn't known she had. "Indeed, I did not."

Four days into their growing relationship, a secret rose between them. Ethan didn't like secrets and, already desperately in love with Margaret, he didn't like keeping a secret from her. But he had to.

He asked her if her parents were wealthy since she had gone to the university and she told him no, that she and her sister attended on a pension voted to them by the Vermont Legislature on the death of her father who, at the time, owned a hardware store in St. Albans.

"He was the only man killed in the Rebel raid," she said. "I was only four years old at the time, but I remember all the shooting and people screaming and the city burning. Those terrible men rounded us all up around the band gazebo in the middle of the park. I just remember my mother crying so hard, and my sister screaming at the Rebels and they just made lewd remarks to her. They said words I had never heard before, nor ever since."

"I think they burned only one shed," Ethan said. "They wanted to burn the city, but that part of the plan failed."

"You know about the raid?"

"Eh-yeah. Furthest north the Confederacy ever operated. They robbed three banks. Got off into Canada with $200,000."

"The damn British," she said, blushing immediately. "I'm sorry, but me and my sister and my mother are ever bitter to this day. Those Johnny Rebs were captured in Canada and jailed, you know, but the government refused to extradite them to Vermont. They were released and went on to deposit our money in the Rebel treasury and no one ever answered for killing my father."

He took her hand and said softly. "That's been... seventeen years ago. People are killed in wars."

"My father wasn't a soldier!" She pulled her hand away from him. "He was an honest working man with a family!"

And so was just about every soldier he ever fought with and against, he thought, including Indians. He took her hand again, slowly. "No matter how tough the roast beef is, you can always cut the gravy." She smiled. "I understand your loss and your frustration. But you have your life to live now and I'm certain your father would want you to live it."

"That's what I've always persevered to do," she said, holding his hand tightly and shaking it with determination. "I know how suddenly a person can be lost. I'm ever resolved to live as much as I can and see the world. My mother was born and will die in Vermont, as will my sister. I refuse to be stifled."

"Good on you," he said, and they had their first kiss in front of her desk in the school house.

But even as he was kissing her, he knew something was now between them. If she was as obsessed with the St. Albans Raid as she appeared, he could never tell her he'd fought with the First Vermont at Gettysburg during the War. The First Vermont was one of the keys in the Federal repulse of Pickett's desperate charge and General James Kemper and Kemper's men had never forgiven the Vermonters for that. Kemper had actually sworn revenge on them, screaming at the top of his lungs on the battlefield so he could be heard over the din of war, just before he was seriously wounded. To add insult to that injury, the First Vermont captured the general during the Rebel retreat.

Margaret probably knew now, as most Vermonters did, that the St. Albans Raid was Kemper's idea, a way to exact revenge he put into action as soon as he was paroled back to Confederate lines. He sent one of his lieutenants, Bennett Young, into Canada with a few handpicked men to sweep down the fifteen miles from the border into Vermont that October and rob the banks and terrorize and burn the town. Get money the Confederacy needed and, hopefully, divert troops toward that undefended Canadian border. Perhaps even draw the British into the conflict if the raiders were pursued across the border, causing an international incident.

If Margaret knew he'd fought with the First Vermont, she might blame him for her father's death. She could never know that.

…his memory was halted abruptly by being lifted off the table and manhandled onto the back of the wagon. The ride was rough and some contents of the buckets around him sloshed over and soaked through the canvas. The wagon halted and Ben's helper and the guard picked up the body bag and tossed it into the bog. Before he sank into the stinking bog, he heard Ben say, "Good luck, old scout," then the wagon drove away.

Ethan quickly cut through the sinking canvas and pulled away the material from his body. He tried to stand, but the muddy bottom sucked at his feet so he leaned forward and swam through the sewage. He rolled onto the edge of the bog and tore off his clothing as quickly as he could. He rolled in the dirt, hoping to rub away most of the smell. When he stood, he saw a small bundle not more than twenty feet down the pathway made by the wagon. Ben had left fresh clothes. He walked around the bog, looking carefully in the quickly fading light for the stream or spring that would create such a place, hoping it wasn't below the bog itself. It wasn't. The trickle of water was no broader than a carrot, but it was fresh. He sat directly over the small stream and bathed as well as he could. He found the clothes bundle in the dark and put them on. They were the right size. Even the shoes. He guessed that some guard would be very upset when he found his spare set of clothing gone.

"Who's that there?" a voice said from behind Ethan. He turned and barely made out Boss Slipher on his horse with a convict walking alongside. Ethan didn't know why Slipher was here but if he recognized him, his days were done. He hunched over and limped to the side of the horse.

"¿Quién es?" Ethan said, hoping the boss would take him for a Mexican farmer.

"Speak white," Slipher demanded, leaning over to get a better look at the man now by his left leg. Ethan reached up, grabbed the reins of the horse and pulled it to the ground. The horse fell with a thud, crushing Slipher's leg and knocking the wind out of the boss. The frightened horse jumped back up quickly and Ethan ordered the convict, "Hold that horse!" The other man managed to calm the horse while Ethan sat on Slipher's chest. He unhooked the man's Big Black Dick and placed the stick against Slipher's throat and pressed as hard as he could. Already gasping for breath and in pain from the fall, the bigger man was nearly helpless and gagged quicker than Ethan thought he would.

"What's— what's going on?" the black convict said, quivering. Ethan picked up Slipher's hat, removed the dead man's gunbelt and pistol. He saw a rifle was in a scabbard attached to the saddle.

"You've got a choice," he told the convict. "You can go back to the camp and tell them what happened and probably be beaten to death for them thinking you were in on this, or you can pronghorn it out of here. I'm taking the horse, so you're on foot. Burgess Springs is the closest town, maybe ten miles to the east. I were you, I'd head to Fort Davis, that's maybe twenty-five miles to the north."

Ethan swung up in the saddle and handed the convict Slipher's canteen. He watched the convict kick Slipher in the teeth then piss on the dead man's face before he walked north. Ethan rode south.

•

Apache Camp, Chisos Mountain Basin

"Are we agreed?" Alsate asked his warriors.

"We are," Lame Coyote answered.

"We are," Four Fingers said. The others nodded.

Yellow Face, Owl Eye's best friend, kicked at the dirt. "We don't like the idea, but we are agreed."

"We have discussed this," Alsate said, impatient.

"We have," Yellow Face said. "And I agree. We should try this treaty. I would prefer to continue the old ways because they were the ways of a warrior. Treaties are the way of women. Talk, talk, talk. You be my friend and I'll be your friend. A warrior takes what he needs, what he wants, from his enemies. The Nacoya have been our enemies for many generations. It is the way of things. It was the way of things. Now things are changing. I understand this. Pale Eyes are coming here in numbers we can't resist. Every time we cross the river, more warriors are killed. We must do as you have said, but I don't have to like doing it. But I do agree."

The other warriors yelled their agreement with Yellow Face. Alsate was contented. They said they would follow him into San Carlos and they would. They would agree to this treaty. Yusn help him if the Nacoya leader could not be trusted. But he felt trust had to begin somewhere or this vicious cycle would continue for more generations until all the Chishi were dead. At least the band could remain free. They wouldn't be confined like their cousins the Mescaleros or the Chihenne, at the mercy of the Pale Eyes. This was the only way to keep his band free and alive.

The travois were packed. Most of the warriors followed Alsate down the trail that led to the desert, the women and children walking behind the travois being pulled by horses ridden by children and old men. Down the mountain, across the desert and the Burned Mountains to the big river by the mouth of the big canyon, cross Tezlingo Creek where the peyote was harvested, cross the big river away from the Nacoya at San Vicente. From there, cross the mountains in Mexico to the plain where the Presidio San Carlos had sat for dozens of generations. Two or three days.

CHAPTER 15

Southern Pacific Railroad Work Camp

Joaquin heard the sounds of the work camp from more than a mile away. The sound of metal on metal, the sound of men hollering, the sound of men singing. As he entered the camp, he looked around for Ethan but didn't see him so he began to ride along the railway bed.

"You better have a God damned good reason to be in this place," one of the guards said as he galloped up to Joaquin. The guard's shotgun was pointed directly at Joaquin's chest.

Joaquin showed the guard his badge and identified himself. "I need to speak to whoever is in charge. I have an order for the release of one of your prisoners."

"I suppose I'm the boss for now. Boss Slipher was brutally murdered by an escaped convict two days ago. Who do you want released and why? Better have some God damned good authorization for it, too."

The Ranger tapped his saddlebags. "I've got a letter from the governor. I hope that'll be good enough."

"Yes, it would." The guard hollered to one of the workers who trotted over as quickly as his ankle chains would allow. "I need you to fetch me a convict," the guard said to the prisoner. Then, to Joaquin, he said, "Who you want?"

"Ethan Allan Twobears. He was assigned to this camp. I'm assuming he's still here."

The guard tipped his shotgun upwards onto his hip, the barrel pointing at the sky. "He was sent here, all right. He's not here now."

"Where is he?"

"I knew I'd shoot the son of a bitch right down the second I saw him. He's the one escaped and killed Boss Slipher. I'm not a betting man, but if I were I'd bet your governor's pardon for that half-breed isn't worth a bucket of warm piss right about now."

Joaquin's stomach convulsed, blood rushed to his head. He said, "You're certain it was him?" but he knew it would be.

"Darky convict escaped with him we caught yesterday. He told us everything. Your man strangled Slipher with the boss's own baton."

"Can I talk to the man you recaptured?"

"If he can, you're welcome to try. Follow me." The guard led Joaquin down the roadbed to where tracks were already laid, then to a freight car. They dismounted. The guard nodded to another guard by the car door who turned and pulled open the door. The three of them climbed into the car. In the center, in air still and foul and blazing like a furnace, was a steel box about four feet on each side with a metal grate on two ends. The guard pounded on the locked door of the box.

"You in there, Ebenezer?"

"You and the hoss you rode in on," was the reply.

"Someone here to talk to you. Texas Ranger. You are polite to him and maybe we'll let you out a day early. You only have three more to go."

"And maybe my momma was a virgin," said the voice.

"He's all yours," the head guard said and left. The other guard jumped out of the car and stood by the door.

"My name's Joaquin, I'm a friend of the man you escaped with," the Ranger said, wishing he could give the convict something, water, food, fresh air. Something.

"You ain't soundin' like any Joaquin I ever spoke with afore."

"Named after my mother's father," he said automatically. "Listen, Ethan was my friend and I'm here to help him."

"Didn't know his name, the bastard. We didn't do no escapin' together. I was out near the bog with the boss and he just comes up and drags the boss's hoss down and next thing I know he's got the boss's Big Black Dick acrost his throat and killin' him."

"Big Black Dick?"

"What the boss calls his bat. All the guards got one. Long stick with leather straps they use to keep us in line with. For some reason, they all got to name them somethin'. That was his name for it."

"And you ran off when all this happened?"

"Shit, yeah, I ran oft. Killin' the boss like that? I ain't hangin' around. Bastard tells me to go north while he took the boss's hoss and rode off south. Used me for the diversion, me on foot. I'm just glad they believed me when I said I didn't do nothin' to the boss. I got me a whippin' and some days in the box and my sentence went and got doubled on up. But I'm here. Like the rock said, 'One day at a time, Sweet Jesus, one day at a time.'"

"Anything I can get you?" Joaquin asked, knowing he probably wouldn't be able to give it to the prisoner anyway.

"Get me reborn as a golden eagle."

Joaquin tapped the top of the box then jumped down from the freight car.

"Can you give him some water?" Joaquin asked the guard. "He's helped me considerably and I'd like to repay him something."

"I reckon I can pee through the grate on him," the guard laughed.

Joaquin grabbed the guard's shoulders and threw him against the side of the car. As the guard's shotgun fell to the ground, Joaquin kneed him in the groin. "I don't need any more shit today," he spat as he threw the guard on the ground. He reached under the freight car where he saw a bucket of water and a ladle, lifted it out and up onto the car.

"Hey, stick your mouth over by this grate, I've got some water for you," he told the prisoner. He heard the man moving inside, then saw his face behind the grate, a swollen, cracked face. Joaquin poured water in on the man who drank as much as he could and splashed the rest over his face.

"Thanks, Ranger," said the convict. "I truly needed that and I appreciate it. But I have a feeling I'll pay for it later."

The bucket empty, Joaquin jumped back out of the car just as the guard was rising to his feet. He hit the guard in the head as hard as he could with the pail, denting both. He slowly lifted himself on his horse, riding south after Ethan. The pardon and letter of passage to the Sandwich Islands, from a king no less, were all worthless now. He was on the trail of a murderer. If this Boss Slipher was like any of the other guards he'd seen, he was certain he deserved whatever Ethan gave him but that didn't make any difference to the law. He was determined to find Ethan before anyone else did, he owed his friend that much.

•

Calamity Creek

Crossing this familiar desert, Ethan longed for a forest of trees. He felt more out of place than he ever had. His dilemma remained — paradise or home — but he knew he would need money to flee to either one. He was confident no one could track him across the desert, except one of the Seminoles or perhaps Joaquin. But they wouldn't be able to get army scouts for a civilian matter so he didn't have to worry about the Seminoles. And he doubted Joaquin would even try to find him. In fact, Joaquin might even point the sheriff in the wrong direction. To make certain he was safe, he traveled off the trails and avoided the road. He moved in a great spiral to confuse anyone who might be tracking him and chose the most difficult path whenever he could. It would take much longer to get where he was going, but he was confident he would get there without confrontation.

Off the mountains now, he rode steadily toward Lajitas, turning to the east before he was in sight of the village. He'd camp in the place they started calling Calamity Creek, the place he'd killed the Comanche. The nearly dry creek bed would provide him cover and water. Tomorrow he would ride to the Chisos, find the cave, get the money he needed, and figure out the rest. As he rode over a hill, though, he found the creek was populated.

A dozen soldiers lollygagged around two large wagons, some of their horses hobbled nearby. In the center of the camp, held to the ground by several long lines, was an enormous green and gold balloon. He'd seen balloons during the war, but never this close. One man was in the basket of the balloon, making adjustments of some sort while he talked to an army officer. Well, he wouldn't camp here tonight. He turned his horse and saw movement behind him.

"Ethan!" Joaquin yelled.

This was the last thing he wanted. His friend had tracked him; he was a Ranger after all. The last thing he wanted was an altercation with Joaquin. He spun his horse back around and galloped toward the army camp as Joaquin hollered, "Stop! Wait!" He hadn't gone thirty feet when his horse stumbled, dropped forward, sending Ethan sprawling over its head. Ethan scrambled a little on his hands and knees, regained his stride, and ran into the camp. Soldiers jumped up, wondering what was happening in front of them. Ethan heard a shot from behind him, one he knew would be fired into the air since the Ranger couldn't risk firing into a group of friendlies. He ran directly to the balloon, pulled the major out of his way, stepped into the basket and with his Bowie knife spun around cutting all the lines holding the balloon.

"You madman!" Travelin' screamed at him. "The cable's not attached! We're free floating!"

And they were. The two men in the balloon rose swiftly into the winds, the soldiers and Joaquin yelling after them.

"Come back here, damn it!" ordered Major Jones.

"No way to," Travelin' hollered down, but he turned and reached for a red cord attached to the neck of the balloon. Ethan grabbed his arm before he could touch it.

"If that's a way to get the balloon back down, you don't want to pull it," Ethan said, twisting Travelin's arm. "Sit."

The aeronaut slumped to the floor of the basket, holding his head in his hands. "You have no idea what you've just done. We're at the mercy of the winds and the air. We have no control over where we'll travel nor how high. Men in balloons have been lost through just such calamities before."

"How appropriate," Ethan said, thinking of the name of the creek.

"You're mad, simply mad," Travelin' said. "Aren't you frightened by what could happen?"

"Eh-yeah. But everyone fears something. Fearless people are the ones who are crazy. Wind's pushing us easterly. Just the way I want to go. Just the way."

Travelin' stood up and watched the motion of his balloon relative to the ground. They rose quickly, now at 1,500 feet if his guess was correct. Ethan looked around, assessing the situation himself. He could see Lajitas, see the Río Grande, he could even see the old Fugawee tepees, three of them in tatters lined up straight like a white man would do it, along the bank of the river upstream from Lajitas. The balloon seemed to rush to the east as it rose more. From here, the ground looked the same where ever Ethan looked, brown and soft, until he saw the scar that he knew had to be Santa Helena Canyon, like a black eel resting on underwater sand, twisting this way and that. As they floated closer, sunlight reflected in a brief flash off the river, giving him a sense of perspective from the nearly sheer cliffs that dropped from the mesa more than 1,000 feet, he guessed.

But the balloon seemed to be following the river, not quite the runaway the pilot had warned of.

Travelin' noticed the same phenomenon at the same time. "Air drafting up from the river. The canyon's walls are directing it and it's creating a sort of a wall of air for us. It's blocking the balloon from crossing the canyon. We'll probably float east until we reach the canyon mouth, then it's either north or south."

"Better south than north," Ethan said.

"We'll die in that Mexican wilderness!"

"You perhaps. Not me."

Ethan was fascinated by the ever-changing sight below him. He could see perhaps three miles of the canyon now, and noticed the narrow passage widened at several spots only to narrow down again. He saw a few side canyons and more dips from the mesas on each side that would be pour-offs from the desert that could create a series of spectacular waterfalls into the canyon after a good rain. The river was completely lost in the cliffs' shadows, brought to life only in an occasional flash of reflected sunlight when it twisted just the right way. The river was heading southerly, but then he saw an abrupt twist to the north and another back to the south.

Travelin' knew he had one chance to save himself. If he could overpower this madman, he could vent air by using the rip cord as judiciously as possible and bring the balloon quickly but safely down. He would wait until they could see the mouth of Santa Helena, then act. He'd seen that area; it was a broad, flat plain. He could land safely there.

They saw the mouth of the canyon at the same time. What Ethan saw that Travelin' didn't notice was a band of Apache heading toward the river. He guessed it was Alsate and he guessed it was their entire village — men, women, and children. He thought, Why? Then he heard the pilot say from behind him, "Get your hands up." He turned to see Travelin' with a gun in his hand, pointed now at Ethan. It was a new model Schofield, the barrel cut down to three inches. The pilot had a hideout. "Your turn to sit," Travelin' ordered, motioning Ethan down with the pistol barrel.

"You don't want to do this," Ethan sighed. "I'm a dangerous man and a survivor. I'll do what I have to in order to survive. Pocket that pistol and if you have a way for us to descend safely, do it. But do it on that side of the river."

"No! Now sit down. After we land, I'm turning you over to the authorities and you'll be put away for good, I'm certain. Sit!"

Ethan squatted down, watching the pilot pull on the red cord very slowly, and as he did so Ethan understood several things all at once:

— People with no experience killing another person were unpredictable. Women would often pull a trigger quicker than they meant to because they were nervous. Nervous and didn't really have much experience with firearms. Men often waited too long to the pull the trigger, having a need before they did to prove to the other who was more powerful.

— The pilot remained within arm's reach.

— Ethan was determined not to go back to the work camp or a prison. He would rather die than be confined.

— Don't pick up a weapon unless you intend to use it.

— Don't use a weapon unless you intend to shoot to kill.

Ethan reached out with both arms, grabbed Travelin's ankles and stood up, tossing the man over the side of the basket. He looked over, watching the pilot fall hundreds of feet as the man unloaded his pistol at the balloon. Ethan turned away just before the body disappeared into the canyon. "I'm sorry," he said, "but I warned you."

The red cord was the way down, Ethan figured, and he yanked it. The balloon dropped quickly, too quickly. He let up on the cord and slowed the descent as he looked up at the envelope. The cord opened a panel, venting its gases to the air. He had no idea how far he should pull the cord so he yanked on it as easily as he could but realized too late that the cord had opened the panel up all at once. The balloon dropped, air catching in the open vent slowing it down a little. The basket bounced against the canyon edge and just before it swirled down into the canyon, Ethan saw how the canyon widened at the mouth giving way to the desert. He looked up to see the south face of the Chisos, just as the balloon hit the cliff, bouncing around several times. The balloon drifted out of the canyon, landing with an abrupt thud on the riverbank. The envelope ripped open further on rocks then air grabbed the fabric and dragged the balloon over more rocks. Ethan's broken ribs stabbed him with each bounce and he passed out before the balloon finally came to a rest. He rolled out of the basket and face down into the river.

●

The Mouth of Santa Helena Canyon on the Río Grande

"We pulled you out of the river after you fell from the sky. What magic is this?" Alsate asked Ethan as the scout opened his eyes. He rested on sand, soaking wet, surrounded by several Chishi warriors.

"No magic, just a balloon," he said, sitting up slowly. He tried to explain what a balloon was and failed, Alsate insisting it was Pale Eye magic. "Well, this time the magic didn't work," Ethan said finally.

"I know you," Alsate said.

"We met a long time ago when I first came into your country," Ethan said, standing now and rubbing his sides to determine if he'd broken any more ribs. He hadn't.

"You brought us four antelope that time. You wished to hunt in our mountains in peace and brought us presents. We were happy to have you as a neighbor. But why are you flying through the sky in this magic boat?"

Ethan told Alsate the entire story, the old man clucking his tongue every now and then at the stupidity of the Pale Eyes. Then Alsate explained where he was taking his band and why.

"Is this a wise thing to do?" Ethan asked. "How well do you know the presidio captain?"

"We do not know him except as an enemy. He is a good enemy. We have agreed."

"I hope it works out," Ethan said. "I'm tempted to go with you, but I have to go in a different direction."

"May Yusn guide you," Alsate said.

"Perhaps you can guide me as well," Ethan said. "A man is following me that I don't want to harm but I need to get away from him. Do you know of a place I may lose him? Perhaps a place I can hide for a few days until he goes away?"

Alsate pursed his lips together, then nodded, giving Ethan directions to a place north of the Chisos. "It is a land much accidented. No one can track in those hills. But you cannot go there on foot. You will need a horse. You will take mine."

"I can't take your horse," Ethan protested.

"One cannot refuse a gift. The horse is no longer mine; it is yours. I will walk to San Carlos. I enjoy walking."

"I like walking, too."

"Yes, but you cannot lose your pursuer while you are without a horse."

"Thank you. I will repay your kindness," Ethan said, watching the band slowly cross into Mexico.

•

Calamity Creek

"Explain yourself, man," Major Jones demanded of Joaquin.

"I'm a Texas Ranger in pursuit of a escaped convict."

"Well, your convict just escaped with my balloon. If it comes to any harm he'll have to face the wrath of the United States government for it."

"I doubt he's too worried about your government," Joaquin said, pulling himself up into his saddle.

"Let me send some of my boys with you," the major said.

"No, I don't need inexperienced men I have to baby sit out here."

"My scouts are some of Bullis's best. They're not inexperienced."

"This is something I need to do myself," Joaquin said and rode as quickly as he could east, to where the balloon had drifted.

"July, Payne, get saddled up and find my damn balloon and Mr. Jones," Major Jones ordered.

"Suh," Private Thomas Payne said, saluting. The two scouts ran to their horses, wondering how they were going to track a balloon flying through the air.

Joaquin figured he didn't have to track anything right now. The balloon seemed to be following the river, so he would ride directly to the mouth of the canyon. If he saw no sign of the balloon there, he'd ride in ever widening circles as Ethan had taught him, on both sides of the river until he found his friend.

The balloon was high enough that Joaquin was able to keep it in sight most of the way but he couldn't keep up with it. The balloon moved further and further away and at one point he saw what had to be a body fall to the canyon. No one could survive such a drop. Was it Ethan or the pilot? He knew the answer to that question before he finished thinking it. Now Ethan had killed two people. The balloon then dropped quickly and he couldn't see it anymore. Had it fallen into the canyon? He spurred his horse into a gallop towards the mouth of Santa Helena.

•

The Mouth of Santa Helena Canyon

He found the balloon immediately—the basket and some of the fabric from the envelope anyway. Dismounting at the mouth of the canyon, he saw a jumble of tracks in the sand: dozens of horses, more people on foot, some of the horses pulling travois. A large group of people had headed into Mexico very recently. Apache, he guessed, the Apache Ethan told him lived up in the Chisos. Maybe this was a regular migration for them, heading south as the weather got cooler. He guessed they cut up as much of the balloon fabric as they could use and took it with them. Did Ethan go with them? That would make sense. He would figure to be free across the border and would be traveling with friends who would protect him.

No, he thought immediately. Ethan taught him to think like his prey. He knew his friend better than he knew any other human being, and his friend wouldn't seek protection by endangering others. And he didn't think he would live in Mexico by choice. What was it he kept saying for the past month or more? Ethan wanted to leave the Big Bend and Texas altogether, to go home or to paradise. Had he decided? Joaquin walked around the tracks until he saw one set of hoof prints going in the opposite direction from all the others. That was Ethan. He was certain of it. He mounted and rode north, following the track.

•

Privates Thomas Payne and Pompey July followed almost the same path that Joaquin had, heading east, keeping the balloon in sight as long as they could. When they rode up to the mouth of the canyon they found the torn remains of the balloon, the broken basket, and a somebody lying on the riverbank gasping for air.

They ran over. "Mistah Jones!" Payne said. "We'd thought yah a goner."

Travelin' Jones looked up a moment, then laid his head back down on the gravel. He couldn't feel anything beyond his lungs wheezing in pain for air.

"Oh, Lord, suh, both your legs are goin' ways they shouldn't," Payne said.

"Can't-feel-them."

"Mebbe broked his back, too," July said.

"Cain't chance on movin' yah, suh, if that might be the case. Pomp, go back and fetch the major and the surgeon," Payne said. Before he finished speaking, July was on his horse, galloping back toward Lajitas.

"No-broke-neck," Travelin' said, waving his arms. "Arms-OK-how-I-swam-out."

"Helluva swim, suh. Helluva swim. Good thing about yah back. Theys can fix the legs."

"Thank-my-Uncle-Tony."

"Suh?"

"He-taught-me-to-swim-when-I-was-a-a-a-boy. Swam-all-the-time-ever-since." He paused and gulped in more air. "Whenever I could. I wouldn't have chosen this way."

"Helluva fall, suh."

"Thought I was a dead man. Guess I hit the water just right. If I just broke both my legs I'll be right thankful."

"Thank God, suh... and yore Unc Tony."

•

San Carlos

Alsate loved the area around San Carlos and was glad to know he would be free to visit as often as he wanted to now. They moved over the mountains, past the waterfall that was barely a trickle now because of the drought, up the San Carlos River, and finally onto the broad mesa where the old presidio was located. Looking back northeast he could see the head of Santa Helena Canyon and over the ridge that formed the canyon he could see the faint, bluish line of the Chisos. It had been years since he'd ventured this far from his home in the Chisos, the home of so many Alsates before him. On the plain surrounding the presidio, several different crops grew. Not too far was the village of San Carlos, but they were riding into the presidio.

It was a large diamond-shaped fortress with two arrowhead bastions facing north and south. The presidio had fallen into ruin over the generations, but was still manned by a small company of soldiers. The main gate on the southwest wall was open with no soldiers in sight. Alsate walked at the head of the band and as he entered the presidio he saw brightly colored papers hanging from ropes, bright fabric hanging from the walls, two beeves barbecuing over deep pits and the aroma from the basted meat thrilled him. As the Chishi entered the grounds, several musicians began playing in front of the chapel on the northwest wall.

"Welcome," Capitan Ulysses Lerdo said to Alsate. Lieutenant Arnulfo Díaz y Paredes stood proudly beside him. "Welcome. Please, have your people feel free to enjoy themselves this evening and tomorrow at noon we will sign our treaty of peace between your people and mine. Enjoy yourselves."

The lieutenant indicated four tables full of fruits and vegetables and bottles of sotol. Alsate didn't like the idea of sotol at this feast, but knew his warriors would so he would give them this reward.

"The barbecue will be succulent. It will be ready soon. Your people may carve off as much as they wish."

The Chishi consumed more of everything than they ever knew they would be able consume. They ate and drank their fill and then drank and ate more. Through it all, soldiers clapped them on their backs and the music played. They all laughed and enjoyed the best night of their lives. Before the moon rose they had all passed out.

CHAPTER 16

Grapevine Hills in the Chihuahuan Desert, north of the Chisos Mountains

Ethan must have passed by these hills hundreds of times on his way into the Chisos but had never paid them any attention. They were uninteresting, just a jumble of rocks many miles to the north with nothing around them. Even as he rode for them, he questioned himself for doing so. Why not ride directly into the high Chisos, get a bag full of coins, and ride on? No. Not yet. Joaquin would assume that's what he had done. The Ranger didn't know the location of the treasure cave, but he did know it was somewhere up in the mountains where they'd hunted many times. The Ranger would track him there and he couldn't risk that.

Perhaps he could throw Joaquin off his trail here. Perhaps. It still didn't seem like an efficient way to do what he had to do.

He rode by a broad dry creek bed that led into the heart of the rocks because his horse smelled water. Water out here? He knew the desert well enough not to doubt it, especially with his horse pulling him strongly a couple more miles north. Water was here, in a small oasis of brambles and mesquite. He dismounted, unsaddled the horse, cached the tack in some thick mesquite. He filled his canteen from the spring. He left the horse behind, untied—it wouldn't wander far from this water and little shade—and walked back to the dry creek bed.

His rifle in one hand, canteen in the other, he hopped up onto a rock as soon as he could then moved up and down from rock to rock deep into the canyon. If he could get high enough, he would be able to survey the desert below the hills and know if anyone approached. No one could follow him across the rocks. At one high point he stopped for a drink, looking around, thinking that this was the place the Apache had in mind when they said after Yusn finished creating the world he took all the leftover parts and threw them into the Big Bend. Here is where that debris from creation went. From here he had a glimpse of the east ridge of the Chisos so he moved further up to the head of the canyon. More rocks to scramble over, all them big and red and worn smooth, some of them with holes worn through and some leaning against others in haphazard fashion. Suddenly, as he rounded one turn, he saw a huge boulder balanced on top of two vertical ones forming a sort of doorway that overlooked the desert. It was a powerful place. He sat with his back against one of the vertical rocks, the larger boulder directly above his head. He drank and watched.

•

Joaquin had little trouble following Ethan's trail at first. *Don't focus on the track. Let your attention wander and take in all the things around you.* It led where he expected it to lead, to the north toward the Chisos, up past Castolon and along the foothills of the Sierra Quemada. Ethan had shown him a way to get into the Chisos from the west climbing near the pour-off from the basin, but horses couldn't make it. He quickly checked that area, found no sign, and kept riding around the Chisos range. *Understand your prey and where he is likely to go.* Confident of where his friend was headed, he wasn't paying close attention to signs. He saw them often enough to build that confidence. But suddenly they were gone. He had ridden around the north face of the mountains, expecting to find some track that would lead into the Chisos through Green Gulch, their usual pathway, but he saw none. He circled out, slowly, and found none. He backtracked slowly, moving out to the north a little. Could Ethan be leaving his coins behind and just running north?

Perhaps, because he crossed a faint sign west of where he'd begun. It wasn't much, just a small rock recently overturned. Joaquin dismounted and kneeled back on his bootheels by the rock, looking around for other sign. *Never pass up a chance to sit down or relieve yourself.* Ethan was moving his mount slowly. The horse wasn't shod—a pony he stole from the Apache or they had given to him. The unshod horse, its deliberate pace, and its path along as rocky a ground as Ethan could find made the trail a nightmare to follow. But he could. A man might be able to hide his tracks, a horse could not. *The ground will not lie to you. Listen to what it has to say.*

The tracks didn't lead towards Burgess Springs but northwards toward an isolated group of small hills and into the Rosillos Mountains. Where was he going? The hills. Had everyone been mistaken all this time about the treasure's location? All the legends said the Spanish gold was hidden in the Chisos, but could it actually be in those forlorn hills? Is that why it had never been found? Or had Ethan moved the treasure there? Or did he have caches scattered all around so that if one were ever discovered, he still had others to rely on? Always have a backup plan. The tracks clearly showed Ethan was heading into those hills. Don't argue with where the sign leads you.

●

His place under the balanced rock was in shade much of the day so he didn't expect the sun to set as quickly as it seemed to. One moment he was looking at the long shadows cast by the mountains in the distance and the next moment was dusk, then darkness and the sky full of stars, and he heard his grandfather sing:

We are the stars which sing;
We sing with our light.
We are the birds of fire;
We fly over the sky.
Our light is a voice.
We make a road for spirits,
For the spirits to pass over.
Among us are three hunters
Who chase a bear.
There was never a time
When they were not hunting.
We look down on the mountains.
This is the song of the stars.

Then he saw Mahealani as clearly as if she were sitting beside him when they used to watch the sky from the beach, the surf a perfect music for the celestial show above them.

"The sky is important to our people because we are great navigators," she explained to him. "We came in great canoes far from the west, guided by Iao, the Eastern Star. One of our first peoples, Kewa, paddled a magical canoe into the sky and scattered the stars so we could always find our way across the sea."

She pointed to the constellation he knew as Scorpio. "That is Uluao, Kewa's canoe. You see the canoe and the outrigger?"

"It's difficult for me because all I've ever seen is a scorpion. Your outrigger is my pinchers," he said. "Our peoples see different things in the same stars."

She giggled and ran a finger down his tattooed chest. "Yes, but wouldn't you rather wake up under the skies and see a magical canoe than a scorpion?"

"Eh-yeah," he said, pulling her hand to his mouth and kissing her palm. He nibbled a little on her fingertips. "I guess our homes are just very different."

"Hawai'i," she explained. "That is our word. Our homeland."

And he thought then, *Your* home. As beautiful as this paradise was, it wasn't his home.

And he thought now: home or paradise?

Margaret was impatient whenever he would sit and look at the night sky. He said he missed the Northern Lights, but seeing the Milky Way so high and clear was comforting.

"You don't have to show off," she said. "I know the names, too. Pleiades, Ursa Major and Minor, Polaris. But what good will they ever do me? I won't ever captain a ship."

"The stars change, you know," he explained. "They're in slightly different places here than at home. Below the equator, they're completely different. Different, but you have to travel so far south."

"I think I've traveled far enough south. The further south I went from home the worse things ever got. Hotter. More crowded. Now desolate. It's not like pictures in a book."

"Eh-yeah. Never are. Pictures can't convey the beauty or the loneliness or heat or cold."

"Nor the dust. I'm ever so tired of the dust," she said. "I don't like it here."

He wasn't certain whether he liked it at Fort Clark or not. Compared to many places in Texas, this was a paradise, with trees and the big pool of cool spring water. Fort Clark just was. Why complain about something you had no control over. Of course, Margaret did have control. He had an enlistment to fulfill, she didn't.

"I wish I could take you away," he told her. "One day I will. I'll take you wherever you wish to go. I promise. But now, I'm bound to the army."

"How long? Oh, how long? Another summer and I'll melt."

He shook his head. He didn't know. He just knew that to make her happy, he had to find her paradise for her.

And he thought again: home or paradise?

He never seemed to fit in wherever he went. He didn't fit in when he was a boy, the whites not wanting anything to do with him nor did the Indians of various tribes—the Abenaki, the Machican, the Mohawk, the Mohican. Only a few Mic Mac lived nearby, most of them were in Maine or Canada. He didn't fit in at college, a "hick from the sticks" they called him. He didn't fit in at the timber camp, those same two groups, white and Indian, ignoring him. That may have been worse than animosity. The army didn't really know what to do with him, finally just making him a scout along with all the other Indians, never mind that as a Vermont Indian he knew nothing about Texas or New Mexico Indian people, knew nothing about the Southwest landscape at all until taught by the black Seminoles. He could have fit in if he'd wanted to. Just keep his father's name, go live with one of his aunts, and he'd be as white as half his cousins. But that would have meant abandoning his grandfather, and he couldn't do that. His grandfather tried to tell him it was a good thing—a foot in both worlds, he said—but now he knew that was dead wrong. Better to belong to one world, even if it was one you didn't like, than belong to none.

He didn't fit in with Margaret, her thinking he was a savage once she'd seen his tattoos and understood just what kind of soldier he was. No marches on manicured fields in a pretty uniform, just dirty desert duty trying to track down other, more blood thirsty, savages. She was educated and wanted desperately to socialize with other educated women, but the officers' wives had little to do with her since she was married to a sergeant. Against fraternization rules for the soldiers, a rule that was informal but more usually followed among the wives. He felt she knew she'd made a mistake by the first night, and the blame she placed on herself only grew with time until they were both glad when he had to go out on patrol. Then David was born and he thought things would be better. They had a bond to hold them together forever, but when she took the baby back to Vermont to visit her family they died there in the influenza epidemic that struck much of the northeast that year. That was his last chance to fit in, by creating his own family.

He tried to ignore not fitting in by drinking, but that only separated him more. Look where he had lived: alone at the top of a hill miles from any other people. He didn't fit in at Lajitas either, confined to a dark, small saloon surrounded by people who preferred to crowd together indoors and breathe smoke and drink alcohol and sweat manly sweat and slip over whores who daydreamed of other places and other men.

He hadn't fit in paradise, either, a haole, a foreigner, no matter how much they liked him.

Everywhere he was an outsider. Where did he fit in? Only one time and place—at his grandfather's side living in a cabin on a bluff overlooking Lake Memphremagog.

He dropped off into a deep sleep, for some reason thinking a phrase in Latin. Veni, vidi, volo in domum redire—I came, I saw, I want to go home.

•

Joaquin found Ethan's horse at the spring but no footprints. He hadn't expected to. His friend would be difficult, if not impossible, to follow now he was on foot. Where is your prey likely to go? Does he have water, shelter, a way to escape? He thought about the dry creek bed he'd passed that came out of a canyon created by the highest of the hills. From the top of those hills a man could observe most of the paths heading into the hills. If you were a man running, you would want to know if anyone was following.

After gorging on water and filling his canteens, he pulled himself into the saddle. He rode into the creek bed, not trying to hide. If Ethan were here, he would know who else was. He looked for signs and saw what could have been a smudged footprint, a day old, pointed toward the rocks. He couldn't track him in the rocks, but he could ride to the highest point and climb up there himself. At the end of the canyon,

Joaquin staked out his horse, grabbed a canteen, made his way up the steep wall of rocks. It was not easy in his boots. At one point he was tempted to take them off but realized trying to scramble around the rocks and cactus in his bare feet would be too dangerous. He slowly made his way to the ridge, seeing a balanced rock that looked as if some giant had placed it there. He walked to the rock and looked south across the desert.

Something moved out there. He wished he had the field glass Ethan always took with him, another lesson to learn. He squinted and strained his eyes at the mote drifting across the landscape more than a mile away. *Before you go into a canyon, know how you're going to get out.* It could be a coyote. It could be a wild horse. Hell, it could even be a camel. But he knew it was Ethan, on foot, headed for the Chisos. For him this meant climbing back down the rocks as carefully as he could, which meant slowly, so he didn't slip and break an ankle or leg, then ride around the hills and across the plain to the Chisos where Ethan would, by that time, already be in those rocks.

•

Before Ethan reached the Chisos, he saw a riderless Apache pony. He approached carefully, talked to the horse in a calming voice for a little bit, then slid onto its back.

"Where's your warrior?" he asked, and let the horse turn around and walk a few rods to the west. He saw one of Alsate's men sitting up by a large ocotillo, blood on his shoulder and leg.

"¿Qué pasa?" he asked.

The warrior said he was Raincrow of the Alsate Chishi and they went to San Carlos to sign a peace treaty and attend a fiesta. When they awoke the next morning, they were all in chains, even the littlest of the children. Two of them managed to escape but the other warrior, Lame Coyote, died along the way back. Raincrow said he was afraid he was dying now because it was difficult for him to breathe and the light was dimming. Ethan asked him what happened to the rest of the band. Raincrow said all but Alsate and Little Moccasins were taken away to work in the silver mines far south in the Nacoya lands. Alsate and Little Moccasins would be executed at sunrise tomorrow at the presidio.

"I will save your chief," Ethan said.

"It does not matter. I will be dead soon and the band is rubbed out forever now. Who can he lead? What difference?" and Raincrow spasmed a fistful of blood and died. Ethan got back on Raincrow's horse and rode as quickly as he dared to Mexico.

•

Chisos Mountain Foothills

Now this didn't make any damn sense, Joaquin thought. A dead Apache and hoof prints leading back toward the Río Grande. Had Ethan killed this man, too? He doubted it, but it was possible if he felt he needed the horse to survive. But why go back to where he'd just been? He still hadn't gone into the Chisos. It just didn't make any damn sense. At least now the tracks were clear; his friend was making no effort to hide them. The first rule of tracking is silence. Silence teaches self-control, courage, endurance, patience, and dignity. Follow where the tracks lead.

•

San Carlos

Ethan watched the presidio from a nearby hill, rain dripping off the brim of his hat. The rain started an hour ago, was hard and steady with occasional thunder and lightning. The lightning helped him see into the presidio, but he knew it would also illuminate him. At least no one moved this late at night, but one guard was posted at the door to a small building next to the old chapel. The old fort's walls in ruins, it was easy for Ethan to slip over one wall and move undetected to one side of the building, between it and the chapel. He rose to a window, looking in to see two shapes huddled in a corner of the old building.

He heard the old man singing slowly enough for him to understand the words, "The night is passing quickly, the firing squad will soon be making ready. Cease your weeping, Little Moccasins, and don't hope for clemency. They will execute us at the first light."

Nobody is executing you, Ethan thought as he pulled himself up onto the window, then to the roof. As he'd hoped, much of the roof had collapsed many years ago. He moved carefully, found an entry and dropped to the dirt floor.

Alsate and Little Moccasin watched in silence as the dark shape approached them. In one eye-blinking sound of thunder, the room was lit momentarily and the chief recognized Ethan.

"You should not be here, my friend," Alsate whispered. "I am an old man and I will die soon anyway."

"You deserve to die at home. So, hush and follow me." He took them by the hands to the hole in the roof, cupping his hands together to lift each one out. He was confident they could do so quietly, and they did. He dropped them carefully to the ground and they slipped in the shadow of the chapel then over the low wall to the horses Ethan had waiting for them.

•

Lerdo couldn't sleep. He was too excited, and the sounds of thunder and falling rain kept him awake. Not only would his actions stop the raids, he had eliminated all of Alsate's band and would deliver Alsate's head and that of the chief's wife personally to General Díaz before the week was out. Yes, his mother had named him Ulysses well. This would get him out of San Carlos finally. And be nothing but an embarrassment to the weasel lieutenant who sought his job. Oh, yes, never serve rabbit stew before you catch the rabbit.

His Panocha slept soundly in his bed, little rivers of sweat pouring off her shoulder and across her soft brown back, down her hip across her backside. He pulled on his trousers and boots, draped his coat across his shoulders, grabbed a couple of cigars and a bottle of tequila and stepped outside under the roof of the short porch. The air was still under the rain. He could see the guard across the courtyard.

He lit a cigar and just as he ground the match under his boot he saw movement from the corner of his eye. What it was, he didn't know, but nothing should be moving out there at this time of night.

He worked his arms quickly into his coat, tucked the tequila bottle in a pocket, grabbed his cap and walked to the guard. "Is everything in order?"

"Sí, mí capitán," the guard said, stifling a yawn.

Lerdo opened the door to the dark room. He lit a match and looked around. He saw nothing. This was an embarrassment to him that would undo everything. He stepped back out. "Make certain no one goes inside," he told the guard.

He strode to the horse corral, saddling his own, then walked the horse to his room where he got his pistols and a rifle. He walked the horse out of the presidio, mounted, and rode north to the river.

As he broke from the carrizo along the riverbank, Lerdo was no more than ten meters from the two fleeing Apaches. As he raised his rifle, he felt cold steel on the back on his neck.

"Softly," the man behind him said in English. "Empty the rifle and place it back in the scabbard. Empty your pistols and reholster them. Once Alsate is safely on his way, in about an hour, I'll let you return to the presidio if you make no trouble. No trouble. Otherwise I'll kill you. I don't want to kill you."

"I cannot let these people go," Lerdo said. The thunder was distant now, the rain letting up.

"Off your horse," the voice commanded. The captain dismounted, facing Ethan.

"Who are you?" Lerdo asked.

"Nemo," he replied. "Nobody. Didn't you read my autobiography?"

"I cannot let these people go."

"You have no choice."

"I am responsible."

"Eh-yeah, well what can an old man and woman do to harm you? I understand you shipped the whole band to the mines. I should kill you just for that. But I'm full up with killing. I was you, I'd go back and say you caught up with them and executed them yourself."

"I would need bodies."

"You shot them in the middle of the river and their bodies floated away in the dark."

"They may not believe me."

"You a captain or ain't you?"

Lerdo nodded. "I have no choice?"

Ethan turned the captain around to face the river and he sat behind him, touching him again with the rifle barrel. "Lie or die."

The rain was gone, only the humidity hung in the air oppressively. Not hearing the gringo say anything for more than an hour, Lerdo asked, "May I go back now?" No response. He asked again. No response. He turned slowly to see no one behind him. He lit one of his cigars and mounted his horse, riding back to the presidio.

It was nearly dawn when he arrived, the fort beginning to stir. He spurred his horse and galloped to the building where the chief had been held, flying out of the saddle, drawing a pistol. He struck the guard sharply across the face with the barrel.

"Careless idiot!" he fumed. The guard was confused, picked himself off the ground and asked what he'd done wrong. "Wrong! Look inside!" and he kicked the door open to the empty room.

"Jefe, what is happening?" Sergeant García asked, pulling braces over his stooped shoulders. Lieutenant Díaz was already by his side, already fully dressed, no doubt anticipating being in command of the firing squad.

"Alsate has escaped in the night."

"How could this have happened? Who is responsible? I'll have his head," Díaz sputtered. "We must pursue them immediately."

"No need," Lerdo said. "I rose a few hours ago and saw they were gone and I trailed them to the river."

"Jefe, why did you not wake us?" Garcia said.

"It would have taken too long. The command was asleep. By the time everyone was mounted and on the trail, they would have been back in the United States. I had already saddled my horse."

"Going for a midnight ride?" the lieutenant sneered. "In the rain?"

"What I do at night is none of your business."

"The capitán often goes for nightly rides when he has trouble sleeping," García lied.

"What happened on your ride tonight?" Díaz asked.

"I caught them as they started to cross the river. I drew my rifle and shot them both down, but their bodies fell into the water and drifted away and sank. I could not retrieve them in the darkness. They are now food for the fishes."

"Very convenient," Díaz said, turned and stomped away.

"Jefe?" García asked.

"They're gone, sargento. They won't be back."

•

Lost Mine Peak, Chisos Mountains

A quarter of the way to the river, Joaquin had turned back. Ethan was leading him on a wild chase, hoping he'd be confused and give up. He wasn't falling for that. His friend needed to flee and flee very far very quickly. He'd need money for that. He was coming back to the high Chisos and Joaquin would be there waiting. He rode to the edge of the basin, staked his horse out of sight, and sat watching back down the trail from behind a large cactus that grew near a hog sized rock. He could doze off but be alert as soon as he heard anything. Listen with your ear to the ground to see if it has anything to say.

It worked, just as Ethan had taught him two years ago. He came wide awake at the sound but didn't move right away. Slowly he moved his head around the cactus, just in time to see a shape start up the side of the mountain to his right, perhaps a quarter of a mile down the trail away from the basin. He knew the trail. Ethan had taken him up there several months ago, teaching him how to track game, how to tell the difference between skunk tracks and those of a raccoon.

He would follow at a safe distance where he wouldn't be seen or heard. Never take a chance you don't have to.

It was a difficult trail, moving up the side of one mountain then crossing to another. Part of it was thickly wooded and at this altitude, more than a mile high, Joaquin was cool but the trail soon gave way to more open country and the afternoon sun oppressed him. Ethan was making no attempt to hide his tracks, so he must not think anyone was following or had become desperate. That was something Joaquin feared.

After a long series of switchbacks, he arrived near the summit. He moved quietly through a thicket of pine and agave and stopped to survey what was ahead. The ground was almost all bare rock from there to the peak. He would have no cover. No sense hiding now. He walked forward, his pistol in his hand.

"Ethan," he said, seeing his friend at the peak. The scout turned toward him.

"Why did you follow me?"

"My job. I didn't want anyone else to catch up with you. They'd kill you on sight. If you want to live, you have to come back with me."

"I'm not going back."

"I know." Joaquin raised his pistol at Ethan. "But I'm not letting you get away, either."

"I know," Ethan said. "But you're not going to shoot me."

"I know," Joaquin said.

"So what do we do?"

"I don't know. I always looked to you for answers."

"Well…," Ethan said, moving backwards. "Bye." And stepped off the cliff.

Joaquin knew the drop was well over a thousand feet. He holstered his pistol, turned, and walked back down the trail.

CHAPTER 17
San Antonio

The interior of San Fernando Cathedral looked lopsided the day after New Year's. The bride's friends and family filled more than a dozen pews on the left while only two couples — one couple with two children — sat on the groom's side. Joaquin Henry Jaxon stood at the altar with his bride's brother standing beside him as best man and Bishop Jean Claude Neraz poised to officiate in golden vestments. He wanted not to have a best man, to preserve that place in memory of Ethan, but his bride insisted so he chose her brother George William. His friends, at least, would understand he wanted Ethan by his side. To emphasize this he had a fiddle player play *Ashoken Farewell*, an old War tune that filled the grand church with a melancholy air. When he finished, the fiddler played *The Wedding March* in a more upbeat tempo. Everyone looked to the back of the nave.

Rachel Judith Burtnett walked down the aisle with her father, William George Burtnett, a businessman whose brewery employed more San Antonians than any other organization short of the United States Army. Her silvery gray dress flowed around her as if she was moving in a glowing cloud. A garland of yellow roses rested easily around her head.

The ceremony was over quickly. The bride and groom kissed. The crowd applauded. The couple turned to the gathering. "Please, Rachel and I would like to invite everyone to her parent's home in King William for our reception," Joaquin said. "A boy at the rear of the cathedral will hand out cards with the address on it as you leave. Everyone is welcome."

Three hours later, after the toasts were completed, the waltzes danced, the petit fours and punch consumed, Joaquin and Rachel stood talking in the kitchen with Karl and Ingrid, Gracey and the Sunrise Kid. Corazon and Alma were sound asleep in a servant's room.

"I'm glad y'all could make our wedding and I wanted to thank you personally," Joaquin said.

"Our pleasure," Karl said with Ingrid nodding agreement.

"It gives me an excuse to see a real city," Gracey said. "I did not know one would be so crowded or so grand. I think all of Lajitas could fit inside that church. But, forgive me for asking this, how long are we going to ignore the elephant?"

"Elephant?" Joaquin said.

"Sí, the elephant that stands in our midst and no one will speak of it, as if it was not here."

Joaquin and Karl shrugged their shoulders at the same time, giving each other bewildered looks.

"You know what she means," Ingrid said. "In all of the three hours we've spent together, and we just can't bring Ethan up?"

"Ingrid, what good can come—" Karl said.

"Shut up, senator," she said. "I want to know what happened."

"I thought Karl would tell you," Joaquin said.

"He showed me the report you filed. Said he jumped off that cliff, fell to his death on the rocks 1,000 feet below. I want to know why you were chasing him in the first place."

"If I didn't, someone else would. And they would have killed him. At the time we thought he'd killed two innocent people, one a state prison guard. That balloonist survived by some miracle but will never walk again, and he was still guilty of murdering that guard. He would have been shot on sight. And there was a sheriff's posse out looking for him, too, along with other Rangers."

"So what good did you do? You killed him anyway."

Joaquin's jaw clenched and Rachel felt him tense up so she patted his arm. "I didn't do anything. He jumped."

"I worry because his body was not recovered," Gracey said. "You did not bring him back."

"I couldn't."

"No one brought him back," she said.

"No one could get to where I said he fell."

"I do not think they tried," Gracey said.

Joaquin shook his head. "I don't think so, either. Didn't expect them to. Like my sergeant said, who was going to risk their own lives for the bones of a killer?"

"He was not a killer," Karl said.

"He was," Gracey corrected him. "But only of those that needed to be killed."

"Amen," Karl said.

"Excuse me," a stranger said from the doorway. He was dressed in a blue and brown striped suit, carrying a briefcase and hat in one hand, an envelope in the other. "Mr. Jaxon?"

"That's me."

The man handed Joaquin the envelope. "My name, sir, is Hiram P. Fischer and I'm an attorney in practice with the East, Bush, and Ramsay firm in our city. We have been charged with holding this for you until the day of your wedding."

"What is it?"

"We do not know, sir. It was delivered to us sealed and with written instructions and payment for our services."

Joaquin turned the envelope over in his hands. "Thank you."

"Thank you, sir. If you would please sign this form declaring that you received this charge on this date, I would appreciate it," the attorney said, pulling a sheet of paper from his briefcase. He produced a pen and small bottle of ink. Joaquin signed and dated it, and as Fischer blotted the signature, Joaquin noticed that the client listed on the paper was Ethan Allan Twobears. The attorney returned the paper to his briefcase.

"How long have you had this?" Joaquin asked.

"I am not privy to that information, sir," Fischer said, bowing to the ladies. He turned and left.

"What on earth is that?" Rachel asked.

Joaquin broke the seal on the back of the envelope, took out the letter and read:

Congratulations to you and your new bride Rachel and your three years as a Texas Ranger.

I wanted to leave you something to remember me by, since I have no further use of it. The Big Bend area is growing a pace now. Mines are being dug and it won't be long before large conglomerates start to rip apart our favorite hills and mountains searching for

gold, silver and quicksilver. With that in mind, I recommend you travel to this location as soon as possible and remove as much as you can and deposit it in
a secure place—probably Brother Karl's new Galveston
bank—and never return to that place again.

Go to the Chisos and find the trail that we took that
one week where I schooled you in tracking game. The
trail you reach before reaching the basin. Go to the very
peak. Fasten a length of rope around your waist and let
yourself over the side. You will discover a narrow ledge
with a mesquite tree growing from the side of the cliff's
face. Behind that mesquite is the mouth of a cave.
Bring something to light your way. Go to the back of
the cave and you will find a large flat rock. Move this
rock and you will discover a second room. In this room
are two casks. One with jewelry for your new bride, one
of coins for you to start your family in comfort. Feel
free to share this wealth as the two of you see fit.

Su Amigo Siempre
Ethan

"Joaquin… what is it?" Rachel said.

He handed the letter to Karl to read and took his bride's hands
in his, a wide smile crossing his face. "Wedding presents from a dead
man."

Lake Memphremagog, Vermont/Quebec

Allan Morris sipped his first cup of coffee as he fried some breakfast hash in the light of the stove and a single candle on his table by the window of his cabin. Dawn was an hour away, but an hour before sunrise was worth two after. Standing by the stove, he ate the hash directly from the pan, glad to have something heavy in his right hand.

The shaking palsy was getting worse now. The iron pan was heavy enough to steady the hand while he ate. He could just ladle the hash into a plate and put the plate on the table and eat like a normal person, but he hated to sit at that table by the large window and not have anything to look at. He was just glad he could stand without getting dizzy. The doctor down in Burlington warned him that was a distinct possibility as the shaking increased or spread. Hadn't happened yet.

He set the pan and fork down in the sink and sipped more coffee. He took the small coffee pot and poured what was left into a flask given to him earlier in the year by James Dewar. It had a glass interior surrounded by a metal exterior, using air between them as insulation. He'd taken the Scotsman and several others out fishing in April, Dewar insisting on fishing only on the Canadian side of the lake.

"I'm proud to be a British subject and when I fish I will fish only for fish which are also British subjects," he said in mock seriousness, waving an authoritative finger in the air above his tam.

Allan made a few extra dollars—money he didn't really need, but it forced him to socialize more than he otherwise would—by guiding outsiders. He'd taken Dewar's party to a small bay just before dawn and everyone caught fish, large fish. Dewar himself landed the largest steelhead Allan had ever seen, along with three good-sized salmon. Dewar was so happy, he presented Allan with his flask at the end of the trip. The flask kept coffee hot for a couple hours, warm for several hours more. Allan told Dewar he should make up more and sell them to outdoorsmen, and the Scotsman thought it was a good idea. But

433

Allan never saw or heard of any such device for sale. Once he screwed the top on the Dewar's flask, he put two pieces of johnny cake to carry along in a small paper bag. He put the flask in one coat pocket, the bag in the other.

Come on legs, he ordered. He was stiff enough with rheumatism, but lately he had difficulty getting his legs to move when he wanted them to. It was as if he were glued to the ground or someone snuck in and nailed his shoes to the floor when he wasn't watching. After a few moments of conscious effort, his left leg finally went in the direction of the front door and once the right leg followed he was OK. He grabbed his paddle by the door.

He shuffled down the familiar path off the bluff onto the lakeshore. The sky was just beginning to lighten, enough to see his dark green canoe. He flipped it over and lifted it into the water, stepping over the gunwale into the seat he'd set just aft of the middle of the canoe when he made it some ten years ago. The canoe was his second big project, after the cabin. When he bought the cabin, it had been abandoned for years and the repairs it needed were serious. The roof had leaked and critters had set up house inside. It took just a month for him to put on a new roof and hire a man from Orleans to come over and tar it. Then Allan replaced rotten boards, swept out the mice, frightened off the porkies and skunks, ordered a new stove he could cook on and warm the one-room cabin with, and replaced the windows. He'd never made a canoe before, but he found an old, broken one on a neighbor's property and studied it carefully, making several drawings. He figured out how to build a rig that would bend the cedar slats for the canoe's body and the cherry wood he'd use for gunwales. He formed ribs from ash, carving two paddles and the seat frame from the ash as well. He laced rawhide for the seat. The difficult part was fitting the canvas around the frame, but he managed that, melted wax and painted it into the fabric. He oiled down the wood and launched the canoe that summer.

He knelt, his knees apart, resting his butt on the edge of the seat. He reached out with the paddle and pulled himself into the lake. Paddling was when he felt most normal. All the stiffness and the shaking and the pain disappeared as his muscles repeated the motions that were as automatic as breathing to him. Reach forward, push down with his upper hand using his lower hand to guide the paddle even with the gunwale until it reached his hip then curl his top hand so the thumb pointed down, giving the paddle a little kick outwards that kept him going smoothly and steadily forward in a straight line.

He kept the canoe moving toward the rising sun, heading for his favorite brook that emptied into the lake. He arrived just before dawn, lifted the canoe up on the shore, and sat cross-legged beside it to watch the first rays of morning cut across the smooth, blue lake water. The light reached out to touch the small islands in the lake, then the base of the mountains, finally reaching the forest of green on each side. The irregular shoreline would remain hidden a few minutes more, until the sun was higher.

As he always did, he poured his second cup of coffee by the brook, its burbling a soothing presence. He huddled over the heat of the cup as he sipped, his eyes watching the lake come to life. He saw the first beaver swim out right on schedule, five minutes past sun-up. Two minutes behind came the second beaver. Two more minutes he watched the third, and two minutes later the fourth beaver. He thought of them as a little family heading out for their day—father, mother, daughter, son. If he had a watch, he could have set it by them. This was the greatest reward of being home, he thought: contentment.

He heard laughing behind him, one of the hazards of summertime. He turned to see two boys walking to the shore along the brook, each carrying fishing gear.

"Hi, mister," one of the boys greeted him. "How're they biting?"

"If you keep your voices down, they should bite just fine for a little while yet."

"Oh, yeah, grampy always says to keep quiet when you're fishing," the other boy whispered.

Allan smiled, reaching into his bag for a johnny cake. "Over there," he said softly, pointing to a shallow bay on the left. "Toss your lines out as far as you can and reel in very slowly."

They did as they were told. The taller boy hooked a trout almost immediately, which surprised Allan a little. After fifteen minutes, the other boy complained he hadn't even had a nibble, and just as he did the taller one hooked another, smaller trout.

"I'm bored," the shorter boy said. He started to reel in his line, but Allan saw he had difficulty. He walked over.

"Lemme see," he told the boy. He turned the reel, feeling significant resistance, guessing the boy had snagged a branch or maybe an old pot. He didn't want to break the line, so he reeled in as carefully as he could. Finally, they saw what was on the end of the line: a bull pout had taken the boy's hook and in an attempt to free itself had spun around and around until it was wrapped up like a mummy in the line. He laughed and dropped the fish by the boy's feet.

"Lousy bull pout," the boy scowled.

"Tastes like chicken," Allan said, handing the rod to the shorter boy.

"Eww, you eat them?"

"Lots of people do."

"Nobody around here," the taller boy said. "My grampy says you shouldn't eat bottom feeders."

"Well, son, place I used to live they were considered a true delicacy."

"Where's that?"

"Texas. You know where Texas is?"

"Gee, sure, I know where Texas is. Doesn't everybody? I was born there! But we moved back to Vermont when I was a baby. Is that where you're from? You don't look like a man from Texas."

"And what does a Texan look like?"

"Gee, wild I guess. That's the Wild West isn't it? You look pretty tame."

"Just because I'm old," Allan said, unwinding the other boy's line from the fish. "I was pretty wild looking in my younger days. But, no, I'm from right here. I grew up on the western shore of this very lake."

"Gee, so why were you in Texas?"

"I was in the Army."

"Really, gosh that's swell," the tall boy said. "My daddy was in the Army."

"Where did he serve?"

"Texas, too. He got killed there. My mommy says he was killed by red Indians before I was born. You ever see any red Indians, mister?"

"You can see plenty of Indians right around this lake."

"Oh, heck, I know. But the Mic Macs and the Abenakis are all tame now. I mean real wild Indians."

"I'm bored," the other boy said, tugging on the taller boy's shirt sleeve. "Let's go."

"Uh-unh. You go on back. I'm going to stay out here a while. If that's OK with you, mister."

"Absolutely," Allan said, handing the pole and bull pout to the other boy, who took the pole but threw the fish on the ground before he ran off. The taller boy picked up the fish and strung it with his two.

"He's stupid sometimes," the taller boy said.

"Don't be too hard on him. We've all got a fight going on inside us all the time," Allan said. "It's a terrible fight between two wolves. One wolf represents fear, anger, envy, sorrow, regret, greed, arrogance, self-pity, guilt, resentment, inferiority, lies, false pride, and superiority. The other stands for joy, peace, love, hope, sharing, serenity, humility, kindness, benevolence, friendship, empathy, generosity, truth, compassion, and faith."

The boy thought about this for a while, squinted his eyes, and asked. "Which wolf will win?"

"The one you feed."

"Well, he shouldn't throw fish away. My grampy says you shouldn't waste food," the boy said.

"Your grandfather was right. Does he live around here?"

"Down the road about a mile, behind that hill. Gordon Hubbarton. He's my daddy's father so he's not my real grandfather but my mommy's father died during the War and he's the only grampy I've got."

Allan's right hand starting shaking in a gentle oscillation. "Don't think I know him, but I don't get around much."

"Oh, that's OK. He just moved here a couple months ago from St. Johnsbury. He doesn't work anymore and my grammy died last winter. How come you're shaking, mister?"

"Old age. Hey, are you hungry? I've got an extra piece of johnny cake."

"Gee, yeah, thanks."

Allan handed him the second piece and sipped more of his coffee. "You drink coffee yet?"

The boy made a face. "Tastes too funny."

"Acquired taste. So do you live around here, too, or down in St. Johnsbury?"

"Oh, no, we live in Burlington," he declared proudly. "My daddy teaches at UVM. He and my mommy go away every summer. He's a historian and they travel to these foreign places and look at historical sites and when they come back he writes about them in books. They're almost always gone part of June and all of July and I stay with my grampy. This is the first time we've ever been here because he only just moved. Sometimes, I used to stay with my other grammy in St. Albans, but she died three years ago. My cousin Terry comes up for a couple of weeks, too. We all have fun."

"My name's Allan Morris, what's yours?" Allan said, offering his hand to the boy.

"David," the boy said, happy to shake a grown-up's hand. "David Hubbarton. I'll be fifteen years old this month."

Allan looked up at the boy, the sun now completely warming the boy's face. He patted the ground, indicating for the boy to sit and he did. "You're a fine looking lad. You know, I had a boy named David."

"Really? Where's he? In Texas?"

"Like your father, he died. He was a baby. At least he and his mother died at home, in Vermont and not in Texas."

"I'll bet you can tell lots of stories about the Wild West, hunh?"

"I suppose."

"I read about it all the time, about Buffalo Bill and the red Indians and Wild Bill Hickok and General Custer and Billy the Kid. Are all those stories true? Did you know Billy the Kid?"

"I knew better people than Billy the Kid, son, but nobody ever wrote about them. And stories, well, stories are just a way to make sense of what happens because what happens is usually pretty strange. The west is wilder than you could ever imagine, but nobody could write it up the way it really is because nobody would believe it. So they write stories to make it all make sense."

"When I grow up I'm going to the Wild West."

Allan shook his head. "It's mostly all tame now. Won't be any wild places left when you're full grown."

"Ah, gee."

He smiled and waved his coffee cup out toward the lake. "Why would you ever want to leave a place like this? This is like living in God's greatest church, it just doesn't have any roof."

"I want to see other places, mister. My mommy and daddy have."

"What are you parents names?"

"Mommy and Daddy."

He laughed and shook his head. "What do other people call them?"

"Professor and Mrs. Hubbarton."

"Don't you know their Christian names?"

"Oh, I'm not allowed to call them by their first names. I'd get in trouble."

"OK. What does your grandfather call them?"

"Harold and Margaret."

Allan nodded his head, smiled, and finished his johnny cake while looking at the boy who kept touching his trout to see them twitch.

"Travel is the greatest education you can have, son, but always remember where your home is. You can live in other places, but your home will always live in you."

"I don't understand."

"I know. Just remember it and sometime when you're grown, you'll understand."

"Well, thanks, mister," David said, standing up. "But I better get back to my grampy's house before he thinks something happened to me. But, hey, do you come here a lot?"

"Often."

"I think it's fun talking to you. Would you mind if I came back and we talked a lot some more?"

Allan finished his second cup of coffee and lifted his canoe back into the water. "I'd like that."

THE END

Other books by Allan C. Kimball

- TEXAS: THE CAPITAL OF CAPITALS

- TEXAS REDNECK ROADTRIPS

- TEXAS MUSEUMS OF DISCOVERY

- TEXAS 107 BEST WALKS

- WHO IS MOTHER NEFF AND WHY IS SHE A STATE PARK?
     THE STORY BEHIND THE NAMES OF THE STATE PARKS OF TEXAS

- BIG BEND GUIDE: TRAVEL TIPS AND SUGGESTED ITINERARIES

- THE LEGEND OF FORT LEATON

- COWGIRL ACTION SHOOTING
  editor, contributor

- HILL COUNTRY TREASURES
  editor, contributor

- MUGGED BY A MOOSE
  contributor

- SUPERHEROES
  contributor

- FUN WITH THE FAMILY IN TEXAS

- *And the first editions of* CALAMITY CREEK, WOMAN HOLLERING CREEK *and* SECOND COFFEE CREEK

ABOUT THE AUTHOR

Allan C. Kimball has been visiting the Big Bend of Texas since 1969 and owns property in Terlingua. He has guided tours through the rugged Chihuahuan Desert and authored THE BIG BEND GUIDE: TRAVEL TIPS AND SUGGESTED ITINERARIES among others.

Allan is an award-winning writer and photographer with a long career at daily newspapers in Texas. Over the years he has interviewed several presidents, discovered clandestine government air strips, and covered stories as diverse as chili cook-offs to prison boot camps, disastrous tornadoes to sea turtle rehabilitation, gubernatorial races to beer-drinking goats. As a member of the Baseball Writers Association of America, he also covered Major League Baseball. And he has chased killer bees throughout Central and South America.

Allan's friends in Cowboy Action Shooting were the inspiration for this trilogy.

He and his wife Madonna live in Wimberley, Texas.

ALLAN C. KIMBALL